SHADOWS

FRANCESCA STANFILL

AND LIGHT

SIMON AND SCHUSTER   NEW YORK

Published by Simon and Schuster
A Division of Simon & Schuster, Inc.
Simon & Schuster Building
Rockefeller Center
1230 Avenue of the Americas
New York, New York 10020
SIMON AND SCHUSTER and colophon are registered trademarks
of Simon & Schuster, Inc.
Designed by Karolina Harris
Manufactured in the United States of America
1   2   3   4   5   6   7   8   9   10
Library of Congress Cataloging in Publication Data

Stanfill, Francesca.
Shadows and light.
I. Title.
PS3569.T33158S5   1984   813'.54   84-10702
ISBN: 0-671-53256-1

Grateful acknowledgment is made to the following for permission to reprint their
copyrighted material.
Excerpts from *Balthazar* by Lawrence Durrell copyright © 1958 by Lawrence Durrell,
and from *Clea* by Lawrence Durrell copyright © 1960 by Lawrence Durrell. Reprinted
by permission of the publisher, E. P. Dutton, Inc. and Faber and Faber, Ltd.

TO MY PARENTS

When you pluck a flower, the branch springs back into place.
This is not true of the heart's affections.
—Lawrence Durrell, *Balthazar*

We know what we are, but know not what we may be.
—Shakespeare, *Hamlet*

PART ONE

Prologue

A young woman gazed at water lapping against high-throated boats, and at men with ancient eyes and taut faces, who urged her to go with them. Sensing they might succeed with her, they continued to beckon: indeed, she did not stop staring—the brazen striped shirts, the ludicrous hats, the Egypt-sleek boats that rocked as the men watched her pass.

Her hand moved to her forehead, as if she had just awakened from a trance. She shivered. She did not know why, at that moment, she should have remembered the dream. For a moment, her eyes remained puzzled, her brow tense. Then she turned and walked on, leaving the gondoliers to mutter their strangely eastern speech. The air was warm and still, the mid-September sky a cloudless blue over Venice.

She was tall and fair, with thick copper-glinted hair that fell below her shoulders, halfway to her waist. She was very thin; one could see the shadow of fine bones beneath her silk shirt. Her mouth was generous, deep pink, her skin pale and freckled. One would have hesitated to call her pretty, and yet one would not have failed to notice her, for her face was at once seraphic and strong, and it was the mixture of those elements, together with the life in her eyes, which gave her a certain strangeness. It was difficult to discern her nationality, even for Italians, who are so expert at appraisals.

The trip from Milan had been long and dry. She felt hungry, almost starving, for in her compulsion to reach Venice she had not stopped for lunch. A craving, as deep and inexplicable as a pregnant woman's, came upon her. She thought of a coffee ice, engulfed in white cream. The white and the dark; the ice-cold and the warm; the bitter and the sweet. "There you have everything that's Italy," she had once said, "all in a small frosty glass."

She glanced at her watch and decided to stop, sensing that the doors would be open this time—unlike the last. Later, Giovanna would be waiting.

Around her were cafés dotted with bright umbrellas. She sat down, gathering her suitcase and a bag of brushes and paints beneath her. *"Una granita di caffè, con panna, per piacere,"* she said to the waiter. Looking past the crowds, she spotted a Gothic balcony trailing with purple flowers. She took out a pencil and notebook and, oblivious to her hunger, began to sketch.

When the ice was brought, one might have expected her to eat in a delicate way; instead she ate quickly and intensely, not stopping until she had finished. Putting down the cold spoon, she wiped some cream from her mouth; paid the check; and, with a light, brisk step, moved on.

At the water's edge, she looked for a water taxi. A man and a woman, impeccably dressed in holiday-correct clothes, came up beside her. They must be French, she thought. Indeed, there was something about the woman's coloring and stance that reminded her, eerily, of Véronique.

The woman had the sure but frugal chic of residential Paris, and a querulous mouth lined in impenetrable lipstick. A burgundy ascot, knotted around her husband's neck, completed the impression that he was accustomed to stately lunches and expensive soap—an habitué, no matter the place or situation.

Making it seem quite natural, he turned to the young woman and said, "May I ask where you are going? We might share a taxi perhaps."

"Oh, that's very kind of you," she answered, "but I'll need my own boat. I have several stops to make."

"You are English, then?" he asked. His question did not surprise her, for she was used to people thinking that in Italy, and, in England, that she was French. "No, I'm American," she said.

They exchanged further pleasantries; Monsieur and Madame de la Nouvelle introduced themselves. The young woman politely inquired about their trip (next stop, Tunisia), and said, yes, she had once lived in Paris, and named the street. Its arrondissement seemed to meet with their approval, which amused her. I wonder what Emily would make of *these* two, she thought to herself. Suddenly she thought of Emily, who was a writer: the mischievous smile, the pen poised above paper, the wicked way with words. Alexander had never liked her. "She's dangerous," he had once said.

Madame de la Nouvelle continued to talk, apparently about the hotel situation. "The last time we stayed at the Bauer Grunwald. *Mon dieu, c'était horrible!* But then we should have known—an Italian hotel with a German name!" She touched her careful hair in disgust, her eyes urging sympathy. Allegra Clayton smiled.

Two boats speeded up to them, slicing the water with froth as they whirred to a stop, and stirring up a gentle breeze. The drivers wore crisp white, their arms as tawny as the wood of the boats. It was always so in Venice, Allegra thought: the driver's arms, warm and tanned against their windblown shirts. Even as a young girl on those early journeys she had remembered that—their arms, and her first bite into a ripe Italian peach.

When the second boat approached her, she quickly gave her destination—an address in the residential neighborhood. The driver was young and blond, good-looking, the hair by his temples bleached by the sun. He seemed surprised by her destination—it was rare for a foreigner to visit that area—but he asked no questions.

A breeze suddenly blew as she entered the boat: the driver glimpsed her white thigh, and the line of full breasts beneath her blouse. He lit a cigarette and started the engine.

They drove past rickety bridges and, for a while, she stood and gazed as one canal and then another unfolded. Then she ducked through the cabin and went outside, to the back, where she settled on the moist cushions. The little doors creaked and swung; a dolphin-stamped flag waved; water leapt up, spraying her skirt.

There was nothing serene about her face now, for a look of pain had come into her eyes. Pressing her fingers to her forehead, she thought, Why won't it go away, when he could rub it out so easily? She remembered his firm touch; his kisses; the caresses that had made her feel so wanted.

She continued to remember, almost reluctantly, as room after room floated through her mind: the yellow and green room of winter, and then another, deep red and gold, with its immense bed. The sheets had been so white, as white as that other room, in Crete. The Hotel Ariadne, it was called—its thick sun, and its terrifying aloneness. "You knew without knowing that you knew," Emily had told her, just days before, in Paris. "But it was too late. You loved the idea of him too much." How changed she had found Emily! As eccentric as ever, yet transformed in a way that even Allegra could not place.

She looked up again, her hand shielding her eyes from the last rays of sun.

The boat moved slowly now, through murky back lanes, past buildings slashed with leftist emblems, painted thickly and clumsily in red. Translucent papers, the foot of a chair, pieces of rotten fruit slid past, sloshing against the boat, and then against the walls of the narrow canal. It had become quiet, strangely quiet, the queer silence of backstage. Beyond, the city was under way, its palaces and piazze set against a gray-green backdrop.

A barge chugged past, pyramided with ripe pears and vegetables, a grizzly cheeked old man at its helm. He waved to the driver, who remained immaculate and unmoved in his uniform, then winked at Allegra.

But it was doubtful whether she had noticed him, for her face was deep in thought. Memories had begun to circle her like phantoms. Each turn of the boat was accompanied by her quickening heartbeat and by fear: that Venice might disappoint, and that those long-imprisoned recollections would now escape to haunt her.

At last, they entered the Grand Canal.

Allegra stood up and caught her breath, as she surrendered to the city's ebb and tint, her eyes wandering across facades with silent, mysterious interiors.

"You knew without knowing that you knew," Emily had said. Perhaps she had chosen not to acknowledge the resonances of doubt, from the beginning—all the coiled, wordless knowledge of a love affair. Still, that he would have treated her so heartlessly in Crete, and used her to his advantage—no, she would never have imagined that. Yet, there were signs: the telephone calls; the strange absences and his malaise in Deauville; the labyrinthine glances between him and Michel, between him and Véronique.

The boat swung past the Ca' d'Oro, the water lapping against blue and white spiraled poles. The sun had begun to dim, and the water darken.

She was thinking of another sea—far away, cold, with waves lashing the sand. The Atlantic. The moment he let my hand go, that afternoon, in the waves. I should have known then. And yet—"My wife," he would say, "my beautiful wife."

The driver, who had lit another cigarette, was looking at her curiously. Meeting his eyes, she blushed and sat down, gazing at the scene before her. The boat was not alone now. Others took up the Grand Canal—*vaporetti* with tourists and neat Venetian children, and the suave *motoscafi* of the best hotels.

How cold and silent that Christmas here had been, two years ago. So different from Switzerland, with its snow, and bells, and bustling teahouses. Still, even that had not satisfied Alexander, for nothing ever did. And so they had left. A long misty drive to Venice. The afternoon when she had walked, the sound of her boots making hard noises as she moved from one alley to another. Finally, she had come to the Bridge of Sighs, the water below churning with what seemed to be dismembered objects.

She caught a last glimpse of an oar as it cut through the water by the Gritti Palace Hotel. The Gritti . . . There she had made love to him. "As if increase of appetite had grown by what it fed on, and yet, within a month . . ." Was it the confusing of love with wanting and fear—and with sex—that had finally brought her to that nightmare room in Crete? A white and silent room against which everything looked so sinister. So unlike Venice, with its glorious colors, and its Byzantine, half-barbaric splendors. The jubilant Tiepolo skies, the pearly pinks and greens of Veronese—you could not help but want to drink them in.

"You think and dream too much," Alexander had told her. The first time they had made love, he had looked at her closely, his elbow in the pillow, his hand stroking her breast—not with lust at that moment. He said gently, "You've got to learn to get your brain out of your cunt." She had blushed; now she smiled to think of it.

She wondered—as she had countless times—whether he had ever really loved her. Yet she knew there would never be an answer to that question; it had even escaped Emily, for all her clairvoyance.

Now she could see all the familiar sights—the red stone of the Campanile, the domes of San Marco, the dusky flocks of pigeons; nothing had changed.

But she had, of course. Certainly from that winter afternoon in Venice with Alexander, when she had come to San Marco—alone, for he despised churches. Lighting a candle, she had glimpsed a flock of peasants, all in black, their cheeks ruddy, the women only too accustomed to their early oldness. The sacristan had led them to the altar, and there they had stood, their rosy cheeks raised, their eyes fixed above, singing an Ave Maria, with joy, a capella. She had cried. It did not take long for them to finish their song. Genuflecting, they had made the sign of the cross, and then, slowly turning, filed out, their faces radiant. As if, in singing that hymn, and in their pilgrimage, they had completed their life's work. Nothing else mattered.

She had once told that story to Véronique, but Véronique had not understood. Her reaction had been a fixed, stiff smile, leaving Allegra to bite her lip, embarrassed. There was nothing worse, Allegra thought, than to confide what moves you, heart-deep, only to have it dismissed so coldly. Emily and her friend Maggie had understood why it had moved her; Alexander had not, but then he had never really understood her painting, either.

She heard the gear click and felt the driver's glance as he increased the boat's speed; then he headed across the widening water. The sea had turned deep blue and steely. The *calle* here were quiet, the water inscrutable.

The motor purred as they passed beneath a small bridge. Allegra looked up to see a fragile Madonna with a few wilting flowers, above a fountain.

Finally, they came to the church. "At last," she said, softly, aloud. It was solitary, high-columned, and shaded by enormous trees. There was something unfinished about its Palladian facade, for the two marble niches were vacant, as if the architect had left them in haste. A bisque-stoned belltower threw an oblique shadow across the walk and *campo*. Her eyes searched for initials carved in the pediment of the belltower: G.R.C., followed by a date, 1967.

Children, rolling out their few English phrases like dice, ran to the water's edge as they saw the boat approach. Some made faces; others called to the driver in dialect; a small girl stood shyly to the side, fingering her embroidered dress.

The driver told them brusquely to leave her alone. His voice was protective, which should not have surprised Allegra, for it was a feeling she often inspired in men. He continued to say other things which she did not understand, nor did she really hear: she had recognized the light, the light of late afternoon which would dim to that of early evening.

He took her hand and watched as her sandals struck the stone. She saw the line of a muscle beneath his shirt. He lit another cigarette as she paid him, and then watched as she walked up the narrow path, her light skirt ballooning behind her.

The immense black-green door of the church had been locked that afternoon in December, when she had come with Alexander, searching for an answer. She had not returned since. But now it opened easily, and beyond the portal it was dark, damp, and strangely inviting. She pushed back the heavy black velvet curtain and then, with one step and then another, she was inside.

How cool and peaceful it was. As she gazed at the windows and arches, she felt the stone floor beneath her; she had forgotten how much it sloped. Walking slowly toward the altar, she kept turning her head, her eyes drawn to immense paintings with swooping figures encased in dark varnish. It was very quiet, and yet it was not nearly as solemn as the place she had remembered. Not nearly as intimidating; even the milky white light streaming through the cupola seemed soothing.

It had been the right decision to return. She knew that now.

An old man with a flat black hat was curled over a pew. She could hear the scuttling of the paunchy caretaker as he swept the altar.

With each step, she remembered all the times she had come here:

first, as a young girl, after the floods so many years ago. The stone slabs had been ripped from the ground like tombstones, the ceiling cracked, the belltower mute. But now it was restored to its original self; her great-aunt Giovanna Contarin, who was Venetian, had given money to repair the belltower.

Now the bells rang, for it was six o'clock—a clear, mellifluous echo across the lagoon, joined by a fugue of notes that rang through the city—distant, close, tinny, shrill, sonorous.

She stood listening and then, after a moment, looked to the right, at the marble Byzantine throne, with its birdtracklike letters and ancient graffiti, and then to the rows of candles flickering before the niche of a patron saint. She went to light a candle, watching as the new wax dripped, then hardened, on the old cold layers.

Kneeling down for a few minutes, her head uptilted, she inhaled the faint scent of incense, the perfume of her childhood, its memories as cutting as stained glass.

She kept walking and looking, and with each moment grew more thoughtful and yet, strangely lighthearted. As if, in returning here, it were truly over, as if those wounds it had seemed no balm could ever reach were finally mended. He could never hurt her again, and were she to meet him now, she would not be frightened. She would not run to destroy herself, nor would she let him destroy her. Even those desolate days in Greece and Istanbul suddenly seemed distant memories that could no longer cut her heart. Those nights in Crete when she lay alone—waiting for him, yet so fearful of him—belonged not to her, but to another, much younger woman.

Passing through the church door once more, she closed the curtain behind her, and stepped out into the early evening. For a moment, she stood gazing at the belltower, but then began to walk, her eyes drawn to the water. Three rats scurried across the layered wall of the canal. She shuddered, remembering an ominous story Maggie had once told her.

A priest appeared, followed by children; he was young and patrician-looking, and, smiling at her, said good evening. But she did not approach him, or introduce herself, as she once might have done. She was older and perhaps more wary now, and even of the church she had come to have different expectations. Not at all the girl who had come here with Alexander that winter. Still less the girl he had first met that September, three years ago in New York. How little I knew then, she thought, and how unprepared I was for what would follow.

She took her bags and walked toward her destination.

It was not yet dark, but dusky. She thought of the church's light, and of the recurrent dreams she had once known—dreams with empty rooms as newly abandoned as a still-warm bed.

She came to a slender palazzo with a lacy wrought-iron gate. Through it one could see a small garden with white roses that crept up terra-cotta walls. Above the entrance, emblazoned with the Contarin family motto, was an emblem depicting a phoenix, and, in the center, a date, 1543. Allegra rang the bell; once, then again.

The butler appeared, welcoming and dignified in his livery and white gloves. The next instant her suitcase was in his hand, as he led her past the entrance, up the marble staircase, and then to the *piano nobile*, which was filled with vases of flowers set against walls of rich faded silk. There were baroque chairs with gilded arms and sepia photographs in silver frames.

"*Un momento, signorina,*" he said, leaving her to wait and gaze at the paintings she knew so well.

She looked at one by Pietro Longhi—*Three Masked Figures Arriving at the Lady's House*—when the butler came to fetch her. Bending over and clicking his heels, he led her through one room and then another; past the red library, with its consoles of *verde antico* marble, its paneled friezes, its dark leather books; and then through a long, damask-lined corridor until they came to a small sitting room, whose doors were just ajar.

He led her in.

Giovanna Contarin had not changed: she sat there, erect, on the sofa—a slender, gray-haired woman in a silk dress, with her rows of baroque pearls, her little dogs, and her lizard purse. Her face was lined, but still sprightly; it had not lost its distinction. It was not a conventionally pretty face, but there was no mistaking its wisdom and cultivation. She wore a rich scent and her makeup, just as Allegra remembered, was careful, perfect.

They fell together into the deep emotion of a wordless embrace, Allegra's eyes blurred with tears. She felt the hand of her great-aunt, with its weighty rings, clasped against her back. And then she heard the familiar throaty voice, with its English accent, say, "Allegra—at last—how lovely to have you back!"

1

It had begun, as had much in Allegra's life, with a letter. Or rather, an invitation—thick, ecru, affluent. She found it nestled among the bills and notices and plucked it from the mailbox.

"Dearest Allegra," the note read, the finishing-school writing sloping and precise. "It's Doug's birthday on September 28 and I'm having a dinner. Tiny. Just good friends. Of course you must come, I simply won't take no for an answer. There's a man I'm dying for you to meet." And then, three x's by the postscript, which read, "It's informal—just look pretty."

Allegra dug into the pocket of her jacket, unwrapped a caramel, and absentmindedly began to chew it. She had folded up the letter and now, as she waited for the elevator, thumbed through the other mail—a note from her godmother, Laura Hilliard, who was a painter; a letter from the head of the Clayton Foundation, explaining some recent donations and scholarships which had been given in her family's name.

Then her key turned inside the lock, and she was home.

She walked into the kitchen first, without taking off her coat, and turned on the teakettle; and then into the living room, where she took out a record of Mozart's Piano Concerto no. 20. It had been given to her a month before by a friend, Harry Chaice, and was already worn and scratched—exhausted by endless playing.

For a moment she stood by the table at the entrance, listening to the music as she sorted the rest of the mail. Then she flung off her shoes and put away her jacket. Her face was flushed, her eyes excited with that inner glow which comes from accomplishment.

It had taken her weeks of research, telephone calls, and study, but she had finally been able to prove it—to prove that a certain painting was (as she had sensed from the beginning) an authentic Corot. She had even had it sent to the world-famous expert, Pierre Dieterle, for his scrutiny. Just a week before the sale at Sotheby's, where she worked, the painting had arrived back at customs, accompanied by the necessary certificate from Dieterle himself. Her instincts had proved right; it was a Corot; and that morning, at the sale, it had fetched a high price.

Carrying her teacup with her, she walked into the living room.

Had her mind not been elsewhere (as it often was), had she really been able to see her apartment, she might have thought it charming. It had a soft look to it, with pale colors, screens, and whimsical furniture, much of which had been found at junk shops; for she enjoyed taking old, homely pieces and repainting them in fanciful ways. In the center of the table before the sofa was a cluster of anemones in an antique vase.

Allegra cared a great deal about the colors and textures of her surroundings; it was a passion she had inherited from her mother. Rooms presented themselves to her as paintings did: a single image that burst upon her mind and willed itself to completion.

She went into the bedroom and sat on the bed, rereading the letter from her godmother.

Around her, on tables and shelves, were photographs of her family—her father, mother, and brother. They had all been killed in an avalanche in Switzerland seven years before, when Allegra was seventeen. Her mother was originally from Milan, her father from Kansas City—a brilliant entrepreneur who had made his fortune in the electronics business. Over the years, the company he had founded,

Forum Industries, had grown into a large, distinguished conglomer-
ate. He had met Allegra's mother at the start of his career—she was
a slender blonde with startling blue eyes, whom he had seen arranging patterned silks in the window of a fabric shop on the Via Monte-
napoleone. He had entered; they spoke; and were married several
months later.

However much she loved her husband, Maria Clayton had never
grown accustomed to the United States, and as the years passed she
grew more elegant, more knowledgeable about art and flowers, and
yet more alone. She spent her time writing letters to Europe, and
filling her New York townhouse with antiques and beautiful objects.
Her children, her husband, and her garden in the country were
everything to her. In a curious way, her daughter's painting came to
be one of her greatest joys—one that verged on consolation.

Allegra began to undress. There was a scar—the result of an
adolescent waterskiing accident—that ran from the base of her neck
across her chest. It haunted her, for she found it ugly. About her own
looks generally, and toward herself as a woman, Allegra had less regard than one might have expected. At some point, she had found it
safer to concentrate on art, and on patterns of color and line that
would spin themselves into her painting. Within her work, she had
achieved a measure of safety and peace; within herself, and particularly with men, she had very little. A fragility of her own inner core
often made intimacy more painful than pleasurable, as if it were an
ice floe that continually threatened to break: the heart driven in one
direction, the self in another.

She got into her painting uniform—an old shirt and blue jeans—
and switched on the lights to the small studio. There were jars of oil
paints and brightly swatched palettes, a paint-encrusted stool, and
rows of old jars with brushes. Art books lined the walls. In the center
of the room stood a half-finished still life of flowers, and an antique
fragment.

She glanced at the clock and thought, Two hours before Harry
comes to pick me up. With that mixture of fear and excitement she
had learned to recognize as the signal to begin, she picked up the
brush. Her first strokes were slow and hesitant, gradually increasing

in speed and sureness. After half an hour, her mind had clicked into that other, magic gear which seemed to have its own momentum, flow, and time-frame. And with it came a cleansing, peaceful feeling, as if those tumbling images had escaped from a dim, subterranean labyrinth to find order and light. Nothing else existed. Not the outside, not her job at Sotheby's, not the terrible loneliness that had pursued her since her family's death.

The doorbell rang, startling her. Wiping some paint from her hands, Allegra went to answer it.

"Harry!" she said, kissing him on the cheek. "Is it really eight o'clock? I was painting, and lost track." She closed the door behind him. "How are you?"

"Fine," he said, walking in—a gangly yet elegant young man with unruly blond hair and dark eyes. He had the youthful authority of one who would, one day, be famous, and looked much older than his thirty years—an impression reinforced by his suits, which always seemed a bit too large. Like Allegra, who specialized in nineteenth-century painting, he too worked at Sotheby's, but in the Old Masters department. During the past several years, a companionable and sexless intimacy had developed between them—a tender friendship that lacked romance, and hence, Allegra knew, any sense of danger or threat of loss.

He pointed to her cheek, an affectionate look on his face. "You've got some paint there." She brushed the spot off. "I heard about the Corot," he said, taking off his tie and putting it in his pocket. "We'll celebrate."

"I was so thrilled, you can't imagine," Allegra said, her voice happy, as she took his arm and stepped into the living room. "Anyway, I was able to come home early and thought I'd do some painting. I've been working on a new still life."

"How's it going?"

"Well—very well. It's been so painless I'm a little suspicious of it. All I can think is that if it's been this easy, it can't be good! I'll show it to you soon, when it's farther along." She glanced in a mirror nearby and made a face. "I really look a fright."

"No you don't. You look great."

She smiled. "I'd better change. Would you like something to drink? There's some white wine, I think."

Brushing some hair from her face, she poured him a glass of wine and went into the other room to change.

In a moment, still dressed in her painting clothes, she returned, drying her hands with a towel. Her eyes looked preoccupied. "Harry," she said, "did you say you were going to Jeannette Howard's for dinner? I got the invitation today."

"Yes," he said, looking up from a magazine. "So's Maggie, I think." Maggie Fitzpatrick owned a flower shop on Madison Avenue.

"I was wondering whether to go," said Allegra. "I never know quite what to make of Jeannette."

"Few people do," he said, with his direct gaze, as he sipped wine and took a handful of nuts from a bowl before him. "But she's harmless, and you've got to admit that her parties are always interesting. Good theater, at least." He put the glass down, looking up. "Why don't you come? We'll have a good time. Besides, a new friend of mine will be there. You'd enjoy meeting her."

"Who is that?"

"Emily Norden. An English girl. Very funny and bright. I met her a few weeks ago, at a lunch."

"What does she do? The name sounds familiar."

"Works for *Vogue*. She's an editor. You should hear her talk . . ." He smiled, as if recalling something amusing. "Well, you'll see for yourself."

Allegra went back into the bedroom, still thinking of the invitation and Jeannette Howard, who belonged to a species she occasionally found frightening—so many layers of lacquer had gone into her existence that it seemed no human parts were left.

But then she remembered that line of the letter—"There's a man I'm dying for you to meet," and she thought, Maybe I *should* go.

A few moments later, she appeared dressed in a hyacinth blue skirt and boluse that matched her eyes. She had swept back her long hair with combs; the blouse had billowing sleeves and the skirt was long and embroidered. Her clothes were usually romantic in cut, and not especially in vogue, but they suited her tall, fine-boned figure and her face. Looking up, Harry said something approving; she smiled tentatively, and went to the mirror to fasten on her earrings.

"Harry," she said, turning to him, "I think I *will* go to Jeannette's."

"Great," he said. "Then we can all brave it together." He stood up with a long, lazy motion. "Now, on to important matters—where should we go for dinner?"

"How about that little Chinese restaurant around the corner?"

Harry, who loathed Chinese food, looked alarmed. "I hope you're joking," he said.

"I am," she said, with a laugh, taking his arm. "Let's try the new Italian restaurant up the street."

After dinner they walked down Lexington Avenue, occasionally stopping to look inside shop windows. The street, with its canopies and signs, was dark and silent now. Below, the subway rumbled.

"What do you think of that?" said Allegra, pointing to a Chippendale chair inside an antique-shop window.

Harry peered inside. "Pretty," he said, "but not the real thing."

"No?" said Allegra, furrowing her brow, momentarily disconcerted by her lack of judgment. "How can you tell?"

"The proportion is wrong. Too much carving on top, not enough on the bottom. There's just something off about it."

They came to a dress shop with mannequins draped in somber, awkwardly cut clothes. "Those are supposed to be very fashionable," Allegra said, "but can't you just see the Red Brigade in them?" She looked up to find Harry smiling, then glanced inside the window again. There was a peach-colored dress, nearly hidden in back, with intricate sleeves that twisted and wrapped. "That one is pretty, though," she said, pointing to it. "What do you think?" Harry nodded. "The color is great."

They continued to walk, Allegra keeping up with his long, regular steps. They spoke of a book on Ingres he had recommended, and of Sotheby's, and then of his older sister, a dancer. She had been in a car accident six months before and was now paralyzed from the waist down. For months, Harry had suffered as he watched her, powerless to do anything.

"How is she now?" asked Allegra, softly.

"Better. Much better."

"With your help . . ."

"Yes," he said, "but she's very strong, you know. Even so, when I see her in that chair, there are moments when I can hardly bear it."

Her apartment was silent—that aching silence to which she had never become accustomed.

She put on the Mozart concerto again and walked to the window, planting her hands on the sill and looking out. But it was only her own inner landscape she saw: restless and—despite all its outward successes—seemingly incomplete. Even the pleasure in the Corot, and in her painting, had slowly begun to fade. It was that tantalizing *elsewhere* that pursued her—the longing to be everywhere she was not.

So it would often happen: that the quiet of her apartment, which should have been womblike, turned into a twisted net instead.

A man and a woman, their arms intertwined, walked below on the street. Allegra thought of her first lover, a young man she had met during her last year at college. He had been infinitely more casual about the romance than she; for her, for months, nothing else really existed. It had ended the following fall, after she had come to New York to work for Sotheby's. "We'll always be friends," he had said to her one afternoon, as they sat in a restaurant. For months those words, the death knell of romance, would ring through her mind; the mere mention of his name would awaken a dull hurt. It had left its mark, as fine and distinct as a thread on her heart.

She walked from room to room, turning off the lights, and finally to the bedroom, with its canopy bed and books. A row of leather-bound classics, given to her by her great-aunt Giovanna Contarin, lined one shelf. She picked up *Wuthering Heights* and leafed through it, wondering how it could possibly have sprung from a girl who most likely had never had a lover.

2

The evening of the Howard dinner was cold and moonlit.

Allegra searched for a taxi as she clutched her cape. It was windy, so windy that the gusts seemed to uproot people from the streets.

She was late and could not see a taxi anywhere. Her feet tapped the ground while her hand gripped the cape closer to her body. At last, a taxi screeched to a stop; she gave an address and slammed the door.

Park Avenue flashed past, a phalanx of canopy and stone. Blinking lights, doormen's arms outstretched, men in black tie ushering silk-toed women into limousines as sleek as barracudas.

The taxi stopped; fortresslike, the building loomed before her.

Grasping the door with his white gloves, the doorman showed her to the entrance, with its black and white marble floor and Georgian tables. Looking into a mirror, Allegra was unexpectedly reassured by her own reflection, and by her dress, which had a slender mauve top tapered at the hips, and wrists edged in lace. She fixed her hair, then walked into the elevator.

A moment later, a maid took her cape and Allegra stepped into the foyer, and then, into the main room.

Before her, the crowd unfolded like a Coromandel screen, its angular characters shifting and clicking. The murmurs, the glances, the clinking of glasses. Men in dark suits, absorbed in women who hovered like rare butterflies, all hollow cheeks and glossy lips, their bodies attritioned to thinness by dieting. Around them spun servants bearing trays that glittered with drinks, as the sound and the chatter assaulted one; talk riddled with names of the famous and of faraway places—Mustique, Sardinia, Sun Valley. It seemed the very air was shrewd.

Standing at the door, Allegra suddenly realized that in the past year the apartment had changed almost beyond recognition: the furniture and paintings had assumed a new smoothness. Indeed, no one, after perusing these rooms, would ever have guessed that Jeannette had grown up in a house where little, if anything, was left unembellished by some sort of horse.

Clearly she—or at least her decorators—had mastered a splendid, if strained look: serpentine banquettes, as cool as pastel ice; spotlit antiquities; a rejection of the decorative, symbolized by steel sculptures and "paintings" of massive clumps of wood. The dining room presented the ultimate challenge: an oval eighteenth-century table, sacrificed to a painting in clinical colors and a quizzical, slit-eyed pre-Columbian head.

But now Jeannette's hand gripped Allegra's wrist. "Oh, Allegra darling, you've come, and how pretty you look!" Hawk-featured and secure in her WASP heritage, Jeannette triumphantly survived her outfit: a vermilion Chinese robe traced with leaping, hot-mouthed dragons and peculiar earrings in tiger's-eye. She had become adept at exceedingly fashionable clothes which also tend to de-sex women. Added to this was her coiffure, with its astounding sense of permanence, and her skin, with its expensive perfection.

Allegra looked at her, returning her kisses, and thought, How she's changed! By sheer force of will, Jeannette had developed a Style. She had gone about this gung-ho, as she did everything else—willing herself, her home, her food, and her clothes into a Look. Even her sex life, which had made strides at about the same time, was conducted with a similar vigor—the sort normally associated with yachting at Newport.

Jeannette continued to concentrate on Allegra. "Where have you been? Working too hard, I'm sure—well, we'll take care of *that*." She took Allegra by the arm, steering her skillfully, as she tilted her head to point out this one or that. "The Clayton girl," someone whispered as they passed.

In one corner lolled the self-styled jeunesse dorée of the city. From another corner came a shrill laugh, as a woman brandished the tissue paper which had puffed up the sleeves to her taffeta dress—a gesture which seemed to amuse the Italian businessman who stood beside her.

Indeed, many famous faces were scattered throughout the rooms: a distinguished ambassador who had recently returned from shooting in Spain; a legendary English beauty (powdered face, steel-blue eyes, feather boa, an incisive wit); an Italian film director with his entourage; a foreign correspondent for the *New York Times*; and a German photographer, whose work Allegra had always admired, who sat quietly apart from the crowd with his wife.

Among them all, the prerequisite European beauties brandished their expertise in evening clothes. Two Parisians, one gray-haired, one young and sinuous, gossiped on a sofa in one corner. They had been discussing Ibiza, but now they turned to sex. The older woman, listening as the other recounted the details of her latest love affair, finally burst out laughing. *"Ah, ces histoires de cul!"* she said, shaking her head. "When I think that I, too, have known such things . . ." She touched her diamond earring, still laughing. "It doesn't seem possible!"

No one could have faulted the perfection of the atmosphere—the rarefied hors d'oeuvres, the elegant flowers, the eclectic guest list. Within its scheme, Allegra, too, filled a slot. She was young and came from a well-known family, and she had a job at Sotheby's.

"We'll get you a little wine. White? Of course." Jeannette gave Allegra's slender form a push. "And then I'll take you around—I want you to meet everyone." Her voice was lacquered with the pride of a big-game hunter unveiling his latest catch.

Allegra nodded to a friend there, an acquaintance here, all the time searching for Harry, and Maggie and Charles Fitzpatrick. At last she spotted Harry. Several people in his group turned as he waved to her— including a tall, pale young woman in red with a cloud of short black hair and the face of a cross angel. She wore high-heeled, pointed shoes and had a way of punctuating her statements with a tilt of her chin and a languorous puff of her cigarette. Whatever she had just said seemed to amuse those around her, and this was not lost on the young woman herself, who had an English accent and one permanently raised eyebrow.

Allegra moved toward them, Jeannette having gone off with another guest.

Kissing her, Harry said, "Let me introduce you to everyone." The fair, black-haired woman was Emily Norden, Harry's English friend.

"I'm so glad to meet you," Allegra said, extending her hand. "Harry has told me about you."

"Yes?" said Emily, looking askance, and puffing on her cigarette. And then, in a throaty voice, "Wicked things, I hope."

"Unfortunately not," Allegra replied, with a slight smile. "He told me to wait and see for myself."

Jeannette approached, interrupting them. "She's needed over *there*," she said, taking Allegra firmly by the arm. "Come."

They passed a dark, mustachioed man chatting with a brunette piped into a black dress. The man looked South American and may have been quite kindly, but he was blighted by the kind of looks that made it impossible for him to appear anything but unscrupulous. Apparently he was a Spanish diplomat, with a last name that twisted the tongue, although his first name was simple enough.

"Roberto," trilled Jeannette, sweeping up to him. "Darling, would you mind if I interrupted a moment to introduce my adorable friend?"

"Of course not," he said, with a warm smile, as he kissed Allegra's hand. The woman uttered an icy greeting. Jeannette whispered something in his ear (the name of Allegra's father, most likely) and, with two steps of a mock samba, said, *"Andiamo,"* and, with a little flip of her hand, moved on.

Jeannette then confessed to Allegra her latest venture: Italian lessons. Anglo-Saxon logic, rather than passion, seemed to have motivated the undertaking, for she ingeniously lumped the effect of Latin languages with that of cold showers and cod-liver oil. "Good for the health," she explained to Allegra. "Makes you loosen up! Cheaper and more effective than a shrink!"

"I've never thought of Italian that way," Allegra said, with a light laugh. "You make it sound like calisthenics, or wheat germ."

"Try it, *cara,*" she said, as a silver tray swooped toward them. And then, "Take a shrimp" as she speared one with a toothpick. "You've got to eat! Especially when I have all of these plans for you. And then there's my *mission.*"

"Mission?" Allegra looked puzzled, wishing she were adept at the sort of badinage people seemed to expect at such moments.

"This charming man I want you to meet. Divine. You've no idea. You'll adore him."

Allegra, remembering the letter, thought, Of course, and began to feel excited, then vaguely uncomfortable. "I've told you, Jeannette," she said, after a moment, "I don't think I'm going to be so easy to marry off."

"Why not?" Jeannette said, indignant. Matchmaking was the last vestige of Jeannette's maternal instinct—the rest had been blotted out as irrelevant. "You're pretty, you're young," she continued. "God only knows you're intelligent—perhaps a bit too *cerebral,* that's all . . ." Her eyes widened, her voice lowered to a hush. "Haven't you ever wanted to have an affair with someone who was just *fascinating?*"

"Is that really what you have in mind?" Allegra looked unconvinced.

"Don't worry, darling, no one's going to mate at table. That I promise." She peered into a mirror, checking her crimson lipstick. "The problem is that you're too serious. It's being among all those paintings and antiques that's done it. I used to tell your mother—too many summers spent touring dank cathedrals! To *think* you never even went to camp! You ought to have been having fun—going to discos, playing field hockey . . ."

"But that *was* fun, Jeannette—going to Europe, I mean. Besides, I hate field hockey."

Jeannette, whose attention had drifted, merely murmured, "Well, then, how about squash?"

"Squash!" Allegra tilted back her head, shaking her thick hair, and laughed.

"Come on, *cara,* let me introduce you to my friend, Mr. Williams. Doug thinks he's terrific—so bright, so *lively.*"

Cradling Allegra's arm, she moved in the direction of the man she mentioned, but not directly, for Jeannette was far too accomplished for that. Stopping here and there, she introduced Allegra to a craggy financier, to an art dealer, and then to a reclusive screenwriter. The rooms were crowded now, with many guests who milled about, talked, whispered, and kissed: real-estate tycoons, who huddled in groups; a well-known television newscaster; a famous clotheshorse, all knobby fingers and bony chest, with a voracious way of absorbing herself in conversation; and, at last, a professor of art history (for Jeannette always found it amusing to include an academic element) whose latest seminar, as he went on to explain, was entitled "The Sistine Chapel before Michelangelo."

As he began to elaborate on that topic, Jeannette slipped away.

She returned, in a moment, with Craig Williams.

He was precisely what Allegra had expected: the young American businessman with a confident air and a forthright face—a veritable confluence of right angles. That is not to say he was unattractive. His eyes—as Allegra immediately noticed—were intelligent and capable; there was a briskness about him. He fancied himself a rather "with-it" banker, and always made an effort to know the latest trends. He had also succeeded in convincing himself that he liked intelligent women, whereas he really came into his own with models, or with the opposite type, the more proper the better.

"Hello," Allegra said. He smiled and took her hand, squeezing it with a bit too much pressure.

She sensed immediately that she was not in the least what he had expected and that the way she looked—her dress, perhaps—put him off. In fact, he found her looks a trifle too European for his taste: the high-bridged nose, with its chiseled bump, for instance ("the nose of a Greek girl," someone had once told her). He had anticipated someone prettier, more Scandinavian-looking; she felt it, and an awkwardness came over her, although she still appeared quite poised.

Sipping his bourbon, and casting his eyes about, he said, "That's a very unusual dress." Searching for another adjective, he came up with "artistic." And then he asked what she did, what she was "into."

"Painting," she said, and then mentioned her job at Sotheby's.

"What's your specialty?"

"Nineteenth century."

They continued to talk, and then he mentioned that he planned to go to Aspen this winter, and did she ski?

"Not anymore," she said quietly, looking away. "I used to." At that, he launched into a detailed comparison of Aspen versus Vail; and Courchevel versus Val d'Isère. With another glance around the room, he went on to discuss music, asking what sort she liked. She murmured something vague in response; she felt reluctant to mention she loved opera.

He sipped his drink, inwardly deciding that Allegra was a challenge, despite her delicate appearance; besides, he might learn something about the art market from her. He was "into" German expressionists, at the moment, and had only yesterday placed a bid on a Kokoschka. His new apartment on Central Park West needed some art—some "serious art," as he would say.

On the other hand, the girl did have nice eyes, he was thinking. He was a fair-skin-and-blue-eyes man himself; he had just told her so.

They continued to talk about art, politics, his years at Harvard, until the moment came when those subjects lay about, used up, dissected. Allegra set down her wine. "Excuse me," she said. A slightly glazed, distant look had come into her eyes.

It was not entirely because he put her off so that she escaped to the bathroom. It was simply that she often retreated, midway through such evenings, seeking a respite from the noise, the effort, the drinking, the stillborn conversations. At such moments, the quiet unoccupied rooms, with their empty beds and silky carpets, drew her like sparkling jewels.

Walking quickly out into the corridor, she passed Emily Norden and heard her murmur something about "lapsed royalty." Then, spotting Maggie Fitzpatrick across the room, Allegra waved, but Maggie did not see her. She came to another corner where two men stood talking: one was flaccid-faced and smoked vigorously, the other trim and tense. Both were partners at prominent investment banks, and had once betrayed Allegra's father. Now, as she passed, they caught her eye: she turned her back and walked away.

At last, she found the bedroom.

It was pale blue, with a creaseless bed banked with that trademark of the New York female establishment: row after row of plump, ruffled pillows.

Such bedrooms never failed to take Allegra by surprise, for she assumed, at least subliminally, that women of Jeannette's breed would retire to far more spartan places. She had not yet learned—as she would later—that the tougher the woman, the more plentiful the pillows. Still, the plethora of lacy cushions seemed incongruous, not to say futile—like an obese woman beautifully groomed.

Standing in the bathroom by the marble sink, she took a hairbrush and swept it across her scalp, then washed her hands and walked back into the bedroom, still reluctant to return to the party. The quiet here was so lovely. A fire burned in the bedroom fireplace, and she went to sit before it, kicking off her shoes. In a moment, her cheeks were flushed with the heat; the logs crackled and glowed.

She heard someone approach, turned, and saw a dark-haired man with a briefcase come through the door. He took off his coat and flung it across the bed, his cheeks ruddy with cold; he was obviously late and in a hurry, for it was nearly nine o'clock.

Broad-shouldered, tall, with a lean, strong face, he wore a white shirt which set off the color of his skin. His eyes were deep-set and of a brilliant dark green, with a certain relentlessness to their gaze. There was nothing in the least hesitant about the way he looked at her, nor did he give the impression of being eager, suddenly, to join the party.

"Shouldn't you be out there with the others?" he asked. He had an English accent, which Allegra found intriguing.

He introduced himself as Alexander Para and took her hand.

"I'm Allegra Clayton."

"You're very pretty."

"Thank you," she said.

"There's no need to thank me. It's the truth. I'm sure you've heard it before."

She smiled, and watched as he turned to the mirror to fix his tie, then to survey the room.

"Do you think that's true?"

"What?" She looked puzzled.

"That." He pointed to a needlepoint pillow tucked on the small sofa, which said, "Old bankers never die, they just fade away."

She laughed softly. "Well, I suppose that may happen to some."

He looked at her intently, as if to say to her, and to himself, that he would never meet that fate. "Would you excuse me?" he said finally. "I should say hello to our hostess."

"Of course."

She pretended to take out her hairbrush as he left, watching as he turned down the corridor. Standing before the fireplace, she thought, I wonder who he is. Where he comes from.

Minutes later, she followed him.

Dinner was perfection itself.

The guests sat around the tables, peering across forests of shimmering glasses and plates. Heads bobbed in conversation while each course, seemingly possessed of its own rhythm, proceeded to them: salmon *en paupiette,* chicken with ginger, and a raspberry *tarte* of breathtaking symmetry. "What, no birthday cake?" someone called, at the end, to Jeannette. "Sweetheart," she answered, raising her champagne glass, "we're not in Grosse Pointe."

Allegra had been seated between Craig Williams and Paul Constantinapoulos, a Greek industrialist with wavy white hair, exquisite manners, thick black glasses, and a famous house in the Aegean. There was a quiet worldliness about him.

However engrossing she found Constantinapoulos, Allegra still kept searching for Alexander Para. At last, she spotted him: he sat between Emily Norden and Maggie Fitzpatrick. Allegra watched how he devoted his attention to each woman—making one laugh, or the other look thoughtful. She hoped to catch his eye, but never succeeded.

Constantinapoulos had just mentioned meeting Allegra's father years ago. "He was a wonderful and unusual man," he said, sipping his wine. "I was so sad when I read what had happened."

"Yes," she said, quietly. And then, after a moment, "You know, he loved Greece so much. He once told me, not long before he died, that I hadn't lived until I'd seen Greece. I'll always remember his saying that, it kept coming back to me. One day, I just walked into a travel agency and booked a trip."

He asked where she had been, and as she told him, she thought of the Aegean islands and their still statues, and of Delphi, where she had climbed the steps to the sanctuary. "I remember the curving shape of the valley, and the wind, and an eagle soaring above. The sun went in and out. You could almost imagine the Greeks making the pilgrimage, and the voice of the oracle . . ."

" 'Know thyself,' " he said.

"Yes."

There was a pause as he sipped the wine again, slowly, as if to savor the taste. "You have been to Turkey, as well?" he asked.

"Only to Troy."

"It is not what one expects, no?"

"No, it isn't, and yet it's very powerful. I remember arriving late in the afternoon, and I kept walking around those small crumbling walls, thinking, were these the 'castles' of the Trojans that I'd read about? It was their littleness that stunned me. They seemed more like huts, or Turkish igloos." He smiled at the description, as she continued. "I kept trying to match what I'd imagined with what I saw before me . . ."

"And of course they were so different," he said. "Ah well, that is something you will grow accustomed to."

"Do you think so?"

"Yes. It is inevitable."

He went on to ask about the Nineteenth Century painting department at Sotheby's, for it seemed his family had a fine impressionist collection—one that also included many Corots. She mentioned the story of the painting she had recently discovered, and as she spoke, her eyes radiated absorption and happiness, for she loved to discuss painting, and indeed, as she did, her face changed: her eyes brightened, and color rushed into her cheeks. Occasionally she would utter a light laugh.

This was not lost on the man at the other table, although she did not know it. He watched her face in animation, how she occasionally rested her chin in her hand, and the way she would draw fine lines with her fork, on the cloth.

"I'll never forget the first time I saw it," she said, still speaking of the Corot. "Everyone said it was a fake, but I wasn't convinced, so I kept working to prove it was authentic. It had a brooding quality I liked, and the light felt right—dry and sunbaked, as it should have been for that period."

"You must call me if you discover another Corot," Constantinapoulos said.

The next moment, they were interrupted by Craig Williams; Allegra turned to him.

From time to time, though, she would glance around the tables, looking at the faces, the colors, and the women with their splendid jewels. There was a rich scent in the air which mingled with that of the food and flowers.

She noticed that Emily Norden was now engrossed in Alexander. They looked at no one else, and Allegra was filled with a sudden uneasiness, even a pang of jealousy. It was difficult not to watch them, for a moment in a silent film could not have been more captivating. Emily puffed on her cigarette, and then, tilting her long neck toward the back of her chair, half closed her eyes. Once or twice she said something which must have amused him, for he smiled and laughed. Until at one point she spoke, looking away quite casually afterward, while he reddened, visibly. Her smile remained a sulky, knowing curve.

"There's something mysterious about her," Allegra thought, looking at the heart-shaped face, and the small, Leonardesque smile. Emily caught Allegra staring, and stared back; the latter blushed.

At last, a glass clinked and, with a theatrical gesture, Jeannette stood up to make a toast. Others followed as her quiet husband—responding in turn—said a few words, tilting his bald head and looking at his plate. The guests listened politely and at last, began to move to other rooms, leaving the napkins lying on the tables like resting birds.

Emily Norden, still holding her champagne glass, passed Allegra as they left the dining room, and as she did, her gold necklace—massive, like a Celtic torque—caught Allegra's eye. In the center of its pendant was a winged, griffinlike creature encircled by a Latin inscription.

Admiring the necklace, Allegra pointed to the inscription and asked, "What does that mean?"

"My motto," Emily said, " 'When in doubt, invent.' " Smiling to herself, she stubbed out her cigarette and muttered, under her breath, "Lord, I'm still starving!"

Allegra began to ask about Alexander Para, but was interrupted by Jeannette, who called to Emily from the other side of the room. Emily excused herself and left.

Coffee was being served. Standing in the library, Allegra scanned the art books, all the while thinking of the man, and hoping she might see him again. The guests had grouped themselves into islands and archipelagos of conversation. Maggie Fitzpatrick seemed to have disappeared; Craig Williams was absorbed in a blonde with high cheekbones and bare shoulders.

Many art books lined the shelves—large volumes with thick pages and erudite print. As Allegra leafed through a book on Cézanne, the pages gave forth a fresh, unopened scent; she inhaled it. After a moment, she heard Harry's voice.

"Well, what do you think of Emily?" he said, coming up to her.

"She's fascinating, and funny," Allegra said, glancing in Emily's direction.

"She's writing a novel."

"Is she?" Allegra smiled. "She's probably here gathering material."

"It's her first under her own name. She's written many under pseudonyms, apparently. She told me she makes up different names and invents a biography for each. Isn't that something?"

"Has Maggie met her?" Allegra asked. "Where *is* Maggie? I haven't spoken to her all night."

"She told me to tell you she had to leave early. Charles had to work late, she went home to see him."

Suddenly Alexander appeared. He barely looked at Harry, and then, with the full force of his eyes and his charm, said, "Ah, *there* she is," and smiled. Allegra was so thrilled that she could barely stammer hello. In the meantime, he quickly and smoothly shook Harry's hand and said, "Hello, I'm Alexander Para."

An unusual name, Allegra thought, watching him.

"And this is Allegra Clayton," Harry said.

"We know each other," he said, and Harry glanced at her.

Alexander began to talk, directing his attention to her intensely; Harry soon excused himself and left. It occurred to Allegra that

Harry's feelings might have been hurt, and that she should go after him, but Alexander was already leading her to a sofa. They sat down.

"I startled you when I walked into the bedroom, didn't I?" he asked.

"Yes. A little."

"I didn't mean to. But you startled me, as well." He paused. "I've been looking for you all night. You have a lovely and unusual name, it suits you."

"Thank you . . ."

"I saw eyes like yours a few weeks ago, when I was in Italy," he said, watching her face. He mentioned that he had been in Positano, and then Naples.

"Naples is wonderful, isn't it? It was the first city I ever visited in Europe."

"Was it?" He sipped cognac, still looking at her. "I spent a memorable holiday there once."

"When was that?"

"Fifteen years ago." He looked thoughtful. "Yes, it must be fifteen years now."

They began to trade impressions; she talked eagerly, while he listened, although, as she spoke, it was her eyes that he noticed, more than her words. Often they would seem to half-close, so that the lashes rimmed them in demimoons. He noticed the freedom and animation which flooded her face when she spoke of something that mattered to her.

She continued to talk about Italy, uncovering memories as she spoke: late dinners at restaurants that floated on the sea; strolling men who sold flowers and smiled, even if one didn't buy ("Charming crooks," her father had once called them); little boys with dusty feet who sang maudlin love songs as one sat at lunch, under scarlet umbrellas, eating peaches . . .

"You're English, then?" Allegra asked.

"No, I'm from Argentina, originally."

"Where in Argentina?"

"Buenos Aires."

"I've traveled a lot, but never in South America. It's fascinating, I hear."

"It can be." There was a slight, abrupt pause; for a moment she felt

she had trespassed, and that perhaps she should not have said what she had.

"I didn't think you were American, when I first saw you," she continued, leaning toward him, her palms pressed against her knees. "You looked much too mysterious—and by your accent I would have said you were English." Suddenly she felt extremely happy; the mood blew over her like a cool breeze.

They continued to talk, until at one point her high-heeled sandals, stitched with gold leaves, began to hurt. She bent over to loosen them, and as she did, he saw the beads of perspiration on her neck, and the lines of her breasts beneath her dress. There was a slight glow, a pinkness to her cheeks; the room had grown warm.

Blue enameled espresso cups, rimmed in gold, were being passed from guest to guest along the banquettes. Alexander watched as she sipped the coffee, seeing how she took a lump of sugar, dipped it in, and sucked on it for an instant. She looked up to find him watching, and reddened, embarrassed at the girlish habit. He made a joke which put her at ease; she laughed, relaxed now, gathering her feet beneath her on the sofa.

Still he kept examining her face. True, he had known many prettier women. But it was her manner, more than any specific feature, that intrigued him. Her voice, which was very clear; her perpetually expectant way of holding her head; and her eyes, with their furtive life and hint of Mediterranean genes. If there was an occasional moment of tension, there was also a gentleness to her gaze; this, too, he noticed.

As he did, she kept questioning him—as she was wont to do—her eyes following the gold spoon that twirled through the potent coffee.

"I think your table was more interesting than mine," she said.

"I doubt it. I kept looking at you."

She realized she had not hoped for as much.

He nodded and smiled, which accentuated the fine lines around his eyes.

"But you seemed so absorbed!" Allegra said.

"Out of habit, I'm afraid. Besides, I had a rather absorbing—or self-absorbed, I should say—partner. Emily Norden, she's called. She's English, or South African." He shrugged his shoulders. "I'm not sure which. A writer."

"I heard she's writing a novel. Harry told me."

"Apparently."

"Do you know her—well?"

"Well?" He stopped, amused by her subtle probing, and then, in an off-hand way, said, "Not well, but I do know her. We had dinner once, but it never amounted to anything. She's odd, unquestionably intelligent, but I doubt anyone really knows her. Although God knows, she's got a reputation." He smiled to himself. "But I wonder if she herself knows who she really is, or even who her several selves are." He had grown serious; her eyes never moved from his face. But then he said briskly, "Enough on Miss Norden. She's really a bit tiresome, you know, and not nearly as pretty as you."

Grasping the cup in his hand—ignoring the little handle as he did—he swallowed the last drops. She watched his strong chin, the line of his neck, and the way his hair curled at the nape. At moments his cheekbones would catch the light, making his face appear almost gaunt. He had a fine, proud nose and a curving mouth; and yet it was not a face distinguished by refinement.

An elderly woman in an eccentric dress approached them. "Ah, Alexander!" she cried, giving him a kiss. He stood up, introduced her to Allegra, and then said to the woman, gallantly, "There's still fire in your eyes."

"That's the only place left!" she replied, sounding rueful, and moving on.

Alexander looked at Allegra, who was laughing. "And now," he said, sitting down and turning to her, "you must tell me where you are from."

"New York."

"I would not have said so." Then, "And your family?"

"My parents are dead," she said, looking down.

"Of course," he said, with an apologetic look that indicated he already knew. "I'm sorry."

Some guests had begun to leave; others, holding brandy glasses, walked about. "Now you must tell me more about you, about Argentina," she said, fearing the moment when their conversation would end.

He did, but only a little, which whetted her appetite for more. He told about his life in South America, and then about his time in London, and his university years at Oxford; and how he had come to New York, where he now worked as a vice-president in the international division of the Atlantic Trust Company, one of the most prestigious banks in New York, a rival of Morgan Guaranty.

He invariably returned the questions to her, however, making her tell him more than she had ever meant to. Suddenly she felt silly, like a schoolgirl, as if her life were a book with thick, unslit pages he had knifed open. Still, she could not seem to leave.

A man, sitting by a woman with an emerald necklace, motioned to Alexander from the other side of the room. Seeing him, Alexander said, "I must go," adding, "Where can I reach you—at Sotheby's?"

She nodded. "I'm so glad to have met you."

"You haven't really met me," he answered, looking at her directly. For a moment he stood with her hand grasped in his, and then, with a confident look, walked away.

As she stood by the elevator waiting, she watched Alexander from a distance—his eyes astute and full of life, each of his steps purposeful, compressed with energy. Now he approached the couple on the sofa: a small, voluptuous woman with beautiful green eyes and a trilling laugh, who would glance from time to time at Alexander, and then at the gray-haired man beside her. Still laughing and talking, she would finger her emerald necklace. The older man smiled indulgently, but missed nothing. Alexander then said something which made the two others quite serious; the three of them exchanged hard, concentrated glances.

As the elevator door closed, Allegra wondered who the other two were. Alexander Para, in the meantime, had already noted her name in the black leather book which he kept, ready, inside the pocket of his jacket.

3

There was a glow to the week that followed; a new brightness in Allegra's eyes. "As if," she said to herself, thinking of Alexander, "everything before were half-lit, empty."

Her life took on a new rhythm. She began to arrive at work very early, walking quickly up Madison Avenue before most of the world was awake, her feet skipping across the sidewalks. Even the most prosaic things acquired a new texture and comfort: the scent of coffee, the articles in the newspaper. She laughed more easily and quickly; everyone noticed it.

It was not entirely that she wanted to *see* Alexander: the pleasure was in the thought of him—a flame to be kindled, and rekindled, at will, in her mind. His eyes, the touch of his hand; his voice.

Now she walked down Madison Avenue on her way home from Sotheby's, her cheeks rosy, her face reflected in the shop windows. A Tang vase in one, a Persian rug in another . . . Her mind drifted to Alexander.

It was six o'clock; the shops were closing up. Butchers in plaid shirts exited from one; a small boy helped his father scrape the stems of roses by a flower stall. Awnings snapped back into place; shopkeepers locked their doors.

Looking at her watch, Allegra decided to stop and see Maggie Fitzpatrick, and quickly began walking in the direction of Maggie's flower shop, Millefleur.

Several blocks away, Maggie Fitzpatrick (née Farinelli) was arranging lavender freesia in a crystal vase. After stepping back to examine the flowers, she went to sit on a tall stool, flipping through a copy of *Apollo* as she smoothed her auburn hair. Her assistant—a small, dark-haired girl—swept the floor. Occasionally Maggie's alert brown eyes would glance at the window as she watched the passersby on Madison Avenue.

There was the damp, sweet earthy smell inside of a flower shop, with all the early signs of winter. Pots of paper-white narcissus, growing in stones, filled the window; there were bunches of anemones, as well, and striped parrot tulips flown in from a Dutch greenhouse. An orderly array of baskets, vases, and bright rolls of streaming ribbons lined the shelves.

In the midst of this, Maggie looked elegant, as she always did, for she was a remarkable-looking woman who had come to learn, late in life, that it was more important to believe one is beautiful than to be so. Her clothes were original and sensual; she mixed her own perfume.

Because she was not conventionally pretty—her mouth was too wide, her nose a bit too large, her bones rather big—Maggie took enormous care with her clothes and skin, which was luminous and tawny. Inside her bedroom closet was a quotation from Stendhal, which she had once come across in a French film: "She took great pains with her clothes in order to forget what she wore." But Maggie could never quite forget, just as she could never quite forget the poor background she came from.

The lively, graceful way she moved and the tone of her voice might have led one to believe that she was a woman of great assurance, whereas this sense of inner security was, in fact, rather new to her. Only now, at thirty-six, had she achieved a measure of confidence and peace, most of which was due to her marriage to Charles Fitzpatrick, a neurosurgeon from an old Baltimore family. They had been married five years; the flower shop had been a present from him.

Together, they had created the one thing she had always most wanted: a home. For Maggie was an utterly domestic creature who had never really liked the notion of having a career, even though her own, as a stylist for several famous photographers, had been quite successful.

When Allegra had first met her, Maggie was pregnant and even more womanly looking than usual, but four months after birth, the baby died. The lost child never left her mind. All Maggie thought of since was replacing it with another; but until now the nursery remained closed, its empty crib stripped of blankets.

Maggie heard the doorbell ring, and looked up to see the tall frame of Allegra, smiling through the door. They kissed and exchanged greetings excitedly. "Do you have time for a cup of tea?" Maggie asked, as she hung up Allegra's coat.

"I'd love one," she said, looking at her friend, and thinking how thin she had become. Maggie had taken to wearing dark colors and clothes that were severe, though fashionable.

"You've been away," Maggie said, bringing out a tray with a blue and white porcelain teapot. "I tried to reach you, but then I saw Harry, and he told me you'd gone up to Boston for something."

"An appraisal," Allegra said, settling on the stool, her hands clutching the warm teacup. "I found some great things."

"Yes, that was it—an appraisal." Maggie offered sugar, and then, "I think Harry's OK now, don't you? I was worried about him a few months ago, after the accident." She looked up, pushing her hair behind her ear. "I went with him to see Clara recently, did he tell you?"

"No."

"Typical of Harry," Maggie said, with a little sigh and a smile. "Stiff upper lip and all that. Well, I *did* go, about a week ago. He is wonderful to her, you know. It touched me. For a while the life had gone completely out of her eyes, but now—at last—she seems to be making headway. She's even begun to talk about teaching." She looked into the bottom of her cup, fingering her pearls. "He has had the most beautiful shoes made for her—all in the finest leather, and tooled in gold—and she wears them so proudly. You feel, at least I did, that in some way they are meant to make up for the feet that can no longer dance."

"He hasn't spoken about her recently. I think it upsets him too much," Allegra said, her chin propped in her hands. "I had dinner with him one night, at that Italian restaurant near me, and then I saw him at the Howards', of course . . ." She stopped suddenly. "What did you think of the dinner? And did you get a chance to talk to Harry's friend, the English woman, Emily . . ."

"Norden," Maggie said. "Yes, yes I did. She was at my table. Clever, but sort of intimidating—at least I thought so. But he seems to like her very much." Maggie looked down, so that the light caught her strong cheekbones. "I must say, Jeannette can be exasperating, but her parties *are* good. I thought the food was wonderful." And then, almost to herself, "I wonder who did it."

Allegra continued to talk about the Howard dinner, until finally, unable to restrain herself any longer, she said, "Maggie, tell me about the man you sat next to. Alexander."

"Why do you want to know?" Her voice was genuinely surprised, at first, and then—suspecting the reason for the question—teasing.

"Because I thought he was wonderful!" Allegra said, leaning forward. "I met him just before the dinner, and then I spoke with him afterwards . . ."

"And he's called you up."

"No," she said slowly, "I'm sure he knows lots of women."

"Well, I liked him very much," Maggie said, wrapping some flowers to take home. "He really looks at you when you speak with him, and he asked interesting questions that got straight to the center of things. The kind most people never do, at a dinner party. We talked a lot about photography." She pushed her hair back again. "I thought I'd met him before, and it turned out I had—at a dinner, awhile ago, at Véronique de Séguiers's."

"Who's that?" Allegra asked, pouring herself some tea.

"She was at Jeannette's too," Maggie said. "She's Swiss—at least I think she's Swiss. Very beautiful." Here she stopped, as if to amend the description. "Very feminine, extremely elegant. She gave a dinner last spring, and I think that's where I met Alexander. At least, he said so." She paused, going over to the sink to wash her hands, and flinging her long strands of pearls to the side. "I hear he's brilliant. Finance." And then, taking a towel, "I'm sure you'll hear from him."

"Do you think so?"

"Yes," she said, with a reassuring smile. Then she glanced at the clock. "I've got to go. Charles is coming home early, and I promised to be finished up here." She wrote a note to her assistant, who had already left, and then asked Allegra, "Which way are you walking?"

"To Bookends, and then home," Allegra said, standing up, and peering inside the vast refrigerator where masses of flowers stood, in buckets. "I ordered a book last week and thought I'd go and pick it up."

"I'll walk with you." Maggie put on her jacket, picked several bunches of anemones for Allegra, and switched off the lights. In a moment the two women were walking down Madison Avenue, carrying flowers, talking, and occasionally stopping before the shop windows. At last, they came to the gray and white striped awning of Bookends.

"You'll come for dinner on Thursday, then?" Maggie said, putting on her gloves as Allegra, holding her flowers, nodded. "Good," Maggie said. "Charles will be so happy to see you. And you can see the dining room, we've just redone it." She paused, her eyes momentarily apprehensive. "I hope you like it. I'm not sure the wallpaper is refined enough." The word "refined" invariably punctuated Maggie's speech, whether it was to describe food, china, or her exquisite, prized linens. "But you'll see for yourself. I'll ask Harry to come, too."

The two women embraced and said good-bye.

Bookends had an esoteric and rather English look. Books of all sorts were tumbled into piles, and salespeople encouraged customers to browse through the stacks. When Allegra entered, she noticed a woman among them who looked bored, fed up. Her short dark hair fluffed around her head like a perverse halo, and every so often her hand, with its red fingernails, would move up languidly to fix it. She was reading and as she read, she smoked, gazing out the front window with each turn of the page. Occasionally she would adjust her feet, with their high-heeled black pumps, on the stepladder where she sat. It occurred to Allegra that the young woman was either remarkably affected or naturally eccentric. I've seen her face before, Allegra thought, trying to catch a closer glimpse. It must be Emily Norden.

Walking to the desk, Allegra asked a salesperson about a book which she had ordered. The clerk looked for it, but when he finally said it must have been sold, she insisted that it was there, and waited until he looked again. Finally she searched the shelves herself, and discovered it in a corner, hidden by other volumes. Content now, and clutching the book, she was beginning to browse around, when she heard a deep laugh from the corner where Emily sat. Allegra glanced in her direction and saw that she was reading a novel, *The Pursuit of Love.* "Oh God, this *is* funny," Emily said, to no one in particular. And indeed, the salespeople ignored her, as if they were accustomed to her. Then she bit into her apple—a resounding crunch—and resumed reading. In a moment, she laughed again.

"That must be a very funny book," said Allegra.

"Oh yes, it's to die over, as they say in the trade," Emily replied, looking up. Her red nails still skipped through the pages as she said, "Here, let me read you a bit." Her mouth formed a queer smile. "Ah, here it is," she said, finding the page. "'Marjorie was an intensely dreary girl, who had so far failed to marry, and seemed to have no biological reason for existing.'" She laughed, snapped the book shut, and looked at Allegra so intensely that the latter blushed.

"We've met, haven't we?" Emily said.

"Yes," Allegra replied. "At Jeannette Howard's."

"That's it." A pause; Emily stubbed out the cigarette and immediately lit another. The smoke whorled through the air. "Poor old Jeannette, trying to shed suburbia like an old skin. Tough old bitch, isn't she? Thank God she's given up those animal tamer's clothes, at least."

Allegra looked puzzled.

"Oh, you know, the jersey capes, over the low-cut dresses. That sort of thing."

Allegra burst out laughing, but not entirely without feeling awkward before the woman's amused, yet piercing gaze; still, there was something intriguing about her. Emily, at the same time, was thinking: A good face. High forehead, long eyes, strong mouth. Perhaps I can use it. Then, with a smile, she said, "Of course, I remember you. I never forget a good quattrocento face when I see one." A pause. "You kept looking over at me and Alex Para. Well, no need to look embarrassed. We must all—at one point in our lives—know an Alexander Para. Good old Alex, I think I gave him quite a start." Her mouth curved into an expression that vaguely resembled a smile—a small, contained curving of the mouth that seemed at once ethereal and lewd. "At the dinner he asked me how I'd been amusing myself. I said I'd been fucking my brains out." Her eyes, slanting as she said this, absorbed Allegra's startled reaction; she would have been disappointed, in fact, had Allegra not blushed (which she did, visibly). It was partly intellectual curiosity, partly perversity, that led Emily to do this: and partly an impish desire to observe the effect of her language on others. Sex was as convenient a subject as any, partly because it came easily to her, which writing did not.

"Actually," she continued, still smoking, and swinging her beautiful narrow ankle this way and that, "I seldom use the word 'fuck.' Very seldom, in fact. Although some might say . . ." (A private joke to herself, and that smile, once more.) "It seems to me a singularly cacophanous way to describe the act of copulation. It also rhymes with 'puck,' which reminds me of field hockey, which in turn reminds me of some of the most hellish and appalling afternoons of my life."

"That's a sport I've never liked, either," Allegra said, still unsure how to respond to her.

"Sport?" Emily's voice was scornful, her eyes incredulous. "Field hockey is too barbaric to be called a sport. But then I loathe sports altogether. When I see all those fools jogging, all of them lurching around the same track, it makes me shudder." Emily paused, tilting her head back slightly as she fingered her earring. The cashier, who was reading Kant, yawned. It had grown dark.

"Funny, she doesn't *look* like a writer," Allegra thought. Emily had a long, curvaceous body, and mischievous eyes that seemed utterly concentrated one moment, utterly vague the next. She wore a slim black skirt, a white silk blouse, and, again, her odd necklace, with its pendant.

"Do you spend much time here?" Allegra asked, wanting to prolong the conversation, as she flipped through another book.

"As much as I can. I live close by, and sometimes I say I'm going to the market—that's Seventh Avenue—and come here instead."

"And they don't mind?"

"At *Vogue*, you mean? Oh Lord, no. Just as long as I drag in the merch, as they call it. That's all the clothes we ferret out from the fashion collections." And then, in a low sarcastic voice, "All the most fashionable items which are then presented in a digestible form to a host of fashion victims."

Allegra, amused by Emily's theatrical delivery, said, "How do you know what to pick? Which things they'll want?"

"I'm very good at it actually," she said. "If it weren't for this knack of mine, I'm sure I would have been booted out long ago." Her voice became newly chatty. "At the beginning, though—that was four years ago—I didn't have a clue. Sometimes I'd bring in something I thought was perfectly beautiful and elegant, only to have it called 'thrift shop.' Other times I'd pluck something from a rack, without even really looking, and the editors would swoon. 'A must have!' they would cry. Now, of course, I've gotten the hang of it. Alas." She turned to Allegra and said suddenly, "And you? Where do you work?"

"At Sotheby's . . ."

"Oh yes, Harry told me," she said, interrupting to hurry on. "He's dear, isn't he, Harry I mean?" And then, crunching into the apple again, "And where are you from?"

"New York . . ."

"But *born* where?" Emily said, narrowing her eyes.

"France, near Tours. My father was working in Paris, and my parents . . ."

"Fancy that," she said, with a sardonic smile, "a frog in disguise."

Allegra, laughing, said, "Do you always grill people this way?"

"Sorry. It's an occupational disease."

"Where are *you* from—England?"

"I was born in Capetown," Emily replied, "but I learned to read in London, so I suppose I should say London." She went on to explain that she considered one's true birthplace to be the place where one learned to read.

"I would never have guessed you were a writer," Allegra said, sitting on a stool, and taking off her scarf, all the time wondering when she would get up the courage to ask about Alexander. "You look too exotic to be an intellectual."

"You Americans have such strange ideas," Emily said, and then, after a moment, "Anyway, I'm not an intellectual, I'm a novelist. They're not at all the same thing."

"Harry told me you're writing a book. Several people at Jeannette's seemed very curious about it."

Emily raised an eyebrow imperiously. "I'm sure they're curious, all right. God knows what they expect—some juicy roman à clef about

New York society, no doubt. Well, I can't think of anything that would be more ghastly." A pause. "All those women running around in their bogus Chanel suits." She drew deeply on her cigarette. "It's a novel," she said slowly, in a different voice, "but it's very far from being finished."

"And the story? What is it about?" Allegra asked, waving the smoke from her face.

"The story and what it is about are hardly the same thing," Emily replied, her tone becoming haughty. A moment later, however, her voice softened as she began to speak, and her eyes lost their brittle look, her manner shedding its carapace of cynicism.

"It's about a writer—a novel within a novel, you might say," she explained slowly, even uneasily, for she almost never discussed her book. "She is married to a man she loves very much. They live in the country, not far from London. He is a remarkable man, supremely understanding, a passionate lover, encouraging to her in her work . . ." Suddenly she stopped. "Oh no, I can't," she said, stubbing out her cigarette. It was the first time Allegra had seen her flustered.

"Please go on," Allegra urged. But then, sensing Emily's ambivalence, said, "Just tell me what happens."

Emily's voice had lowered to a hush. "You see, she finishes the book he has encouraged her to write, and then he falls in love with one of her characters, no longer satisfied with his wife. He leaves her to search for the likeness of his wife's own creation!"

There was a silence. "Go on," Allegra said softly, "Tell me what happens."

"I don't know the ending. I only know it will be cryptic. I don't like cut and dried conclusions."

"Will it have a happy ending?"

"Of course not. If it did, it wouldn't be romantic."

Allegra's eyes were questioning, even though by this time, she was becoming accustomed to Emily's enigmatic pronouncements.

"You need some suffering, some obstacle, otherwise the story would be humdrum." Emily stopped for a moment, looking pensive, "What would Juliet have been, had she ended up happily married to Romeo? A nouveau riche housewife from Verona. The real tragedy would have been if she had wound up with him, eternally together. Don't you see? You need something drastic for it to be a bona fide romance."

Suddenly she looked impatient. "Well, what do you think?"

"Well," said Allegra slowly, "I'm not sure it feels completely right."

"What do you mean?" Emily's voice had taken on a defensive edge.

"Do you think that's really why he left her? Because he fell in love with what she had created, I mean?" Allegra shrugged her shoulders. "Maybe he was repelled by it." A moment's pause, then she said quickly, "But of course, I'm not a writer. I don't know about these things." Emily did not respond, and merely lit another cigarette. Allegra saw that her hand was shaking and immediately regretted her words; still, she could not lie to Emily. That, she had sensed from the beginning.

"And this book," asked Allegra quietly, "is it autobiographical?"

"No."

"You were never married?" Allegra said insistently.

"Once."

"And what happened?"

"We parted." Emily's manner returned to its original acerbity, as she added, "Which is what happens in all good marriages."

A woman swathed in scarves and a fur boa approached, looking for a particular book, and finally asked for the latest pulp novel. Emily made a scornful noise, glancing at the woman so superciliously that the woman quickly took the book, paid for it, and fled.

Allegra, who had observed this, laughed.

Emily raised an eyebrow. "There's no reason to *encourage* such hideous taste, after all."

Allegra wrapped her scarf around her neck, preparing to leave, and Emily began to put on her coat.

"Which way are you going?" Allegra asked.

"A few blocks away, towards Lexington," Emily said. "And you?"

"Nearby. I'll walk with you."

It was dark outside, and the rush of automobile lights cast an eery glow on Madison Avenue. Emily stopped for a moment to look inside a jewelry shop window, while Allegra put on her gloves and buttoned her coat.

Still waiting to ask the last, and most important question, Allegra said, as casually as she could, "How long have you known Alexander Para? A long time?"

"Oh, a while," Emily said, walking swiftly. "A year I should say.

We were up at Oxford at the same time, although funnily enough I didn't know him there. I was at Lady Margaret Hall; he was at Magdalen College. I've had dinner with him a couple of times, here, in New York." She smiled. "God knows, I do love to watch him. He knows it, and I suspect it makes him rather uneasy. He isn't used to irreverence." She lit a cigarette, shielding the tip from the wind, and then looked at Allegra. "He's no worse than most men, and I've known some real bastards in my time, mind you."

They came to an ungainly-looking brownstone in the middle of the block. Emily said good-bye and began to walk up the steps. Suddenly she turned around and called to Allegra, "Be careful!"

"Why?"

"A storm, they say."

"Oh yes, of course."

4

For a moment Emily watched as Allegra disappeared down the street; then she walked up the steps to her apartment, which was on the first floor of the brownstone on Seventy-fifth Street. Although the street was quite elegant, the building was shabby, and the apartment itself was small, faced an overgrown garden, and did not get much light. Its atmosphere of genteel poverty suited her very well, and its very mustiness reminded her of home—of England.

Invitations were stacked on the dusty mantelpiece, and pillows in exotic colors were piled along two sagging sofas; odd pieces of furniture were strewn about. Much of the atmosphere had been inspired by photographs she had seen of Lesley Blanch's home. ("All I need now is a lover named Casimir," she had once said with a smirk.) There were books everywhere, stacked under tables, on shelves, in the kitchen. It was clearly not the apartment of one who cared in the least about housekeeping. What flowers there were had wilted long ago, and stacks of English tabloids had turned quite yellow. "Don't care much for the proper papers," she would say in a mock cockney accent, "but I love me rags—catch up on the murders and the Queen Mum."

Only one corner of the room was tidy—the baskets that contained her stationery: stacks of papers in various colors, sizes, and shapes, that were arranged with a perfect, almost Oriental order.

Baskets brimming with antique jewelry lined one shelf, and photographs of Emily at Oxford, in various Shakespearean roles, lined another. She shared the same birthday with Shakespeare—April 23—and claimed a spiritual affinity. "Your genius, I suppose," someone had once remarked to her sarcastically. "No," she had replied, with dignity. "The fact that we are both highly sexed and share a fondness for strange words."

On her desk—the only piece of "good" furniture in the room—were rows of dictionaries and stacks of bills ("The dread piles," as she called them, for money terrified her). Beyond it was a bulletin board, lined with quotations from various writers: "Guilt is squalid" (Elizabeth Bowen); "The lapse into despair of a writer who cannot write" (Marguerite Yourcenar); "It is in the nature of a novelist to make private life public" (Philip Roth); "I can only write about the truth and I am the only truth I know" (Jean Rhys); and, curiously, "I dress for the stranger across a crowded room" (Antonia Fraser). As Emily wrote, she would occasionally glance at these passages; one or another would invariably be found inside the covers of her journals, about thirty of which were heaped under her desk.

The many books toppling on the shelves clearly belonged to one with eclectic tastes. There were biographies, novels, and literary criticism: *What Shakespeare Read and Thought; Love in the Western World*. One corner, in particular, ran the gamut from Harlequin romances to crime novels, murder mysteries, and historical romances. These books, about eight in all, had been written by Emily under a variety of pseudonyms simply to pay her bills. There was a book by Jack "Snakebite" McConnell, for instance, entitled *A Slash of Red* (McConnell was described as a father of six from Moose, Wyoming—an avid mountain climber and elk hunter). Another—*Sultry Smoldering Passions*—was by Fiammetta Wallis. This last had a fuchsia cover depicting a nightgown-clad woman, a French château, several obelisks, and in great swirling script: INTOXICATING DESIRE!/SPLENDOROUS LOVE!/SEARING PASSION! The book belonged to a genre known as the "bodice ripper" and had sold exceedingly well, making "Fiammetta Wallis" the toast of the recent Romance Writers Convention—a success which Emily commemorated by purchasing a pair of Regency earrings.

Emily had written these books quickly, a month or two for each. It was only now as she began to write a novel under her own name that she confronted a *horror scribendi*, a real fear of setting words to paper. She was concerned about how her work would be received, and it was at these moments that she became blocked. (In this she differed from Allegra, whose joy in painting was almost solely the absorption of the process, rather than the end result, a refuge-place where she had the freedom to express those feelings—sorrow, hurt, disappointment— which had no outlet elsewhere.)

At this moment Emily sat on the sofa smoking, draped in a caftan and wearing dangling earrings, as she wrote in her journal. Damedith, her cat, was curled at her feet. Occasionally, as she wrote, Emily would take a sip of her particular brand of cheap red wine.

"The girl Harry Chaice introduced me to came into Bookends to-day," she wrote. "I was struck again by her looks, and thought, as I did at the Howards', that I should use her for my book. Hers is an interesting face, European, and yet I would never call it Latin. Long neck; manner at once elusive and intense; tall, very fair, somewhat proud, and yet somewhat vulnerable. Clear voice; good diction, far better than most Americans one runs into. A voice, and a propensity to foreign languages, perhaps several. Her general impression is one of fragility.

"Were she to cross the pages of my novel—as, no doubt, she will— how would I describe her? It would not always be easy, for whatever one sees on the surface, one senses something else below. No doubt she is complicated—a mass of contradictions. There is both a gentle-ness and a fierceness about her, as there is, curiously enough, about Harry. (He, too, is an interesting case—father a minor rich man from an old Protestant family, mother Jewish. One senses, occasionally, the schism within him.) I'm sure she's driven to intense attachments; there's a feeling of the sensuous intellect about her—it is partly those eyes that convey it. That she knows without knowing that she knows.

"I watched her, though she did not know it, as she looked through the books with great concentration. Like the fingers of a blind woman, pressing over Braille, searching and searching through the titles and pages. She told me that she seldom reads fiction now, and that she's 'crazy about biographies—artists, queens, eccentrics.' She was so intent as she said this; one doesn't know whether to confront it with a similar earnestness or to smile.

"When she first entered the shop, she caused a commotion, for she insisted that there was a book put aside under her name. They said, no, it wasn't there. But she wouldn't give up, continuing to insist, very firmly I thought, that they *did* have it and that she *would* find it. She then went through the shelves until she emerged, triumphant, with the object of her quest.

"She told me she worked at Sotheby's, but never mentioned that she also painted, which surprised me. Harry had mentioned that she's gifted and had, in fact, shown me some of her work. Hers is a style that is highly coloured, even hallucinatory, and yet, despite that, has a certain tightness about it, as if she wanted to go further but didn't dare.

"When she returned, we continued to discuss this and that. I think I shocked her when I told the story about Alex—my retort about fucking my brains out. She blushed. Then I told her the plot of my book. She didn't find the ending right, and that, I must admit, disturbed me.

"I wonder if she's right." She stopped, nervously nibbling her pen, and then continued. "But the question she burned to ask—about Alex Para—she saved until last. Shyness, I suppose; or fear; perhaps she was afraid of knowing what he's really like. And who knows what I am capable of saying, after all?

"As regards Alex, she is clearly infatuated—and yet, what an unlikely pair! For him, of course, it would be a coup (his social ambitions and lust for money). What's in it for her, though? Sex, of course, and yet that is only part of it, I'd guess. *Le coeur a ses raisons que la raison ne connaît pas,* etc. One senses that she is given to romance, perhaps to a dangerous degree, for she seems rather sheltered. And while I'm sure she has had a great deal of experience appraising those paintings, she is clearly a novice in other areas. It's her eagerness that interests me.

"She radiates loneliness, and that's dangerous . . ."

It was precisely in those "other areas" that Emily herself was hardly a novice. Her love affairs were notorious in New York; many people called her promiscuous. And yet it was not always pleasure, but often pain she sought—the pain that would propel her to write.

She liked men, and she liked novelty, but she had become adept at using them too—not for power, or money, but for her work. "You see," she had once confided in a rare moment, "after I sleep with them, or leave them, all I want to do is *get it on paper*." This "using" of her affairs haunted her as an addiction might, for it seemed to her that reality only existed in its capacity for transformation. But for that, she never really "lived" at all.

She was only really happy when she wrote, for there was a part of her that only came alive when confronted with a typewriter, or a pen. ("When the dry creek suddenly becomes fluid, and the thoughts flow and the syntax rumbles"—a note from her journal.) It was partly the erotic aspects of writing that drew her—the movement of pen upon paper, the sound of words, the feeling of thick white envelopes etched with ink—and partly that she loved to lie. ("What did Faulkner say about novelists? That they are congenital liars?") It was the failed actress—not, as some might say, the failed poet—that had turned her to novel-writing.

She had made it a point to observe Alexander Para and had, in fact, slept with him once. They had had dinner, and he had asked about her book. She told him that she had written very little and was still in the material gathering stage. "I'll give you material," he said. "What kind?" she asked, playfully. "Sensate," he replied, taking her hand across the table. Later—in the elevator to his apartment—he had pushed her against the chrome railing, as he gripped her buttocks and kissed her hard. He gave her a push as the door opened at his floor.

The next morning he lay in bed watching her as she dressed; it was cold, and she felt uncharacteristically uneasy. It disturbed her that she felt she knew him in some inexplicable way, that she knew exactly what he would do, and when, and to whom.

And yet it was not really so curious, for the two were rather alike in some ways: ambitious, fascinated by the opposite sex, supremely restless, scornful of rules. Each had developed his own particular way of dealing with the truth.

It was questionable whether either was truly capable of tenderness.

5

Another week passed.

The ringing of the telephone interrupted Allegra, who was watching a film of *Macbeth*. She turned down the television to answer. It was Alexander Para.

Her heart jumped at the sound of his voice. "Dinner next Monday? Yes, I'd love to . . . But I think I have an invitation to something that night, at the Metropolitan Museum. Yes, the installation of the new Egyptian wing. Shall we go to that first?"

A moment's pause; he could not see the excitement in her eyes.

"Monday at seven-thirty, in the main hall? Fine, I'll see you then."

Monday evening came—slowly, it seemed to her. Yet now she rushed to get ready. The dress she had seen in the shop on Lexington Avenue now lay on her bed, its silk top the color of pale tiger lilies, its intricate wrists designed to twist and wrap. Trying again and again to get the sleeves right, Allegra suddenly remembered the words of the saleswoman who had sold the dress to her. "Yes, my dear," she had said, bending over to help her, "you've got to have a husband or a lover for this dress!"

Exasperated, Allegra continued trying to tie the wrists. Too tight one time, too loose another.

It was the doorman who finally finished the task. "Thanks, Frank," she said, with a grateful smile, as he helped her into a taxi.

When Allegra and Alexander met later that evening in the vast, flower-filled hall of the Metropolitan Museum of Art, she thought he looked somewhat different from the man she had remembered—older, more poised. He stood with one hand in his pocket, his black-green eyes grave, the light catching the gray in his hair, as he looked for her.

She stepped up quickly, her cheeks and hands still cold, and as he took her cape and saw her dress, he said, "What a wonderful color." She smiled, realizing how much she had wanted to please him.

As they moved toward the Egyptian wing, she was aware of his hand, lightly on the small of her back, as he guided her through the crowds. Friends waved, and several museum officials came to greet her. The Clayton Foundation had been a generous donor to the Metropolitan and had, in fact, contributed to the new installations.

The new Egyptian wing was beautiful. The amulets and scarabs Allegra had known since childhood glistened from new settings: beaten lunulae in gold next to tiny sphinxes in turquoise and faïence; pharaohs' falcons in lapis; signet rings in garnet.

Peering through the glass, she was taken back to childhood visits here, when she would come to the museum with her father. They would ride the subway and then walk down the vast corridors to the old Egyptian wing. In glass cases, like those before her now, were pearly blue-green jars that had been buried with bodies; some had held hearts. There were paintings of child kings and queens (not much bigger than Allegra then, it seemed). At four o'clock, bundled in boots and gloves, they would start back home, her father bending his head to talk about the paintings, or the hall with flags and armor. Beside him, Allegra would walk—a lively little girl, yet with a certain reserve, like a child out of Velásquez. It always seemed that her questions would come back to Egypt, and to those dead and buried kings and queens, guarded by immense, windchafed sphinxes.

Now, as she looked at them, she thought, Only their jewelry has lasted . . . And then, suddenly turning to Alexander, "To think that these have been buried and that they have lasted, for how many centuries? Why is that?"

"The climate, they say," he said, taking her hand and leading her to a case with golden rings and bracelets. "The dryness preserves everything—even papyrus." He went on to add that the history of Egypt was smoother, less interrupted than that, say, of Greece, where invasions and earthquakes had often destroyed cities and islands. Looking again through the cases he said, thoughtfully, "And of course, they had the good fortune to be hidden." An object had caught his eye. "Look at this one. It's especially lovely." He pointed to a small clay statue of a girl with a headdress, and a straight lunar gaze. "There's something about her that reminds me of you. The profile. What do you think?"

Bending over, she gazed at it, but she could not see much of a resemblance. "Really?" she asked, with a smile. He nodded, and led her to the next case, with the mummies.

"What are you thinking?" he asked, watching her as she stood by the immense coffins.

"I came her many times, as a child . . ." she said, her voice trailing off, as she turned to him and touched his arm. He took her hand, and then held her, briefly, around the waist.

The moment passed.

The guard, pointing to his watch, said the museum was closing. "I wonder how it affects you, being a guard all day with these mummies," she said, with a little shudder. "I can't imagine it."

They passed into the Byzantine gallery, where the faces seemed to speak: wise eyes, knowing mouths, ears hung with golden loot. He watched her as she walked, this tall, slender Madonna at his side, with her gentle contradictions. "Come," he said, taking her hand, and feeling its small bones in his.

They left the Metropolitan and walked across the street, to a hotel, for dinner.

She ordered fish; he, a steak. The maître d'hôtel uncorked the bottle of burgundy which Alexander had chosen. It was delicious—a warming burgundy on a cold mid-October night. The wind had swept them down the steps of the museum and into the quiet restaurant with its pink-skirted tables and staid flowers. A pianist ran through a repertoire of bland melodies.

As their talk ebbed and flowed, she asked about his life—how he had left Argentina, how he had escaped to England.

"I was thirteen when we left—my mother, my father, and myself. My father had supported the wrong general—we were forced to leave. We went to England, to London."

"You have no brothers or sisters?"

"No. I had a sister who died when I was very young."

Allegra paused. "And how did you get out?"

"We paid the right people. Like most things in those countries, it all comes to money, you know. You can buy anything—anything at all."

He paused, sipping the wine; she watched him, thinking that his voice, a moment ago, had changed, had become cynical, tough. In a strange way, this excited her. She leaned toward him, her eyes scanning his face and mouth.

"But I had always known we would leave," he continued. "It was just a question of when, and how. I grew up on it, you see."

"And your parents?"

"They are both dead." He paused. "My father lost heart when he came to England. He missed the life he had left behind, and never grew to like London. He had owned several shoe factories in Argentina, and had made enough money to dabble in politics. And my mother"—he stopped, a look of tender disdain on his face—"my mother was never the same. She became old so quickly, and settled for a life that was not at all what we had known before." His eyes looked hard, impenetrable; he began to eat quickly.

She noticed his hands: they were square and rough, ill-proportioned. Had they not belonged to him, they might have repelled her; as if to forget them, she began to search his eyes.

"And you?" he said, turning to her with a warm expression. "Do you have brothers, sisters?"

"No," she said quietly. "I had a brother, but he was killed, with my parents, in Switzerland."

"Of course," he said gently. "Now I remember reading . . . But you never talk about it, do you? I can tell that from your face." He brushed some strands of hair from her eyes. "Perhaps you should talk about it, rather than bury those feelings. The pain will only survive that way, like those things from the tombs."

She managed a little smile. "One day," she said, "but not now."

"You haven't been back to Switzerland since, I take it?" he asked, after a moment.

"No, I haven't been back, and I haven't skied since then. I don't think I ever want to ski again." She paused, her finger running across the rim of the wine glass. "It's strange, you know, because I used to love it more than anything. I used to love to ski very fast, so that I had that wonderful feeling of speed, and wind, and cold, and the edges of the skis cutting through the snow."

"You *will* ski again," he said, in a way that was at once reassuring and commanding, as he took her hand. "You will come and ski with me, and you won't be frightened. I will hold you, and take you down the best runs, and you'll follow my tracks and forget all the rest." A pause. "There must be a part of you that misses it, because you used to love to ski." And then, still holding her hand, "And you are so lonely now."

She looked startled. For a moment they said nothing. He let her hand go.

"I feel very much alone sometimes," she said slowly, "but I'm not sure that's the same as being lonely . . ."

"You are very lonely, Allegra. There's no need to be ashamed of it. I sensed that the moment I first saw you."

"Sometimes, yes," she admitted, "but not when I paint—that's the amazing thing. I can paint and paint for hours, and be so absorbed that everything else vanishes—even loneliness."

He asked when she had first begun to paint.

"I always remember having a sketchpad, or a box of paints, from the time I was a little girl," she said. "My mother encouraged me, and so did my great-aunt, Giovanna Contarin, who lives in Venice. She was a great influence on my mother, and had taught her all she knew about painting, about art. When I was growing up, I spent a lot of time with Giovanna, and with my godmother, too, who's a painter. So you see, it always seemed quite natural to go off by myself and try to capture those images. Even when we traveled"—she paused— "even more so when we traveled, because those images are always that much more vivid and fresh. We'd go to Venice every summer, and stay on the Lido, and I remember every morning I'd get up—before anyone else—and go to the beach with my sketchpad and paints, and set up my easel. I used to love the early morning feeling of the sea, the light, and the footprints of the *bagnini,* setting up tents. Later, it would become very noisy—lots of children, and bored-looking signoras. I used to dread the beginning of September, when we'd have to come back." She was quiet for a moment, still thinking of those foreign feasts which would, seemingly out of ritual, end with Venice. Then, realizing she had rambled, she blushed. "But that was long ago. You asked about my painting."

"You need to do it," he said, "I can tell from your eyes. I want you to show me some of your work."

Her eyes shone. "I will, if you like."

He nodded, and then asked what genre she preferred—portraits, landscapes. "It varies from time to time," she said. "Sometimes I'll do nothing but still lifes for months, and then I may switch to portraits." She looked at him closely, as if something had just occurred to her. "I would like to do a portrait of *you.*"

"Yes?" He smiled, "And how do you see it—my portrait?"

"Very strong," she said, looking at his eyes. "Deep brushstrokes, earthy colors. Heroic. Like those Byzantine paintings we just saw."

"Really?" he asked, as if struck by the idea. "Well, I know appallingly little about painting. You'll have to teach me." He glanced at her plate. "But now you've got to eat. You haven't touched a thing."

She took a few bites, hardly even tasting the food, as Alexander told funny stories about England, and his first experiences in New York. She was laughing; it seemed she had never laughed so hard, or so long. Finally, he paused, looking at her; she was relaxed, leaning back in her chair.

The waiter came to clear the plates. The wine was nearly finished, and, as the new bottle was being uncorked, they began to talk about Oxford. "In a way, I suppose that was the real beginning of my life," he said. "It changed me in a way that only Oxford can. Have you ever been there?"

"No. But I've seen photographs and it looks impossibly beautiful and medieval."

"It is." And then, "Now finish your wine, and I'll pour you some from this bottle."

He continued to discuss Oxford—how he had read history, and studied the career of Disraeli—and then, about his arrival in New York.

"Did you know anyone—anyone at all—when you came?"

"As it turned out, yes," he said slowly. "The stepmother of a friend of mine, a Swiss fellow I knew. We'd met once at Oxford, and I happened to see her on the street one day—walking up Fifth Avenue— and before long she invited me here and there, to dinners, and openings. She was very kind, and, as it turned out, very helpful."

"What's her name? I may know her."

"I doubt it." And then, "Tell me more about Sotheby's." She said she had begun working there almost immediately after college. "I had never really worked before," she told him, almost apologetically, for she so admired those like Alexander who had made their own way. Then she added, "The money you make on your own is different from any other—at least, it seems to me."

"I wouldn't know," he said. "It's the only kind I ever had."

She looked at her plate, feeling silly. "And your job at Atlantic Trust," she finally said. "You must travel a lot because of it."

"Yes," he said, motioning to the waiter. "To Italy and France. A great deal to Paris." He mentioned he had spent much of the past summer there, working on a merger, and that he would probably return in the winter.

"I studied there once, for six months," she said. "It was wonderful, it was hard to return." She told how she had rented a room from an ancient, eccentric widow called the Vicomtesse de Cahuzac, who owned a *hôtel particulier* on the Left Bank; and then about the building itself, with its colorful family members and Balzac-like intrigues. He smiled at her descriptions.

"And of course you had a lover," he said, as he sipped his wine. "A Frenchman called Henri or Marcel—very suave, with a mustache." His voice was teasing.

"No," she said, "I never did."

"I don't believe it. You must have had a lover, especially in Paris."

She shook her head, feeling curiously ashamed, as if she had not "done" a famous monument or museum. For a moment she looked away, still feeling his eyes on her.

"And when did you have a lover?" he finally asked, in a quiet, probing way.

"When I returned. I fell in love."

"And what has happened to him?"

"I'm not sure. It ended when I came to New York."

"And since then . . ."

"Since then, I have met a lot of men." She paused, and then asked—all the while fearing the response—"And you? You have known many women, I'm sure. Many beautiful women."

"I suppose I have," he said, directly, "but the most beautiful women are those who are not aware of it. Like you." He drank the wine again, tilting up the glass, his eyes on her. "You have a great deal of passion, Allegra. You shouldn't try to hide it."

Their eyes met for an instant. She was unable to respond. "And you," she said at last, "aren't you lonely sometimes, too?"

"Sometimes. Though I have been alone a great deal, you know."

"And there is no one in your life?"

He paused. "No one serious."

The waiter had come with the dessert: a chocolate mousse for her, and a *mille-feuille* for him, its layers of flaky pastry lined with thick white cream.

He caught her looking at it and said, "You must have a taste," as he took a forkful and held it to her mouth, watching as she ate. She felt strangely thrilled, for his eyes never left her, and the dessert was sweet, delicious. He wiped the cream from her mouth. Then she took her spoon and fed him some chocolate; he asked for more. Her spoon was still warm from his mouth when she tasted from it.

For a moment their talk drifted, until at one point they began to discuss old films. He mentioned his favorite, *Rashomon*, which she had never seen. "You must," he said. "It's fascinating. The same story—the story of a rape—told from three different points of view." A pause. "Although I wonder if it appeals to women as much as it does to men."

"Why do you say that?"

"Because of the subject. It would appeal to men's fantasies."

"But not to women's, too?" She had said this without thinking; he looked up, sharply.

"Why, Allegra, is that your fantasy?"

"I'd say more of a dream"—she stopped, realizing her slip—"I mean, nightmare."

"Ah yes, of course."

It was quiet now, in the restaurant, as they stood up to leave. Alexander gave the coatcheck girl a large tip; she put down her book and went to find Allegra's cape.

After several minutes had passed, the girl had not yet returned. Alexander grew impatient, calling the headwaiter over. "Where is she?" he said, abruptly. "It can't take anyone that long to find a coat." Allegra became uncomfortable; she noticed his hands again, as he brushed back his hair.

At last the girl returned. Alexander took the cape, wrapping it around Allegra. "Here, button it up," he said, his voice now gentle. "It's cold out. You'll get chilled." She did as he said, and then put on her gloves. He took one of her hands, kissing it, and holding it tightly as he led her outside, into the night.

He hailed a taxi, and they rode together wordlessly through Manhattan, his hand on hers. She longed to stare at him, yet she gazed out the window. They were silent, Allegra wondering what would become of her strange feelings for this man.

They passed skyscrapers and the florid faces of beaux-arts buildings, all lit by the pointilliste lights of nighttime Manhattan.

Once, he reached over to stroke her hair, but he did not—as she wished so much that he would—try to caress or kiss her. He had decided that it would be more effective to wait.

6

It was two o'clock and Allegra, who had worked through lunch, put down her pen, leaned back in her chair, and took a long stretch. It had been a busy morning at Sotheby's; she had arrived at the office around eight o'clock, and worked nonstop to complete a catalog for an upcoming sale. Now the deadline had been met, the catalog sent to the printer's, and she was alone. She took out a sheet of paper and idly began to sketch, quickly filling the sheet with clusters of flowers.

A week had passed since the dinner with Alexander. She had not heard from him since, and lived increasingly in the hope he might call—it seemed it was only his voice and attention that would give her life meaning. The telephone had begun to exert its own tyranny: thrilling, with the expectation it might be Alexander, agonizing, when it was not. She had stopped painting and had begun to daydream and drift; colors seemed brighter, the taste of food more intense.

An assistant entered with a letter Allegra had drafted to a client in Los Angeles. She handed the letter to Allegra, who began to read it, at one point making a correction.

"I thought that would be OK," interjected the girl.

"I'm afraid it isn't," Allegra said quietly, but firmly. And then, looking up, "Just make this change, please, and bring it back for me to sign. And let's be sure there's a copy of the December fifth catalog to go with it."

The assistant left and Allegra stood up, glancing at the clock. It was nearly two-thirty, time to meet Harry. She took the elevator and went downstairs to the exhibition floor, where an upcoming sale of nineteenth-century paintings was on view.

It was a quiet, damp afternoon in early November. Harry stood at the opposite end of the room, absorbed in looking at a portrait by Jacques-Louis David. "Hi," Allegra said, approaching him, then glancing at the painting. "This one's great, isn't it? And the provenance is interesting, too." Then they went from painting to painting, with Allegra listening—as she always did—to Harry's opinions about the quality and condition of each. He was extremely opinionated in all matters of taste, which never failed to amuse her. After a moment, they came to the side room, hung with a group of impressionist paintings. "Oh, this one's right up your alley," Allegra said, with a teasing smile, as she led him to a gauzy portrait by Renoir. Harry grimaced, then laughed, for she knew he despised Renoir, particularly late Renoir, which he considered, together with Chinese food, as epitomizing middle-class taste.

Nearby, a tall turbaned woman with a long, narrow face went from one painting to another, followed by a small, toadying decorator. "Questo è un amore," she kept saying, in a high-pitched voice. Harry turned to Allegra. "That's the baroness of such-and-such. And that's her sidekick. Of course, who knows what she really is? There are a lot of bogus titles floating around." He was inordinately suspicious of the new breed of Europeans living in New York—"Euro-trash," he called them—and often treated them quite contemptuously. "What would you do if you had her as a client?" Allegra whispered. "Barely tolerate her," he said, with a wry glance in the woman's direction.

They returned to the main room, which was nearly empty, and very quiet. A young man carrying an umbrella, his coat draped around his shoulders, gazed at a harem scene by Benjamin Constant. The guard, sitting by the taupe velvet curtain, hummed a tune under his breath.

Several moments later, a woman entered: it was her scent, actually, that Allegra noticed first, a rich lingering perfume that seemed to have been created from unknown flowers. She was dressed in a beautiful suit and a blouse that framed her face, and carried an auction catalog, in which she checked off items from time to time with a thin gold pen. She wore sheer, spotted stockings and a deep green cape with a sable collar that swung over the many layers of her outfit. Stepping delicately in her high heels, she gazed at the paintings. Each canvas came under the scrutiny of her pretty eyes: a bacchanal by Fantin-Latour; a portrait by Boldini; a Degas pastel; and finally a picture by Courtois of a young woman, dreamily reclining before an Oriental mask. At last, she approached Allegra and Harry, who stood before a nude by Jean-Jacques Henner; the subject's flesh seemed at once weightless and marmoreal, masses of red hair floating around her head.

Allegra—noticing that the woman had suddenly approached them—thought that her face, with its dainty nose, rounded cheeks, and little curved mouth, looked as if it had emerged from a painting itself. "How elegant she looks, how European," Allegra thought, as she smoothed her sweater and fixed her hair, which she had hurriedly tied back with a ribbon.

The woman turned to her with a vivid look, her mouth forming a smile. "Excuse me," she said, "I was wondering about this one." She pointed to the Henner. "It's lovely, no? Not as amusing as some of the others, but how much do you think it will fetch?" She spoke quickly, with a slight accent Allegra could not place.

"We've had a good deal of interest in it," said Allegra, as Harry looked on, then moved away. She quoted the estimate. "But I'd say it would probably go closer to the top. It's very finely painted, quite a good rendition. If you look closely, you'll see that the varnish has a beautiful, jewellike quality. And it's in extremely good condition." Allegra stopped, her eyes still focused on the painting. "Look at the way the light is cast, so that it creates a chiaroscuro effect." Her finger, which had moved to the surface, lightly traced the outline. "And then the way the figure has been molded with shadows and light; it has a wonderful sense of mystery."

"I hardly know a thing about the artist," the woman said, untying the knot at her neck, her green eyes darting from the painting to Allegra. "Henner, did you say?"

"Yes," said Allegra, nodding. "Well, he's very typical of nineteenth-century painters, actually. That feeling of languor . . ." She looked again at the painting, and then at the woman, "Is she asleep, or caught in a daydream? It's hard to tell."

The woman continued to ask more questions: indeed, she was such a knowledgeable and appreciative audience that Allegra began to give her a tour, pointing out a Parisian scene by Béraud ("Interesting for the details, rather like a cover of *Vogue* from the time"); a plein-air scene from the Barbizon school ("Not my sort of thing, I admit—all those sheep and swinging buckets"); and finally a group of small genre scenes of farmers milking cows or drinking beer ("Very big with the Germans," she said, with a laugh).

As Allegra moved from one painting to another—giving a description, anecdote, or appraisal—there was a mounting authority and excitement in her voice. The stranger noticed it.

"Ah, here's my favorite." Allegra pointed to a small painting by Alma-Tadema, called *Among the Ruins*. It was painted in iris blues, and depicted a woman with a neoclassical hair style and braceleted wrists reaching for flowers among tumbled blocks of carved marble.

"Marvelous!" said the woman, "What colors!"

"You see," said Allegra, pleased at her reaction. "At that point his technique was beautifully evolved, with all the nineteenth-century attention to detail. Heavenly, isn't it?"

She asked whether the woman would be interested in seeing the section of Russian and Eastern European paintings. She nodded, yes, and followed Allegra to the small, side gallery.

"They have their own power, don't they?" Allegra said, looking at a landscape by Ivan Choultse, and another of a dacha in winter. "Even the light and the colors are different from those of the French paintings. The pale greens, the blues, the heaviness of the snow. The silence."

She motioned to another winter scene on the opposite wall, and quickly walked toward it. Véronique de Séguiers, her cape swinging, followed. "And then here," Allegra continued, "is quite a good one. It needs a bit of inpainting, but it's charming, don't you think?" Véronique nodded, making a note in the catalog. Allegra had moved to another painting nearby, an enormous after-dinner scene by Karlovsky. "Here's a really marvelous one. It's by a Hungarian, which is unusual; we don't often get them. And again, there's a difference in its coloration—the burgundies, the teal blues." She looked at it closely. "I love the man's bored expression as he looks at her, don't you? The technique is very painterly, but unfortunately the painting is in bad condition. Lots of creases here (she traced one) and here (another)."

She looked up, only to find the woman staring at her, not at all at the painting. A smile had appeared on Véronique's face, and then she said, "You were at the Howards' dinner, weren't you? I'm quite sure I saw you there."

"Yes, yes I was," said Allegra, surprised, then shy.

Véronique introduced herself; Allegra felt the bones of her large hand in hers.

"You are American, then?" the woman asked.

"Yes, yes of course," she replied, thinking, What an odd question, just as Véronique thought, Strange, he usually prefers Europeans, and this one isn't even chic. Although there is something interesting about her.

But instead, Véronique answered, "Yes, I was sure I'd seen you there. You talked with Alexander Para, didn't you? I thought so. I asked him afterwards who you were; you were so divine looking, I said. And how marvelous to find that you work at Sotheby's." The two women went on to discuss nineteenth-century painting, and, as they did, Allegra grew impressed with Véronique's knowledge. It seemed she shared her own interest in the neoclassical period, especially the painters of the *Directoire*.

"I've a very fine Prud'hon," said Véronique, slowly walking into the main gallery. "You must come and see it, it's quite atypical of his work. And then I've a pair of exquisite paintings, in my bedroom, very much in the style of Ingres, by Chassériau." She went on to describe the twin portraits: the women's languid costumes and the enamellike colors of the settings.

"Have you always collected?" Allegra asked, watching Véronique's expressive face, and her wrist, with its fine ruby and gold bracelets.

"Oh yes, quite a lot, that's why I came here today. I'm always scouting around for things." And then, after a moment, "Do you think I should bid on the nude, the Henner? I do think she's rather wonderful." They came to the painting again, standing before it a moment together, Allegra offering her critique, as Véronique listened. "If you like it, I'd certainly place a bid," Allegra finally said. "It's very fine, you couldn't go wrong with it."

"And the other?" Véronique walked to the painting of the woman among the ruins. "I rather like this one, too. But the estimate seems high. What do you think?"

"I'd bid just in the middle of the estimate . . ."

"Yes," said Véronique, mentioning the sum she had considered.

"That would be more than enough."

"May I leave it with you, then?"

"If you like," Allegra said. "I'd be very happy to help you."

"I'll call you this week about it," Véronique said, knotting the tie of her cape. She smiled in that rapturous curved way again, closed the catalog with a snap, glanced at the last painting, and then looked at Allegra, as if something had been concluded in her mind. "When is the best time to reach you?"

"The mornings, usually."

"Perfect," she said, pulling the leather of her gloves over each finger one by one. "And then perhaps one day, you will come and see my collection, and tell me what you think. I'm sure I've some gaps, you can advise me." She extended her hand to Allegra and, with a little nod and a warm smile, walked away.

Allegra returned to her office, intending to ask Harry, immediately, what he knew about this charming and rather fascinating European woman.

In the meantime, Véronique walked toward the painting she had not sufficiently studied—the portrait of the woman with the Oriental mask.

7

Later that day, Alexander Para was talking on the telephone. He had just come from a meeting during which he had presented an analysis for the collateral of a financing. The meeting had not gone well, his proposal had been challenged, and he was tense and angry. His secretary had left his messages on his desk and, as he spoke, he sorted them quickly and decisively: those calls he would return at once, those he would return at leisure, and those he would not bother to return at all.

He said little during this present conversation; an occasional "yes," or "we'll see if that's possible," and "yes, yes, quite, I understand." He would smooth his hair, or sit back in his chair, his handsome dark head staring straight ahead. At last, he put down the telephone and rang for his secretary, saying, "Get me the number for Sotheby's."

In the meantime, the message slip from his last call was slowly being crumpled in his hand—a small pink paper on which his secretary had written "Mrs. de Séguiers."

8

After speaking with Alexander that afternoon, Véronique de Séguiers walked into her dressing room, with its *faux bois* walls and neoclassical touches, and changed into a silk robe. For a moment she stood before the mirrors, caught by her own reflection: a small, supremely feminine woman, with exquisite green eyes, slender arms, and an incisive, yet voluptuous figure that was particularly devastating to the rich men in her circle. It was only her large, square-tipped hands that were not beautiful; she knew it, and had spent a lifetime devising ways to hide them.

Knotting the robe around her waist, she then switched on the chandelier and entered her bedroom. It was large, with high ceilings, pale striped walls, and heavy apricot silk curtains that fell in luxurious folds to the floor. Eighteenth-century drawings framed tall, corniced windows; a pair of paintings by Chassériau, a follower of Ingres, flanked each side of the bed—"my follies," as she called them. Each portrayed a woman—dark-eyed and languid—reclining on a bed draped in the same creamy white satin of her negligée, a silk of gleaming insidiousness. The eyes of the women shone with provocative, defiant stares. They rather resembled Véronique, in fact.

There was a glazed serenity about Véronique's looks, a seeming in-dolence that was extremely seductive. It was partly intrinsic, partly cultivated—inspired, as well, by her fascination with the Empress Josephine. As a young woman, Véronique had decided that there was simply no one else she would rather emulate—enamored, as she was, by the courtesan-like ways, and the involvement with the house and the presentation of the self. And indeed, her own *Directoire* features and manner lent themselves perfectly to those of her heroine.

Before her dressing table was a gilt bench, its seat of ice-blue silk embroidered with Josephine's insignia, the swan. Véronique sat down, taking a silver brush to her hair, and glancing once or twice at the treasures before her—a profusion of crystal perfume bottles and boxes, some in gold, others in lapis and vermeil, still others carved like shells or fruit. Several had come from the Empress's collection. ("If you want me, find me something of Josephine's," she had once said to a particularly rich lover. He did, and was suitably rewarded.)

Her hair arranged, she applied a last touch of lipstick and looked intently at her face.

The conspiratorial glance she reserved for this moment was unlike the flirtatious sort that punctuated, say, her time at a dinner party, or one of her soirées. Now, as she gazed into the mirror, alone, on the Empire bench, her look was hard and unsparing. It missed nothing.

It had become more difficult, of late, to stare into the little oval mirror: fine lines creased the smooth skin around her eyes and mouth—what she saw, quite simply, was a lovely face slowly turning old.

She picked up a steel-blue Fabergé compact chased with a gold dragonfly, opened the catch, and looked into its mirror.

One would have been frightened—wary, certainly—to see the ex-pression in her eyes.

Later, the maid knocked at the door and announced that Mr. Para, who had been invited for a drink, had arrived.

"Alexander! So late—I'd nearly given up. Come, let me take your coat," Véronique said, with a delighted smile, as she helped him. Rubbing his cold hands together, he kissed her, noticing, as he did, the circles under her eyes which makeup had not quite concealed, although the scent of her perfume almost caused him to forget them. As she moved, her robe rustled, its red silk imparting a glow to her face.

Taking his arm, she pointed to a table, and then to a painting she had recently bought. "A beauty, no?" she said, walking with him into the drawing room. A fire crackled and the sound of Chopin nocturnes filled the air.

There was a subtle, luxurious feeling to Véronique's apartment: each room flowed into the other like the courses of a harmonious meal; one never felt engorged by too much color, or pattern, or a glut of objects. Its mood was one of European richness, yet restraint, created by a woman whose intellectual impulses had been channeled to the furniture and art around her.

Splendid chairs, mostly in the Consulate *retour d'Égypte* style, were poised in each room. Alexander sat down in one now, as the maid entered and inquired what he would like to drink. "A whiskey and soda," he said, loosening his tie.

Véronique, settling on the sofa opposite, asked about his work; he mentioned some details of a deal in progress and, as was his wont, asked her advice. "It would be helpful for me to meet Sidney Garis," he said at one point. "Do you think it could be arranged?" She nodded, for she knew the Pittsburgh industrialist well. "I'll have him come to dine," she said.

Theirs was a relaxed conversation, one with all the ease and complicity of old friends, for they had known each other for years, and had met at Oxford, through her stepson.

At Oxford, Alexander had been an eager, gifted young man in the midst of a world which, miraculously, had opened up to him. No one knew much about his background, nor did he encourage questions about his family, or schooling. About his past he spoke little, even to the many women who slept with him. As his family never visited, few asked questions; they merely sensed a difference.

During his second year, he met Jean Dubois, the son of Véronique's first husband. One afternoon in May, Véronique came to visit—a moment that Alexander would always remember. She was dressed in delphinium blue, and wore a swooping hat quite unlike anything he had ever seen. Crossing the lawn and stone courtyard, she looked like a vision. Within an instant, her arm was within his and they were tour-ing the grounds of Magdalen College.

She left that afternoon.

Throughout his last year at Oxford, and later, in London, Véronique never reappeared. Jean became increasingly distant, settling into an easy life with his true social peers. Only once or twice did Alexander inquire about Jean's stepmother. The answers, vague at first, gradu-ally became evasive and frosty at the very mention of her name. Later he learned she had moved to New York.

Several years passed.

Alexander was working in London at the Rothschild Bank, and liv-ing in a small flat near Gore Street. He had become restless, and his broken engagement to a red-haired beauty, Lady Camilla Warwick, had left him wounded and humiliated. He felt limited. He would try New York.

One day, as he walked along Fifth Avenue, he saw a familiar figure—one wearing the same exquisite blue he had remembered. He stopped her; she smiled; they spoke.

Véronique invited him for dinner. They became friends, then lovers (clandestinely, however, for she did not want the liaison to spoil her chances elsewhere); and afterward, she to him, something of a mentor. All the while, his debt to her remained unspoken, but in fact she introduced him to everyone and succeeded in teaching him a great deal; it "amused" her. "We're cut from the same cloth," she would say. She had a keen eye for talent and drive, and had sensed, from the beginning, that he could be useful to her. And, indeed, she proved right. He eventually introduced her to Edward Stern, the vastly rich oil baron from Kansas; she had been Stern's mistress for the past year.

Now, sipping her vodka, her eyes on Alexander, she said, "I went to Sotheby's today." He looked up; their eyes met. "Oh?" he said, knowing exactly what she burned to ask, but not replying.

"Yes," she said, with a deliberate smile. "I met the Clayton girl. She seems to know you—so you took my advice, after all. Why didn't you say anything? I would have done as much."

"It slipped my mind." His voice had become cool.

"I told her I'd come to look at some paintings." And then, ironically, "I think I quite impressed her with my knowledge." She stood up, smiling to herself. "How fortunate you met her. I gather from Edward that her father started Forum Industries—she is the major shareholder. That makes her very rich—did you know that?"

"I read the papers."

Tilting back her head and glancing at herself in the mirror, she lit a cigarette, her gold lighter making a sharp snap. "It would be good for you—for us—to get to know her, Alex," she finally said, looking up. "Surely you could. Her eyes lit up when I mentioned your name, it would have touched you! Truly. I said I would call her tomorrow—about a bid, I said. Should I ask her to dinner?"

"If you like," he replied, turning the pages of the *Wall Street Journal*. Her love of circuitousness, which had at first intrigued him, had now begun to be irksome. Still, he said nothing, which infuriated her, although she did not show it.

"She seems a bit of a bluestocking," she continued, in her lilting voice, as she twisted a strand of pearls. "Apparently the whole family was killed. It happened in Switzerland, Edward said." There was a pause; and then, lowering her voice, "She could be useful, Alex. She may be exactly what you need at this moment, in several ways. You should marry her."

"Why?" He went to the window and looked out, his back turned to her.

"She would take the edge off your newness, first of all." Véronique ran her hand across the pillows. "And she would help to hide the amount of money you've been spending. No one would wonder where it was coming from if you were married to her; they would assume you were using her money. And then her family is so respectable, it would make you very hard to touch." Her voice changed almost imperceptibly, became more commanding. "You've been a little careless about money, Alex. People will start to wonder. Even Nazif has mentioned it to me."

"Has he? When?" He took another sip of whiskey.

"Last month, in Paris."

"I see." He paused. "So you think I should marry her," he said, almost pensively. "She isn't quite what I think you think she is, Véronique. She is very intelligent, first of all."

"I'm sure she is," she said, "but she's also rich. You could marry her and then, afterwards—if not before—use the money to placate Nazif. He is getting restless, you know. I worry about it for you."

"I spoke with him only last week. I didn't get a feeling of that, not in the least."

For a moment there was silence. Then Véronique, her eyes ruminative, said, "I can't decide whether she's pretty. Do you think she is, Alex? That auction gallery look, those droopy clothes, the hair." Her eyes did not move from his face, watching his reaction. For Véronique's was an intense, but unresolved competitiveness—a deadly speargun with no fixed goal, poised through vast, dark water. "Even so," she continued, "you could make her into something." She lit another cigarette. "Let's have her come to dinner. What do you think? Edward, too, would be so appreciative, and that of course would be good for me. He'd take it as a sign of . . ."

"Of what?"

"Of . . ." An instant's pause. "Of caring. He told me he's had his eye on Forum Industries. He's thinking of buying some stock. Well, you know how these things work."

"I had already planned to call her," he said, in a low voice.

Véronique smiled, but then the expression vanished, replaced by another that was utterly serious. The room suddenly seemed preternaturally quiet. Alexander sipped his drink and sat down again. "And if I should marry her," he said, "what would become of the rest?"

"It would exist as before. Nothing need change." Then, her voice tinged with sarcasm, she said, "You wouldn't be marrying her out of passion, after all. It would simply be a marvelous . . . arrangement."

The telephone rang in a distant room. The maid entered. "It is Monsieur Stern calling, Madame."

After a few moments Véronique returned, her face slightly drawn, but the look disappeared as she settled on the sofa. It was dark now, and the room's glittering surfaces made her seem all the more ravishing; indeed, she looked so utterly worldly and complete that it would have been difficult to discern that, deep within her, was an acute sense of defeat—for her life had not lived up to her dreams. The magnate, the sheik (in short, the Napoleon) she should have married—and for whom she would have made the perfect wife—alas, she had never found him. She had known many powerful men, but none had ignited in her what she had always dreamt of: sexual passion, submission, and, most importantly, the unity of twin ambitions.

The clock struck eight. "I've got to go," said Alexander, standing up and putting on his jacket.

"You'll think about all of this?" she said cheerfully, taking his arm. "Yes."

While the maid went to fetch his coat, Véronique escorted him to the front hall, with its bare, shining floor and vaulted ceiling. The light here was bright, brighter than elsewhere in the apartment, where crystal girandoles scattered and deflected it.

She straightened his collar and fixed the hair on his nape; then he turned around, looking at her full face, closely, and kissed her—holding her, for a moment, around her waist. Suddenly she turned away.

He had seen the paper-thin creases around her mouth, seen that her arms, for the first time, hinted of flaccidity; no longer were they the firm limbs of a young woman. She went to kiss him again, but he brushed his mouth away from hers, giving her his cheek instead.

She felt his glance, said nothing; but she would never forget it.

As the elevator descended with Alexander, the maid entered the drawing room to smooth the couches and clear the ashtrays. She had expected to find the room empty. Instead, what she discovered was Madame de Séguiers, with a strange expression, fixing herself a drink.

9

When Alexander called, he did not invite Allegra to dinner, or lunch, or to a film. He asked whether she would go running with him in Central Park.

She had only been running once or twice before, yet she said yes, immediately. They were to meet the next morning, Saturday, by the reservoir.

Saturday was a perfect November day. The sky was cloudless, and the cold was still merely hesitant, the shadows lacy.

She arrived early and, as she waited for him, idly crunched the leaves beneath her feet and watched the others jog past. Many people were out—runners, bicyclers, mothers with baby carriages—set against the fluttering trees and the gleam of cold water. The lines of the buildings cutting into the sky had a movie-set splendor; all around her the green was interrupted and confused by the mingling of bright athletic outfits.

She tried to appear casual, standing by the rail, but she felt awkward, afraid that her blue jogging suit made her look too tall and thin. Sweating men eyed her as they bent over the rail to stretch; she looked away and stared at the sky and trees. People touched their toes, some breathing out in great gasps. Others muttered. There was an inherent madness about the scene; suddenly, with a smile, Allegra thought of Emily Norden and what she had said about jogging.

"What a funny conglomeration of bodies," Allegra kept thinking as people ran past. She saw the slim buttocks of men, the jiggling hips of women, the thin thighs of young girls, and the slow, mangled steps of an old man, with a dazed expression and painful-looking leather shoes that flapped with each movement. A pleasant-faced young man with only one arm—his other, an empty sleeve flapping in the breeze—ran past her. It touched her to see him running; she watched until he became no more than a tiny figure in the distance.

Still, there was no sign of Alexander; she kept looking about. Where could he be? she thought, fidgeting with her hands. It crossed her mind—as it often did with men—that he might have forgotten, and that he would not arrive at all.

But suddenly she saw him running up—a tall, ruddy figure with an expectant smile. Healthier-looking and leaner than the man she had remembered; another man, again, from the one who had met her at the Metropolitan. "Hi," he said, grasping her shoulder and kissing her on the cheek; the force of it startled her; she blushed.

He seemed so perfectly attuned to this atmosphere that she was quite willing to do exactly as he told her. He had already sensed that she was a novice and said, "Here, this is where we stretch." He put his leg up to the rail and pulsed the muscle softly, and then more strongly, with his hand against his leg, pushing his foot down and bending over, breathing deeply. She followed his example, but her muscles were not as agile as his, and her leg felt stiff and tight. Still, she yielded to his instructions. Next he bent down and stretched, touching one hand to the opposite toe, and then the other. She did the same. At last, he stood up, ready to run.

"Ready?"

"Ready."

He ran in a rhythmic way, bounding slightly on each foot as he stepped; it appeared effortless. And he ran fast; she had to struggle to keep up. Her breath seemed short; she felt a pull in the back of her calves.

They ran and ran, their feet pounding the track, as they passed other people and then, rocks etched with graffiti.

He watched her as she ran, touched that she tried so hard to keep up, thinking that she looked pretty with her blue suit and pink cheeks, now moist with sweat.

He began to talk; she gasped as she answered and continued to breathe fast. "Too much on your heels," he told her. "Pitch yourself forward, like this . . ." She did, and found that it helped. "Now," he said, "think of something. Anything. But keep your mind on it—not on running. For instance, I am thinking of you."

People brushed past; the sky had grown gray, cloudy. Their breaths flowed out in milky white puffs against the increasingly cold air. The water of the reservoir gleamed with all the density of autumn.

They had run about two-thirds of the way when Allegra felt the heat slowly beginning to build up in her body, the sweat mounting through the pinpricks of her skin. She pulled off her hat, and then her gloves, and wiped the beads of perspiration from her forehead and told Alexander that, please, she had to stop.

"No," he said. "Keep going. You can do it. You can stop only when you reach a fixed goal—that lamp ahead, do you see? To there." She nodded.

When they reached it they walked a moment until she recovered her breath.

"You're not breathing deeply enough," he said, as he bent down to fix the lace of her shoe. "Breathe out, breathe in—deeply, more deeply, ah, that's it."

They continued to walk; he watched her. "You need to run more," he told her. "Now, let's go."

Off he went again, watching her even more closely this time, and telling her again and again to breathe in, breathe out.

She did, and it was better; she smiled, as if she had discovered a great secret. The running became easier.

"Now you go ahead," she said, "I'll catch up." It was difficult to get the words out, and her breath, despite the deep-breathing, was short and clutched.

He set off before her as she watched: the springy step, the lean legs, the hair on the nape of his neck edging over the back of his collar, his buttocks tensed with each step of his tall figure. She watched and watched until he grew less and less distinct. She felt sad, suddenly, for she had grown used to his pace side by side with hers, and now, as she moved among the relentless strangers, she felt lost. Feeling a pain in her calf muscle, she came to a stop; then she continued.

At last, at the end, he stood waiting. "Good girl," he said, wrapping his arms around her waist. And then, "Your heart is beating fast." She felt the coolness of his cheek suddenly, and the salty moistness of his skin and damp clothes, against hers. He took her hand for a moment, then let it go. They began to walk. Gradually the heat and the sweat dissipated as the cold air hit their faces.

Soon they came to the Metropolitan Museum—a white-faced mime enthralling the crowds on the steps—and then, crossing the street, to Madison Avenue.

He asked whether she was hungry; she nodded. "Good," he said. "I'm going to fatten you up."

They passed a small food shop, bought some sandwiches, and walked in the direction of his apartment building.

It was not far from the Park—a tall, modern building with an entrance lined with mirrors, set at angles, from floor to ceiling. There was no color, no flowers; it seemed the only brightness was the doorman's crop of red hair.

Alexander turned the key in the door, picked up a stack of mail, and showed Allegra in.

She immediately felt an emptiness and a sense of impermanence in his apartment—no sense of a home. It was no more than a place through which one wandered, to awaken in the morning, and to return to at night. Its atmosphere possessed that combination of slickness and disarray which often characterizes a bachelor retreat. Modern, serviceable furniture, with touches of glass and chrome; books and records piled in great jacketless stacks. She walked around, looking with curiosity, her eyes drawn to the one arresting piece of furniture in the room: a table in the *Directoire* style, carved in front with a gilded swan motif.

She asked about it, thinking it odd amid the rest, her fingers running over its elaborately carved front. "A gift from an old friend," he told her.

They walked into the kitchen to unwrap the packages; he opened a bottle of wine. "Do you have a pot?" she asked, with one of her grave looks. "For the soup?" He smiled at her expression and handed her a pot; she stood by the stove, watching the soup as it warmed.

He arranged the other food on a tray and went into the living room. Suddenly Allegra, still in the kitchen, heard music; jazz played, very softly.

Whistling a fragment of the tune, he returned to the kitchen and—standing behind her—gently kissed her on the neck (for he had been thinking, while running, that her neck was especially pretty—long, solitary, pale, as if it needed the nourishment of kisses). She became completely mesmerized as she felt his lips. But then he stopped, took two wine glasses from a shelf, and went into the living room.

They talked little during lunch, for they were hungry, and their appetite seemed to have staunched any need for real conversation. "I'm starving," she said, biting into her sandwich. "So am I," he said, laughing. Afterward he asked her about Sotheby's, and a film she had seen, and then about Forum Industries, the company her father had founded. She spoke to him unusually openly.

He asked her, then, if she was still painting.

"Very little the last week or so."

"Why?"

"Sotheby's, I guess," she said, not able to confess that it was he who had preoccupied her so. "And somehow the desire to lock myself away to do it. It's hard, in New York; hard to be contemplative, I mean. It's as if you should always be springing to action—why, I don't know. Don't you feel that? When we had a house in the country, I used to paint there a lot. But that was home, nothing but peacefulness. There it was always quiet . . ."

"And here, you are alone," he said, interrupting her, his voice soft. Moments passed.

He looked at her plate, which was still heaped with food. "Don't you like it?" he asked. She nodded that she did, but said she was no longer hungry. "You've got to eat some more," he said. She took another bite; he watched; and then, taking his fork, he made her bend her mouth to eat from it.

She blushed, not knowing why, and he noticed.

He went into the kitchen to make coffee. She looked around the room again, and wondered whether, when he returned, he would touch her. Her gaze drifted to an empty picture frame on a table . . . And then she thought of his mouth, and the way his hand had felt, slipped into hers, after running.

When he returned, he went to the chair opposite, put down the coffee cups, and bent over to stir in the sugar. She noticed again how he grasped the cup, ignoring the little handle.

At that moment he was wondering exactly what he should do; whether it would be better to take her and kiss her, and make love to her here, on the sofa; or simply do nothing at all and make her wait. The clock struck three.

The record stopped; quiet, again, filtered through the rooms. They put away the plates in the kitchen, with its haphazard sets of dishes and utensils.

"What would you like to do now?" he said, sensing what she hoped.

"Oh"—she tried to appear casual—"nothing very much. Run a few errands—on my way home, you know." She glanced at her running shoes and thought, suddenly, how strange the blue foam shapes looked. Like martian feet.

When he turned to her and said, "Shall I walk you, then?," her heart stung with disappointment.

"Yes, of course, I'd like that," she said.

10

She did not hear from him for another week; there was something about their last meeting which had left her disturbed. She did not know why and kept trying to place it, like the strains of some forgotten tune, weaving through her mind.

She kept thinking of his apartment: its masculine colors, the absence of any domestic touches. Sitting at her desk, she would suddenly recall the empty picture frames, and the swan-carved table, and she would feel depressed, not knowing why.

Other men called to invite her to dinner, only to find her preoccupied and uncustomarily distant, the softness in her eyes transformed into a look which prompted others to say, "She's charming, but elusive." All she could think of was Alexander.

It grew much colder—the wind slicing and beating the buildings, the streets, the sooty roofs—and she found it increasingly difficult to stay home alone at night.

Craig Williams took her to a fashionable club with long red-velvet-lined corridors, called Charades. He seemed to know everyone there; many pretty women approached him as he dined with Allegra. The atmosphere was strangely cold for a room all in red, and the music, pulsing through the night, lent it an even chillier, frenetic atmosphere.

After dinner, they danced, but she found him a stiff and awkward dancer with little sense of rhythm, and soon grew tired and impatient. No matter how she moved with him, her eyes half-closed, she could not imagine he was Alexander. And the music seemed plodding and tame; she longed for sultry Brazilian rhythms! At last, he motioned to her, and they sat down. She had grown sleepy, her eyes in listless half-moons. Before midnight, he hailed a taxi and took her home.

The following week, after another such evening, she returned home to find a large package, tied with streaming lavender ribbons, that had been left with her doorman. She unwrapped it: inside, on a fanciful tray, was a pot of purple crocuses beside a small package—one which contained a tiny nineteenth-century still life of a basket of fruit poised on top of a table with one locked drawer. She had mentioned the painting to Alexander the day they had gone jogging.

With it came a card, engraved just with his name.

11

"Mr. Para, please?" Allegra asked.

"Twenty C," said the doorman.

Passing a phalanx of mirrors, she walked to the elevator and pressed the button. The lobby was peaceful; it was the third Saturday in November, and many people had left for the weekend. In an instant, she arrived at the twentieth floor.

She held a basket of food carefully in one of her hands, stamping the ice off her boots as she rang the doorbell. No answer. She waited, then rang again.

Finally she set the basket down, unwrapped her white scarf, and took off her gloves. When she looked up, Alexander stood at the door, dressed in a robe.

"Hi," he said, kissing her on the cheek and beckoning her to come in. And then: "Your cheeks are all rosy. You look beautiful."

"And you—you still look pale," she said, thrilled that he had called her beautiful. "Are you OK?"

"I am now, though still a little tired. Which is why I thought I'd work at home today." He took her coat. "Just over the flu, I'm afraid. But I feel much better, not nearly as bad as my secretary probably made it seem. Here, let me take this. What is it?"

"Lunch—a care package for you," she said. Then, glancing at the basket, with its red napkin, "It reminds me of the painting you sent me. Don't you think?" She went on to thank him effusively for it, once more, her eyes shining.

"I wanted you to have it. You seemed to love it so much. I remember the way you described it that day, when you pointed it out in the catalog."

"But it was so thoughtful—such a surprise!"

"I'm glad you like it, that it made you happy," he said, taking her hand and looking into her eyes. "I want you to be happy." For a moment he stroked her hair, almost absentmindedly. She said nothing, wishing only that he would kiss her.

Instead, he led her into the living room, which sparkled with sunlight, and then into the kitchen, where he set down the basket. A lovely stillness filtered through the rooms. Allegra breathed it in, for there were few things she found more peaceful and serene than warm, domestic order.

Then he led her to the small corridor that led to the bedroom. "I've been working in here," he said, smiling and almost apologetic, as Allegra looked around. "I can see that," she said, laughing. There were stacks of things on the bed: copies of the *Wall Street Journal*, notepads, pens, and dossiers.

She began to fold up the newspapers and plump the pillows. "Here, lie down and I'll do the rest. I'm a good nurse, you know. Majored in it at Princeton."

"I'll bet you did."

He sat down as she smoothed the covers, leaning back as she bent over to fix the pillows behind him, as she held his head. "You are uncommonly gentle for an American woman," he said, his eyes scanning her brow.

She smiled, too flustered to respond, and continued to smooth the blanket and fold the papers that lay about—returning to him, once more, to fix the pillows, so that she might hold his head, and feel his skin and hair, or touch the collar of his shirt. As she did, he watched— the slender waist, the roundness of her breasts in her sweater, the slight furrowing of her brow, as she concentrated on the homely tasks. Suddenly he started to laugh. "You look as if you were contemplating the destruction of the universe."

"Do I?" She stopped, brushing some hair from her face. "Well, I know . . . People tell me that I tend to go at things with a vengeance. Maybe it's true; I don't know any other way, really."

"Good. I like that."

They sat a moment and talked, Allegra at the foot of the bed. It was a busy time at Sotheby's, and there were several funny anecdotes to tell (a Boldini that had been discovered by a guest on the walls of her bedroom at an Arizona health spa; a Mary Cassatt that had been bought by an old lady who thought it the work of a great-aunt). The clock struck one.

"Would you like something to eat?" she asked. "Some soup, or something hot?" She stopped and smiled, remembering what he had once told her. "I'm going to fatten you up," she said.

He said yes he was hungry, for he had not really eaten in several days. But now he had an appetite and soup sounded very good.

She returned with a tray, spread with a bright napkin, and a bowl of steaming minestrone. There was a plate of sliced meat, as well, and some chunks of bread, a pot of tea, and some honey.

"This is a feast," he said, biting into the bread, his eyes on her. She smiled, delighted.

Indeed, he must have been ravenous. In an instant, the soup was finished and he asked for more, which thrilled her. She returned with another steaming bowl.

"Still painting?" he asked her.

"A bit more, now, yes. I began something last week which I kind of like."

"And my portrait?" he asked, teasingly.

"As soon as you will sit for me."

"I think I'm probably too restless." And then: "I love it that you paint."

"Do you?"

"Yes."

"You said you painted a great deal after your parents died . . ."

"That's true."

He continued to watch her, his eyes urging her to continue, for he liked to hear her speak.

"After my family was killed, yes, I did paint," she said slowly, taking away the tray. "Almost crazily at first, there was an enormous energy to it. I couldn't seem to stop, day and night at the country house we had then, in Connecticut. But then, gradually, the obsession seemed to wane." A moment's silence. "And yet I know it would make my parents sad, to know that I had stopped—or nearly stopped. My mother encouraged me so, and in some ways I feel that it is a borrowed passion, or at least one that she nurtured. So that there is a part of her in it, you see. In everything I paint." Her head was slightly bent, her eyes troubled; he took her hand and pressed it against the blanket. And then, suddenly, her eyes filled with tears, she looked up, and said, in a voice hoarse with pain, "I miss them so much, Alex! You've no idea!" Tears ran down her face. She felt profoundly embarrassed, yet she could not stop crying, and it seemed an eternity before she could speak again.

"How did it happen?"

"Seven years ago, in Zermatt. We were skiing in the spring. In early March. The weather had been strange, I remember, very warm during the day, and then at night, a terrible iciness would set in. We were staying at a hotel. I remember the day very well—we were all in the dining room, having breakfast, deciding where we'd ski. I said I'd take the day off; I'd fallen hard, on my arm, the day before, and it ached still. I said I'd read and walk. I remember my brother was so disappointed; he had grown into a wonderful skier, very lean and fast. But no, I said, not today.

"My mother skied only a little. She was a graceful skier, but not a strong one, and I almost always went with her. She seldom went out for more than a few hours a day, and when she did, she followed my father and me. He, too, skied very well—fast, like my brother. My mother hesitated to go—'I'll stay here with you and take a walk,' she said to me. But I encouraged her to go ahead. 'You'll have fun,' I said. 'Go.'

"After breakfast, I went up to my room—how well I remember it! It had sprigged wallpaper, an eiderdown, red carpet. I stared out at the window, at the mountains. The sky was blue, cloudless, and I looked at the Matterhorn. I remember thinking that it looked craggy and knifelike, almost ominous that day. There was a knock at the door, it was my brother, with his clanking ski boots. 'So you're copping out on me,' he said. I ruffled his hair and said, no, I wasn't copping out, it was my arm, it hurt. And anyway, we'd all meet for lunch.

"He wore a red hat and I remember when I came back to the room later, I could still see where his boots had marred the carpet." She paused, deep in thought; her sentences, as she spoke, spun themselves in a strangely disjointed rhythm.

"I went downstairs and watched the three of them leave, walking up the narrow street—up, past the fountain and the church, and then, towards the lift. I remember my mother turning around, calling to me, 'We'll be back for lunch,' she said. 'Save me a piece of *Apfelkuchen, mit Schlag!*' She had a funny way of pronouncing German—it always made me laugh. My father waved and took her hand. And then they disappeared.

"I went for a long walk that morning, near the town. The mountains were green, and there were flowers starting to come up. Above, of course, the snow was high and thick. I remember looking up again and again at the mountains—seeing the Matterhorn, all blue and white, gleaming in the sun. Like a rapier covered in snow. I sketched a little, bought some books, nothing much.

"It came time for lunch. The tables, the white cloths, the jokes with the waiters, who were all from Naples, but still, no sign of them. Strange, I thought, because my father was always on time. I kept looking at my watch. Finally, I went ahead and had lunch. I'd nearly finished when I heard some people—Frenchmen—say, 'You haven't heard? An avalanche, a terrible accident. Six people, just standing there, killed like that . . . The snow came hurtling down through the trees, above the lift near Findeln. They've got the dogs out there now.'

"The first thing that flashed through my mind, strangely enough, was my mother's fear about being engulfed; she wouldn't even go in the water, if there were waves.

"I heard the dogs barking and went outside to see them racing up the streets with the Swiss men.

"They took me in a helicopter, later, to the place . . . The stillness, that awful stillness, the quiet of all that whiteness. It took hours to dig them out while the dogs circled and the men made their way through. I don't remember much of that, I suppose I've blocked it out. I wanted to take a shovel myself, but they wouldn't let me." She paused, her eyes dazed, "There was so much snow!

"We found them dead and buried." She stopped, pressing her fingers to her eyelids, and then looked up. "My father's poles were still around his wrist, my mother's face was lifted, with that childlike smile—even her little ruby earrings . . ." She thought of them now, small red stones entombed in frost. "My brother's arms were wrapped around a tree, his mouth stuffed with snow, his hat all twisted . . . I wept and wept. I cried until I thought it was not possible for any more tears to exist."

Alexander let her finish, handed her his handkerchief. "And then you returned—to college?"

"Yes. It was hard, though, to concentrate on anything. The summer was the worst time, without them. I went to our house, but . . . All my mother's things seemed like ghosts! The chairs, the paintings, the flowers which we continued to arrange just as she would have liked them . . ."

She stopped, her voice still shaken, her features distorted from tears and sadness. "Every night, after dinner, I'd walk down to the stream. The house had lawns sloping down to it. There was a small gazebo where you could sit and read, or look at the moon. My godmother and her husband came to stay with me, that summer . . . Sometimes, before I went to bed, I'd look out as I closed the shutters to my bedroom, and I'd think I'd see my father, with his fly rod. Sometimes at night, you see, he would go down there, after dinner, and practice— I'd hear that whooshing sound as it streaked through the air."

The clock kept ticking—louder now, it seemed.

"Your mother must have been a remarkable woman," Alexander said at last.

"She was, though I'm not sure she knew it. My father was, too, but in a totally different way. Few people really knew him, or who he really was. He was warm and had a great touch with people—all sorts of people." A moment's pause; he watched her hand, stroking the blanket. "To know how to go about knowing—this my father considered the greatest gift. They were both full of life. My mother loved to dance, and read, and travel, and she always encouraged me to do the same. 'I don't want my children to be provincial,' she'd say.

And yet she was full of fears, and very insecure. I doubt she ever really knew how beautiful she was, or how gifted. Everything I feel about art comes from her."

"And your father?"

"From my father . . ." she said, speaking slowly, "my father had the will to get through. An enormous determination and vision. He could be reserved, and yet I know he felt so deeply . . ."

"You resemble him, then," said Alexander.

"They say I am a mix of them both," she said. Looking around the room, she noticed that the sun had dimmed. What few rays were left threw a ladder of shadows across the bed.

"My father always wanted me to have everything he never had—to be able to travel, to spend the summer by the beach. As a child, he'd been poor. French lessons, drawing lessons, all those things he wanted us to have. I always remember how happy he'd look when my brother and I came home each day from skiing; he'd ask how many runs we did, and how we'd skied. He was very much of a family animal, my father—in some ways, even more than my mother. She had . . ." But she left the thought unfinished, suddenly talking quickly, as if memories had rushed back, and she were unable to contain them. Her thoughts rambled in a way which would have annoyed Alexander in another woman, but not in her, strangely.

"I remember we rented a house by the beach once; this was years ago, when my father was just starting to build Forum Industries. Money had become less of a problem then . . . Anyway, the house had rickety walls lined with bushes, and great decks that faced a bay." She thought of the smooth bay, and then of the long stretches of sand, and the foam-laced waves that licked the beaches with a lovely rhythmic rumble. The glistening sheets of aquamarine that would slowly curl, then crash upon the sand.

"My father taught me how to swim that summer—how to take the waves. My mother would watch as we swam and dove, as the waves crashed around us. She seemed so delighted, even anxious that I learn to swim, and *like* to swim. I remember her sitting on the beach, a book in her lap, watching us as we came out of the water. She never went in herself.

"Not long after she died, I came across one of her books, a novel.

Funny, I can't remember the name of it . . . But she must have been reading it during that time, because there was a date written in front, and a sentence she had underlined inside: 'If a girl does not like dancing and swimming she will never be able to make love.' " Allegra suddenly drew back, for she had not intended to tell Alexander this.

"Do you think that's true?" he asked.

"Yes, I think there is probably something to it," she said, her voice so soft that he could barely hear it. And then, standing up, she felt his forehead and said, in a different voice, "You feel a little warm, don't you think you should take some aspirin? Is there some in there?" She motioned to the bathroom.

"Yes. In the cabinet."

"I'll get some." She went into the small room, with its mismatched towels and haphazard bottles of shampoos and pills. "Where is it?" she called to Alexander.

"On the right."

With his eyes fixed on her, he gulped down the pills with the water she had brought, and then said, in an even voice, "Do you like to dance?"

"Yes." Her eyes joined his.

"Do you like to swim?"

"Very much, yes."

"I thought so," he said quietly. Then he knelt up, above her, taking her face in his hands and kissing her, holding her fast against him, and gradually moving his tongue and fingers all over her—her mouth, her breasts, her neck. She felt his warm mouth and cheeks, and all the weakness seemed to have ended; suddenly he seemed much stronger than she, strong enough to take her here, in the afternoon, amid the waning light.

She wanted to melt into him, never to leave the feel and scent of his skin, and the mouth that kept pressing against hers. The ceaseless exploration of his tongue and hands . . . She wanting him so much, a surge of desire that pressed her against him, feeling his hardness, wanting him to undress her . . . Now he had taken off her sweater, and pulled off her boots, and for a moment stood, kneeling, gazing at her slender body, at the full breasts; and then, swiftly bending down, to enclose her again.

She kept searching for his mouth, and holding him tightly at the neck, and at the small of his back, feeling the hard insistent kisses all over her face; the darting tongue that made her go warm and tense with pleasure.

"Touch me," he said, and she did, gathering the stiffness, her fingers moving softly, then more insistently around him. Taking off his robe, he gave himself over to the movement of her fingers—gentle, wanting, unaccustomed. His hands, around her waist, then moving across her buttocks and to her neck and breasts. Her nipples tensed, dark pink now in his mouth, as his eyes scanned the pale blue veins crossing her chest. The sound of his mouth, sucking; the warm moistness between her thighs. He pushed her down, apart from him, his hand moving to her sex, to its juices, and feeling the space he knew he would soon carve out for himself. "Look at you," he kept saying. "Look . . ." His mouth and face fierce with wanting, her own eyes shining with desire.

But then he was inside her, a split-second that smoothed into his undulating thrusts. She gasped and felt him moving inside the innermost valleys of her body, in places she had never known or felt. Mauve shadows cast across the ceiling; the wetness of his back, the tensed muscles of his buttocks. The gentle, then violent movements within her, his hand with its hard grasp, his mouth tasting, tasting her face and body.

His cry echoed through the silent room, a shudder that seemed to rip him from her, even as it joined them together. Then, slowly, he began to recede, nestling his head in the cavern of her neck, so that she could feel the sweat on his forehead, and a moist hair against her cheek.

Her arms, which had clasped him so closely, now rested on the bed.

They lay like that for many moments—spent, moved, and grave. She, drawing up the sheet to cover her scar, and thinking that if the world had stopped there, at that moment, she would not have minded at all.

12

Emily Norden was slightly drunk. Not so drunk that she did not see or speak coherently (in fact, her thoughts flowed more fluently than ever), but a bit—as she put it—"warm in the head," her movements woozy. She tossed her scarlet coat on the sofa, and then flung off her black silk shoes, and poked the cold fireplace, with its mounds of dust and ashes. One electric light glowed—she had not bothered to turn the others on, and reveled in the semidarkness for a moment, smiling to herself. Sitting down on the sofa, she lit a cigarette.

"How perfect, how incredibly perfect," she said suddenly aloud, and then, in a deeper voice, "And how clever. It's worthy of . . ." But she did not say what it was worthy of, and simply continued to think and smoke. Then, yawning, she went to her desk and picked up her journal. It was made of red leather, and inside, in an elegant hand, was written: "EMILY NORDEN. PRIVATE. JOURNAL."

She wrote the date first, December 6, 1977, and next, the time. Then she began to write:

"I've just come from a dinner at Véronique de Séguiers's, a woman of several voices, assumed to be Swiss. No dearth of material tonight. In fact, I kept disappearing into the bathroom, with my notebook, just to jot down some of the juicier details. The food was delicious and chic—La Nouvelle Cuisine has swept the city—which means that I'm dying of hunger. Dying. I'd eat Damedith at this moment, but I don't expect she'd be too tasty. The wine, though, was good, rich, and very mellow; I expect it was supplied by the ever-generous Mr. Stern. He didn't appear, apparently kept away by his wife's charity ball in Los Angeles. I trust this explains the slightly tight look around Madame de S.'s mouth? Anyway, for me the chief objects of interest were Alexander Para and Allegra—I'm not sure what they intend by this (Alex and Madame de S., I mean). It's like a play—one watches eagerly for the next scene. It couldn't amount to good. But Allegra clearly adores him, and he, on the other hand, treats her with an unexpected gentleness. So perhaps he's what she needed, after all—oxygen to a closed rose. But then it's only a few weeks, apparently, that they've been seeing each other.

"I was wildly disappointed by the nonappearance of Stern. I'd met him once and—after all—I *need* a tycoon in my book. I was counting on him to be good copy.

"The evening came about rather serendipitously. A few weeks before, in the midst of a workblock one Saturday, I decided to go gemming. I called Harry Chaice and Allegra, asking whether they'd like to join me, and have lunch. They said yes. First, though, they dragged me to antique shops, and then we stopped off at Millefleur, a flower shop owned by their friend, Maggie Fitzpatrick—a bright, housekeeperish sort of person from a poor background who has turned herself into a splendid *belle laide*. From there, we set off for the jewel shops.

"Allegra was in great form—endlessly curious, and always teasing Harry." Here, Emily paused, reflecting a moment. "It's strange. I'd expected, at the start, to simply observe her for my book; *use* her for it; and now I find that I've grown immensely fond of her. Occasionally I call her Emma. 'Why Emma?' she asked, the first time, wrinkling her nose. 'That's a bit too Anglo-Saxon for my taste.' Jane Austen's Emma, I told her: 'Handsome, clever, and rich.' She laughed, surprised at this. I don't think she thinks of herself that way at all.

"Anyway, we began with Bulgari, and then lingered some at Harry Winston's—all the windows wet with gems, the promise of those inside treasures! I *do* like Winston's. You get the impression that this is where the sheiks shop, where the magnates come to stone-hunt. Compared to it, the other shops look like poor pickings—all that bone-shaped silver, and those anemic necklaces and earrings; not for me. From Winston's we went on to David Webb. What a menagerie of sparkling stones! I'd love a conch shell *minaudière* and a bracelet with a gold tiger, wrapped around my wrist.

"Hell, even now, it makes me shiver with lust.

"Afterwards—it was two o'clock by then—we went to lunch at the Plaza, and had a splendid feast, which was finished off by some whopping pieces of cheesecake. Allegra fairly bolted down her food, which surprised me.

"The two of them left, after that, and I went off, alone. I'd saved my favorite shop until last—James Robinson. The antique jewels are, to me at least, the most beautiful, although it has occurred to me that there might be something slightly ghoulish in my predilection for the trinkets of dead—albeit antique—women. After admiring a granulated Etruscan-style cuff, and then a lovely amethyst ring in the window, I was about to move on, when suddenly, through the window, I spotted Véronique de Séguiers and Edward Stern. Still thinking of the tycoon for my book, I put on my dark glasses and went in. I went straight to the jewelry cases, and peered at the dazzling array, pretending to be as absorbed as possible, so that Véronique and Stern wouldn't notice me. They stood at the opposite end, the whole ambience one of SALT Talks reverence.

" 'Ah, I'm sure it was hers!' Véronique kept saying vehemently. Turning to her side, she held up a necklace—and Lord, it *was* splendid. Masses of pearls suspended on the most beautifully worked looped chains, interspersed with emeralds and diamonds. The remarkable thing was that the emeralds were exactly the color of Véronique's eyes, for I could see them hazily reflected in the mirror.

"And then I heard the salesman say, 'Yes, there seems to be good reason to believe that this did belong to her. We bought it from a French estate, from a family whose château is not far from Malmaison. Of course, no one can be absolutely sure, without documentation, but we have found a portrait in which the Empress Josephine seems to be wearing the necklace, or at least one so similar that it seems likely to be the same.' He then held up a book with coloured illustrations. 'Ah, by Prud'hon,' Véronique whispered, bending her head to look. And then, with the most charming, though slightly fearsome smile, she turned to Stern and said, 'Oh, Edward, you *are* dear!' That seemed to settle it; the necklace was clasped at her nape and she peered into the mirror. There was silence. No one moved. The next moment, the necklace was placed in a burgundy velvet box and Stern—lean, tall, with shorn gray hair and steely eyes—signed what I assumed to be a discreet but astronomical bill.

"It's at moments like those when I wish I were a Kept Woman!

"Why I should have been so transfixed by the scene I don't know, but I stood there, unable to focus on anything else, even on the jewels. Deep in talk, the two of them did not see me; and indeed, I stayed in the other part of the store, hoping they wouldn't (I looked quite a sight). Véronique has that peculiar tendency to make any woman she encounters feel badly dressed and imperfectly groomed. (It is a talent for intimidation that certain European women have.) Anyway, I was just getting ready to leave, when I heard a voice say, 'Emily, Emily Norden, is that you?'

"I looked up and pretended to be delighted to see her. I asked how she was. 'Marvelous,' she said, clutching her red snakeskin purse in that assured way of hers. 'Such a beautiful day!'

"I nodded. Her companion came toward us. I found his height rather startling, but it was his serpentine stare that unsettled me more; still looking at him, I realized that one of his eyes was fake, and inwardly shuddered. She introduced him—Edward Stern, a near billionaire, known to be ruthless. His house, usually described in square feet, is a paradise of malachite, with television cameras scanning every room. He's supposed to be fanatically private, which makes his avidity for social position strange. The wife (there is, indeed, a wife) is one of those women whose appearance seems to telegraph her extraordinary insecurities; she invariably wears garish sequins and massive necklaces of gems so huge they look fake. (Inescapable vision of Véronique, bet she can't wait to be dressed in same!) The wife also has a battery of press agents who are paid to get her name into the newspapers and magazines. I know; they often call me.

"Stern said almost nothing, but looked at me so intently with his no-colour eyes, while Véronique spoke, that I soon grew uncomfortable.

"Wonder what he sees in Véronique. Could be sex—the final fuck, as it were. For her, of course, it's money—what else? Certainly not love, or even sex. Anyway, when you're really bent on marrying a fortune, you usually have to forfeit all notions of a lusty sex life. Some women of her breed mistakenly try to have it all, which is rather touchingly romantic, no? The problem is that you can seldom have both—the fortune and the fucking, I mean. Any woman who's ever married for money has known that for the screwing she's had to look elsewhere. There are exceptions, of course, but very few.

"But back to the twosome. We continued to talk—V. and I, that is, she moving about on her high heels, his arms motionless at his sides. It's clear that he's one of those men who doesn't really like women. (Although Véronique may have a chance, simply because she may be able to outscheme him.)

"She knows, of course, that I'm in the press, in a manner of speaking, otherwise it's obvious she wouldn't pay any attention to me. I don't think she has any use for women; they do not figure in her life, except in their capacity for being used toward some end. Why *me*? I kept asking myself, as she continued to turn those green eyes on me. But then it occurred to me that *Vogue* had once included her in its Aging Beauties issue, so perhaps she was after another moment of airbrushed splendour?

"Oh, but she did continue to talk, her eyes glowing as the clerk finally presented the beribboned box with her treasure. 'It was Josephine's,' she said, confidingly, in a low voice, as if she'd seen a ghost. There was something so odd in her look that for a moment I thought I was in the presence of a mad woman! Josephine who? I asked, goading her on. 'The Empress,' she told me, with a combination of disbelief and reverence. She went on to explain that it was her passion to collect the dead Empress's things.

"She asked me, then, what was going on at *Vogue*. I told her that everything was 'divine'; we'd uncovered lots of 'major dresses' and were busy at work on our annual beauty issue. (I just tossed that in, curious to see her reaction.) At that, her ears perked up. 'You must come to dine,' she said, in that honeyed voice. I said I'd love to, with my most charming and duplicitous smile (thinking of the tycoon I needed for my book, first; and secondly, hoping to get an entrée to her friend, Ardeshir Zahedi, the Iranian ambassador, whom I'd like to interview). 'Good,' she answered, and said she'd call. Smiling again, she wrapped her red talons around Stern's arm and left.

"I watched the two of them exit—Véronique with her arm firmly under his, clutching the box so tightly that her large white hands looked strained and tight.

"Now to the dinner itself. As usual, I arrived late. I'd borrowed a dress from the *Vogue* sample closet and didn't look too dreadful, even though it was green, a colour I usually loathe. It had a rather snug skirt with a high slit, which caused some glances, I must say.

"There was something extraordinarily intimidating about the atmosphere. That I noticed first off, even as I entered. The baroque sconces, the way the light shone from the gleaming bare floors, the maid in her gray uniform, and the assemblage of guests, all in black tie. The commanding chairs and the splendid furniture and paintings. All with an enormous sense of luxury, and yet spareness—a high-styled decor that challenged, rather than comforted the eye. It wasn't a large dinner—never is, apparently, *chez* la Séguiers—but it was meticulously thought out. Everything glistened; that was my first impression, of the *pearliness* of everything. Even the petals of the flowers—orchids and a variety of esoteric blossoms—seemed to be invested with some supernatural glow. I began to realize that this setting—its sensuousness, originality, and studied intellectual quality—was precisely what distinguished Véronique from other women with similar goals, in New York: women of a certain age, as the French say, whom one can often see at the best restaurants, escorted by rich men they hope to marry.

"When I entered the living room, the group was assembled in such a way that I thought, for a moment, of a *tableau vivant*. The faces with expressions that nearly resembled smiles and some sort of animation. The voices in a low murmur. That curious pinched look of American upper-class women; the assurance of their bejeweled European counterparts; the powerful faces of the men.

"There were several people I knew, and if I were to dissect the guest list, I'd say it was a mixture of the fashionable glittery types, who amuse and intrigue the Establishment; the Establishment, who impress the fashionable; and the small, but no less powerful group which caters to both—the inevitable interior decorator (or designer, I should say), or the fellow from the auction house who's got the inside track on the next English furniture sale. For 'amusement,' a few *National Geographic* types tossed in, accompanied by their desensualized WASP wives.

"That's the usual New York mix, isn't it?

"That Stern wasn't in evidence struck me immediately, but the peculiar thing was that Véronique wasn't either. I asked about this, and was informed that this was often the procedure; in fact, there were times when she didn't appear until moments before dinner. Michel Haran, Islamic antiques dealer with a penchant for the darker side of life, told me why: 'She's so particular about her appearance, you know. The colour of her lipstick, her makeup, her dress. I've known evenings when she hasn't appeared at all, and has simply sent an excuse, at the last minute!'

"Even without the hostess, there was an awful lot to take in: Chantal Clarigny, the French film actress of the glacial profile, talking with Sidney Garis, the Pittsburgh industrialist; James Richards, the political columnist, talking with some English banker I didn't know; and then Lewis Shepherd, the English film director I admire, speaking with Bill Rafaelson, the biographer, and Clara Moretti, the Italian heiress. When I put this all on paper, it may sound quite ordinary, but the apartment itself is so seductive that it seemed to impart an extraordinary glamour and importance to everything.

"After a moment, Michel Haran introduced me to Tom Fields, a Detroit real estate tycoon who is building a house in Florida that resembles a ship; very Bauhaus, apparently. 'It's going to shock 'em all,' he told me, gleefully. I found him charming—an engaging combination of immense power with a certain childlike delight; a 'can-do' sort of person. He invited me to visit him (perhaps I will, if I don't get Stern for the tycoon model, in my book).

"I had spotted Alex and Allegra first, actually, but only went up to them later. They sat on a small sofa and seemed to speak with almost no one but each other. That I noticed at once—strange, for Alex, who's usually making the rounds. No; for once he seemed to devote all of his attention to her; and she, on the other hand, looked lovely, as if a certain serenity had come to her."

Here, Emily stopped, bit the tip of her pen and smiled slightly. "They've probably been doing nothing but screwing.

"I was curious to have a closer look at them—always thinking of my book, naturally—so I went up, glass in hand, trying to be nonchalant, and said hello. They looked up together at once, his hooded eyes dark, hers light and fringed with lashes. I don't know why it startled me so; if I had obeyed the look in Alex's eyes, no doubt I should have leapt out the window. Hers, on the other hand, were warm and welcoming.

"I asked Allegra what she'd been up to, as I hadn't seen her since the weekend we went gemming with Harry. She said they'd been on Long Island during the weekends. 'Alex has a house in Sagaponack.'

"Alex knows me, of course, and he knows I make a point of knowing everyone, for my job and my book. So he didn't hesitate to ask me who this person was, or that, while Allegra listened.

" 'And the man talking to Lewis Shepherd?' Alex said, looking in his direction. I told him it was Bill Rafaelson, and that he'd just written a biography of Nasser. And then he asked me about Chantal Clarigny, and which films she'd been in, and then about James Richards. Finally, seizing the moment, I said, 'And where's Edward Stern? I was sure he'd be here.'

" 'Who's that?' asked Allegra. But Alex cut in and said to me, 'How's your book coming?'

" 'Very well,' said I, lying. I told him that I hoped the critics wouldn't be blinded by its brilliance. They both laughed.

" 'You must be so disciplined, Emily,' said Allegra, turning those disarming eyes on me.

" 'Why?' I answered, never having associated myself with that lofty quality.

" 'To write! To get up every day and go at it alone—alone with darling self, as someone once said.'

" 'Well, you paint, don't you?' I answered, smiling at the expression she had used. 'It's much the same thing. Besides, it has nothing to do with discipline, and everything to do with obsession.'

"She nodded, thoughtfully. 'Yes, I understand that.'

" 'You do, do you?' said Alex, slightly amused and surprised, as if a child had just pronounced a new word. He meets her ruminations with a combination of fascination and disdain, that of an analytical mind toward one that is artistic, or intuitive.

" 'Yes, I understand,' she said, not really acknowledging his tone. 'The flashes of inspiration; the times when you just have to lock yourself up, and get it right! See it to the end.' A moment's pause, and then she repeated, 'I do understand that.' Then she asked me, again, about the ending to my book. So she hadn't forgotten!

"It is one of her more endearing characteristics that she devotes all of herself to the talker. Alex can, too (and at this point he does, to her), but only when it suits him.

"We talked some more about writing and painting, but Alex cut in again, caressing her hair and making some joke. When he is bored, there is no use in trying to engage him. He is curiously unintellectual for someone who was at Oxford—all action-oriented. I watched his hand, which lay gently on her thigh.

"(I wonder if Allegra thinks she is pretty. I doubt it. There are moments when an extraordinary anxiety crosses her face, and then a moment later, completely disappears, leaving her forehead so serene that you wonder if that split-second of tension wasn't a mirage.)

"But the next moment, Véronique appeared, and an electric stillness seemed to galvanize the room. She clutched a long black lace handkerchief and wore a sheer décolleté dress in the Empire style, that showed off her white skin and full breasts.

"Again, everything about her gleamed in that peculiar way—her dress, the ropes of her pearls, the sheen of her cheekbones, the edges of her tiny teeth. Moving from group to group, she kissed this guest or that; you would have thought they were all sisters or long-lost brothers, so intense was her apparent affection.

"I waited to see what would happen as she approached our corner. It occurred to me that it was strange how she and Alex had concealed their relationship; she isn't so old, after all. But I suppose she doesn't want to be linked with anyone who might spoil her chances with someone established and moneyed (or 'loaded,' as they say here), and he, on the other hand, knows exactly what she is about and has, in regard to her, no illusions whatever; he's seen too much." Here Emily stopped and thought, before continuing to write. "No, that's wrong, he may still have one or two illusions left.

"From one to another Véronique went; an outstretched hand here, a cheek proffered there, the clinking of ice within glasses, and then—

finally—to our corner, accompanied by Sidney Garis, whom she immediately introduced to Alex. They began to talk business.

"She had given Alex a chaste kiss, but not so chaste that she didn't let Allegra and myself see how, for a moment, she *would* linger. Then she kissed Allegra, too, going on about how pretty and divine and intelligent she is. (The lady doth protest too much, methought.) For a moment they spoke about some paintings Véronique had bought through Allegra, and how delighted she was with them. 'They fill in my collection,' Véronique said, smiling and fingering her necklace. 'Allegra has such a marvelous eye, you know.' As she spoke, she gracefully took the ends of Allegra's long hair and held them up, so that they cascaded, in a fanlike motion, to her shoulders.

"She *hates* Allegra, that's clear! And the more she enveloped her in compliments the more it became obvious. To me at least.

" 'Emily,' she suddenly said, 'don't you think she's divine?'

"I nodded. What else could I do?

" 'But you're the fashion expert,' she continued. 'Don't you think she should do something to her hair?'

" 'Not really,' said I. 'It suits her.' Allegra, in the meantime, looked rather softly and pleadingly at Alex.

" 'Oh, but just a few snips here and there. At the edges. It would be so much more'—and here, her eyes looked dangerously concentrated—'chic.'

"She sat down and began to devote all of her attention to me. (She must want to be in that issue very much.) I tried to slip in Zahedi's name, and, in fact, succeeded. (Perhaps I will get that interview, after all!) I suddenly realized how comfortable Alex looked; he said little during all of this, and glanced about. Then Véronique began to ask questions about Allegra's family, her father, his company. She seemed so interested that I became fascinated, but wary, watching them. I suddenly wanted to shake Allegra's shoulders and say, 'Oh, you stupid sweet girl, be careful!'

"Finally she left, leaving a trace of that heavy perfume. Allegra said something to Alex—which I didn't hear—and kissed him, thinking I hadn't seen.

"We walked into dinner, Alex's arm around Allegra's waist, his movements energetic and lean, as if possessed by a hidden purpose.

He looked extraordinarily handsome at that moment—he doesn't always, at least not quite so much. It depends on the light and the expression of his eyes.

"Allegra looked about at the ubiquitous white orchids. 'Harry would be in seventh heaven,' she said, and expatiated on Harry's near mania for orchids. 'He raises them himself at his family's country house. You can't really *know* Harry until you've seen him there, tending them.' The profusion of other flowers had lent the air a heady, provocative scent. She took a breath and said, quite out of the blue, 'The scent here reminds me of being in church, I don't know why.'

" 'Church?' said I, with my best sardonic smile. 'Talk about opposite settings!'

" 'I guess,' she said, smiling, 'I always remember—much as I hated some things about church—how I loved the smell of incense, and the colours, and the processions. Unfortunately, there seemed no way to have the beauty and the ritual, without the guilt.'

" 'But that would be defeating the purpose, no?' I asked.

" 'I suppose. The priests, the nuns, those dour faces.' She gave a mock shiver. 'So different from Italy, from Europe. There it seems to be warmer, tied in with art, part of the neighborhood.'

"Interested to see her reaction, I said, 'Well, I wouldn't know. I'm Jewish.' Indeed, she seemed surprised to learn this. Then I asked, 'And Alex—what's he? What religion, that is?'

" 'He says he wasn't raised with any,' she said.

" 'A heathen then, I take it.'

"She laughed, tilting her head toward Alex, who had returned from another conversation with Sidney Garis, and finally said, 'I didn't know they turned out pagans in England.'

"I looked at Alex, and then at her, and said, 'They *specialize* in it,' as I stubbed out my cigarette. She laughed again.

"Curiously enough, I was seated at the head table (which only confirmed to me, again, how much Véronique wants to be in that issue). It fascinated me to see her perform, to see her matchless ease and interest in everyone. Among the city's hostesses, she is perhaps the most cultivated: turning to Bill Rafaelson, she professed a love of Egyptian history and began to discuss the art of the Ptolemaic period. On her right sat Enrico Vespucci, the Venetian aristocrat. With him she began to talk—quite knowledgeably, it seemed to me—about Palladio, and the villas of the Veneto.

"I must say the dining room was marvelously elegant: the walls a deep, neoclassical terra-cotta colour, the three tables gleaming, the proud gilt and ivory chairs covered in striped silk. There were no flowers: instead, rare Chinese porcelains from her collection sat in the center of each table—at mine, a luminous white-on-white bowl mounted in bronze (eighteenth-century *blanc de chine*, according to Allegra). The tables were set with vermeil and Venetian glasses, each course served on different sorts of antique china. The food was decidedly delicate, as satisfying to the eye as to the old *estomac*.

"She had seated me beside Henri Duprais, the French publisher—a rather Dickensian figure, with a brilliant mind; I enjoyed talking to him immensely. On my other side was a young architect, John Durham, who looked almost too straightforward to be included in this gathering. Brown hair, deep voice with a particularly engaging American accent, a touch of the Irish about his features; an athletic build which dissuaded me from my original impression—that he might have been a professor. It occurred to me that an architect might be the very thing for my book, so I began to question him relentlessly. He responded to this in a good-natured way, but soon succeeded in turning all the attention to me—asking about my work, my background. Even so, I sensed that it was really Allegra who interested him. Several times he turned to her, on his other side, to include her in the discussion, but so besotted is she with Alexander that she responded only vaguely, even perfunctorily at best, her eyes moving restlessly to Alex.

"Alex sat near Sidney Garis and sloe-eyed Chantal Clarigny, who wore the most astounding diamond earrings. He seemed quite absorbed in both her and Garis, only occasionally looking—rather proudly, I thought—at Allegra.

"At one point, Bill Rafaelson took up the conversation. Véronique had asked him about Nasser, and then about Anwar Sadat, of whom he proceeded to give an interesting portrait. Throughout it, Alex listened closely, his eyes never moving; he did not even see Véronique's gaze directed at *his*. I wondered at Alex's close attention to the Sadat story, for he had never professed any interest in politics or world affairs—except, of course, in their connection to business and money-making. But then I realized it was the clandestine nature of Sadat's ambition, while under Nasser, that drew him in. Otherwise, he could care less about politics. I remember the night we had dinner, and his totally noncommittal attitude; it rather shocked me. He told me that he doesn't even vote, even though he is now an American citizen. I suspect this is because he doesn't want to be affiliated with one political party or another; it might limit him in his climb at Atlantic Trust.

"Dessert came—exquisite, but nothing lush. It's not in these days. Instead, what was presented before me resembled a still life rather than a sweet—a dab of pear *sorbet* next to a few artfully arranged mint leaves, the whole confection christened with a bit of raspberry purée. I was dreadfully disappointed.

"The moment came for the toasts and the champagne, served in sheer, fluted glasses. I adore champagne, so that at least made up for the spartan sweet.

"Not long afterward, we went into the main salon. Here, Véronique swept up to Allegra once more. I heard them discussing painting, and the two pictures Véronique had purchased from Allegra's sale: a haunting nude, very chiaroscuro, and another—more colourful and enigmatic—of a woman before a screen, holding an Oriental mask.

"The next moment, Véronique took both our arms (Allegra's and mine) and gave us a tour of the apartment. We were shown the bedroom first—pale striped walls and two enormous, provocative paintings of nineteenth-century sirens. Then she led us through a corridor to still another room. Opening the doors, she announced, 'This is the library.' It was, to my mind, the most chillingly beautiful room I have ever seen: the walls an incandescent deep stone-gray; tall *faux marbre* cases with row upon row of leatherbound books gleaming with gilt titles; and three graceful, attenuated chaises longues, each about nine feet and covered in gray velvet. We stood a moment, silent, the flames from the candles throwing long shadows on the walls, narcissus and tuberoses emitting their powerful perfume. I began to walk slowly around, noticing the books on the Napoleonic period in one section, those on Catherine de Medici (another of Véronique's heroines, it seems) in another. Then she went to a shelf and opened a volume, her finger pointing to her book plate, taken from an eighteenth-century design, with its swan motif and swirling script. 'How breath-taking,' Allegra said, after a moment, fingering it. Véronique's eyes, coolly triumphant, watched us both.

"The first to leave were Alex and Allegra, she resting slightly on his arm, and talking to him softly, as she often does—something funny, no doubt, because he smiled. It was the first time I've ever known him to be the first to leave. Nor was I the only one to notice this: I saw Véronique's eyes as she watched them descend in the elevator. *Exeunt omnes.*"

13

Alexander had told her again and again that she was beautiful, and in the whirl of those weeks before Christmas, Allegra grew to almost feel she was.

She seldom slept at her own apartment anymore, for she ached for him always: even the thought of his kiss, his whispers in her ear, or of him spooning dessert into her mouth filled her with inner shivers. When he worked late at his office, or was engaged in a business dinner, the hours dragged by. Lying in bed, forcing herself to read, she would watch the clock until the moment came when she thought he might be home; call him; and moments later—even if it were past midnight—she would arrive at his door, carrying a bag full of breakfast provisions: the exotic jams and shapely croissants that he loved. It seemed at once safer, more exciting and more romantic to awake enfolded in the arms of the man she loved, than to greet the early morning light alone in her own bed.

To be apart seemed a cruel and unnatural deprivation; when she was not with him, he absorbed all her thoughts. Her appearance changed perceptibly—her mouth looked fuller, color often flushed her face. Her colleagues at Sotheby's often found her idly sketching when she ought to have been working, or tapping the desk with a pencil, her face lost in languor, her eyes far away.

She broke lunch dates with Harry, arrived late at work stifling yawns, and began to wear pale silk blouses and jasmine-scented cologne.

They sometimes went running at lunchtime and often—gleaming with sweat—they would return to her apartment, have lunch, and make love. There were moments when they could not even wait for lunch, when he would grab her, and pull her to the floor, that strange look in his eyes, his strong arm around her waist, embracing her so that she gasped; her mouth searching for his, her back rubbing again and again into the carpet, causing a pain she never even noticed. Afterward they would lie there, exhausted and breathing deeply, her hand stroking his wet back, his finger brushing the hair from her eyes as he kept kissing her cheeks, and then her moist shoulders and neck.

One day, as she undressed, he noticed a large scab on the small of her back; he mentioned it and teased her. She blushed, but was actually rather proud of her wound.

Now every afternoon she could hardly wait to leave work, and watched the clock as it ticked to the moment when she could escape, to be with him. She would go home and bathe first, rubbing an almond-scented cream over her body, washing her hair carefully, anointing her cheeks with rouge, and flecking her lashes with mascara. She would brush her scalp hard, and took great pains with her appearance; he noticed it, and showered her with kisses, saying that she was the prettiest girl in the world.

She dreamt of taking care of him, of having his child; she began to live for his approval. When they jogged around the reservoir, she forced herself to keep up with him. She searched for books he might like and experimented with perfumes which might attract him. (One day, in fact, she asked him if there wasn't one, in particular, he liked; "I'd tell you," he said, "but it would be someone else's.")

They tried different restaurants, never returning to the same one twice, even if they had had a good meal. He liked change, he explained, and there were so many fine places in New York, it seemed ridiculous to limit oneself to one, or two, or even several. He encouraged her to eat ("I'm going to fatten you up"), taught her about wine, and had her order desserts—watching as she licked *crème brûlée* off a spoon. He told her he loved her mouth and never tired of kissing it.

They went out for dinner almost every evening. Once or twice, when they did not, they ate at his apartment, she in a silk robe she had taken from his closet. Sometimes, midway through the meal, he would beckon for her to sit on his lap, and the dinner would end— dessertless—in bed.

Assuming that he would like for her to cook, one day she spent hours learning to prepare chicken breasts with paprika and cream. Instead, he grew rather tense when he saw her in the kitchen and said that it was a waste of her time. The dinner passed rather silently, instead, with Allegra withdrawn and near tears, fearing that she had displeased him.

Afterward, when they made love, though, it hardly seemed to matter, for he was as tender as ever.

When they went dancing, they were often the last to leave the nightclubs. He was a wonderful dancer with a sure sense of rhythm and a seductive way of guiding her through the beat. She told him that she loved Brazilian music, and, as it turned out, so did he. In its quest they went from place to place, their favorite being Bocachica, which featured sultry music, couples who moved as if their hips were carved of one piece, and a singer in tight, filmy pants that outlined every curve of flesh.

They drank thick orange liqueurs with foreign names that tasted of bitter fruits—Alexander watching as she sipped hers from an immense, bulb-shaped glass.

During the day, there were moments when she suddenly felt she *had* to see him; it might be in the middle of an appraisal, or as she toured the paintings on exhibition with some client. At the first available moment, she would run upstairs to the telephone, breathlessly dialing his number, her voice rather impatient when she reached his secretary. When she finally heard him, a deep relief and pleasure would fill her; sometimes he would invite her for lunch. Stepping lightly, nearly running down Fifth Avenue, she would meet him on a corner, her cheeks flushed with cold, her eyes sparkling, her hands white and icy—for, most likely, she had forgotten her gloves in her excitement.

Then, as they sat at lunch, all appetite would escape her, although moments before, she had been famished! It hardly seemed to matter what they ate—it was being with him that thrilled her, talking to him about the events of the morning, asking the advice she soon learned he loved to give, or joking about something she had seen, or a funny incident with a client.

Then they would part: she, tugging his collar and begging for more kisses; he, laughing and smiling but still protesting (they were on the street, after all). After watching him disappear among the crowds, she would walk slowly back to Sotheby's, and her afternoon would pass in a haze.

There seemed no greater pleasure than waking up with him in the morning, when the light had just come through the curtains and the sheets and blankets were warm and languid; the mind still suffused with drowsiness and dreams, so that love-making seemed almost an extension of that sleeping state.

Soon she hardly minded whether his doorman knew she had spent the night there, or whether, at eight-thirty in the morning, she entered her own building wearing what were, quite obviously, evening clothes.

Sometimes he would escort her downstairs, in the elevator.

Once he said, "Who is this beautiful woman next to me?," as he buttoned his coat. "She must have just slept with me."

"Why?" she asked.

"Because her eyes are sparkling."

After a brisk walk, she would click open the door to her apartment, pick up the newspaper, and feel the awful stillness. The bed, still made. The rays of light crisscrossing the floor. And then she would look into the bathroom mirror to see her mouth still warm, slightly swollen, her hair scented with the previous evening's perfume (to wash it and eradicate the scent, or to let it linger?); her body fragrant with his pungent, slightly saline wetness still within her.

Before this time, it seemed that sex had only existed as a lacuna in her life; she had skipped over it as one would a hunter's trap along a leaf-strewn path—for who knew what lay beneath its camouflage of branches?

Yet, as a young girl, it had never dawned on her to discipline her growing lust for romantic literature; nor to inhibit her mind from racing and feeling its way through brooding nineteenth-century stories.

Her first lover had been an astonishingly handsome young man: tall, blond, and hard to fathom. She had slept with him after their second meeting. His tweed jackets, his vivid blue eyes, the expert way he sailed—his presence was as disturbingly physical as it was, in the end, remote.

He gave her a compass once: "For direction," he told her.

The first night they made love had left her perplexed, for she had somehow expected *more,* and after, he had hardly even kissed her. She, on the other hand, lay awake, startled and still tense. The next morning—after a restless sleep with dreams of empty seas and endless wanderings—she lay staring at the ceiling, like a marble-sculpted lady carved atop some medieval crypt.

Months later, there had been that other unforgettable night: they had lain sunburnt on cold hotel sheets, as she turned to him and told him that she loved him. In response, only an asplike silence that bit off her desire.

She had known several other men since then, yet her experiences had remained eerily the same.

And so, how different it was with Alexander! She thought about it endlessly—how tenderly he held and caressed her, how he stroked her hips and seemed concerned for her pleasure, how he kissed and held her and telephoned her at perfect moments. And then he made love to her so much, in such unexpected places! In the kitchen, he would kiss her neck, as she stood by the stove, and it would end in bed; or, in the early morning, as they finished coffee, he would take her on the sofa, untying the loose silk robe and kissing her breasts; in the elevator, he would stroke her and she would become so excited that she could hardly bear the thought of work.

Their talk on the telephone was like that of any other lovers—

listless, often unimaginative, riddled with pauses. "My heady package," he would often call her.

In bed, his language was sometimes gentle; other times, he would use words which she once would have considered rough and coarse, but which now, in a strange way, excited her. "You want to be fucked hard," he would say, pressing down on her shoulders and watching as she welcomed him, her head turning from side to side. Or he would say, softly in her ear, as he thrust inside her, "You like to fuck, you do."

Her sleep, which had once been fitful, now became almost uniformly long and deep. When she awakened before he did, the quiet of the early morning seemed almost painfully wonderful. She would look at him, his hair tousled in the pillow, and slowly, as he awakened, he would gather her to him, and they would lie for a moment, her fingers tracing the pattern of hair on his chest, to his hard thighs and penis, as she touched and stroked until—very quickly—he became erect.

His ardor for her filled her with an almost mystical sense of attainment, as if her life had suddenly accomplished her fantasies, becoming as breathless and romantic as the stories which had fed her imagination.

Allegra was perhaps the most innocent woman Alexander had ever known, which was partly why he found her fascinating. He watched her face, which was—more than most women's—a barometer of her moods, thoughts, and feelings. She soon learned that the restraint she tended to practice with others was useless with him; she could not dissemble, for he seemed to have an uncanny ability to decipher her mind.

There was a certain lack of embellishment about her that also intrigued him—her fresh pink nails, her fine skin, but most of all her face in animation, when the rush of ideas, or the emotion of a memory, or the delight in some beautiful object flooded it with feeling.

Nevertheless, this delight in her bewildered him, for he was a man who had always been easily bored, who liked change, and who had never really known a woman who satisfied him. And, in a curious way, Allegra taught him things. "I always learn from listening to you," he once said, as she finished describing a painting, or explained the technique of an artist. When he first heard her speak French, pride swept over his face; his friends, rather amused, remarked about it.

It was her combination of earnestness, dreaminess, and determination that appealed to him, and which often made him inwardly laugh. It amused him to watch her, waiting so impatiently, for the tea water to boil—her chin nestled in her hand, her feet tapping the floor. Sometimes he would stare at her, in the early morning, while she slept, her hair spread upon the pillow, her face tilted up.

Most of all it excited him to see her hunger for him, to know that her preoccupied eyes were filled with desire.

On the Saturday before Christmas they went shopping. The streets were filled with impatient crowds, the sound of bells, and the scent of roasting chestnuts. From store to store they went, gathering boxes and bags, until they could carry no more.

At last, they went to the St. Regis Hotel, for a late lunch.

She had been there before, but now everything about the atmosphere seemed to incise her with pleasure: the lengths of shiplike brass rails; the thick pink cloths; the flame-stitched seats; the high, cavernous ceiling; and the crystal chandeliers. Even the frescoes—which had once seemed to her like weird Art Deco parodies of Piero della Francesca—assumed a funny, baroque glamor.

They drank wine, and ate steaming hot soup, and picked plump rolls from brimming baskets as they laughed and talked and spread the bread with butter shaped like rosettes.

Allegra was suddenly filled with such a deep, unutterable happiness that she turned to Alexander and said, "I wouldn't mind if my life stopped here, at this moment, at this table." She then took his hands and kissed them, fervently, again and again, so that the maître d'hôtel turned, and looked the other way.

It grew dusky, but they were both reluctant to leave the hotel, which was at its most merry and bustling.

He took a suite.

Moments later, they were making love in an immense room with a vast bed which Allegra said looked as if it had come from the set of

Gone with the Wind. It had a gilded, tufted red velvet headboard and flat, soft pillows; through the small hall was a high-ceilinged room with a fireplace and formidable sofa.

She wore his shirt the next morning as they ate breakfast in bed.

That day, there was an article in the newspaper about Princeton, which mentioned a professor of art history who had once taught Allegra.

"You know, he once told me that I was the most gifted pupil he ever had."

Alexander, holding up the newspaper, looked at her, smiling. "Why, that's exactly what I tell everyone," he said, gathering her into his arms and covering her with kisses.

14

Véronique stood by a blazing fire clutching an icy glass of vodka. She wore a long purple dress, belted in gold, with a petallike collar that framed her face. Every so often she would poke the burning embers with a long brass rod.

"And so, how is it going?" she said, looking at Alexander. The light was dim, making his hair appear darker.

"My work?" he asked, knowing exactly what her question meant.

"Yes," she answered, pretending she had.

His hand grasped a glass of bourbon. "We had an interesting deal come to us, actually," he said, sipping his drink. "A Milanese pharmaceutical company that wants to start investing here. Riffner has given it to me to handle; I may have to go to Italy soon." He went on to tell something amusing that had happened only the other day at Atlantic Trust. "How extraordinary," she said, uttering a light laugh.

A moment later, her face serious, she asked, "When do you see Michel?"

"Next week . . ."

"So soon?"

"Yes." He paused. "And where will you be?"

"Here, with Edward." And then, after a second had elapsed, "And the girl—you've been seeing her, haven't you?"

"Yes. Why?"

"I went to see her yesterday at Sotheby's. I told her there was a painting I was interested in. I thought she looked . . . changed." She went to the sofa, sinking among the cushions, pillows massed around her. An ironic smile lingered on her face. "I think she's quite taken with you."

"She is someone who feels deeply," Alexander said quietly.

She had not anticipated that response. "And you will marry her?"

"That remains to be seen."

"You should—soon."

"There's no rush," he said, looking into his drink, "We can wait."

15

Allegra spent Christmas in New York, waiting for Alexander's telephone calls. He had gone to Paris, on a business trip. "The Garis deal has come through," he had explained.

She had pleaded with him to let her come. "No, not this time," he had said, kissing her. "Another trip, I promise, when I don't have so much work. I'll take you then."

On the Thursday before Christmas they rode to the airport, Allegra laden with gifts for him. She sat silent, looking out the window, dreading the moment when they would part, and the desolation of her own apartment. "What are you thinking?" he finally said, squeezing her hand, an amusement and slight annoyance in his voice. "You are always *thinking*."

She looked at him, her eyes sad, her face pale above her white scarf. "I was thinking how much I'll miss you. How I don't know what to do without you."

He drew her close and kissed her, wiping the tears from her face with his handkerchief. "I'll miss you too," he said gently, lifting her chin with his finger, and stroking her hair. "I'll be back in a week, that isn't so long, is it?" She shook her head, trying to look convinced, all the time thinking that it sounded like a century.

That weekend she tried to read and sketch, but did almost nothing of either. Her paintings—the product of her unfocused mind—remained unfinished.

On Saturday morning, she stood before the canvas of a painting she had begun in mid-September. She had pulled her hair back and put on her old clothes, but her hands moved only half-heartedly to the canvas. It seemed that the images that had once flowed so freely now lay clotted in her head; her hand, with the brush, felt petrified. She stood before the easel, her thoughts wandering, occasionally yawning or walking to the window. Finally, she put down the brush and lay on the bed, staring at the ceiling.

It occurred to her to call Harry, who was in the country with his family. But she had hardly seen him recently and had noticed, when she had, a coolness in his eyes at the mention of Alexander. Then she thought of Laura Hilliard, her godmother; she had invited Allegra for Christmas, but Allegra had declined, feeling certain, then, that she would be with Alexander. Suddenly she remembered that it was months since she had written Laura, and that she had neglected to send on a book she had promised.

She was invited to the Fitzpatricks' for lunch on the Sunday before Christmas, and walked up Park Avenue on a cold, but bright-nooned day. Everyone seemed intoxicated by the lapse of routine. Doormen nodded and tipped their hats; Christmas trees shone in many of the windows.

Allegra returned home at three o'clock, her cheeks red, her hands icy from the walk, and immediately went to the kitchen to make tea. She stood by the stove, near the flames, waiting for the water to boil. Moments passed; again and again she thought of Alexander, until a burning smell, and then some flames, startled her. Her coat! The cuff was on fire! She frenziedly dashed out the flames and ruefully held up the sleeve, but it was only imperceptibly singed—she sighed, relieved that she had caught it soon enough.

It was three-thirty now, a good time to call Paris. She would surprise Alexander, and then, afterward, she would try to paint again. Walking quickly and humming a tune, she went into her bedroom and dialed the number of his hotel. She was excited, as she always was, to think that she might hear his voice, and clutched the telephone tightly as she waited, almost holding her breath.

There was a moment's pause, and then a ringing—the gurgly, irregular sound of a foreign connection.

A woman answered in his room, a voice Allegra did not recognize. Startled so that she could hardly think or speak, Allegra merely repeated, "Is Mr. Para there? No? When do you expect him?"

She left a message, spelling her name with a painful precision. He had met someone else! Slowly she put down the telephone, and then, thinking there must be some mistake, rang again. There was no answer.

She lay down on her bed, her muscles aching, her mind suddenly exhausted.

That night, she made her way through Christmas Eve dinner as one might grope through fog—hardly seeing anything. She felt ugly; the food seemed tasteless; she barely sipped her wine.

When she returned home, the telephone was ringing. It was Alexander.

"How are you?" he said, in a booming, cheerful voice. "I miss you!"

"But I called," she said, her eyes wide, frightened for what she might be capable of saying. "Didn't you get the message? A woman answered . . ."

"A woman? What woman? Did you ask her name? Well, why ever not?"

"No," she said, "I didn't, it was stupid of me, but no . . . I was so surprised that . . . Are you sure there's no message? She said she would leave one."

He laughed. "It must have been the maid," he said, as he joked about the "phantom woman." And then he began to tell her about a restaurant where he had had dinner, and a walk he had taken. "But I miss you!" he kept repeating, with such warmth and vehemence that she thought, How silly of me to get so upset, and told him that she missed him terribly, too, and could hardly wait to be with him again.

He told her how much he thought about waking up with her, and making love to her, and how much he loved touching her body; such things that excited her, that filled her with such wanting that, as she lay in bed that night, her arm propped under her head, her eyes fixed on the ceiling, she could think of little else but how his body felt next to hers; or how he looked, when he wanted her; the things he said and the pleasure he gave her as he kissed her and held her and touched her, so that she grew restless and too aroused to sleep.

Hours later, when she did, she dreamt.

There was a beach and a boat, slipping through waveless water. So clear and blue was the sea! By her side, in the boat, stood a figure draped in black. Allegra kept watching the water, and longed to dive in; but what would she do with her favorite ring? Perhaps it would slip off as she dove, for her hands were slippery with tanning oil. Surely it might . . . So the figure—man or woman, she did not know—turned to her and said, "Give it to me, I will keep it for you." Allegra took it off, and watched how it disappeared into the other's fist, like a magician's trick. Then she sprang into the cold blue water. Swimming and swimming, she came to the island that lay beyond, its palm trees bending their fronds over the white—such white—sand. Water dripped from her as she stood, gleaming like a seal, in the hot sun. At last the boat arrived with the figure that held her ring. "Now," Allegra asked, "may I have it please? Surely you've finished with it." But the fist that opened before her was empty. "What happened?" she asked, looking up to the veiled, triumphant eyes. "I let it go," it answered. "Accidentally, you understand, but those things happen." The hooded figure drifted off, leaving Allegra to search and search the sand for the single band of gold and sparkle. The sun began to fall, and then to turn crimson; and then the sky blackened out of recognition. Everyone had left her, and the ring was nowhere to be found. Divers, surely, could find it, she thought; with their spearguns they would know where to dig and sift. The night grew blacker than any she had ever experienced, and finally, with her vacant hand, she left the sand to follow, to go, she did not know where, for there was no one now . . .

Allegra awoke, clutching her fingers, her mind hazed with fear, until she remembered that it was only a dream, nothing more, and that her ring lay in a basket, on the table. Still she could not fall asleep again, and stood, until dawn, looking out the window at the forsaken streets.

16

A part of Allegra was drawn to separation almost as much as she feared it: the voluptuousness of anticipation, and the intensity of the long-imagined meeting afterward.

Late in the afternoon of the third of January, she hailed a taxi for Kennedy airport, for she had told Alexander, who was to arrive from Paris, that she would meet him. Indeed, he had expected her to come. "Of course I'll be there!" she had said, when he had called with his flight information. "I'd already planned to."

The plane was late; and then it took time to clear customs, so that she waited, endlessly it seemed, among the crowd of brightly dressed strangers.

She had dressed as carefully as an actress preparing for a role. Her hair shone, and there was a pinkish gleam to her eyelids; as she moved, those around her smelled jasmine and lavender. The tips of her fingernails had been filed into a smooth almond shape. Men gave her appreciative glances. She wore a peach-colored sweater, a coral bracelet, and carried a book, which remained closed.

Someone bumped into her. "Excuse me," she said.

A moment later, a man asked, "You got the time, lady?" "Yes," she said, with a short breath that sometimes punctuated her speech.

Never did an hour drag by so slowly; never did it seem that so many airplanes could have unloaded with so many passengers, and none of them Alexander.

As she glimpsed each tall man in a dark suit, her breaths grew faster, her eyes widened; until, spent with anticipation, she sat down, her eyes fixed to the clock.

At last, when he arrived, she hardly grasped the moment, for she had flown to him, and his embrace had nearly choked her; his arms, gripped around her waist, seemed eternally locked. Kisses erupted from their lips; she stroked and stroked his face, his hair, his back, wordless with happiness.

He looked relaxed and well, more handsome than she had ever seen him. Laughing, and grasping her hand, he gave her a dossier to carry; in his other hand was a glossy bag lettered "Christian Dior." "Presents for you," he said; and then, "Did you miss me?"

"So much! I don't think I even thought of anything else."

"Good. That's how it should be." Stopping suddenly, he looked at her blue eyes, seized her again, so that she felt his warm chest, and his hardness, and her own moist, unstoppable passion.

They sped from the airport to Manhattan in one long uninterrupted kiss.

For weeks she would not work; all she wanted to do was make love and bake cakes.

At Sotheby's, everyone wondered what had happened to Allegra, for she had always followed the progress of each sale with a crusader-like zeal—eager to know who had bought which item, anxious that her favorites should find the right home; thrilled when the items of best quality fetched prices equal to their worth. Now she hardly seemed to care.

When, that January, an exquisite Mary Cassatt went to her least favorite client (a Frenchman she had once described as "that frog with the common taste"), she did not seem perturbed at all. When, after the same sale, she had to telephone the woman who had consigned a superb Millet and tell her that it had not sold, Allegra's voice—though gentle—verged on the matter-of-fact. After putting down the telephone, she simply resumed her cataloging, gathered her things, and quietly went home, an hour early.

She, who had always begged to go on appraisals, now seemed to shun them; she began to avoid distant trips to other cities, willingly—even eagerly—letting someone else take her place. A robust young German woman in the department—Lisa von Schecter, with whom she had a subtle rivalry—began to call those who had always been considered Allegra's clients.

"What's this, I hear?" said Harry to Allegra, one day as they left for lunch. "Lisa's calling the Mortons and the Rosses now, not you? What's the matter with you?"

"Oh, who cares?" said Allegra, nervously looking at her hands as she attempted a laugh. "Let the Baroness"—which Lisa was, in fact—"have her day."

It seemed to Allegra that all sense of pleasure was linked with Alexander, and that her work, which had once provided joy, now seemed a nuisance bordering on deprivation.

Everyone said she looked different.

Her gestures seemed to have shaken off their skittishness; her face had changed—her mouth was riper-looking, her eyes radiant. Her cheeks and hips had grown slightly fuller, which—as Harry observed—gave her a charming, pre-Raphaelite look. She almost never pulled her hair back now, began to collect beautiful shoes, and was meticulous—to the point of fearful—in regard to clothes.

But then, Alexander was so particular! She could tell instantly if a dress, or style of blouse, displeased him. An unfavorable comment from him, or even the most gentle suggestion, made her quick to chastise herself, and once or twice, silently angry. "I want you to be beautiful tonight," he would say before an evening with an important client, and the pressure would blow upon her like a cold wind.

Still, when he told her how lovely she was, and how perfect, she felt she had never known such happiness!

She spent so little time at her apartment that she hardly knew it anymore; for she saw it in the morning, as she dressed for work, and then again in the evening, before she went to Alexander. It had assumed the anonymity of a hotel room, with a hotel room's stillness and foreign textures. The neutral colors of his apartment, with its modern furniture—to these she had grown quite accustomed. She associated his apartment with adventure, and hers with emptiness and isolation.

The rare evenings without him were spent thinking of him, or trying to paint him a present; and in steamy, perfumed baths during which she scrubbed every inch of her body with a rough, scratchy cloth which, if used assiduously, supposedly softened the skin.

She who was gifted in languages now learned another. Sex seized her mind and her senses, a restless blue tide advancing and ebbing, at times as violent as a thunderclap, at others as diaphanous as a darting shadow.

He teased her about her lust, and said he could tell when she looked "hungry." "Your eyes," he told her, "give you away." But it was not only her eyes that mirrored her desire, but her entire body, which suddenly felt ripe and open, purling with needs she had never recognized before.

She would often find herself at her office lost in the thought of him, her nipples suddenly tensed under her sweater.

Sitting across the table from him at a restaurant, she would recall the way he had been with her only that morning: the tremor she had felt as he unknotted the soft robe from her waist; his hand, parting her thighs; the hot flashes of naked flesh and silk. And the murmurs that accompanied the robe, dropping in folds to the floor . . .

Morning teacups on a table. She might have been talking about something quite earnestly; the two of them stretched out on a sofa, her head in his lap. Interrupting her streaming sentences, he would say, "Come here," in a voice gone low and deep in the register of sex. "But I was *talking* to you," she would say, adopting a tone of playful annoyance to mask her thrill. He would gather her into his arms, and they would begin again: questing tongues, his dark head moving between her thighs, groping hands, hot keen kisses mounting to the crimson chills of climax.

The cool panting of the exhaustion, afterward, as his face nestled in her hair, her hand on his moist chest.

Before she had met Alexander, she had come to dread Sundays—

their emptiness of purpose, their scheduleless hours, their aimless walks and absentminded museum visits, their aloneness—but now she lamented Sundays' end, for she loved their new mood of ceaseless lingering . . .

Newspapers scattered on a floor, the thick sections merely glanced at; sheets spotted with tea stains and brushed with crumbs. The disarray from the previous night: one murky half-finished glass of wine, another ringed with lipstick. Light, drifting through curtains; the feast to feast of caresses with breakfast. She, groping through the dark tunnel of his affections as his strong arms wove around her.

He knew it was he who had carved the place within her, for it had been eager and wanting, but tight at first, its stopped juices unable to articulate how much she desired him. But gradually it had yielded to a warm, fluid space that craved and welcomed his thrusts, newly slippery, quickly moist.

The utter relief of postcoital satiation: furrowed pillows and slow, ruptured breaths.

She loved the smell of his sweat, the feel of his skin, the rounded muscles of his arms; and the hard, but faraway look in his eyes as he grew erect, absorbed in her.

Her "ravishments," as he called them: for the idea of her submission excited him, as it did to see her kneeling on the floor, all his stiffness gathered into her lips; her little sucking sounds, his low moans, her cream—for that is what he called it—flowing. He never made love to her the same way; he liked to see her body turn according to his desire.

To see her high round breasts, the upturned nipples, and the incisive curve of the waist yielding to the softness of her hips; or the round buttocks moving, free-willed, against the lean, flecked shadows of her back, as he pushed and thrusted so that she gasped. The seeming eternal closeness of those moments, the early morning sun gone blue-green with stillness.

Like fences ripped apart, so too were shattered all the inhibitions that strangle intimate language.

His gentleness soothed her and made her feel safe, but it was often his roughness that excited her and made her eyes beg for more. The explicit words, breathed into her ear, as he lay atop her, pressing down her shoulders. "You know you love to fuck but you couldn't admit it," he would say in that voice. "You need a lot of cock." Words that brought to life some dark, sealed-off part of her.

Her foot, slipping through a transparent stocking as she dresses for dinner. He watches, and then she says, with a small smile, "Why are you looking at me so strangely?"

"Not strangely at all—pure lust."

Her knees, moving to the floor, as he stands, satisfied, watching . . .

For her, leaving him meant a march into the abyss; how could she have felt complete before?

Her key, slowly turning into the lock; memories of a chaste, unsatisfying bed.

Gradually she learned to tell him what she wanted, which pleased and aroused him.

"I need you," she would say, in a hoarse whisper. "Please, now." Her fingers, prying open the buttons of his fresh shirt; loosening the knot of his tie; and the thrill—to her, to him—as the zipper slowly yielded, leaving her to feel him bursting against it, as she slowly sank to the floor . . .

In the mornings now, she no longer waited for his desirous gestures, or for the firm, tongue-darting kisses that signaled the beginning. Her hand, now more expert, knew how and where to arouse him, and her mouth—no longer intimidated—moved about him beautifully. (Then, his head, sinking into the pillow, and the cool-hot shimmers that shot between her thighs.)

Now he seldom needed the sleeping pills which he had occasionally resorted to using. "Mine are better," she would say, with a tender smile, her lips grazing his. Pulling off the sheets, she would cover his body, from neck to feet, with kisses; his arms, his nipples, the flanks of his hips, the tensed muscles of his calves . . . His body would relax, and the tension that sometimes crossed his face and neck would disappear. He would say nothing, for he felt too much. She would take his feet and caress them, kneading them across the arches, kissing all his toes.

No one had ever kissed his feet before, he told her, taking her up again into his arms, and kissing her so lovingly and drowsily that she fell—as he did—immediately back to sleep.

The following morning: her shiny, just-washed face at odds with her black stockings and high heels. *Diamanté* earrings hidden in the side pocket of her handbag.

They spoke about their desires at moments when it was impossible to fulfill them, each watching the other's reaction. She had learned this from him.

He, to her, at a formal dinner amid candelabras and stiff linen napkins. "Let's go home and fuck." Her face, reddening; the sudden flush of inner thigh warmth, again.

Or:

Pressed against him, dancing, she would murmur in his ear and feel him harden, his eyes lowering, his cheek suddenly hot. He would draw her closer, so that their hips locked, their steps reduced to a slow, lingering motion.

And there were times when sex—which had once seemed so august and insurmountable to her—assumed a strangely lighthearted air.

At dinner, one night: The waiter who brought him a pear tart and, brandishing a small silver bowl, asked if he cared for whipped cream.

"He only likes *crème fraîche*," she had said, interrupting, her eyes shining and laughing as she watched him. His smile; and her hand, creeping to his thighs, under the table.

PART TWO

17

Emily wrote in her journal:

"January 17. She must be good in bed; otherwise I'm not sure she'd get anywhere with him, despite the money and the 'class' (a vulgar word, but here it applies). I say this because I saw Allegra today and thought, something has changed about her.

"Hard to pin down, but absolutely true.

"She'd called me and asked whether I'd like to have an early dinner. 'Alex is working tonight,' she explained. We planned to meet at Bookends and go from there to the bistro around the corner.

"I happened to be in a rather sour mood—as I usually am, during the damn collections—but she, on the other hand, looked fresh, almost impish; her skin totally translucent, her cheeks glowing pink. She looked quite tall, because of the rather high heels she was wearing. 'Hi, Emily,' she said, in a jolly voice, as she saw me, and then asked whether I would mind if she looked for a few books, before we left for dinner. She wore a fluffy purple scarf which framed her face, and looked so spruced up and I thought, ah, that's Alex. Such is the transforming nature of a love affair.

"Taking off her scarf, and fixing her long hair a bit, she asked for some books: history, finance, that sort of thing. I looked at this fair creature with the Rapunzel hair, and I thought, is *this* the same girl who was searching for books on obscure Italian queens? But again, I thought—it's Alex—and sure enough, I heard her tell the clerk that they were for a 'friend.'

"A 'friend'! That's marvelous. They probably haven't stopping fucking since Véronique's dinner.

"The clerk led her around and spent a good deal of time helping her find the books (this irked me; when *I* ask for help, they won't take five seconds!). She thanked him repeatedly and then made her way to the back, where I saw her look at all the popular trash—titles which, I'm sure, she would never have bothered to glance at a month ago. She hardly even looked in the Art section; in fact, I thought I saw her yawn as she approached it; and then went to another corner, where they keep all the How-To books (this section has grown recently; even old Bookends has had to succumb to this peculiar American mania). Included among these, of course, were all the sex books. (All with very discreet covers and the most circuitous titles, whereas they'd do a damn lot better if they just came out and said, *How to Masturbate*, or *The Joy of Cock Sucking*, etc.) She looked around— ah ha, I caught her—and I saw her gingerly but eagerly pick up *The Joy of Sex II*, which seemed to hold her attention. When last seen at the cash register, however, she had settled on *Delta of Venus Erotica* (a compromise, I suppose, between one's baser urges and the calling of lit-rature), as well as those worthy tomes for Alex.

"We left for dinner shortly afterward. At one point, looking up over her glass of wine, she asked how my book was coming. Oh, that question—how I dread it! I gave a very sarcastic answer. I think I went too far, though, and I felt badly, for my voice was really much too cutting, and she looked hurt. Indeed, I think she is genuinely curious, fascinated by my project, and I shouldn't have been so mean, but, alas, I can't always control my tongue. When she is hurt, she tries not to show it; her eyes suddenly look sealed off; one senses that she has to surmount the pain in some way. She tried to continue the conversation as if nothing had happened, but I could tell that I'd cut off something inside her.

"Why does New York do this to one? To me, I mean?

"I asked about Alex. She said very little and what she did say was guarded, this due to my own idiocy.

"I mentioned the dinner at Véronique's again; she smiled, and then asked how long I'd known the Bonbon (my name for Véronique). 'As long as I've known Alex,' I said. She did not reply, as if she were digesting those words, but then she turned to me just as we were leaving, and asked me another question.

" 'Emily, tell me something. How can you write a love story if you're not in love?'

"A damn good question, and one I've tried to come to terms with myself. But I answered: 'How can you write one if you *are?* It's a contradiction in terms. It's not for nothing that Flaubert kept his mistress at a distance.'

" 'Funny,' she said, wrapping her scarf around, 'I'd think it would be the opposite. That you'd need the material fresh—newly molten, I mean.'

"She did not wait for me to answer, but merely said good-bye, for we'd just arrived at my building.

"Her words at once disturbed me and made me feel guilty. I suddenly remembered the first time we met at Bookends, when she had asked about the ending. She was right, then.

"I came home and tried to read, but without much luck.

"I wonder if she is really happy, and how much longer she can go with him, until he blots something of her out."

18

Alexander was the most restless man Allegra had ever known. His life whirled with activity, business meetings, appointments, and calls hurriedly placed in telephone booths as he sent coins rattling down their metal throats. He never stopped moving, thinking, or planning; nor did he ever seem to need, as she did, quiet and solitude.

There were moments when Allegra's nerves—unaccustomed to this vortex of movement and constant company—felt seared, red-hot. He was not drawn to—as she was—long walks, or stretches of contemplation. She had always been energetic, but had always known periods of peacefulness as well, and this ceaseless activity and unsparing use of time occasionally made her feel engulfed and oddly irritable. Sometimes she would not know why, except that her mind would be starved for reflection, for moments when she could read, or think, or paint.

He owned a small house, by the sea, in Sagaponack, and it was there they often spent their weekends. It sat among the dunes; on a windy day, the reeds swayed and the sand blew onto the porch as waves pitched and churned, tendriled with froth.

The house was painted gray and, apart from its setting, was nondescript. There was a lake behind it, within view—Lake Crystal, it was called. Years before it had teemed with fish and wildlife, but one summer the algae had grown uncontrollably, and all the fish, gasping for oxygen, had died. Birds and swans now shunned Lake Crystal and its silent, smooth surface—no clanking sounds of geese, no strutting of ducks.

On the third weekend of January, the houses, with their lonely fronts, stood boarded up and tenantless, the beach deserted, and the lawns mounded with thick white snow. On the other side, the dune grass swayed and the ocean thundered with a cold, menacing power.

There were no sounds, except for that of the waves; no people; the town deserted; the tiny cluttered newspaper shop animated only by the bell that rang as one entered. The icy stillness of the lake, and the low thumping of the waves, beyond the dunes.

That Saturday, they took a long walk on the beach, Allegra looking out at the winter water—an indeterminate blue-black that afternoon, very dense, seasick-making. One sensed it harbored a multitude of sharp-teethed, thrashing fish.

She had always associated each sea with a distinct spirit; that of Long Island, it seemed, had no lushness. There was a hardiness, a newness, even an asceticism about it; it had always left her with a relentless and unfriendly impression, its waves changeable, and its tides capable of destruction. Even in summer, it always appeared eager to return to its former desolate state, as if it could not accommodate itself to the onslaught of human beings and status seekers.

"The water here seems to have no particular tint," she said now, as they walked along the beach. "As if it were too restless to attach itself to one color." She watched Alexander pulling his hat down over his ears, his feet kicking pebbles, and his breath, blowing hard white clouds through the air. Squeezing her hand, he bent down, picked up a piece of driftwood, and hurled it out to sea.

A few moments passed; the sky had gone blue-gray, the wind had come up. She turned to him again and said, "You know, I read once—somewhere—that the two great lessons in life are to learn how to make love honestly, and how to reflect." Her eyes bright blue, her cheeks rosy with cold. "Do you think that's true?"

He took her around the waist, kissed her, and uttered a response in a tone that did not encourage her to pursue the discussion. Still thinking, her eyes drifted into what he called "that look," as if some spell had taken over. He was always quick to notice this sudden absorption that would seize her, and that made him uncomfortable, as· if there were a part of her he would never know, a pocket of her mind that would remain inaccessible to his scrutiny.

He began to tease her, then to say things that were irreverent, to jolt her out of it.

They were near the house now, and stood for a moment looking toward the sea. The sky was ominous; there were no other people on the beach. A lone black dog barked.

"Did I tell you," she said, clutching her collar, "about the portrait I found last week?"

"No," he answered, drawing his arm around her shoulder.

"I'd gone to see Mrs. Wentworth on an appraisal. She has an apartment on Fifth Avenue. Quite a good collection of nineteenth-century things, although the place itself has a kind of motley feeling. All dusty and full of swagged curtains and furniture. Anyway, I went into the library, which was deep red, and full of the most unlikely stuff. Things she'd picked up from trips, and little souvenir Mexican sombreros . . ."

"What is the *point*, Allegra?" he said suddenly, interrupting her, his voice impatient. "You lose people's attention when you add all those details. What possible difference does it make if the room was blue or red, or what it contained?"

"But I just wanted to get the feeling right," she said, her voice trailing off, embarrassment, and then a resolve not to do it again, coming over her.

Later that day, when he reproached her for the same habit, she burst into tears.

He gently took her into his arms and kissed her, for he could not bear to see her cry. Her tears knifed him in a way those of no other woman had done before.

During that weekend, they took early morning walks across Lake Crystal: the surface now totally frozen and covered with a powdery film of snow, as fine and dry as diamond dust; the air, crystal-faceted; and their breaths, leaving milky clouds as they walked. Hearing the ice moan, Allegra would laugh with fright and, stepping more carefully, would watch as he pointed to the geese, beyond, flying in a V-pattern.

He came upon a huge horseshoe crab which had been tossed up by waves. Its legs were twisted and gnarled—struggling for life, it seemed. Picking it up, and watching its legs dangling, Alexander said, "This is one of the oldest living creatures. It has no eyes." "No eyes," she repeated, horrified, incredulous. "Only a spot that used to be an eye," he said, hurling it back onto the sand, as they continued to talk, his arm in hers, while her eyes, still turning to the creature, continued to stare.

She was in the midst of tidying some shelves later that afternoon when she came across some photograph albums. She picked one up, slowly opening its cover, and then, still curious, turned from one page to another, her heart suddenly feeling pinched, her throat dry. There were so many women who decorated the pages! A tall redhead who looked like a model; an ivory-skinned brunette, photographed in Paris; another, a blonde; and finally, a photograph of Alexander in the garden of Magdalen College, with two men she did not recognize—one who was slight, with a jaunty cap, and another with a smooth gray-flannel suit and a confident stance.

Slowly putting the book back on the shelf, she had the uncomfortable feeling of one who has unwittingly come across something she would have preferred not to know at all. All day, the faces pursued her.

At dinner, she was very quiet, drawing lines on the tablecloth with her knife, and eating little.

When at last they went to bed, he asked if there wasn't something troubling her. "Yes," she said, with relief, as she told him about the pictures. "I feel as if I've joined a chorus line!" He laughed, kissed the top of her head, said she was silly, and went to get the book. "Look," he said, opening it. "This is all in the past. Nothing at all to do with you." Then he went from page to page, until she thought she could not bear to look at it anymore. Still, he continued to explain—who this one was, or that, and where he had met her, and how long "it" had lasted.

They came to the photograph of Alexander with the two other men. "Who are they?" she asked, pointing to them.

"That's Jean Dubois, the son of Véronique's first husband," Alexander said, pointing to the man with the cap. And then, in an even voice, "And that's a French friend of Jean's. He's called Michel Théron."

"What does he do?"

Alexander smiled. "He manages his family's money. His uncle was very rich." And then, snapping the book shut, "You may meet him one day, in Paris."

He fell asleep before her, turning his back as he did. Finally her eyes began to close, and she too slept, but fitfully. Again, that night, she dreamt—of the hooded figure, the ring, the beach.

The next morning—Sunday—they went running very early, before breakfast. As usual, he was impatient to get started. "Please," she said, standing by the gurgling teakettle. "I need a cup of tea first. It only takes a second." Then, puffy-breathed and swinging their arms back and forth to keep warm, they walked outside, past the dunes, to the edge of the water. Slowly their bodies stirred to life, as they stretched and bent over to limber up.

He ran swiftly, and it was still difficult for her to keep up with him, even though her pace had quickened considerably since their first run in autumn. "If I don't make it, Alex won't love me anymore," she would tell herself. She had grown accustomed to the quick heartbeats, and the pull of the calves, and the sudden mounting of the sweat through the skin. And then, at the end, the breathless feeling of hot damp clothes against the body as the wind cooled the face and hands.

He wanted, even demanded that she run with him. "It's good for you," he said at the end, kissing her cheeks and pinching her buttocks. And then, with an appraising look, "We're going to make you a ten."

They returned to the house for breakfast, with the newspaper.

"Come here," said Alexander, looking at her, as she emerged from the shower in a fluffy white robe. "Your cheeks are still flushed from the running." Taking her in his arms and kissing her, he led her to the sofa, where she lay down. As he began to untie her robe, she tensed, feeling his eyes upon her scar. "Haven't you ever thought of doing something about this?" he asked. Still he continued to touch her, her mouth reaching for his.

The telephone rang. Reluctantly she picked it up.

"Who is it?" Alexander said, his hand still moving across her breasts.

"Someone who says he's Mr. Sidney. From Europe."

Immediately Alexander sat up, his expression no longer languid, and walked briskly into the bedroom, returning a half-hour later, his eyes steely, preoccupied.

"Who is Mr. Sidney?" she asked, biting into a piece of toast.

"A client," he said, rifling through the newspaper. Then he looked up, holding the business section, "Is breakfast ready? I'm famished."

Late that afternoon he went running again, coins clinking in his pocket. "I may need to make a phone call," he explained, kissing her as he left.

19

Alexander loved to gamble, to travel, and to ski—all of which they did that winter and spring with an intensity which, at times, left her breathless. He took her to an illicit gambling spot on Manhattan's West Side where men with tense faces played blackjack, and to Atlantic City one weekend, with a Lebanese client, the two of them bent over the baccarat tables, stacking chips amid the greenish light.

Allegra had come to learn that Alexander loved, even craved adventure and variety. He could not be in one place for too long before he began to plan to leave it for another. Luxurious places made him dream, after a certain time, of wild spots with danger and hardship— of South America, where he had once roamed the jungles, or of Mexico, where he had hunted jaguars. Yet, once his appetite for adventure had been sated, he would yearn for soft beds, sophisticated food, and all the worldly comforts of civilization.

In February, he took her on a long weekend to the Caribbean resort of Cap du Loup, and in the spring, on a longer vacation, to Europe.

On the trip to Europe with Alexander that May, she truly realized she had a lover. The atmosphere of airplanes, foreign hotels, and restaurants seemed to affirm it—a thrilling realization that blew siroccolike upon her senses.

The first time they registered together at a hotel, she was overcome with deep delight, her eyes following him as he filled out the registration card, showed the passports, and took the key. The porter had only just arrived with their suitcases and shut the door, when she threw her arms around him and told him, again and again, that she loved him, loosening his tie, as she did, and asking whether they could make love before dinner.

As they went from Sardinia to Paris, she wondered if having a lover was not why Europe looked subtly different, infinitely more ripe, sensual, complex. For she too had always been lured by the druglike pleasure of travel—that endlessly aspiring sense of being en route, and never quite arriving.

When she was a young girl, her European trips with her parents had always had about them an air of concentration and learning, as if one would emerge from them newly minted, cultivated, accomplished. She had seen the continent from a colorful, if diligent vantage point—one of carefully mapped-out itineraries, meticulous entries in her daily journal, sage walks with guides, tours of Gothic cathedrals, and late afternoon visits to cafés, her feet aching, her head buried in the *Guide Michelin*.

And yet it was invariably the wilder, unexpected moments which had seared her memory: the trip to Yorkshire; or the afternoon, in Italy, when she and her brother had got lost in Lucania; or the day when—older, but no less enamored of such adventures—she had made her way in a rocking boat through a treacherous sea, to Samothrace.

On these trips, France, and particularly Italy had always resembled a school with forbidden courses, or a word with multiple meanings of which she knew only one. She simply sensed there was *more;* whatever it was enticed her.

Years later, these recollections would return as she glimpsed a certain color, or inhaled a passing scent: the windows of Parisian *parfumeries* with faceted bottles and rich perfumes; the profusion of Do Not Disturb signs along the corridor of an Italian hotel, one afternoon. All of which hinted at other aspects to these travels, ones

which had nothing to do with Romanesque architecture or the petrified treasures of the Louvre.

For her, there was little or nothing about Europe which did not
seem fraught with romance. The towns, the scents, the slotted tombs
of the Etruscans, even the exhaust fumes of the rumbling early
mornings at San Remo—these she drank up greedily, like caresses in
the middle of the night.

There was that evening, long ago, in Positano—the town on the
Amalfi coast with pink and blue villas that seemed to tumble down
the steep cliffs to the bay, with its beach of gray stones. Her family
had stayed at a hotel with cool white-tile passageways and a terrace
restaurant with climbing vines, bougainvillea, and jutting balconies.
Allegra was just thirteen. The first evening, midway through dinner,
a couple had appeared—she, a tall, tanned blonde with distant blue
eyes, in a raspberry dress, her pale hair drawn back; he, with grave
manners, dark eyes. He had taken her hand across the table; she had
watched him taste the wine; and then, after a nod to the headwaiter,
their heads had descended in conversation, their eyes never parting.

Allegra had not been able to stop staring. But when she looked for
them the next evening, they had vanished.

She hardly slept their first night in Sardinia. The jet lag had made
him restless and he kept wakening her through the night, pulling her
over and kissing her so that she, too, soon felt awake, and then wanting. She had turned to him, and pulled his head to her breast, watching as his head moved and his hands, holding her buttocks, pulled
her hard against him. And so the night passed, in darkness and sex—
she, falling asleep with a wistful, sated smile, only to be awakened, a
few hours later, by his caresses.

Afterward, he would turn on his side to sleep, pulling her over to
feel her buttocks grazing his, and reaching back to feel her breasts. "I
want you close, come here," he would say, words that thrilled her and
eased her, almost immediately, into a profound sleep.

The following morning, when she reached through the sheets to
find him, he was gone.

She sat up, startled, looking around the room. Where could he be?
she was thinking, her eyes still searching, as if she were seeing the

room for the first time, its shining tile floors, and naïve rustic touches. Where could he have gone?

They had arrived late the evening before, exhausted by the flight, and by the long wait for the bumpy plane ride to Olbia. There had been a short drive to the hotel, through desolate roads and shaggy, windblown hills. When they arrived at the hotel, the concierge, who had been reading, quickly shut his book and assumed his best professional smile. A waiter swept the floor of the restaurant; a few throbbing sounds emanated from the basement discotheque.

Now she walked to the balcony in her blue robe, looking out to the water; the walks that led to it were pale and smooth, the color of terra-cotta. The light shot up from the sea; a man swept the ground before the large white, thatched-roof building that stood by the swimming pool.

She heard the door click open. It was Alexander, a faraway look on his face.

She ran to kiss him, her head, with its tousled early morning hair, nestled against his shirt. She felt his mouth sweeping against hers, and then his hand, grasping her neck. His eyes were preoccupied.

"Where were you?" she said, thinking how full the room now felt.

He gave her a kiss on the forehead, his eyes focused outside as he did. "I had to call New York, there have been some problems with the deal. You know, the Behrman deal I mentioned." She looked puzzled, for she could not recall hearing about it. "I told you," he said, insistently.

"Did you? I don't remember."

He nodded, brushing her hair away, his eyes suddenly concentrated. "Then you've forgotten. Come on, put something warmer on, you must be freezing."

She kissed him again, softly and slowly, holding his collar as she did; his mouth relaxed. "Have you had breakfast?"

"Yes."

"Without me?" She meant to sound teasing, but in fact she was disappointed that he had not waited. Even so, she merely said, "Come back to bed," her mouth imploring, her head tilting to the side, her hands pulling his. Resisting her, he laughed, and then smiling, said, "Wasn't the night enough?" She felt his mouth, newly warm.

"Nothing could be enough." She pulled him closer. "You kept waking me up to make love to me," she said, with quiet delight; and then, seeing she had his attention, began to repeat the details as he listened appreciatively. His hand tightened around her neck. She felt him grow hard.

"You really wanted me, didn't you?" His voice had grown lower, urging her to continue, even as it submitted to her lulling re-creation.

And yet it excited her, as well, to tell how he had taken her, caressed her, what she had felt as he parted her thighs. "I love it when you do that," she said, repeating some explicit details, and kissing his face softly, so that her tongue felt his flesh. "When you keep waking me up like that, again and again, when you need me."

"I was bored," he said, with a short laugh, and a quick kiss.

Her mouth sprung back; then she turned, her eyes to the wall, as if to wince away the pain of an incision.

Immediately he turned her around, drawing her close, his fingers propping up her chin. "That was a joke," he said, "only a joke!" His voice was soft, convincing.

The next moment he lay atop her on the unmade bed, covering her mouth and then her breasts with deep, obliterating kisses. Her hand grasped him at the small of his back; then—with a force that made her forget—he came.

They took long drives through Sardinia, past small towns with rough white light and poor flat houses; ghostlike, in the afternoon, when everything closed for the siesta. They would often take a swim in the late morning, at the hotel; have a lunch of grilled fish, white wine, and salads laced with olives; and in the afternoon, they would drive, to the island of Maddalena, once, taking a small ferryboat there.

The sun seemed perplexed, darting in and out of the clouds, and leaving only a trace of the numbing heat that would invariably be banished by a cool breeze. It was not the season in Sardinia, and the peace of the place only made Alexander grow more restless. Indeed, the hotel was very quiet. In the morning, when they awoke, hardly a sound could be heard: the steps of a waiter, or a maid carrying towels, or the lapping of water. Nothing more.

She sketched and wrote postcards to Harry and Emily, her back propped against a small tree. He made telephone calls and drove to Olbia, once, alone, to exchange some money. He returned from that trip relaxed and full of affection and jokes; even so, he soon grew restless. She had begun to feel as if his restlessness were an easily communicable disease, as if her happiness at being with him was always tempered by the pressure that he wanted to move on, to get going, to be elsewhere, that time pressed.

After his telephone calls, he would often be preoccupied. But she had learned to accept these moods, and also knew when it was best not to ask questions, or even to inquire about the progress of some transaction underway in New York.

They visited the town, where she bought gifts for Laura and Maggie; played tennis (she gracefully, but badly; he very aggressively); made love in the afternoons; and swam. Every evening they would have dinner very late, afterward holding each other tightly as they danced in the hotel's small discotheque—"Underground," it was called—with its ivory pillows and jewel-colored drinks.

The discotheque had been created with a subterranean feeling; there was a sense of descent as one entered it, music pounding, and seats carved from seemingly cavelike walls. Most of the music came from American records, which gave the place a familiar, yet foreign atmosphere; as if, without knowing it, one had been there before.

Other couples danced, or wandered by with a drink. It did not take long for Alexander to meet nearly everyone: an Englishman called Henry Sheffield (tall, with remnants of a distinguished face, now dissipated; drinking pernod), and a young woman called Jenny, also English, who wore tight pants and soft-breasted blouses, and had the determined air of an aging King's Road ingenue. She worked as a cook at a local restaurant and had once been an au pair girl in Brussels. Her long hair looked as if it had been ironed; her two favorite adjectives were "gorgeous" and "smashing."

Alexander sipped a drink at the bar, watching Jenny as she danced—the lines of her buttocks outlined by her white pants, the pointed edges of her hair grazing the places her shirt had left bare. Allegra watched, too, for an instant; and then watched Alexander, watching; until at last she took a mirror from her purse and, staring into it, fixed her lipstick. She said something to Alexander, but he answered her brusquely, not turning around to face her.

"She's very sexy," he said, turning to Allegra. "Don't you think so?"

She shrugged her shoulders, her eyes darting in Jenny's direction, her voice with the strained objectivity of one who is battling the most insidious emotions.

He continued to watch, as she sipped her drink.

The beat of the music suddenly changed from a song that was raucous to another, more lilting, sensuous, and plaintive—the music from a recent Brazilian film, *Dona Flor and Her Two Husbands*.

Allegra beckoned to him, "Come, let's dance."

But he hesitated, saying that they would dance later, but not now. Henry Sheffield had entered, his open shirt showing a chest matted with gray hair. Nodding to Alexander and Allegra, he made his way to the bar.

That evening, Alexander made it clear that he was amused by Henry and Jenny, and spent much time talking to them, and dancing with Jenny, when she asked him, a guileless expression on her face, as she shouted over the music. Alexander introduced Allegra as his "friend," leaving her to stand by the bar with Henry, who offered her a pernod, as they danced. She tried not to watch, but her eyes were drawn to Alexander and Jenny, as one would stare at a car accident, or a mangled dog on the road; his arm, around her waist.

They stayed for not one, but four songs, the last being that of *Dona Flor*.

When they returned, Henry asked Alexander and Allegra if they would like to have a drink, later, at the house of a friend, an architect, called Louis Vetter.

It was a compact, fortresslike place built into the rocks on the hills. There were steps in unexpected places, and windows where one could look out, as if from the towers of some medieval castle. Louis Vetter himself was ingratiating and stylish, wore white, and smelled of an expensive eau de cologne. His teeth were white and fine, and he asked Allegra many questions—where she was from, where she worked. As it turned out, he knew many of the people at Sotheby's.

Jenny arrived later, slightly drunk and dressed in pink with high, shiny sandals, the alcohol exaggerating her flirtatiousness. Sitting on the edge of a table, her mouth set into a pout, she swung her legs. It seemed that she was Louis's "guest" for the week, at least that was the way it was explained to the others, with a smile. Alexander had eased into a chair with huge white cushions; Allegra, sitting beside him, her feet curled beneath her, had gathered a shawl around her shoulders. It had grown cold, and the wind outside rushed against the walls with a swirling, primeval force.

"So it's your first time here?" Louis asked, standing by the bar as he stirred his drink with a tall silver rod.

"In Sardinia, yes," Alexander answered.

"You seem to have made yourself at home."

"That's not difficult; from what I can see, all you need to do is know Henry and Jenny."

"Right." Louis smiled.

Jenny wandered over, swinging her hair and sipping a drink. "We've got to take them to the Club Med," she said. "It's smashing. Ever been?"

"No, never," said Alexander.

"But you must, even if it's just for the day," Louis said, sitting down, and smiling.

"Isn't that where they go around with no clothes and trade beads?" said Allegra, who was becoming bored and irked by the evening.

"Everyone becomes terribly friendly, from what I've heard," Henry said, emphasizing the word "friendly" with an unctuous tone, so that it assumed a multitude of meanings. "Lots of affairs. This one's famous for the ménage à trois. Terribly free, mind you."

"Where did you say it was?" said Alexander, which made everyone laugh, except for Allegra, who felt embarrassed for herself and for him. Louis, walking to the mirrored bar, opened another bottle of champagne and poured another round of drinks.

It grew late. Jenny lounged in one corner, among white pillows, sipping from a cloudy glass rimmed in lipstick. Henry grew increasingly garrulous—his face flushed, his talk rippling with forced enthusiasm.

As they drove back to the hotel, the wind whipped through the dry, rough plants and fields of stunted trees. The hotel was silent as they entered; even the sounds from Underground had abated. They walked in, Allegra yawning, leaning on Alexander. Their steps made hard sounds across the tile floor.

With great dignity, the concierge handed them several messages. "I should return these calls now," Alexander said, seemingly galvanized by the slips of paper, as if the effect of the wine, which had been coursing through his veins, had suddenly stopped. "Don't call now, it's too late," Allegra urged him. "Do it tomorrow. Let's go to bed."

They walked through the large cool hall to the small twisting staircase that led to the second floor, Allegra holding his hand, and occasionally looking back, behind her, trying to erase the evening from her mind.

The room was dark and cool, and the beds turned down, the sheets folded in such a way that the edges looked knifelike. Something about the evening had made Allegra want to make love very much, and yet it was not so much out of desire, but out of some uneasy feeling that she herself could hardly identify, or even acknowledge.

Hours later she finally fell asleep, with her arm around his waist and her hair spread upon the pillow.

Even in late spring, the light in Sardinia was brutal—mounting to a constant white hardness early in the morning and only descending, in the late afternoon, to a lazy softness. Allegra, who was sensitive to light, was struck by its unsparing quality; even in the morning, it lacked all gentleness. Each day, on awakening, she would pull open the shuttered doors that kept the room as dark as midnight, and look outside, standing on the balcony in her robe, her elbows poised girlishly on the rail. Alexander would still be in bed, or in the bathroom, shaving; sometimes he would catch her off-guard, as she daydreamed, and she would jump, startled to feel his arms around her waist.

Throughout the stay in Sardinia, she did not know quite how to *see* Alexander. There were moments when aspects of him seemed to wane and flicker like the light, as if a strange chameleonlike phenomenon had occurred—his image changing, as if the stable, marble-like essence were not marble at all, but a substance so ephemeral it could not be counted on for constancy. She kept thinking of the evening at Underground with Jenny and Henry, and of Alexander's arm around Jenny's waist; but then she would dust the images from her mind. "Oh, what does it matter," she would say to herself, and then, "I'm probably much too sensitive." And it was often at the times when she recalled the most unsettling memories that she would run to him, and kiss him, and be at her most vivacious, driven by a confusion of feelings, often by a demonic hurt that alchemized into desire.

She would have been surprised if someone had turned to her and said that it was fear. And yet she had begun at times to fear him very much. She feared not pleasing him; or losing him; or disappointing him; or not living up to his expectations. However uninhibited she was with him in bed, she found—face-to-face, or worse, over the telephone—that her own fears and anxious thoughts were difficult, even impossible, to disclose. He might laugh. He might not understand. And when his occasional, crackling-edged comment would come, she would again be seized by such uneasiness that her mind would spin and she would again be unable to think, or work, or paint. To be at peace. Often, then, she would be haunted by the presence of the scar across her chest. If only it would disappear, she would think, then all the other thoughts would vanish with it.

She had begun to notice his shifting moods, as one tends to, with particular acuteness, when traveling. He would be loving, and then suddenly removed, when business matters preoccupied him, or when Mr. Sidney called. Sometimes he would disappear for hours, making notes in the telephone booth of the lobby, only to return later, with hard eyes and an absentminded kiss. She had learned not to press her questions too much, or even to appear too lighthearted at such moments. It would only make his moods worse.

His remarks, however tender to her in bed, were often sarcastic among others, or edged with impatience. Sometimes, as a "joke," he would call her spoiled. And yet Allegra did not know if she ought to trust her own instincts, or whether she was simply too vulnerable. There were nights—the time after Louis Vetter's was one—when she would lie sleepless, her body knotted with an anger and tension that she had thought sex would mollify. Toward Alexander, she would feel nothing but a deep, immovable hostility, even when, moments before, she had been caressing him. Or it would happen the other way: that she might be angry, until he began to touch her . . . And so she would sink, quicksandlike, into desire, eagerly leaving the other feelings to disappear.

She wondered whether one grew resistant to the insensitivities of men, and to the incisions of romance, whether one developed a second skin, an immunity.

She began to take a great deal of time with her appearance and often, before dressing, stared into the mirror. Increasingly, though, she did not see her skin, or eyes, or hair, but only the scar. The long, seemingly irreparable line across her chest.

Only a week had passed.

When it came time to leave Sardinia, her sleep was still disturbed, and she was waking at odd hours. She attributed this to jet lag, and to dreams—one, in particular, frightened her, making her awaken shaken and hot. And yet she could not remember what she had dreamt. She said nothing to Alexander; indeed, he did not even notice her flushed face, or her trembling hands.

They left for Paris the following Tuesday, the twenty-second of May, and were met at the airport by Michel Théron, Alexander's friend from Oxford. He wore a creaseless gray suit, was tanned and good-looking, with a careless poise and small, fine features. A deracinated sense about his eyes hinted of high finance and multinational transactions. Smoking, and standing by his black Mercedes, he waved as they approached.

Once the bags were in the trunk, Michel and Alexander got into the front seat, Allegra into the back. His hands on the steering wheel and the light catching the gold pen in his pocket, Michel turned to her, offering her a suave stare. "What beautiful eyes she has," he said, approvingly. Alexander reached back and pressed her hand, his face proud.

They came to the center of Paris—luminous and bisque-stoned in springtime, the boulevards dotted with tables and busy cafés—and finally to the Rue de Varenne, on the Left Bank, where Michel's family had a townhouse. It stood in the midst of one of the loveliest parts of eighteenth-century Paris: the seventh arrondissement, with its graceful embassies manned by guards with inscrutable faces and beautiful uniforms. Allegra had lived just around the corner, when she had studied in Paris.

They entered the cobblestone courtyard, Michel walking jauntily with Alexander, his arm around his shoulder. "You look very well, my friend," he said, in his precise English. Alexander said something in response which Allegra did not hear, but then a moment later, she heard Alexander say, "Where will we go for dinner tonight?"

In a hearty voice, Michel answered, "Why, to Taillevent—as always."

They drove to Normandy that weekend. It was damp and strangely cold, the countryside supernaturally green and moist; beyond stretched the Channel, gray and choppy, hit by wind.

At Honfleur, they stopped for lunch at a famous inn that had once been the haunt of impressionist painters. It sat on a small hill, hidden by trees, and inside the rooms were cozy, bourgeois, the walls lined with porcelain plates and the second-rate paintings that always seem to fill the best French restaurants. Large families ate with utter seriousness.

Michel was polished and amusing, ordering the best wines—"For Alex," he said—and talking at length about painting. Unlike Alexander, Michel knew a great deal about art, a fact which he made clear, albeit subtly, both to Allegra and to Alexander, who listened on.

From there they went to Deauville, now empty and forlorn, the Normandy Hotel cavernous and luxurious, the shop windows closed up. A rain had left the sidewalks and the huge white casino glistening.

Allegra and Alexander went running on the beach late that day, the light tinged with pink and yellow, the sea a minatory color, the rocks that tumbled near the cliffs a mossy gray-green. She thought of seascapes by Courbet, an impression she never mentioned to Alexander.

They had dinner at the Casino that night; a small band played in the latticed dining room, which was filled with huge beribboned pots of hydrangeas. Alexander was relaxed and affectionate, taking Allegra's hand and kissing it, and dancing with her between each course. Michel had ordered champagne. "A drink to my friend, who only likes the best," he said, with a wink at Allegra.

The two men spoke about their days at Oxford, and how they met, and the good times they had had together. "He was always the star," said Michel, looking at his friend. "The most ambitious, and a great success with the ladies, who found his manner devastating." Smiling, he sipped some champagne. "And he finished with a first—didn't you, Alex?—which, God knows, Jean and I didn't." Then he mentioned his recent trip to Turkey, and a friend, Nazif Keskin, whom Alexander seemed to know only vaguely. "You must meet him," Michel said to Allegra, his elegant fingers circling the glass. "He has the most fantastic apartment overlooking the Bosphorus. Great taste. He took me to the digs at Aphrodisias, when I was there; I must arrange for you to go one day." He lifted his glass, drinking, his eyes still on her.

Afterward, they went to the immense gambling room, where croupiers' hands moved deftly across tables amid the dim light. Michel and Alexander stood by the baccarat tables, their faces lean and serious. For a while, Alexander held Allegra's hand, but when the stakes became higher and his eyes even more concentrated, he let it go.

The following day, they drove back to the Paris airport, Michel waving to them from the curb.

Toward the end of the flight, they were handed a customs declaration form. Allegra, who had bought some things in Paris, began to fill it out.

Alexander, seeing her, said, "That isn't really necessary, you know. No one would question you. Not with your face, my angel."

20

That week, Véronique had secretly slipped away to the Clinique d'Harcourt, not far from Lausanne, in Switzerland. It was a quiet, meticulous place, renowned for the discreet upkeep of international beauties. She had known Doctor d'Harcourt, the famous plastic surgeon, for many years.

Two days after her face-lift, Véronique lay in a small white room—some wild flowers on the table beside the bottles of painkillers and a cup of tisane—and thought. It was rare for Véronique really to think, for she mostly plotted; but now, with the dizzying aftereffects of the anesthesia, and the nausea in her stomach, and her swollen face, she merely wanted to reflect. "I look like a mummy, *tiens*," she said to herself, glimpsing her face in the mirror which she kept at her side. There were great patches of black and blue around her eyes, her nostrils looked aboriginal, her neck was a strange greenish-yellow.

She sat in the room, the pillows plumped behind her, gazing at the green mountains and feeling the delicious cool air. In the morning a young blond nurse with crisp movements would come to smooth the sheets and help her bathe, and then, leaving her to read, would close the door. But so far the stack of books remained untouched, as

Véronique thought and thought, her mind curiously renewed by the psychic chill of Switzerland.

She was preoccupied with Alexander and Allegra, and considered that he would soon tire of the girl. Then it would be time to provide him with someone else, and for her to resume her role as his guide and mentor. Even so, it disturbed her that he seemed to need her less and less, and that his late-night visits had all but ended, and that a vaguely sarcastic look would enter his eyes at the mention of Ed Stern. He had suddenly made her feel not only old, but useless, which was worse.

Even Michel had mentioned it to her, not long before, that Alexander seemed distant; not quite *there,* he had said. It's the girl, she had answered, the American.

Had Véronique known herself better, she might have realized that it was precisely what she thought she disdained in Allegra that she actually envied—her naïveté, her lack of experience, her enthusiasm. For the fact remained—and this Véronique knew—that she herself had become a fixture on the New York scene. People knew who she was, and what she was about; whereas Allegra's life still waited to be formed. But Véronique's life, as far as she had always imagined it, was now nearly over. What remained of it would be decided by her machinations, and by the actions of others.

By Stern's, for instance. She thought of her Josephine treasures— the little boxes, the necklace, the antique pieces of silk—and then she thought of Stern himself, and gave a deep sigh. His raucous taste, the silly woman who was his wife; a feeling of dread came over Véronique with these thoughts, and the sudden sense that everything was threatening to go askew, and that her life, which had been going along so promisingly, had all but ended. Still, she would never give up, for her determination was as unflagging as her discipline.

As she lay there, she thought of Henri Dubois, whom she had married years before. He had been much older than she, and had adored and spoiled her, obsessed with the idea of fathering her child. Even then, decades earlier, she had been as deliberate as she was now; and after she convinced him that she, too, wanted nothing but a quiet family life and children, they were married.

Soon afterward, when she did indeed become pregnant, secretly she had an abortion, for she had never intended to have children and abhorred the idea of pregnancy. "There is something degrading about it," she had once remarked to a friend.

Now, the vestiges of her beauty and taste were virtually all she had left: no children, no husband; even her home had a faintly museum-like quality. But she would not remain dispirited for long, even so; the mood would pass, and in a moment she would think of her beauty, and her bone structure! Those remained, which was why she had given herself over to Doctor d'Harcourt with the trust of a religious fanatic to a high priest.

And yet, with the subtle tucks, she also felt a despair, even as she felt a renewal, for she knew that the doctor's scalpel and sutures could only do so much. Nothing could eradicate the fact that she had been around for too long, with too many men, with motives that were becoming too transparent. Nothing could alter that, as it was a question not only of age, but also of character and reputation. Those things were now set. And yet it was her doing, after all; from the time she was a young woman what she had most wanted in life was to be beautiful and immensely rich. Nothing else had mattered.

Again, her thoughts turned to Alexander. No, she had never dreamt he would actually become enamored of the girl. It was to have been a business alliance, a means toward an end, nothing more. And if that changed—here, she paused—then, she would simply go about setting things straight.

"Why, we're looking very serious today," said the nurse, in French, as she entered.

21

Ben Mulligen, the messenger, had just shuffled into Allegra's office at Sotheby's. He was a singular character, ridden with prejudices, with a lumbering walk and suspicious eyes. Every newcomer to the department was subject to his scrutiny. No one knew his age—or, for that matter, much about him, except that he had served in the navy during World War II and that he was a faithful parishioner of his church, where he occasionally attended "bowling banquets."

He had a thin, stooped frame, grizzly hair, and a lean, gaping-toothed smile. His habitual outfit was a corduroy jacket of a grayish-blue color, so stained with soot that it appeared to have taken on a pattern.

Those he did not like knew it immediately. In fact, his brutal, almost childlike honesty perturbed many, even in judging paintings. (He likened the art world itself, for which he had nothing but contempt, to "spraying a garbage can with perfume.") Once, when a particularly fey Bouguereau, depicting two infants sleeping, arrived in the department, he commented that "the guy can paint, but who'd want to have a picture of two fat babies in bed?" Allegra had stifled her laughter while the others looked nervously down at their feet.

Allegra happened to be among the people he liked: partly because she was polite, partly because she was a Catholic, and partly because she did not smoke, and hence could never be accused of borrowing his treasured ashtray, a heavy block of green glass he had stolen from an Irish bar. If someone did take it, he was treated with such contemptuous belligerence that he seldom dared to do it again.

His manner on the telephone was gruff, and occasionally surly. He liked to characterize those who telephoned Allegra—her "heartsick admirers," as he called them. "Sounds like a real sexy Frenchman," he would say, adding, "C'est la guerre." Once, when Alexander called, Ben, passing the receiver to her, said, "Sounds like some phony Brit," while her face reddened.

On this morning in the first week of June, Ben entered at nine-thirty to find Allegra already at her desk, reading the New York Times and sipping a cup of coffee. "Morning," he said, shuffling to the coatrack, where he hung up his cap. "What's the matter? You couldn't sleep at home last night?" She laughed, and said she had come early to catch up on some work. Lately Allegra had been very diligent, for she had realized, on her return from Europe, how much she had let her work slip. The previous week, on an appraisal, she had discovered a portrait bust she believed to be the work of a Renaissance artist; now she was trying to prove its authenticity. There was something frenzied about her quest; even her colleagues had noticed it.

"I'm going to get some coffee," Ben said, stuffing the Daily News (the "real" newspaper, as he called it) into his back pocket. "You want anything?"

"A muffin with another cup of coffee, I'd really appreciate it," she said. There was an exaggerated decorousness in her voice, for she knew that one small presumption would be enough to land her on his black list.

"Sure, no problem," he said. Searching in her purse, she took out some money and gave it to him. Fifteen minutes later, he returned.

Thanking him, she took off the lid from the cup, and, unwrapping the muffin, said, "I don't know why I'm so hungry this morning." Ben merely grunted something.

There was a stack of mail on her desk—letters from clients, a request for a catalog, and a package from Giovanna Contarin, which contained a large folder covered in blue-green marbelized paper, and fastened at each end with ribbons. "A little remembrance of Venice for you to keep your sketches in, dearest Allegra," said the note. Allegra gazed at the handwriting, thinking of Giovanna, touched by the present. But then her mind wandered—as it often did, these days—to Sardinia, and to the week in Paris, with Michel. The house on the Rue de Varenne, and its strange, musty atmosphere. Michel's mother—a frail, nervous woman—who had led Allegra through the house, one day after lunch, leading her to her late husband's room, with its rows of beautifully arranged shoes and shirts. Michel, with his smooth gestures, watching . . .

At last, Allegra cleared her desk—for it was ten o'clock now—and dialed Harry's number.

"Harry? Hi." A pause. "What do you mean? I'm always here early. No? You just don't see me then." There was a playful shade of defensiveness in her voice, but it softened, almost immediately, to a quick, newly excited cadence. "Do you remember when I told you about the Marbury apartment, and coming across that marble portrait bust? Of course you do. You know, the one I found in with all that awful junk. Anyway, it's just arrived, and I'm sure it's by Francesco Laurana. It's just like the one at the Frick—except more beautiful, I think. It's got a slight crack, but otherwise it's in fine condition. Come and see it with me."

A pause, while she listened, her hand, holding a pen, tapping the desk.

"Well, I know it's not my department." Another pause. "What do you mean, it's not my field? I know his work, and I'm sure this is the Lost Lady that everyone's been looking for, for years. It was supposed to have been commissioned in Lucca. She's exquisite, wait till you see. Anyway, I know my first instinct was right. Now I just have to prove it."

She listened for a moment, again, and then said, "At eleven-thirty? Upstairs? OK."

At eleven-thirty, Allegra told Ben that she was "off to the catacombs" (her expression for the storage rooms) and would be back before lunch.

There was an odd, jumbled atmosphere to these rooms. "Exactly like being backstage at some eccentric play," she had once said. After the relative homogeneity of the painting department, with its concentration on one century, it was a pleasant shock to enter this space, with its dismembered feeling of loose objects from various periods. Stickered paintings lined the racks; in other corners of the room stood tables, suits of armor, teapots, Oriental screens.

The bust sat on a shelf in a distant corner; nothing else surrounded it. The lady (or the "Lost Lady," as Allegra insisted on calling it) was carved in white marble, her face suspended in an expression where sleep and wakefulness merge, her smile at once serene and ambiguous.

Allegra stopped before it now, her hand touching the diminutive frieze of maenads and satyrs around the base, and then the planes of the face itself, with its smooth, high cheekbones, lofty forehead, and chipped nose.

"There you are."

She jumped. "Harry! You startled me."

"Not nearly as much as you do me." He paused, stepped back a moment, and, looking at the bust, said, "So there she is." One hand in his pocket, he circled the sculpture, touching the marble and examining the plinth. "Pretty. Not remarkable, but a nice rendition."

"What do you mean—'nice'?"

"Just that."

"Look at the carving," she said insistently, almost pleadingly. "And the way the face has been molded. Here. And here." Her fingers pointed to the shape of the neck and the relief below it. "Don't you think it's extraordinary? The expression?"

He examined the fine crack which ran above the frieze. "I told you, Allegra—pretty, yes. Good quality, certainly. Fifteenth century? I doubt it. I'd say it's a copy. It's obviously been executed by someone good, someone who's aped Laurana's style. But still, I'd say it's slightly too realistic; it's got a bit too much of Desiderio da Settignano about it. The rondures aren't eery enough."

"You're wrong," she said, her voice bruised.

"I may be. It's possible." He looked at her a moment, and then, leaning back against the wall, he said, "Why *this*, Allegra? Why are you making such a production about it? I could understand if it were a painting in your area, although, even then, this *idée fixe* would still seem ludicrous. But this!" He looked at her, then at the sculpture, and back again. "I think you identify with her in some strange way. I think you really do."

"Don't be ridiculous."

"We'll see," he said, going to the shelf. "Let's move it over here, we'll be able to see it better." They did. He walked around it again, examining the frieze, the contours of the face, and the way the hair was bound beneath its *cuffia*.

"Harry," she finally said, sputtering out her thoughts, "you know so much about sculpture, much more than I do. Can't you see that it's authentic, that it isn't a fake? I just don't think you find that kind of work . . ." Her voice trailed off.

He said nothing for a moment, while she stood to the side, her hands twisting together. And then he said softly, "Allegra, tell me something. You've got a big sale coming up. You've done very little for it; from what I've heard, Lisa has wooed away all your favorite clients. And here you are, obsessed by something that has absolutely nothing to do with your field, that's out of your range, that's highly dubious—that really isn't important! And all your thoughts and energy and time are directed to *this!*" He nodded at the piece. "If I were you, I'd drop it. Let the right department make the appraisal and just let it be."

"And that's what you think I should do?" She looked pale, her mouth tense.

"Yes. Skip it. It's fruitless—you're making an ass out of yourself."

"Since when? Is that what they're saying?"

"That's what I'm saying." A moment's pause. "Have you been painting at all?"

"No, not much. I've been too busy."

"Too busy. I see." There was a note of sarcasm in his voice.

They could hear the sound of porters moving paintings in the next room, and of a table being lugged into a corner. Harry looked at his watch. "I've got to go."

"Harry," she pleaded, tugging his arm, "I'm not doing this to make any trouble, I'm just . . ."

"I know, you're just making trouble. You've taken this on as a cause célèbre; you've already stepped on people's toes in a department that has nothing to do with yours, and I think you're beginning to look like an ass. That's right—an ass. You know I've never lied to you, and I'm not about to start now. You've asked my advice. I've given it. What you do from here is up to you."

"But Harry . . ."

"I'm late." He looked one last time at the bust, and then, at Allegra, shaking his head slowly, as if to show his lack of comprehension.

She watched him disappear down the corridor.

A Chinese garden bench sat opposite the sculpture. She sat on it, her chin resting in her hand, a vacant look in her eyes, her hand idly picking a thread from her skirt. Looking at the face of the marble woman—the white cheeks, the knowing lines of the unflustered mouth—she wondered for a moment if Harry wasn't right. If this isn't some sort of crazy obsession, and out of my range, to boot! Standing up, she moved to the sculpture itself, her hand moving over its face, her eyes examining the frieze, with its tiny pagan figures dancing in abandon.

From each angle, it seemed the woman looked different, for she was not a perfect beauty, and there were even some sides that revealed a touching plainness. It was even difficult to know her age, and whether this might be a marriage portrait, or, for that matter, some sort of funeral remembrance.

Suddenly, Allegra's entire stance changed: her back straightened, her eyes fixed with a new resolve. He's wrong, she thought. And I won't give up. She's real, I know it. I've felt it from the beginning, just as I did about the Corot. And the fact that she needs some repair shouldn't matter that much, not if she's a real Laurana.

Brushing the dust from her hands, Allegra walked past the other rooms, and then to the elevator.

Ben was waiting with the message when she returned. "It's from the phony Brit," he told her. She took the slip from his hand and, without a word, dialed Alexander's number.

The next week, Allegra was called into the office of the head of her department. He told her that the bust was a fake; a good one, he said, but a fake nonetheless. A test had revealed that the marble came from an Italian quarry which had only been mined since the nineteenth century.

In a firm, low voice he reprimanded her for having neglected her work and having spent so much time on an object which was, without question, completely beyond her field of specialty. He then told her that if it happened again, serious measures would have to be taken.

The office door opened before her, and she was ushered out.

She returned to her office near tears, humiliated, and nearly nauseous with a sense of failure. It was four-thirty. Her head was bent over her desk, images of the Lost Lady whirling within her mind's eye. She began to gather her things and then she left, without saying a word to anyone.

Tears ran down her cheeks as she walked down Madison Avenue, the street reeling before her as crowds brushed past. She thought of calling Harry, but was too ashamed. She would go and see Maggie; Maggie would understand. But when she reached Millefleur, the shop was empty, and Allegra stood by the locked door, wondering what to do next.

22

Emily had just begun to write:

"June 12. Clearly this is not the same girl as the one I met last September. If so, she has changed a great deal. Allegra, that is. There's *une espèce de lassitude,* as the French say, in her eyes—a trapped look. As if the initial radiance has dissolved into grim sparks.

"We went to Maggie's exercise class today, which is why I had a chance to observe her. First off, I noticed her hair, and thought, so the Bonbon has had her way—gone are the pre-Raphaelite tresses! She looks fashionable, all right, but it doesn't really suit her; the haircut is too stark for her face. I have a feeling that she senses it herself, for she continually brushes it aside, as if—in that gesture—to recover the shorn strands.

"Of course, she dresses very fashionably now; Alex has obviously seen to that, for it matters to him very much. And yet, in a curious way, I rather preferred her other clothes. They suited her beauty, which is that of another century. Instead, he has turned her into a mannequin, with all a mannequin's slickness, and it really isn't her at all. Cheapens her, in fact.

"It's not every day that one gets to see this kind of perverted metamorphosis.

"She had rung me up a few days ago to ask if I'd come with her to Maggie's gym for a five-thirty class. I said yes, and then—thinking of background material for my book—volunteered to meet her at Sotheby's. Fine, she said, and told me the floor of her office. It was a busy day at Vogue, but I managed to escape early by telling them I had an appointment to investigate a possible auction-house story.

"When I arrived, Allegra came out to the main desk and greeted me, looking brisk and rather self-possessed in this office atmosphere. She was just in the midst of examining some things that people had brought in, she said, and would I mind waiting. Of course not, I said, and immediately took out my pad to jot down some notes.

"She went into a small room to the side, where an elderly woman with a frowsy hat was waiting for her; piled on the table was what looked to me like utter junk. Allegra began to sort through the things, dismissing the most hideous among them in a polite, professional way. She came to the last item—a small canvas, an almost mystical still life of a bowl of lemons and shells. It was incredibly dusty and very old; carefully she wiped it off. 'This is very good, very nice quality,' she said, the woman hanging on her every word. 'Yes,' Allegra continued, still scrutinizing it. 'This should fetch several thousand, at least.'

"I wandered around a bit more, still taking notes. Finally Allegra came out, holding her handbag, and said she was ready.

"We talked for a moment, but she seemed preoccupied. There were pale, bluish circles under her eyes. I asked about her job, but she gave me only a vague answer, saying that it was OK, but that unfortunately some marble portrait bust she'd spent a lot of time on had turned out to be a fake. 'A good one,' she said, 'but a fake. Harry told me so, but I didn't listen.' There was a pained expression in her eyes as she said this; I didn't pursue it.

"As she pressed the elevator button, I noticed her hands. They, too, have changed. I had remembered them as white and fine, but untouched before, their nails the colour of a pale shell. But now the nails are tapered in bright red varnish, and seem so incongruous on this creature—sad, common. She's begun to wear more makeup, too, and even that, as subtly as she does it, doesn't really do her justice. She looks far more striking without it.

"We walked down Madison Avenue about ten blocks to the Lotte

Barclay studio. Maggie, very trim and wearing a black leotard, was waiting for us. 'Come,' she said, with a broad smile. 'I'll show you where to put your things.' She led us to a changing room with pale pink walls and spotless showers—very 'refined,' as Maggie put it— and we began to undress. As we did, I noticed how self-conscious Allegra suddenly seemed. I couldn't understand it, until I noticed, for the first time, a thin scar across her chest. 'It's from an old accident,' she said in a confiding voice. 'Waterskiing, when I was a teenager.' I told her that it really wasn't so noticeable. 'Funny,' she said. 'It never used to bother me so much, but now it does. Terribly. Still . . .' She shrugged, and then, making some joke, went upstairs, where we were joined by Maggie.

"There were about ten women in the class, all of them exceedingly svelte, very well kept up indeed. The instructor was a tall, striking young woman with dark waist-length hair and the uplifted posture of a ballerina (it seems she had once danced with Balanchine). I felt a wreck; I'm in miserable shape and every stretch seemed an agony (a fact reiterated by the music, which chanted, 'Can you *feel* it? Can you *feel* it?'). Maggie, through sheer determination and practice, did very well; so did Allegra. 'I go running with Alex quite a lot,' she explained, as we headed downstairs afterward.

"We took showers and then walked up Madison Avenue together, the three of us with that feeling of inner peace, even catharsis, which comes from exercise. Maggie left us near her apartment. Allegra and I continued toward Lexington to Chez Madeleine's, for a light supper. Harry had told us he'd meet us there later, for coffee. 'Let's have something fattening,' Allegra said, with a wicked look. I'd been skipping lunch recently—to save money—and was starving, so I readily agreed. Besides, I was dying to probe further—about her and Alex, that is—partly out of curiosity, but mostly for the book.

"We walked down Seventy-fifth Street, and then over to Chez M.'s—fortunately, it wasn't crowded. The smell of the *pâtisseries* and croissants always makes me swoon. We ordered *croque-monsieurs*, salads, and white wine; then, at the end, a cappuccino—pleasantly bitter and white with foam. 'Let's have something else, Emily,' Allegra urged, so we ordered little chocolate cakes with dense, sweet icing. 'These are called *mystères*, did you know that?' she said to me, as the waitress, a scowling-faced woman in a tiny green-striped apron, placed them before us.

"I tried to eat daintily, imagining she would, too; after all, she's a well-brought-up thing. But in fact, she finished hers before I did mine and even scraped the plate! 'Wouldn't you like another?' she said, the colour coming back into her cheeks. I nodded, and she ordered a second round. (Her French is lovely. I was rather envious, as mine has never been able to shed its British flatness.) I kept looking at her as we drank and ate, wondering at her, eating so heartily. I suppose I had half-expected her to pick at her food, which she did not. She really dug in—that was the amusing thing! But then she is a creature of opposites: her face, for one thing, is both delicate and strong (the lines of the nose, the jaws, the wide mouth), and if you look closely— as I did—you will see great plump veins running beneath the white skin of those delicate arms!

"I asked her about Sotheby's again, and was met by a surprising lethargy. But then I asked about her painting, and when she had first begun to do it, and, as she began to discuss it, her eyes sparkled and a whole other being suddenly seemed infused in her place! Extraordinary. I felt it, too, when I asked about Alex. She obviously adores him, although when she speaks of him it is with a warmth touched with a certain feverishness.

"I asked more about her painting, and when she had first become interested in it. She told me that she had always loved colour, and that she had read, as a child, all about the lives of artists; and that she had a godmother, who was English, a painter called Laura Hilliard.

" 'She lived—or lives, I should say—not far from the ocean, on Cape Cod,' Allegra told me. 'I often spent the summer with her there, in a rambling white house. I remember it so well!

" 'The days were given their rhythm by Laura, by her riding and her painting. She was an artist, you see, with a studio of her own, and her own time to work. Portraits and landscapes, mostly.

" 'She always awoke very early. I'd hear her going down the stairs, calling to the dogs, and then I'd hear her horse, Much Ado, as he made his way down the road.

" 'About an hour later, she'd return, and the house would come alive with all the morning noises. The doors banging, the teakettle whistling. Laura would stand at the stove, scrambling eggs, and I'd watch the toast as I read the comics. And then at about nine, she would disappear to her studio. It had a closed door and always seemed hushed. No one else was ever allowed to go in it.

" 'Once or twice, I managed to get a glimpse inside, and see what that other Laura did there. She looked strangely dazed when I peeked in—absorbed and serious—so different from the woman who made my breakfast and organized boat trips! But at lunchtime she'd become her old self again, and return to the kitchen, whistling. And then most likely she'd ask if I wouldn't like to have a picnic.

" 'She'd do this every day.

" 'One morning, when she went out riding, I crept down to the studio, still in my nightgown, and slowly opened the door. There they were, all the paintings she'd done! Some finished, some needing more touches. All the people and flowers of her own creation. There were pots of paint, and cigarette stubs on plates by vases of lilacs that looked sad, neglected, as if they needed nourishment.

" 'I remember going through the pictures, one by one, with the feeling of someone who's secretly reading a friend's private letters. When I reached the last, I looked down and saw a name I didn't recognize, at least not for an instant. Laura Kent! She had her own name for painting, you see—that struck me as the most remarkable thing. It has often come back to me.'

"We sat for a moment, sipping our coffee, when Harry arrived. He fairly pounced on the table, planting his elbows down, his eyes not wavering from Allegra. 'What the hell have you done to your hair?' he said at once. She looked completely flustered. 'Alex likes it,' she stammered. Harry said nothing.

"For a while they talked shop, but I could tell that something has happened between them. Harry has his own life and his own friends, of course; even so, he loves her in a special way, and cares for her thoughts. They don't see each other so much anymore. 'She's always busy,' he told me recently.

"About a half hour later, Allegra looked at her watch and made a motion to leave. 'I've got to go,' she said, calling for the check. 'Why?' Harry asked. 'I promised to meet Alex,' she said, almost reluctantly. Then she kissed us and left.

"I watched Harry watching her through the large front window, his eyes following her down the street, as if to trace her footsteps. His expression was disconsolate. For a long while he said nothing.

"Finally, as if to no one in particular, he murmured, 'Her hair . . . She never paints anymore.' And then, turning to me, 'Have some more wine,' he said."

23

new love affair is rather like a fresh waxen tablet—as yet unmarred by etching, and eagerly waiting to be written upon. But increasingly, Allegra's love affair seemed to be marked by the imprints of hurt and confusion, and by her own waning sense of self, as if the steel cord within her had suddenly snapped.

She had begun to feel tired on her return from Europe, a fatigue that worsened after the Laurana incident. She often found it difficult to awaken in the morning, and dreaded the ringing of the alarm clock and the unraveling of her first dream-throttled thoughts. She would dress slowly, hesitating to see her face, and especially the scar, in the mirror.

She had grown self-conscious about her physical self—including her height—and began to imagine, in the presence of every diminutive woman, that Alexander wished that she, too, resembled a small Dresden doll. She relegated her high heels to the back of her closet; was seldom seen without makeup; and, before going to bed, religiously applied a cream that promised to fade the freckles she thought he disliked.

At dinner with him, there would be moments when she would be seized by an inner silence, as if something inside her had suddenly frozen. And paradoxically, it was often at such moments that she would reach for his hand, or touch his face, or his hair, as if to reassure herself that he were there, and that whatever it was between them lay intact.

They had begun to circle one another like two people groping in the dark, their words and actions like arrows flung into an abyss. There were moments when he was extraordinarily sensitive toward her, and others when he seemed oblivious to what would wound. "Don't tell me the facts," he would say in a moment of emotional largesse. "Tell me what you are feeling." At other times, when she did, she would be rebuffed, or treated in a patronizing way that only sparked her anger.

Yet often her anger, too, would dissolve into desire, or it would become suffused with her aching admiration for him—for the fact that he, unlike her, had begun from nothing. This was a test she would never know, and she came to distrust herself for it, feeling weak, where she should have felt fortunate.

Throughout this, the Fitzpatricks were a comfort: their steady life, their delight in each other, the warmth of their home—this cheered Allegra and made her think that a relationship of lovingkindness was truly possible. She saw them mostly alone, when Alexander was occupied elsewhere, or when she had asked for a few days of solitude, to try to paint. ("You're trying to get rid of me," he would say. "No, that's not it at all," would be her response, uttered in a voice heavy with denial as she stroked the back of his neck.)

But inevitably, the demons would creep back into what was to have been peace: perhaps she had done wrong, she would think; and then the fear of losing him would become so intense, as would the imaginings of a wrenching separation—the anxiety of not having his arm around her waist, or his mouth to kiss, or his lips brushing her temples and breasts. That she might never bask in the serenity of his physical affection . . . A day would seem a month; two days, a year.

He thought he understood her. "She's a dreamer," he once said to a friend, when asked to describe her. "You always sense she is seeing what we are not." He had smiled as he said this, not in amusement, but in exasperated fascination.

Their arguments would usually begin late at night, in bed, or on the telephone, she at her apartment, he at his; to be ended the following night, stifled by love-making.

In between, in the afternoon, they would meet in a small, darkened restaurant, the tables clustered together with people eating and talking animatedly. Allegra would be unable to really look at him, her head still hazed by the sleeping pill she had taken the night before, her words escaping in a tremulous pattern. Almost always, by the end, she would relent—perhaps she had simply acted stupidly! "You take things and twist them," he would say quietly, looking at her directly.

And it was at moments like those when sex would assuage all the troubled feelings, like ebbing water erasing frantic etchings in the sand. In bed, they spoke a language of skin and touch that was common to both. After a night of making love, it was as if a lovely nacreous film had curtained off any disruption.

She grew used to this rhythm, and to sex as the balm that soothed the most painful emotions.

But her joy in painting! She hardly remembered when she had painted. Her canvases stood about her like mementoes of a past life— the landscapes and faces she had created, the flowers whose petals she had lovingly depicted. Now her concentration was too often interrupted by the pricking memory of something hurtful he had said, or the fear that she herself had committed a gaffe; or she would think of a dress she ought to buy, or a new cosmetic. She convinced herself that it was because she was no longer alone that she could not shut herself away to paint, or that sex had staunched her appetite for creative solitude. She no longer cared to be "with darling self," since it was precisely from that self she wanted to flee.

It was worse when she saw Emily, for she felt the latter's piercing glances, and her tone of voice when she spoke of Alexander, all of which prompted Allegra to look into herself, asking questions which made her uneasy.

It was not until July that she saw Emily again, at a dinner at the Iranian embassy in Washington.

24

"J uly 6," Emily wrote. "Washington.

"Have just returned from a splendid dinner at the Iranian embassy—Lord, what a night! I managed to wrest an invitation through Véronique: New York and Washington are towns of such mutual using; all I'd done was let it be known that I was planning to do a story on Ardeshir Zahedi.

"He's a *numéro*, by the way, this Iranian ambassador: great dark eyes that miss nothing; the air of a bon vivant that probably conceals the most Machiavellian mind on earth. His eyes glancing at the décolletés, and yet there's nothing which I would call distinctly sexual about him.

"I flew down here late this afternoon; took the shuttle, and dragged down a dress, or rather a caftan, which I'd borrowed from Vogue. (This one bright red, which I thought suitably garish for the embassy. I'd seen pictures of the place and knew that I'd have to wear something bright in order to be noticed.) I'd decided to look as exotic as possible—kohl circling the eyes, and great dangling earrings.

"I came alone, which made little difference, as there were many people I recognized; lots of New Yorkers had been invited. I felt as if I were at the Bonbon's, actually.

"Washington is really quite amusing. The women, for the most part, are rather dowdy. The men all looked the same—white-haired, craggy, deep-voiced, hard, earnest handshakes, eyes darting about. I couldn't tell one from the other.

"I arrived at around eight and found the place already swirling (unlike New York, where no one would have dared appear so early). Was met by Zahedi, who gave me quite a welcome; found that flattering, until I realized that of course he does that to everyone. Part of the job. Then I got a drink, and wandered from room to room, mentally taking notes (I may need an embassy for my book). The place is fascinating—an attempt at real grandeur and voluptuousness of colour that just misses. The colours are off; too much ormolu, and there's something cheap-looking about the much-vaunted Persian room. Too much turquoise, perhaps?

"I'd become suitably relaxed by the time most of the others arrived; time to mingle. Lots of famous Washington faces, and then—to one side—Alex and Allegra (she had told me she would be here, which is another reason I'd come). I thought Allegra looked subdued. She was all in white, and had very long gold earrings. There was something Greek about her dress, which suited her. Alex, too, looked well; both of them had a slight tan.

"As I sauntered up, Allegra—looking amused and astonished—said, 'Is this the new look?' I told her it was *my* new look—'Very Justine, don't you think?' said I. 'All I need now is a perfume called Jamais de la Vie.' She laughed.

"I asked if they had been away, for I hadn't seen her since the dinner at Chez Madeleine's. Allegra said yes, 'Bermuda,' and then wrinkled her nose. 'You'd love it, Emily,' she said, with a mischievous look. 'The middle-aged women lie on the beach all day reading trashy novels. You'd spend your whole time burning books.' I laughed, and then looked at Alex, but he was occupied elsewhere.

"The immense room—shimmering with mirrors and chandeliers and garish blues and marvelous silky rugs—was quite full of life by then. Many people. The intermingling of perfume. Eyes cast here and there to see who was worth talking to; lobbyists and pols with their noses out for money. That sort of party.

"The women were a sight to behold. I met one who looked particularly mousy—an ex-stripper, apparently, married to a billionaire.

Of course, now she is simply too ladylike, and rather buttoned up, as they tend to be when there's a dubious past. And then an heiress from Minnesota, whose money comes from shredded wheat.

"If the splendid red wine hadn't gone to my head, I would remember all of this much better. Several aging movie stars, the sort who are trotted out for everyone to examine, great rocklike pendants trickling down their formidable fronts, and antiquated eyeshadow giving them a slightly Manchurian aspect. Many newscasters; you'd think they'd be good at making conversation, whereas the opposite is true. They don't *need* to make an effort, they already hold so much power in this town. Members of the cabinet; several famous ballet dancers; cinema people; a claque of socialites (one of them, bent on appearing in *Vogue,* pursuing me). Everyone assembled in the Arabian nights room to gather information, make some sort of contact, and find out which cabinet member's head will be on the chopping block next. All of this in an atmosphere tinged with the most hedonistic feeling of corruption.

"At one point, while standing with Allegra and Alex, I spotted Lillian Riddell, the Oriental rug dealer who has a shop on Madison Avenue. Everyone said hello, while La Riddell assumed her most distinguished air—knowledgeable, haughty, draping her shawl over her bosom in her best pseudo-bohemian manner. She must have sensed that they—unlike me—were potential customers.

"La Riddell continued to talk, stalking about, pointing here and there, and looking, for all the world, like a carpet-dazed Sarah Siddons. 'In my own house,' she intoned, 'I always change my rugs constantly. Of course, that is one of the advantages of being in the business. The eye wearies, you know; if I have something around for too long, in the same place, I cease to notice it . . .' Here, Alex cut in. 'I can see the point of that; it would be tiresome to have the same thing underfoot all the time.' She laughed, although I doubt she really got his point (as for me, I took note—the book, of course). Allegra, who was speaking with someone else, did not hear.

"However, Allegra returned in a moment, and asked about a small Persian rug by the staircase—where it had come from, why one design was considered finer and more rare than the others; how one could tell whether it had been created for the European market. La

Riddell—impressed by her questions—answered at length. Alex listened, his eyes with their customary alertness. He seemed impatient, though, and wanted more exacting information: what caused the expense, how much labor was required, and the knots per square inch. The knots per square inch! I thought he *had* Riddell there, but she came back right again, and told him that in a Tabriz, for instance, there were approximately two thousand knots to the square inch. That subdued him for the instant.

"At last, we were informed that dinner was served; the crowd, assembling, had begun to take on the same multicoloured dazzle as the mosaic-patterned walls. The seragliolike setting quite undid me, and as the evening wore on, and the wine performed its magic, I began to see the power of this, its utter seductiveness.

"The doors opened to a massive room of mosquelike proportions with great round tables, weighted by heavy cloths, gleaming with gold services, and fragrant bunches of violets and white flowers. I looked for my table, number 23, and found—as I'd tried to arrange—that I was across from Allegra and Alex. Next to me, a senator—Mount Rushmore face, straight out of central casting—with a rather meek wife (next to her, a Harvard-educated curator from the National Gallery). The senator, who is from what is known here as the Deep South, is apparently Very Powerful (this, uttered in hushed tones). This was told me by the man on my other side, who was obese, and whose fingers were lined with rings—a lobbyist, apparently. ('Very glad to meet you,' said I. 'Same here,' he said.) I asked him what he lobbied and he burst out in great guffaws; it was at that moment that I turned to the senator.

"Bits of conversation followed. Gossip about a congressman who, on a recent goodwill trip to Argentina, spent the whole time 'getting laid' (didn't even bother with the introductory ceremonies, simply made his priorities clear from the moment he disembarked). Also, talk of China. One member of our table, a fiftyish woman of obvious D.A.R. ancestry, kept saying, in the most annoyingly sheepish voice, 'Oh, but you know, you have to take all your own *amenities.*' This she said frantically, at least three times, so that I finally piped up: 'Do you mean to say you had to take *toilet paper?*' She turned red and focused on her caviar.

"For the rest of the time, I tried to be good, but found it immensely difficult to understand the senator, with his Deep Southern accent, so that I wound up shouting, 'What? What?' at the top of my lungs. There was also a pouty-voiced woman, a reformed socialite from Chicago, with a dreadful, tough voice and language which even I thought crude; she's famous, it seems. Apparently she has the turnstile approach to sex—nearly everyone has passed through, so to speak. I found her revolting. She tried to impose her views on nearly every discussion—the oil crisis, whether Kissinger would come back to power, etc.

"Ah, but then the dinner had already started, and it *was* heavenly. First: blue and gold Czar-size tins of caviar, mounted in enormous crystal bowls massed with cracked ice, and served by waiters in white gloves. With this we drank iced vodka. The rest of the meal I hardly noticed; my mind was too glazed with alcohol, and my voice hoarse with saying, 'What? What?' to the senator.

"I spent some time watching Alexander and Allegra. He seems rather good to her—still! That surprises me. As for her: she quite devotes herself to him, and listened, with great concentration, as he spoke on one subject or another, to the senator. About Iran, mostly, and the Shah. It got quite heated at one moment, and I saw Allegra looking down at her plate. Alex can be insistent, overbearingly so, at times, I think. She drank rather a lot of wine, which surprised me.

"Dessert came—a foamy chocolate mousse, which quite slipped down my throat. *Une merveille.* I looked at Allegra, and then at Alex, as they ate.

"I think he is enchanted and intrigued with her; not really 'in love.' He's not capable of it. He'll only really want her when there's a danger of losing her. It reminds me of that Chinese proverb, 'Beware of what you want; you may actually get it.'

"A svelte blonde with an hourglass figure came over to meet me at one point. From Kentucky—I've read about her. It seems she gave a rather raucous Old West party last summer, all the socialites turning out in their fringe and headdresses; she had wanted me to cover it for *Vogue*. To continue: the woman went to Alexander next, spoke with him, offering her hand in a simpering manner to Allegra, and left. Alex then turned to Allegra and said something; she laughed, and gave him a kiss.

"There were many toasts: one by the senator, one by a rather prominent pollster with a toupee, and one by Zahedi himself.

"(Indeed, I *do* think he'll make a rather good story.)

"Music was playing as we left the dining room and went into the large salon, where after-dinner drinks were being served. I looked for Alex and Allegra, thought they had slipped away, but finally spotted them.

"Another man had joined them: slightly plump, with a red and black paisley evening jacket. Little black silk pumps. I went over and Alex—hesitantly, I sensed—introduced me. They seemed to know one another vaguely. He was called Nazif Keskin, and he's from Istanbul. Ah, that's a magical city; we began to talk about it. 'Have you ever seen the belly dancers?' he asked. 'Only once,' said I. He went on to tell a story about one who was very famous, and whom he had seen dance many times. Finally—and this was recounted with a gleam of his distinguished, albeit lascivious eyes—he said he had asked the dancer, 'Can you dance as well as this—in private?' 'Yes,' she had told him, 'but in that case you have to work harder!' He uttered a low laugh as he told me this, the ice clinking in his whiskey. Alex and Allegra had gone off by then, but I stood there, strangely fascinated by him. He's a young, fortyish man who looks much older; his voice, his balding head. Educated in England, I'd guess.

"Alex and Allegra were dancing. I watched them as they did. Everyone was gyrating to a rock-music beat, but not they. They danced slowly, his arm tight across her waist. I could see the long line of her back, and that of her neck, for her dress was quite bare, different from the sort she usually wears.

"The next moment, a man came over and asked Allegra to dance. Alex stood to the side, watching; I wonder if he was jealous. He would never admit it, of course, but in fact I think he's terribly jealous, and protective of her in a way which is curious in one who has seen so much.

"It got quite mad by the end, everyone swirling and drinking, the blond Swedish ambassador's family making a scene dancing, as well. The senators and congressmen had all but abandoned the place . . . The mosaics shone more brilliantly and the patterns of the Persian rugs and the vast mother-of-pearl mirrors began to move and reflect it all in an undulating motion. Suddenly it did not seem garish at all—

the colours, the mixture of patterns, the carnal richness that had seemed, at first sight, too heavy for the eye to digest.

"And so by the time I left, I found that I had come to rather *like* the place. The atmosphere which had revolted me, at first, now seduced me so entirely that I will—if invited—return. It made me forget—and oh, the ambrosian power of forgetfulness!

"I left about one in the morning, but before I did, went to the loo, where I found Allegra standing before the mirror, a blue enamel compact in her hand, fixing her lipstick. I mentioned I had just read a book I thought she might like. 'One of your sex books, I hope,' she said, with a slight smile. No, said I, I didn't expect she needed that; I said she may have when I first met her, but that I guessed Alex has taken care of *that*. As she laughed, I suddenly looked at her face and remembered how she had appeared the first time I met her—the very long hair, the face clean of makeup, her whole person glowing with the feeling of one from another era. She asked me about my book; I noticed that her eyes looked tired. 'Late nights,' she explained. I asked where she would be spending the summer. 'Long Island,' she said. She asked whether I ever go there, and I said only occasionally, and that I found it amusing in small doses. She smiled again, and said, 'Give me a call,' as she wrote down the telephone number, adding, 'And then you can fill me in on your book.'

" 'And you can show me your new paintings,' I said.

" 'My new paintings?' There was a touch of self-mockery in her voice. 'Did I ever paint?' Then she snapped the compact shut, embraced me, and, with a soft movement of her skirt, she left."

25

Emily made it a point to visit Sagaponack early that August. Arriving one Friday night, she called Allegra, and was immediately invited to lunch the following day.

It had been a dark, terrifying month for Emily. She had all but discarded the original plot of her book. Now it hung about her—those pages written at another stage of her life—like the dead embryo of a foreign organism. Paragraphs she had once loved revolted her; a character who had caused her sleepless nights of excitement now spun her into an intense boredom. Often she would fall asleep in the early evening hours, over her manuscript, only to awaken later, too dispirited to continue.

Most of all she missed the feeling of daily release that she had once achieved through her writing: the rush of ideas which would come when her thoughts, fueled by black coffee, would explode in an orderly procession onto the typewriter.

As June, July, and then August passed, it seemed there was no more point to her life, and all her most tiresome and hypochondriacal symptoms unleashed themselves in the face of her workblock; as if the demon within her *would* be free, or would take revenge on her in other ways she hardly recognized. She grew preoccupied by nourishment and yet by diets, none of which seemed stringent enough to satisfy her growing appetite for self-chastisement. She spent too much money and lusted for clothes; at night, she stayed out very late with men she did not like, simply as an escape, and as another form of self-punishment.

On Saturday, August 12, she wrote:

"I arrived at Alex's house about noontime and was met by Allegra—barefoot, in a white bikini, tanned and looking rather heavenly, I thought. A scent of jasmine and lilies of the valley trailed about her. She seemed happy to see me, though a bit surprised, for I was early. 'Alex is running on the beach,' she told me, taking my arm; in her other arm was a basket of fruit and vegetables. She'd been to the market, she said. Would I like to go for a swim? I declined. I've gained a bit of weight—one of the more depressing symptoms of *horror scribendi*—and feel quite porcine in a bathing suit. I felt it especially because Allegra is so slender, although she has lost the painful thinness she once had. Her hair has gone lighter, with the sun, more copper-coloured, almost reddish. She wore no makeup, and I thought how much prettier and more distinctive she looks without it.

"I asked about the rather flashy Jaguar in the driveway. 'Oh,' she said, 'that's Alex's. He bought it a few months ago. It goes hellishly fast. Good-looking, though, isn't it?' I nodded, for the shiny bordeaux sports car in question was terribly sleek. It must have cost a pretty fortune.

"She then brought me some wine in the most fanciful glass. Sheer green and white crystal, wafer-thin, and etched with an extraordinary design of pagodas and lotuslike flowers. 'Italian,' she explained. 'From my great-aunt, who's Venetian.'

"She told me that two other couples would be coming for lunch: Maggie and Charles Fitzpatrick, and then a friend of Alex's, Mark Goodman, and his girlfriend. 'A business friend,' she said, this time making a wry face.

"We stood on the porch and looked toward the beach: the sky opalescent, radiant and clear; the water a constant and dazzling series of sparkles; the waves much more gentle than I ever remember seeing them, for they can be quite savage here. The porch was small, and there was a table set up in one corner with cushions in a pale terracotta colour along the railings. All the colours gave the house a Mediterranean feeling. That's Allegra, I suspect.

"She asked me about my book, and then about my job ('And the major coats?' with a smile). I told her about *Vogue*—the 'prophetic dresses,' and so on—using the fashion jargon which never fails to make her laugh. Again, it was her listening so intently and with a rather tender expression on her face that affected me. I'm such an awful egocentric creature, and yet I feel an affinity with her, strangely enough. I even feel that I've betrayed her in sleeping with Alex long before she met him, though I would never dare tell her. (I wonder if he has. I doubt it.)

"She led me into the kitchen, and I asked if I might see the rest of the house. It's a simple and yet cozy place with her touches everywhere. Along the walls were paintings I recognized to be by Allegra. Her style is distinctive: strong and yet dreamlike, rippling with colour; some small interior scenes that owe something to Vuillard. I asked about them. 'Oh, these were done a long time ago,' she said, rather disparagingly, stepping up closer to look at one. 'Do you think they're good? Sometimes I think so, and sometimes I don't. There are days when I swear to take them down and others when I just can't bear to part with them. Has that ever happened to you?' I said that it had, and that there were moments when rereading my own writing left me nauseous. 'Really?' she said, her eyes widening, so that they seemed to overwhelm the small, oval face with its pointed chin. 'That's fascinating. But you see, *you* just get on with it. That's discipline. I look at these paintings and it's as if another person had done them. Not me at all . . .' and then, abruptly, 'Emily, do you have a cigarette?'

"I was startled when she asked. I'd never seen her smoke before, but of course I had several packs of them, cigarette fiend that I am. She took one, lit it, and stood there, looking out to the water, her face reflective. I asked about the smoking. 'I started about a month ago. Alex hates it! I've promised to stop, but it's become an addiction, and as long as I do it quietly . . .' Her voice tapered off. She smiled and excused herself, for a moment, and went to change.

"She emerged from the bedroom wearing a pale aquamarine T-shirt.

'I don't often go without something covering me on top, you know. My scar,' she said quietly, then adding, 'I don't like people to have to look at it. It seems unfair to inflict it on others—men, particularly.' I reassured her again that it's really not very noticeable, even in her bikini, which was very bare. 'Well,' she murmured, and went into the kitchen. Most of the work, from what I could see, had been done. There was a lobster salad, and marvelous breads, and great plump tomatoes dashed with basil. It all looked delicious.

"I really wondered at all of this. She looked so charmingly incapable when I first met her, yet here she was, quite efficiently putting this luncheon together. Food, flowers, the house, the lovely table setting that resembled a painting: a basket of white flowers, sea-blue napkins, small wine goblets painted with a coral-branch design.

"I heard Alex's voice next. He'd been running, and then had gone for a swim. He stood dripping wet, a happy expression on his face as he blotted himself with a towel. He looked handsome and happy. 'How are you, Emily?' he said in a surprisingly friendly voice. 'Still dipping your pen in venom?' I told him that I'd been utterly angelic lately, and had even been remarkably well behaved at the fashion showings, which usually bring out the very worst in me. He greeted Allegra next, giving her a strong kiss; took a tomato from the salad; and went to change.

"I noticed that she had stubbed out her cigarette.

"In a moment Alex came out, still shaking his hair of water, and smoothing it out with his hand. I suddenly thought that, with his intense black-green eyes and his tan, he was wildly good-looking (although funnily enough, he actually isn't), and that, together with her, they made a remarkable-looking couple. The Apollonian and the Dionysiac, as it were.

"He went to Allegra, holding her from the back, as he asked her some question. She looked at him, contemplating an answer, while he stood watching her, almost amused.

"Suddenly he remembered that he'd left his tennis racket in the car, and went to get it. 'I played at the Maidstone this morning,' he told me, when he returned. He then made a great point of saying that he was a member there now, and what a terrific club it was. I glanced in Allegra's direction and thought she seemed a bit embarrassed, although surely it was because of her and her family that he was admitted to the club at all!

"For a moment I stood with him, looking at the ocean, at one point asking him why he had chosen Sagaponack as a place for a summer house. He replied that it was a good investment, that the land prices were stable, and that, in the future, sites by the water would become increasingly desirable, especially with the advent of European investors. And, too, he knew a lot of people here; it permitted him to 'make contact,' as he put it, with those in the banking world he might not meet in New York, or through his job. And of course, the ocean was beautiful, that was another reason.

"I smiled to myself.

"Allegra came out from the kitchen and he poured some wine for them both. Noticing her T-shirt, he said, 'It's so hot, you don't really need to wear that, angel.' But then, sensing the reason for it, he turned to me and added, 'Allegra's become so self-conscious about that damn scar. I've told her it's not so bad, but she won't listen.' And then, to her, 'Will you, my love?' He took her in his arms and, kissing her gently, said, 'I've told her that if it bothers her so much we ought to do something about it. I'll find a doctor, and we'll see if it can't be removed. Right?' He lifted her chin and kissed her again, her eyes shining.

"Then, in an exuberant, proud voice, he said, 'Have you seen Allegra's paintings? They're all hers, you know. All of them.' I said that I had, but he continued to point out this one or that, nonetheless: 'Aren't the colours here marvelous?' or 'Look at the way she *caught* that child's face.' This rather touched me, even though I think it is mostly through the eyes of others that he has come to appreciate her talent, and her gifts in realms where he knows little.

"He took my arm, led me to the porch, but immediately went back, calling, 'Allegra, where are my shoes?' 'In the bottom of the closet, righthand side,' she answered. He reappeared with the shoes and said, shaking his head, 'Impossible to walk out there without shoes, the splinters on the deck are something terrible.' I hadn't noticed, because I was wearing sandals, but then I looked at Allegra, who was chopping celery, and saw that she was barefoot. I was about to remind her, when I suddenly realized that it was because of Alex that she had gone without them. With them, she looked taller—so this little measure was in deference to him. I didn't know whether to be touched or appalled.

"I went with him to the porch. We sat sipping our drinks, saying little (the awkwardness that engulfs former lovers who now find themselves 'friends') and looking at the rhythm of the turquoise sea. The air undulated with beach noises, and the sand was dotted with coloured umbrellas, some of them striped, others that threw shades of tinted light on the white sand. Children shouted; couples strutted by, beyond, near the water's edge—young, old, beautiful, trim, sagging, homosexual.

"Not much later, the Fitzpatricks arrived, Maggie looking a bit too fashionably and carefully dressed, as she sometimes does. Toward Allegra and myself she is warm, even a little deferential at moments (she never went to college and is, I think, quite self-conscious about it). Her husband, Charles, smokes a pipe, is rather reserved, and almost nondescript-looking until he begins to speak—then his face becomes wonderfully arresting. He has the quiet obsessiveness of a surgeon, together with the confidence that comes from intrinsic self-discipline.

"A moment later, Alex's business friend, Mark Goodman, arrived. He works for Goldman-Sachs and was accompanied by a juicy little blonde, utterly vapid, with an astounding figure, from Virginia.

"As we sat and drank the wine—Allegra having joined us by then—I suddenly felt very much the bookworm among the beauties. But then I often do.

"At last, we went to the table—thank God, because I was starving. 'Don't you want to sit by Allegra?' Maggie said, as Alex helped her to her seat. 'Oh no,' he said. 'I sit by her often enough.' I saw Allegra's eyes, and her glance, but in a moment it seemed forgotten.

"Alex began to talk with Charles and Maggie. I sense he is careful to be good to them, since he knows they mean so much to Allegra. Indeed, he has quite won over Maggie, in particular.

"A few moments later, Maggie brought up Véronique. 'I haven't seen her in so long,' she said, looking at us all. 'Have you?' Alex remained silent; and then Allegra said, 'We don't see her much, but I hear from her fairly often. She's become a good client, actually; I'm helping her with her collection.' And then, rather guardedly, 'It's amazing how much she knows about painting.'

"Alex changed the subject.

"Maggie picked up the conversation again, saying that she and Charles were looking to buy a house nearby, in Water Mill. I kept watching her as she spoke: she is really rather affecting in her own way, although funnily enough I didn't take to her at first. But since then, I've come to appreciate that this is a woman who has worked very hard to make something of herself; I also began to suspect that she had, at one point, sustained a terrible loss in her life. (I was right, as it turned out. Later, in the kitchen, Allegra said sadly, 'Her baby. She lost her baby about a year and a half ago.') Charles is indulgent toward her, and clearly adores her. As for him, he is very kind, and has wonderful, fine hands. I watched, fascinated, as he cut his meat with a surgeon's meticulousness.

"During much of the lunch, Alex and Mark talked business—the stock market, an Italian merger Alex is putting together, and a new venture with a Canadian ship-building company. Mark's girlfriend looked vacantly around, while Allegra tried in vain to engage her in some sort of conversation. At last, giving up, she turned to Maggie, while I spoke with Charles.

"It had grown quite, quite hot by the time we came to dessert— ripe figs covered with *crème anglaise*. I gobbled them up. Alex looked contentedly about, in the meantime. Getting up to pour the wine, he suddenly went over to Allegra, giving her a great kiss, and saying, 'She's the best, isn't she?'; her eyes were radiant.

"Then we began to talk about Europe; the Fitzpatricks had just returned from several weeks' holiday in Italy. The hill towns, Siena, and, at the end, Venice.

" 'I couldn't have been happier,' said Maggie. 'Harry joined us for a few days. He stayed at the Europa. We were at the Gritti—it was wonderful.' Then she stopped, sipping her wine, and said, in an excited voice, 'Did I tell you about the wedding we saw in Venice? No?'

" 'Tell us,' Allegra said, leaning forward, her elbows on the table.

" 'We were taking a walk late one afternoon, far from the center of the city,' Maggie said. 'There weren't many tourists around. It wasn't far from the arsenal, was it, love?' Charles nodded. 'We came to a church—or rather, a cathedral—and saw lots of people gathered, talking, whispering. I asked someone what was happening. A wedding, they said. I should have known—the trees were strung with flowers and small white lights. I told Charles, "We've got to stay. How many times do you get to see a wedding in Venice?" So we did.

" 'About five-thirty, the boat came up. It was gilded all around the edges and prow, and fitted inside with bright yellow and white striped cushions. What a sight! As it approached, the crowds rushed to the edge of the water, to see the bride. She was tall, with very dark hair and a delicate face, a northern Italian face. The skirt of her dress was so enormous that it seemed to fill the boat. The people went wild. There must have been hundreds there by that time; the trees seemed to shake with their shouts. *"Bella sposa!"* they cried. *"Sempre amore!"* ' Maggie smiled, almost to herself. 'All the old men smelling of wine, and the young girls with wide eyes.'

" 'And then?' I asked.

" 'Well, the music started and the bride went slowly, very very slowly, to the church, past the huge doors, and then inside. We followed, although it was hard to make our way through the crowd. Inside, it was beautiful, you can't imagine—just like a painting! Red damask draped along the pews, and garlands of lilies and wild flowers, intertwined with tiny pears. Two enormous gold chairs were set up for the couple, side by side, on the altar. The music had begun by the time we entered—I recognized a few of the pieces—one by Albinoni, another by Vivaldi, with a lovely haunting part played by a violinist.

" 'It was so moving,' she continued. 'All the parishioners, family, and strangers gathered together. There was something very impressive and yet human about the mass: the sound of the choirboys' voices, the colours, the burning candles, the feeling of the ancientness all around us.

" 'Finally, the bride and groom—both of them smiling, radiant— made their way down the aisle, through the church, and, outside, to the wedding boat. It was nearly dusk then, and the lights had gone on, and as the bride and groom came out, everyone threw almonds and rice·and shouted and shouted.

" 'They made their way to the boat, followed by the flower girl, a tiny little thing with braids and glasses. And then, as the bride stepped into the boat, I heard the little girl say to her, "Look! Even the rats have come out for your wedding!" And she was right! You could see three or four of them scurrying below, on the layers of the canal. The water had gone very low, you see . . . And then, still waving from the boat, the couple moved away, under the bridge, and then past the Riva degli Schiavoni. The sky had turned a strange colour, tinged with pink and yellow. We were able to get a boat, so we could watch, and wave, and follow the procession.' A moment's pause. 'It was wonderful, wasn't it, Charles?'

"He nodded, tapping his pipe on the table, as if to remember. His response couldn't have equaled that of his wife, however—Maggie's was rapturous. And so, in fact, was Allegra. Indeed, we had all listened closely to the story, there was something hypnotic about it. But finally the conversation did turn from the wedding, to Italy itself. 'Oh I *wish* I could speak better Italian!' Maggie said. 'I love to hear it spoken, it's like music.' Then Alex, turning to Allegra, said, 'Why don't *you* ever speak Italian to me?' She: 'But you wouldn't understand me, if I did.' He: 'But I don't often, anyway.'

"There was a long silence, I saw Allegra bite her lip. But then Charles came quickly into the breach, and began to talk of traveling in general, and asked which places everyone wanted to visit. 'Egypt,' said Allegra, instantly. 'Back to Spain,' said Charles. 'To Scandinavia,' said Alexander. 'To look at the women.' Glancing at Allegra, he then said, 'You'd give me a dispensation for that, wouldn't you?' He laughed, but only Mark Goodman joined him; as for me, I watched Allegra's eyes. It was terrible, for she tried to act stoical and modern, but he had really hurt her. 'Sure,' she said, in a nearly inaudible voice. 'If you really wanted to.' Charles looked embarrassed, lit his pipe, then glanced at Maggie, who fidgeted. I could see that Alex had suddenly realized his mistake. 'Oh, why would I want to look at *them?*' he said (for he had gone over to kiss Allegra). 'I was only joking.' I could tell that the kiss and purring words had placated her, but only surface-deep. I would have exploded if I'd been her, but she's too proud. She had already put on a smile and, brightening her voice, said, 'Would anyone like some more dessert?'

"We had coffee, and talked some more, until the sun began to wane. 'Some music?' suggested Alex. He put on a Brazilian record and suddenly took Allegra in his arms, tightly, and began to dance. There was something so intimate and exclusive about the way he held her that I could barely watch, as if I had caught a glimpse of them making love.

"Maggie and Charles had gone walking on the beach. Mark Goodman and girlfriend were outside doing God knows what. The telephone rang, and Allegra went to get it. 'Alex,' she said, 'it's for you. Mr. Sidney.'

"His countenance seemed to change, and he went into the bedroom, and closed the door."

26

Later that night, it grew very cool. The moon appeared white and hot against the cold indigo sky, now starless, as if the crescent of bright superior light had swept all else away.

After the guests had left, Allegra returned to the kitchen. Alexander remained on the telephone, for several calls had followed that of Mr. Sidney. She had cleared the table, washed the dishes, and put the things away; and then, after wandering to the deck, walked down the steps to the beach. There was almost no one out now, for it was nearly eight-thirty. A man ambled past with a cavorting dog; and then a pregnant woman, her arm around a man's waist.

Allegra sat on the sand, hugging her knees and looking out at the water, thinking how crystalline the sea had seemed in the afternoon, and now, how dark and unfathomable. The sky threw a mauve light on the sand's surface as the waves rolled, pounded, and hissed, leaving the grains glistening.

Allegra felt so exhausted and dispirited that she could hardly move; each movement of the waves made her edgy, each ebb and flow made her head pound. Her mind ached with the small repeated heart-stabs of remembered hurt and anger. There were moments when she suddenly did not *know* Alexander. When she resented him, even hated him for his capacity to hurt her. The needling comments clothed as jokes; the attentions to other women; the way he often made her feel incapable. The less she painted, the more susceptible she seemed to feel to the emotional attrition. He would tell her that he wanted her to paint, and yet he chipped away at the inner resources she needed to create.

She thought of the lunch, and his humiliating remarks, and the way he had cut her short when, after Emily's departure, she had mentioned Michel Théron to the Fitzpatricks. Had she confronted him then, she might have exploded; at least, she thought, that would have brought an end to this silent, knifing hurt. But now it had all metamorphosed into another emotion—one that left her spent and listless.

She brushed some hair from her face and drew a circle in the sand.

Suddenly, hands grasped her shoulders; she looked up; it was Alexander.

"Where have you been?" he asked, sitting down beside her. He looked almost disturbingly handsome and vigorous; she turned her eyes from him, almost wishing him otherwise. "Aren't you cold?" he said, beginning to button her sweater—a brisk, compensatory gesture she knew all too well. "No," she said, her voice cool. "I'm not cold. It feels good. The wind, after the sun today."

"Lunch was delicious."

She did not look up. "I'm glad."

He paused, and then said, "I really don't understand why Emily had to be invited, though. I understand even less why you seem to like her, even to be fascinated by her."

"I find her interesting—eccentric and wounded."

"Wounded?" He laughed sarcastically. "She's brittle and single-minded . . . Believe me, I know, and if *you* knew . . ." But here, he stopped; for a split second it occurred to him to tell the details of their affair. Instead, he merely went on to say, "She suffers from a multiplicity of selves, and none of them can be trusted."

"I'll keep that in mind." Her voice was woven with hurt, and with bruised pride, not only from his words just then, but from the way he had treated her during lunch. She could feel the rage spinning up again inside her, and could not bring herself to look in his direction.

"Why did you cut in when I mentioned Michel?" she said, after a moment had passed.

"I'd prefer you didn't talk about him; he's very private, you know, and always worried about his family's visibility. He likes to keep a low profile—I've told you that."

She hugged her knees again and looked up at him, suddenly: the light had hidden his eyes, so that she saw only the shape of his face, and his dark hair, and the precise lines of his mouth. "Alex," she said, "you were so rude to me this afternoon. I was embarrassed. You embarrassed me in front of them. I felt . . ." She began to cry.

"Allegra, please. How can you say that? You know I adore you, although sometimes, I really don't understand you. Please. Please stop." He hugged her and wiped her face of tears, then kissed the tip of her nose, saying, "You get in these moods and you make me feel, as if I were alone again." He picked up some sand and threw it toward the water. "You know how much I care about you." He hugged her again.

"Do you love me?" she asked, in spite of herself.

There came the pause that she had feared.

"I care about you," he said. "I'm very loving to you. You know that."

"I don't, sometimes. What you say makes me think that you're never satisfied with what I am, as if you were always searching for something better. It's like the way we travel, from place to place, searching . . . There are moments when I feel that I'm some city you are getting ready to abandon."

"This kind of talk is degrading," he said, in a disgusted voice. He stood up, his hands dropping from her shoulders. "You know how I feel. I've told you, and nothing I've done has indicated anything less."

He walked back to the house.

She kept listening to the waves, and breathing slowly, so slowly, as if to vanquish the fatigue that infused every vein of her body. Her questions had been a way of searching for emotional sustenance from him, and they had only been met by a marble wall of logic, and by answers that confused her. Part of her knew this, and yet knowing it did not prevent her from being devastated by it.

Her tears would no longer come.

It grew too cool to stay outside, and she stood up, vowing that she would let him know what she felt, that she did not care if he left her, that she would tell him he was selfish and careless, and that she hated the way he had treated her among her friends.

But by the time she reached the house, her resolve had stopped at her throat. She would wait for a better moment, she told herself. Not now. Another time.

She saw a light in the bedroom, and walked toward it.

27

It seemed, by the beginning of September, that they had changed camps: it was she who was pursuing him—fearful that he might leave her, eager to do anything for him, and yet resentful of what she thought it took to keep him; and if she did not do the expected, what would happen? Her work, her painting, she had again quite tossed aside. "What do you do?" people would ask, and her answer would come out all choked, for she had come to feel that she did very little, and it began to show on her face. An embarrassment would sweep over her, a sense of despair and worthlessness, as she felt Alexander watching.

He, on the other hand (and was this not true of men in general? she wondered), seemed to have recovered himself—his goals, his work, his discipline. It frightened her that she seemed to need and desire him more than he needed her; at least she did not seem to be the utmost matter on his mind, nor did she preoccupy him as he did her.

A nervousness, a palpable physical tension—over the muscles in her neck, in her back—came into her body and, once again, she would be unable to *see* anything. She ran to him, depended on his calls, wanted to make love to him, often more out of reassurance than out of desire.

And then she wanted so much to sleep, to sleep and sleep. "Perhaps it's good," she said to herself, "that I don't want to leap out of bed in the morning. That the sleep is now so deep, and the dreams so absorbing that I can't leave them. Like a good book." On the weekends, she was listless. She would suddenly fall asleep, and then sleep for hours, on the porch, waking up in the early evening, the sun quite dim, the cool breeze making her shoulders shiver. She sensed that he disapproved of this: where was the energy of the girl he had first met? Most often, though, he merely teased her, or said nothing.

She was in love, and yet she felt lonely. There was a threat to it, a safeness that was missing.

And then, there were Michel and Véronique—two profiles enameled on the missing panels of a triptych. In the background, always: so seemingly concerned, so desirous that it "work out" between them.

It began to be difficult for Allegra even to read, to concentrate at all. Books collected dust; pages remained closed; her paintbrushes lay dry and unused in their holders. Sometimes she would try to work an hour or two after returning from the office, only to find herself, at seven o'clock, standing in the kitchen making herself a drink. The telephone would ring: Alexander. Once she mentioned, in passing, that she had just made herself a drink. "A drink? Alone?" he had said. "Ah, the first stage of alcoholism." He had laughed, and yet what he had said shocked her, as if she had done something wicked, unholy, and that—worse—she had no personal discipline.

Errands, small tasks, getting ready to go out—these became increasingly difficult and fraught with fear. Anything creative that demanded a return to herself seemed overwhelming and made her want to flee, as if her own emotions were too chaotic for her to confront the kaleidoscope of options and feelings that painting demanded.

And yet, she looked so elegant and composed! Surely she had never been so well-dressed, so well-groomed. Her hands, with their oval, polished nails; her hair, an even shorter length; and the concern—which she had never seriously felt before she met him—of how she would appeal to men, through her appearance. "I don't like that dress," he would say, and she would immediately take it off. Or, at a dinner, he would look at another woman, one who was quite fashionable and say, "Why don't you get *that* style of pants? They're very sexy." The next instant, she would think, Surely I must look silly, in my dress, and the following day, search for a copy of what he had admired.

Gradually, his comments came to awaken in her latent feelings of anger, even spite: the sickly triumphs of destructiveness that seemed her only armor against his power to hurt her and make her feel inadequate. She would smoke incessantly, because she knew he hated it; or wear a dress she knew he disliked, simply to see his reaction; or, at a business dinner, compliment one of his rivals, just to see him smart. At such moments, she hardly recognized herself.

As for her mind: it felt cluttered, confused, misguided, and most of all, lonely. The rivulets of learning, of reading, and of the safe port within the self, these she seldom knew anymore. Turbulence was all.

And then she had always had such a different notion about the evolution of a love affair; for in the antechamber of her mind she equated romance with courtship, and with a fluent series of commitments. Here she found none. Did he love her, she had asked that night at the beach. The small, biting silence that had followed!

There were times when she simply ached for him to go away. Sometimes, when he did, she would feel the most immense freedom and relief, as if, then, there was a chance of recovering the self that had been, and no reason, really, to worry about anything. Let him go, she would say to herself. Until the moment came when, perhaps, he did not call. Perhaps his tone when he did was not right, not loving enough?—and the old anxiety would mount again.

The abandoned paintbrush, the closed book once more.

She had always assumed that love meant safety; that romance was exhilaration; and that, having both, she would have no need to look elsewhere. She suddenly found herself in a part of the woods she did not recognize, where the trees looked forbidding, and she seemed to have lost the path she had dreamt of.

She began to think that only marriage would assuage the restlessness and fear; a panacea to the lostness, to "this limboish feeling of mine." Marriage would give her the peace, the inner security, and the safety she craved; the sense of the family she had lost, to be married, yes! It began to consume all her thoughts.

The following Sunday, the second weekend of September, was beautiful and hot. On the beach, there was a cool breeze that seemed to offset the warmth of the sand, and the sudden absence of crowds made the water look even more majestic and luminous. Choppy and rough, the waves seemed to have escaped all order, darting here and there in a sluicing, chaotic rhythm.

It was Allegra's favorite season at the beach: the bittersweet moments of the waning summer, the first falling leaves, and the moon, at night, high, overripe.

Alexander stood on the porch, his hands planted on the railing, looking out to the ocean. Allegra had gone inside; he waited for her, impatient that she had not yet reappeared, and looking from the water to the sky, which was full of high, puffy clouds.

He had gone into the water earlier that day, and had felt the sudden, ledgelike drop of the sand on the ocean floor, his body buffeted by the waves and their powerful, relentless motion—briskly, as if they knew autumn was approaching. The swim had thrilled him, and he had returned—tired and exhilarated—for breakfast.

But now Allegra appeared, carrying a book and smoking a cigarette, her hand shielding her eyes from the sun. "Come, let's go in the water," he said, disregarding her smoking, for the moment. Her eyes moved to the water. There was no one swimming now, and a warning about the undertow had been posted. "Not now," she said, still looking out. "You go ahead, I'll watch."

But he had already taken her hand, and snatched her book, setting it down on a chair. "Come on," he urged her again. "I'll go in with you and hold your hand. There's nothing to be afraid of."

She murmured "OK," smiled reluctantly, stubbed out the cigarette, and followed him down the steps, for the thought that she might disappoint him was more harrowing to her than the waves. And indeed, her acquiescence always made him more affectionate; he slipped his arm around her waist, drew her closer, and kissed her.

She suddenly thought of skiing, and of that moment when—pitched high above a steep slope—one's eyes wandered through the descent as one picked a path, the stomach knotted with the tantalizing mix of thrill and fear that made the speed so exciting.

They came closer to the edge of the water. The waves rose and crashed, faster and faster, it seemed, one cutting into the other.

She pointed to the warning that had been posted. "Oh, they always do that," he said, disregarding it and holding her hand more tightly. "Come on."

"Please stay close, so I can feel your hand!"

"Of course." He gave her a salty kiss, her memory of it warm and fresh as they strode through the froth. "Come on, come on," he said, his knees plunging through as he turned back to smile at her.

It was difficult to pass through the point beyond the breaking line of the waves. Normally, it would have taken a short, brisk swim, but now they went slowly, so that, for a long time, she could still stand on the sand—one wave approaching, curling itself to a peak, and then crashing. She dove through one, then another, the cold thrilling her throat as she felt his hand in hers, moving up and back again as it pulled her. But suddenly she felt herself being tugged out, deeper into the waves, as if she would lose the rhythm of the dives, yet still she felt his hand, anchorlike in hers, and the fright abated. She swam for a moment, her head just above the water, with him, waiting; two bobbing heads, two hands entwined, the waves swirling around them.

Gradually the waves grew larger, swifter, more powerful, more potent in the way they broke. She clutched his hand, and looked up to see the crest of a wave approach; dove; emerged. But then came another tug which exhausted her, weakening her for the next—and suddenly there was no hand to sustain her, only the silent blue-black terror of the water churning and churning above her. Rolling and tumbling in the underwater current, she stifled a scream, for what seemed to be endless hours. Waves rushed on, sealing her inside a vast underwater world; above it the pitching froth . . . Her life sweeping past, the beach she would never see again; no escape; no breath; and her head and body pounding, swirling . . .

They said it was only moments later when they reached her. She opened her eyes to see the face of a strange man holding her head and looking with concern into her eyes. The lifeguard. Her eyes opened in small flecking movements; was it the waves of pain in her arm (the snap she had felt), that made the sun seem so bright? Another face, Alexander's, stared at her, and then kissed her, his hand again in hers. Gently he kept kissing her, stroking her hair. "You let it go," she murmured. "My hand. You let me go." "I couldn't help it," he said softly. "I was pulled away. Please, don't talk now, Allegra. Please. Stay quiet."

He kissed and kissed her, holding her, murmuring that it was the tide that had pulled them apart; the waves that had done it. He helped her to the house and then, to the hospital.

She sat in a cool corner of the living room, her arm in a cast, her head nodding over a book, her thoughts roaming. She tried not to think of his hand letting go of hers, yet she linked it, inexplicably, with that other moment of stinging silence on the beach.

The painkillers had made her drowsy, bringing with them a welcome sleep and a host of bizarre dreams . . .

She lay awake in a cold, empty cave to which there was no entrance, no exit. Wind blew; she heard the sound of a knife slicing the air. It was black and dark all around her. What colors did exist were too dark to name. No light, no illumination, not a single candle; the walls and the floor were of deep, cold earth. A sharp wind made her shiver, for she was curled on a small sheetless cot of hard, splintered wood. The cover was thin and the air was dark and damp. A rough, skimpy brown blanket, strung up haphazardly, divided the cave in two; in the other part she felt—but did not know—that another person was sleeping.

She wore no clothes and the wind was merciless; she pulled the meager blanket closer.

At last she fell asleep, deeply and profoundly, a deep and dreamless sleep, until she awakened suddenly, startled and fearful, to find a man—dark-haired, in a striped shirt—standing above her. Looking up, she thought she saw a flash of a knife through the air and then his hand, streaking back, so that it was held, behind him, concealed . . . It was nothing, he said, go back to sleep; his eyes smiled; they were friendly, in fact . . . Perhaps he would sleep with her, too, would she mind? It did not matter that she wore no clothes;

it may be better, he told her. Suddenly she did not like his smile, which was at once merry and lascivious. Whether she knew him or whether he was a stranger she did not know; and when she asked whether someone was sleeping in the other part of the cave, he did not answer. A sudden vision in her mind's eye of the knife, blackened with the other's blood! So perhaps there was no one now; no soft breathing of sleeping in the other part.

And perhaps she was next; to sleep with him, or to be knifed? She did not know; she could not sleep, for her eyes were wide and her body tense; and as he crawled beneath the covers with her, she could feel the rounded muscles of his arms, and then his cock, for it had brushed against her thigh, making her shiver, but not with cold this time. She was suddenly afraid that she would desire him, that he would fuck her, and that she would want him to fuck her; and that, exhausted from the pleasure his biting and thrusting had given her, she would fall asleep again, and while he watched her sleep, the knife would slice through the air and then . . .

Allegra awakened, murmuring, her hands hot, only to find Alexander's face above hers, asking what was wrong.

For months she would remember that dream with a deep and dreadful fear.

28

Allegra was awakened one morning several weeks later by the telephone. She groped for it in the darkness.

"Allegra?" said a voice.

"Yes," she said sleepily, sheets tumbled on top of her.

"It's Emily."

"Emily?" For a moment the name escaped her, but then, remembering, said, "Emily! Where are you?"

"Allegra, I need your help. I didn't know who else to call and I thought . . ."

"What is it? What time is it?" The urgency in Emily's voice made Allegra sit up. "Tell me, Emily, what's the matter?"

"I'm at the hospital."

"The hospital! Why?"

"I came here yesterday, but they won't let me leave unless someone comes to take me home. Will you come?"

"Yes, yes of course. But what's happened?"

"I had an abortion. Yesterday. Please, I'll explain later—just come, will you?"

"Of course. What time?"

"Eleven."

"Where?" She took a pen and jotted down the directions: which entrance; what wing; what floor; which desk to ask for. And then, "Emily, are you OK?" she asked again, anxious now.

"Yes, I'm fine. I'll see you at eleven."

The call had so unnerved Allegra that she was unable to work at all that morning. Cataloging details and the minutiae of an upcoming sale spun before her eyes. Her stomach jumped and she felt withdrawn—the voice on the other end of the telephone had not sounded like Emily's at all!

At ten-thirty she left for the hospital, saying that she had a doctor's appointment and would return shortly. Outside, on Madison Avenue, it was cool and sunny, with that cleansed feeling that comes from a rain the previous night. People brushed past—eyes glancing at watches, fists tensed around briefcases—as Allegra continued to walk. It suddenly occurred to her she ought to take Emily something—some flowers. She stopped at Millefleur.

Maggie was in the shop moving some buckets of roses, her hair tied back, an apron around her waist. Seeing Allegra, she went to open the door. "This is a surprise," Maggie said, kissing her, and then, glancing at Allegra's left arm, which was still in a cast, "I hope that's coming off soon." "It is, in a few weeks," replied Allegra, who then explained why she had come. "Emily's had some sort of stomach bug," she said hesitantly, "and I thought some flowers might cheer her up."

"What do you think she'd like?" Maggie asked, her hand on her hip, her eyes scanning the flowers. "Some lilies? We just got some beauties in today."

Allegra gave a slight smile. "I don't think Emily is really the lily type, do you?"

"You're right. Something red, or purple would be better . . ."

"What about tiger lilies?" Allegra said suddenly. "They'd be perfect. A big bunch."

The flowers wrapped, Maggie handed them to Allegra. "How pretty," she murmured, taking the lavender package with its multicolored ribbons. "Tell her I hope she's better," Maggie said, walking Allegra to the door. "Give her my love."

"I will," she said, kissing her, then walking out to the street, where she hailed a taxi.

Soon after, Allegra reached the entrance of the hospital, with its formidable blue awning that shielded the door from all traces of the late September sun. Through one revolving door she went, and then another, clutching the cone-shaped parcel of flowers. All around her was the terrible, inescapable hospital atmosphere: a catacomb of rooms, and, in the air, what one imagined to be the smell of anesthetic. She inhaled the institutional odors and noticed the walls, which were painted a turgid green. The light seemed pale and grim.

Walking to the elevator at the end of the hall, she pressed the button and arrived in a few moments at Emily's floor. It had a labyrinthine feeling, with signs and arrows posted everywhere, and an enveloping aura of sickness.

Allegra came to a desk, knowing it was not the right place, but she was lost and needed to ask directions. The woman who sat there had an officious face and fleshy hands that rummaged through stacks of papers.

At last, she found the right room. Inside, a nurse sat quietly at the desk and opposite her, on a hard chair, Emily. She looked drained, weak, and lost.

"Emily!" said Allegra, hardly able to think of anything to say and standing there for a moment awkwardly, until she thrust the flowers forward. "Here, these are for you."

"Thanks," she said. "Thanks for coming." And then, seeing Allegra's arm in the cast, she asked, "What the hell have you done to your arm?"

"I hurt it, swimming at the beach . . . Tore a tendon. Nothing serious."

"We make a fine pair." Emily gave a weak smile.

"How are you feeling?" Allegra asked, after a moment.

"Fine. Considering. Really a miracle of modern medicine, you know . . ." She stood up, unsteadily, and for a moment Allegra saw the struggle in her eyes and on her face. Emily murmured something again and Allegra smelled her breath, which was stale; her clothes were rumpled and her whole being looked dejected. The doors swung behind them as they left.

Allegra let Emily walk ahead, watching to see if she faltered, and occasionally extending a hand to help her. Emily said very little; that in itself seemed strange to Allegra, who had grown so accustomed to

Emily's quips and stories. Instead, utter silence and wan smiles. Allegra also said little, but kept looking at her friend's face—at her thin, high nose and the small lines around her eyes, and the bluish color of her mouth against the white skin. Her tousled hair looked darker and blacker than usual.

They took the elevator, going downstairs to the place where patients collected prescriptions. Many people clutching papers queued ahead of them. They came to the window, Emily handing over her prescription to a young bearded man. "OK," he said, glancing at it, and giving her a number. "Just watch the board and wait till yours comes up."

The two women walked to the bright-colored chairs, which were made of hard plastic and scooped out like shells.

Allegra kept noticing inconsequential details—the linoleum floor, the face of a child playing, an old woman with a bandaged eye—as if to avoid looking into Emily's eyes. She dreaded seeing her like this! And, indeed, Emily had turned her head away, as if she sensed this.

"How did it happen?" Allegra finally asked.

"What do you mean, how did it happen? How does it usually happen?" Her voice sounded weak, exasperated.

"You know what I mean."

"I noticed it Friday, the strangest thing," Emily said slowly, her hand brushing beneath her eye. "I suddenly knew I was pregnant. There was no doubt about it in my mind at all; it was so eerily recognizable and yet . . . My breasts were all full, very sore. I went to the doctor."

"What did he say?"

"To come and have a test done." She paused, coughing slightly and covering her mouth with her hand. "By Sunday, I had started to feel very unwell. Nauseated, vomiting. I *knew* then I was pregnant. Knew it. I called Monday to find the test results. Positive. I came here late that afternoon; the good doctors did their work, and so here I am, back to normal operating procedure." She looked at Allegra, shaking her head slightly, a wan smile on her face, but the cavalier remarks could not mask the despair in her eyes, the confusion, and the self-disgust.

Then Emily suddenly said, "The pathetic thing is that I'm not even sure whose baby it was."

"Emily! You must."

She looked down, and said, in a weary voice, "I really don't. Although I think . . ." She stopped and looked directly at Allegra, her face annoyed. "Oh, please let's not talk about it now. Please."

At last the number flashed on the screen. Allegra went to get the medicine—several small bottles in a white bag.

And then—past the children, the old people, and the crowd of waiting patients—they left the room, and finally were outside. It was a clear day, the sun jubilant and holidaylike, the trees in Central Park a glorious burnished color. Allegra breathed deeply as she stood for a moment on the street, and, looking around, hailed a taxi.

They sped down Fifth Avenue, and then Seventy-ninth Street, arriving soon at Emily's brownstone. Allegra paid the driver and helped Emily up the steps.

There were old newspapers in front of the door, which Allegra picked up. Emily stood unsteadily, the flowers drooping in one hand, her keys in another. In the dim light of the hall, she looked even more pale and worn.

It had never really occurred to Allegra to imagine what Emily's apartment would look like, much as she tended to fantasize about the homes of others. In a curious way, she was delighted by what she now saw: the tumbles of books, the faded silk pillows, the ink-stained sofa, the invitations on the mantelpiece, the stacks of yellowing theater programs (the sources of names for Emily's characters)—all of this enchanted her, as if she had entered some bohemian retreat, a writer's domain, with all its idiosyncrasies.

Emily, seeing her looking around, said in an amused tone, *"Architectural Digest* was going to photograph it, you know, but then they decided it was a bit too *purist."* Allegra laughed, and for a moment Emily smiled too, but the smile soon vanished as she sat down on the sofa, her head in her hands.

"Are you all right?" Allegra said, kneeling down to her. "Is there anything you'd like?"

Emily looked up. "For my book to be finished and my bills paid."

"No, no I mean now," said Allegra, furrowing her brow, as she managed a smile. She helped Emily stretch out on the sofa and put some pillows behind her head, as Damedith, the cat, scampered over. It was obvious that Emily had not eaten for days, for her stomach looked painfully concave. It upset Allegra even to look at her.

"How do you feel?" she asked.

"Empty," said Emily, in a voice Allegra had never heard before. "Terribly, terribly empty. The odd thing was that—even for those few days—I felt I had company. Can you imagine?" She gave a small, self-mocking smile. "Merely a little fetus, of course, but at least *there*." She closed her eyes and said, "Oh God," in a low voice, and then she began to cry. Allegra held her shoulders and murmured, "Emily, don't worry, it will all be OK. Really." For a moment, the tears continued to pour down her cheeks, and her face looked remarkably ugly. She stopped abruptly, wiping her face and trying to regain her composure.

"Let's talk about something else," she said, after a moment had passed. "How's Alex?"

"He's in Los Angeles, on business."

"Los Angeles?" Emily smiled, that peculiar Leonardesque expression on her face which Allegra had noticed the first evening they had met.

"You've been to L.A.?" Allegra asked.

"Yes," Emily replied. "But only once. I always imagined that I'd be greeted by an enormous billboard that read: Welcome to Los Angeles. Home of the Identity Crisis."

"Why do you say that?" said Allegra, smiling.

"Oh you know, the bean sprouts, the shrinks, that sort of thing." A pause. "Why do I say most of the things I do?"

"Would you like a cup of tea?"

"Yes, I'd like that, actually. There's a tin in the kitchen, on the counter."

Allegra went into the tiny kitchen—no more than an enlarged closet—and found the tin of Russian Caravan tea, which seemed to be as ancient as the Victorian teacups, their edges chipped and paint faded.

Moments later, she brought in the tea on a tray. Emily sipped slowly, the color slowly coming back into her cheeks. Allegra, turning to her said, "You know, I remember going to Los Angeles a few years ago. Funny how vivid my memories of it are. I'd been sent on an appraisal. There's a remarkable collector there, who lives on the beach, called Rupert Tuchman. Nineteenth century, as well as some wonderful furniture. A beautiful Tiepolo, too . . ." She continued to describe the collection, but noticed that she had lost Emily's attention. "I'm boring you," she finally said.

"Not at all," Emily said, sitting up.

"Anyway, one night I'd been invited to a dance at a movie studio. Have you ever been to one? I hadn't. It was a costume party—very very fanciful. You passed through the gates, and then through a street that looked like Montmartre—they'd just used the set for a film—and then into an enormous sound stage. I felt as if I were entering some feudal kingdom; all it needed was a moat!"

"And you met film stars, and people like that?"

"Some." She stopped, lit a cigarette, and said, "It was sort of a shock. They were so different from the way I'd pictured them."

"Yes," said Emily, her thoughts wandering. "All those attempts at sybaritism that somehow flop . . . What's Alex doing there?"

"Working on a deal. He didn't say which. He never—or rarely—discusses his work with me. And if he did, I wouldn't understand anything about it. Business doesn't interest me at all."

"He is difficult to know, your Alex."

"Do you think so?" Allegra looked out, past the windows, to the overgrown garden.

Emily nodded. "The queer thing is that I do think he loves you, at least in his own way—oh, don't look hurt! You're entirely lovable, that's not what I mean. It's Alex I'm talking about. I would imagine that . . ." But she stopped, midsentence, her eyes rolling to the ceiling, her voice exploding, "God, I'm frightfully hungry all of a sudden! Really starving!"

"What would you like?"

"Some soup, some nice comforting soup. All thick and potatoey—the kind my nanny used to make. Dear old Nan, if only she could see me now." She smiled ruefully. "Would you go around the corner? There's a shop where you can get some soup and cheese. Here, get me my purse and I'll give you some money . . ." But Allegra refused, pushing the wallet away; she returned a few minutes later with vegetable soup, cheese, and an apricot pie.

At the end of the lunch, Emily patted her stomach and gave a long, satiated sigh. Allegra smiled. "You're feeling better?"

"Much." And then: "Allegra, tell me—and this is purely intellectual curiosity, you understand. Is Alex a good lover to you?"

Had anyone else asked Allegra that question, she would have been astonished, but not so with Emily. "Yes," she said slowly, not quite looking up. "He is . . . and tender."

"I would expect that he's very experienced."

"He's very loving."

"Loving? That's good. He's been with a great many women, and I'm just trying to figure out the allure. It's the novelist in me, you understand. I can't help it. It's just that you're rather different from the sort of women I associate with him; they're a tougher breed, altogether. You're not tough. And I worry about you sometimes. He is—very. You know that, don't you?"

"I'm sure, in business, he . . ."

"I'm not talking about business. I'm talking about—well, let's get off the subject." Emily reached for a cigarette. "How is your painting? You shouldn't let it drop, you know. Especially now."

"Why, now?"

"It gives you an edge, don't you see? You'll be sorry if you cast it aside."

Allegra said nothing, her eyes thoughtful, as she lit another cigarette. Still silent, she looked around the room, with its dusty bookshelves packed with volumes of all vintage, size, and shape. Some tumbled down; others leaned precariously against their frailer neighbors.

"You've got so many books," said Allegra at last, her eyes still scanning the helter-skelter array of titles.

"Books," said Emily slowly, "are really the best companions. On trips, especially. Then it really doesn't matter where you are."

"If that's the case, why travel at all?"

"That's a point. I've been to so few places that have lived up to my fantasies that I've wondered about that myself. Once I was booked on a trip to Singapore. Oh, the visions I had of Singapore! The mystique! The hotels. The dark, handsome strangers . . . When I got there, it was the most incredible disappointment! The only thing I remember was being in the bazaar and watching people chop up bats. They eat them, you know. All those little bats in cages, waiting to be sliced up. I stood, fascinated, and even took some photographs." She paused. "Sometimes I'd really rather preserve the place in my mind—as it exists there, all golden and whole—rather than disrupt it with reality. Do you know what I mean?"

"Yes, yes I do . . . Sometimes I'm not really sure I'm even seeing what exists, but instead, what I thought would, or what I would prefer to see."

"Ah, the perils of a romantic," said Emily, sipping her tea, and leaning back.

"Do you think that's it?"

"Yes. It takes a while to wean yourself from it, but eventually you do. I don't think that men, in general, have the same problem. It's peculiar to women, I think; not exclusively so, but certainly more intrinsic. It takes years to cut the cord."

"How many?"

"How would I know? I'm not even sure I've done it myself. Sometimes I think I have, but then some little romantic stirring will surface and *voilà*—back to square one."

"Maybe that isn't so bad," said Allegra, smiling.

"It's not that it's bad, it's just that it can be blinding." Emily felt the teapot, which had grown cold. "Some more tea?"

"I'll do it," said Allegra.

"No, let me. I'm OK, really."

As she went into the kitchen, Allegra stood up and wandered to Emily's desk. There was a series of leather folders, with titles inscribed in gold. "On the handkerchief motif in *Othello*," read one. "On food imagery in *Antony and Cleopatra*," "On Canto V of *The Inferno*."

"What are these?" she asked, as Emily returned from the kitchen.

"Oh, nothing much—just some old essays from Oxford." She sat down on the sofa, bending over to pour the tea. "I got them out the other day, it's so strange to reread them! Quite another period of my life. It was just at that time when I fell in love, desperately, with an older man—quite a well-known publisher in England. I'd shown him these essays, and later, we began to see one another. I was totally besotted, so in love that I could hardly see straight!" Her eyes looked almost wistful.

"And then what happened?"

"Oh, you know, after a while I noticed that he seemed rather distant; he always had excuses. I'd moved to London by then, and was just starting out. Anyway, I returned to my flat one day and found a letter from him. Ending it. He'd gotten engaged—to a very famous writer, quite a beauty, too—and of course, how could I have competed with that?" She stopped abruptly, sensing that Allegra was trying to decipher the effect the incident had had on her life. Then, changing the subject, Emily began to talk about her job at Vogue, and the reaction to her article on Ardeshir Zahedi, which had recently appeared.

"I loved it," Allegra said. "I kept laughing when I sensed your *eye*, and that edge between the lines. You got all the details."

Emily looked pleased. "Well, *you* got the tone; so many people didn't. Funnily enough, some thought it an encomium, some thought it quite acerbic. But each preson seemed to come away with a different picture of what Zahedi is, and what he's after. So you see"—here, a gesture of her hand—"I achieved my goal, to make it true to life."

"Everyone's been talking about the story. Even Véronique."

"She's been lying low lately."

"Why do you say that?"

"I don't know," Emily said. "It's just that the Bonbon is usually a bit more in evidence. The dinners, and all of that."

"I've hardly seen her, that's true . . ."

"And Alex? Has he seen her?"

"I don't know. I don't ask him. I doubt it; he would have mentioned it."

"Do you really think so?"

"Yes." And then, disquieted by Emily's persistent tone, she asked, "Why wouldn't he?" and lit a cigarette.

"I'm glad you think that of him," said Emily, her eyes not moving from Allegra's, as she watched the smoke vanish in the air. "But I wouldn't leave too much to chance, you know. He is rather difficult, Alex. Charming, but impenetrable. You should know that by now."

"But you hardly know him."

"But I *do* know him."

For a moment the two women sat in silence, smoking, the remnants of lunch on the table before them.

Emily stood up, uncertainly. "Thanks so much, Allegra. Thanks. It's something—something I won't ever forget."

"It's nothing, nothing at all," Allegra said. "Don't think about it, just rest."

She gathered her things and then, glancing at the tiger lilies she had placed in a vase, said, "Funny. I brought some once to Alex when he was sick. It seems such a long time ago!"

Emily, who had been watching her, said, in a voice suddenly much stronger, "Allegra, remember what I told you. Don't give up your painting. You'll be sorry if you cast it aside. Is it that Alex discourages you?"

"No, not at all, at least I don't think so." Allegra's eyes moved slowly from the floor and then to Emily's. "But I need a certain peace of mind, you know, and at the moment . . ." She stood face to face with Emily now. "You see, I feel that the self that paints and the self that exists with Alex are two different selves." And then, in a tremulous voice, "Do you know what I mean?"

Emily nodded, slowly, her eyes still fixed on the small head, with its thick hair and thoughtful face.

"Do they ever come together, *ever?*" said Allegra; and then, looking up, "I think you do understand." She took her handbag, went to the door, turned the knob, and looked back. "Call me if you need anything."

29

The following week, Véronique—sitting on an antique chair with arms carved like swans—picked up the telephone and dialed a number. "Mr. Para, please," she said, and then, after a moment, "Alex, it's me." There was a pause. "I spoke with Michel this morning. He's very impatient, you should know that. He could be very troublesome. He mentioned that he had met with you, in Bermuda, and that you seemed . . ." Another pause. "He had just dined with Nazif, in Paris. Michel keeps saying that he needs more money, and why can't you do something about it?"

She paused again. "What about the girl? I saw her yesterday at Sotheby's. She looked . . . not quite right." She listened, poising her foot on the silk ottoman. "Surely you don't have to wait until you're married—if you do marry." And then, "Come for a drink tomorrow." Her mouth tightened. "Why not? Wednesday, then, for dinner." Her green eyes had taken on a chilly look; her voice, however, retained its warmth. "I think you must decide, Alex. About her. About Michel. And Nazif."

Her hand grasping the chair, she said, "Good. Wednesday, then, at eight."

30

September passed, and then the bronze-leafed months of autumn, months that grew colder, and darker. Gradually one grew accustomed to the inky light of early morning, and to the frost that assailed the face.

Allegra's life was all confusion, as if she had drifted to some unknown sea, where the currents were overwhelming, and where all hopes of arriving at a safe, peaceful inlet had vanished. There were moments when—at dinner with him, or during their talks—she would feel such confusion and despair! His implacable self against hers—doubting, relenting, wondering all the time if he really knew who she was, or what she felt. Many of their friends saw the tension between them, although Alexander himself usually seemed quite oblivious to it. It was his work, or a business deal, that preoccupied him, and only that, it seemed, which had the capacity truly to trouble him.

At Sotheby's, her colleagues whispered about this new person who was pale, often tired, more than occasionally irritable. There would be moments when they would see her hand listlessly poised on the telephone, after one of his calls; or her eyes exhausted, even in the morning.

It was simply that Allegra did not know what a love affair should be; she had even begun to be confused as to what love itself was, although she thought she had once known. Its real essence seemed to have been crowded out by other aspects, like invading scents: sex, loneliness, the fear of losing him. "But of losing what?" she would ask herself; and to that question she hardly knew the answer. Slowly she succumbed to the numbing disillusionment of an ambivalent love affair, blinding her, as it were, to real pleasure and peace.

As for Alexander: his moods, like hers, had undergone some sort of transformation, although this was not due so much to Allegra, as to his work. She sensed, rightly, that this was so. One evening he would be brusque and distant; the next, loving and effusive. But beneath it all lay an undercurrent of cutting remarks which were unfailing in their capacity to hurt her.

Increasingly, he would go running alone. "It's too cold for you," he would tell her. On the weekends, even when it had grown bitter, he would bundle up and head down the beach, stretching, panting, coins rattling in his pockets. She seldom went with him anymore, nor did he encourage her. Instead, she would read, or try to read, but most likely she would flip through the pages of an art magazine, or glance at a cookbook.

During one of these mornings when he had gone running, she inadvertently knocked his date book to the floor, and picked it up, glancing at one of its pages. There were many days when appointments had been erased with a thick, chalk-white liquid. Visions immediately flashed through her mind—of his having an affair with another woman, of his being elsewhere when she called his office. She put the book down, and, a half-hour later, when he returned, he saw her placidly reading a magazine. But if he had known what coursed within her! Anger, self-loathing, hurt! And yet she said nothing. It was she who had trespassed, after all.

She had begun to turn on her physical self, castigating it for what she thought to be its flaws—her height, the scar, even her freckles. Previously, her competitiveness had been only with herself; now, destructively, it turned toward other women. Almost invariably, even those who were, by any measure, her inferiors she thought prettier, more intelligent, more accomplished than she; and certainly, in bed, were they not more expert, more voluptuous? The consciousness of what she conceived as her own failings became a relentless burden that colored their relationship.

And yet she was unable to express this; just as, at a dinner or cocktail party, she would be unable to rally against the occasional arrow-sharp comment. There had been that evening with Harry Chaice, at a bistro, the three of them together. Harry had talked about Italy and his trip to Florence; Alexander had hardly listened, and what he had said was curt, and to Allegra, embarrassing.

Harry: "I saw all your favorite Botticellis, Allegra—they reminded me of you."

Allegra, smiling: "Me, a Botticelli?"

Alexander, abruptly: "She's too tall to be a Botticelli."

All night long his words had cut through her. The next morning, Harry had called her at the office. "You tell me that he loves you. If he did, how could he possibly talk to you that way?" Her voice, stammering, as she attempted to find some explanation.

Her work at Sotheby's had slipped so much that it was now taken for granted that she was not given the choice clients or trips. There were days when she was so absentminded, and her eyes so tense, that her colleagues avoided her.

Friends came to visit. Michel Théron arrived from Paris in late November. They took him to lunch one rainy Sunday at a restaurant in the country, a few hours' drive from New York. The cold had deadened the woods; rain had drenched the leaves. Allegra asked Alexander why it was necessary to go so far away for lunch, on such a dreary day. "Michel prefers the country," he told her. "Crowded restaurants get on his nerves, this will be a good change."

Toward Alexander, Allegra grew increasingly rebellious: smoking constantly, drinking more than she had ever done before. Now, when he criticized one of her dresses, she might react in an absurdly violent way. One night she greeted him wearing an ivory silk dress with billowing sleeves. "What's that?" he said. "You look like Snow White." She slapped him hard across the face, flew into her bedroom, bolted the door, and wept, refusing for a while to go out. Eventually, she gave in.

Other weeks passed. He grew increasingly careless toward her, and subtly mocking. She began to draw away, plunging into her work; he telephoned more frequently. In bed, she was uncustomarily cool; he redoubled his caresses. But when, one night, the subject of the Laurana bust came up among friends, he humiliated her in a way she thought impossible ever to forget—as if, with an ax, he had dismembered her.

That night she told him that it was over between them; ended; and that she did not want to see him again, that they would be better off as friends, that they were not good for one another; and that he needed someone tougher, more resilient, less fragile than she; and that she hated him at times, that she resented the comparisons he made of her with others, and that she wanted him to leave immediately, and never speak with her again.

When he left, she crumpled to the floor, a heap of tired aching limbs, devastated emotions, emptiness, endless tears.

She never slept.

The next morning, a letter for her had been left with the doorman. It was written on long yellow sheets lined in blue, in a strong, jagged hand:

"December 1.
"Dearest Allegra, ·
"You must know how much I love you, and that I cannot live without you. I beg you to reconsider this drastic step, before you shatter what I treasure most: our life together, and my love for you.

"Please understand, I do not take your accusations lightly, nor do I minimize the extent of your 'wounded' feelings. I am not perfect! I consider our relationship something of a partnership in progress. Within it, I concede that I have made mistakes, and ask your forgiveness. I will try to be more sensitive to your feelings, just as I implore you to have compassion for the pressures which I must deal with.

"As you may have surmised, I have been through quite a lot in my life. Some of it you know, some you probably have no conception of, and some of it I choose to forget myself. In any event, like most people, I have developed certain mechanisms which allow me to cope with difficult situations. You should not misinterpret those for lack of caring, or involvement, or sensitivity, just as I will try not to interpret your actions last night as demonstrating a lack of love.

"We all have fantasies of those we are in love with. It pains me to think I have disappointed you, that I may not always have been the man you wanted me to be. Please give me another chance, my darling! Our time together has been—for me at least—such a dream. Do not turn it into a nightmare!

"I love you, I need you, I cannot live without you,

Alexander."

He appeared on her doorstep that night, shaking, and kissing her so hard he drew blood from her mouth, nearly choking her as he grasped her waist, telling her how much he loved her, that he could not imagine life without her, and that she must forgive him; and that he would take her someplace far, far away for Christmas.

Never had he seemed so passionate, so full of love. She wanted to drink him in—every kiss, every tender word, every muscle of the arms that held her, and the mouth that swept her neck, her face, her cheeks, her breasts.

They made love, and in that night it seemed that their love-making had assumed another, deeper meaning: healing the wounds, merging them, as if every motion of her mouth around him, and every thrust of him inside her, were an affirmation of them together, and of their union and love.

Later, her head on his chest, he asked whether she would like to go skiing for Christmas: Switzerland, first, and then Italy. And it was the thought of Europe, and traveling with him once more, that came as the final balm. They would begin again.

Two weeks later, they left for Geneva.

31

Cosseted, luxurious, insulated from the cares of the world, Saint Moritz lay nestled in the mountains—a Fabergé egg glistening with snow. Late in the afternoon, a week before Christmas, the streets bustled with Europeans shopping: Italian magnates with farouche hats and great furry boots; subfusc Arabs escorting beautiful, bored-looking young women; nannies, clutching the small hands of demanding charges. At Hanselman's, cups of steaming hot chocolate were being carried on trays to a laughing, gossiping clientele; in other shops, necklaces, watches and diamonds lay on red velvet trays, as clients, rifling through, selected gems.

Not far away, the Palace Hotel stood like a fin de siècle sentinel: proud, yet yellowing at the edges—*usé,* as the French say. It was difficult to know whether this added to or subtracted from its charm: certainly it did not affect the character of its hotel life, with its multilingual concierges, and the vast upholstered chairs of its immense salon. There, in the late afternoon, tea would be served to those who had descended from the slopes, and to the many others who had simply spent the day ambling and resting. Later, plump Middle-Eastern women would play cards, their black eyes scrutinizing the felt tables; others, strolling arm in arm with their children, looked at displays of shops. In another corner, a Frenchman—his small puffy eyes reflecting his appetite, his hand on the lace covering of the chair's arm—hesitated between a chocolate éclair and a flaky apple strudel.

The most worldly resorts have the most seductive routines; certainly this was true of Saint Moritz. The rhythm began in the early morning, in the quiet dining room of the Palace which looked out to the mountains—chiseled and bluish in the light—and to the terrace, immersed in soft mounds of pink-tinged snow. As guests in sweaters and boots prepared to go skiing, hardly a sound could be heard, and even then, only the most civilized sort: a knife scraping toast, or the brittle voice of an Englishman, inquiring after his favorite marmalade.

Later, as skiers descended the slopes, all sense of embonpoint would be surrendered to the frosty air, and to the wind that exhilarated the senses. The face, assaulted by the elements; snow screeching beneath speeding skis.

By late afternoon, the skiers returned to the warmth and comfort of the town, slowly descending the mountain and watching as the streets and buildings came into view, like an exquisite miniature—the fanciful railroad station, the Palace Hotel, the winding streets. Soon the cold, the ice, and the falls that rattled the limbs would be left behind for the cavernous warmth of the grand hotels.

It had been four days since Allegra and Alexander had arrived in Saint Moritz, but so enveloping was the atmosphere that it seemed they had been there infinitely longer. Each day they would follow the same schedule: breakfast at eight o'clock, and then to the slopes, walking up the narrow streets, surrounded by a cacophany of foreign voices. And then, after a morning of hard skiing, a hearty lunch with wine and delicious food. About four o'clock or so, they would begin to ski down, stopping to watch a horse-drawn carriage, perhaps. Deepening shadows, the gentle sound of bells, the proud waving flags in the distance. After a long walk through the streets, with their glistening shop windows, they would return to the hotel sore, exhausted, ravenous, happy.

Allegra had not skied in Europe since her family's death. At first— still haunted by that terrible spring in Zermatt—she had been reluctant to come. But so sensitive had Alexander been to her fears, and so protective, that she had, at last, acquiesed. "It will be different this time," he had said, "I'll be with you—you won't think about the other."

Even so, it was still Zermatt—not Saint Moritz—she saw, after arriving. The narrow cobblestone streets, the bustling skiers, the lights against the mountains at night, the sound of German, French, and Italian on the tram. It seemed she could not escape the memory of that morning: her mother's ruby earrings embedded in the snow, her dead brother's twisted arms.

She would not ski the first day, nor the second, much as Alexander coaxed her. "You must put the past behind you," he would say, holding both her hands, and kissing her. "Let it go! They would *want* you to ski again." At the beginning, she would walk with him to the tram, carrying his poles and kissing him goodbye, as she promised to meet him for lunch. Only on the third day did she agree to take one run. "But just one," she told him, "to see how it feels." They took a T-bar to the slope. The cold was brutal that morning, the fog so thick it obscured the mountain peaks. Her body felt frozen; silently she began to cry, tears making her goggles misty.

She thought, she could not stop thinking, of that spring: the trees brazenly green, the sparkling light powder whooshing against one's knees. But now it was winter, as cold as it had been unnaturally warm that fatal March, the light invested with a chilly blue-gray, skis making a scraping sound against the icy, ungiving surface of the snow.

Still, after the tentative first moments, it felt so good to ski again, to feel the freedom and the peace of wind and movement. The rhythm came back quickly. Allegra had not forgotten the dancelike *Wedel* turns, or how and when to plant each pole. Soon her body and skis moved as one; the pleasure was addictive. She took one run, and then—surprising herself—another, until, at last, she felt the letting go.

From that moment on, it seemed she could not ski enough.

During those days, all the hurt of the past few months—the emotional buffeting, the destructive comments, the ups and downs—all of this had suddenly melted in the light of his new consideration, and the obfuscatory power of European travel. Was she dressed warmly enough, he would ask her in the morning, as he helped to button her parka; did the rented skis work properly? Was she too tired to make another run? Later, he would draw her bath, and soap her back, planting a sudsy kiss on her cheek. (Once, while he did, she asked him half in jest, "Alex, would you have taught me to ski, if I hadn't known how? Been patient, and taken me to the bunny slope?" "No," he scoffed, his eyes mischievous. "Why not?" she asked. "I've already done that with sex," he said.) One afternoon, he arranged for her to have a massage (eyes half-closing in the darkness; the sensuality of a stranger caressing warm muscles). He bought her a watch and had it inscribed ("To my darling Allegra, December 1978"), and took her dancing at the Kings Club. He serenaded her with stories about England and South America, and his travels; and told her of his last, clandestine visit to Argentina, where he had gone to rescue hidden possessions from his family's house, which had been seized by that government. ("Wasn't that a great risk?" she asked. "Of course," he replied, his eyes strangely exhilarated.) But most of all he listened with an attentiveness that reminded her of their first meeting, so that she would talk in a new relaxed way about Europe, about painting, about her feelings, about their life together.

And yet he had her ski hard! So hard that her ankles would be raw and red at the day's end, for they would ski from early morning until the time the lifts closed, racing down one trail, only to mount another; breathing deeply on the lifts as they prepared to descend again, Allegra following the coiled patterns of his tracks, for she had learned his rhythm, and how to follow him expertly. And indeed, he led her well. She would sometimes try to guess which route he would take through the moguls; when he would turn, and when he would shoot down the fall line. He almost always surprised her.

Late one afternoon, he told her that he was going out to buy the *Herald Tribune*. He returned several hours later.

She looked up as the door opened and saw his tense eyes, but then, meeting hers, the look vanished. He put down his coat and glanced out the window, his hands clutching the sill, his forehead furrowed, as she sat drying her just-washed hair. Then he settled in a chair, his feet on the ottoman before her, and told her—opening the *Tribune* as he did so—that he had happened to run into an old friend, someone he had known in London. They had stopped to have a drink. His voice was casual, as he said, "I hope you don't mind," his eyes scanning the stock market pages.

"Not really," she said, inwardly annoyed that he had not called. She put aside the towel and looked at him. "Why didn't you invite him to dinner with us, here, at the hotel, or somewhere else?"

"He couldn't," he said, turning a page. "He's leaving tomorrow and he'd already made plans." Alexander stood up and walked to the window, where darkness had fallen. The lights were lit; the streets were suddenly quiet.

He looked at her again—intently, this time, as if to study her—and then lingering as he kissed her. Her robe fell open, and his eyes went to the line of the scar. She quickly gathered up the robe around her.

Suddenly he said, "I've got to make a phone call," and put the newspaper on the bed table. "I'll do it downstairs, so I won't bother you."

"You won't bother me, make it here."

"No, it's faster if I do it downstairs."

He left, only to return an hour later.

During the days that followed, Alexander seemed to grow increasingly preoccupied and impatient—looking repeatedly at his watch while they rode the lifts, suddenly bored with the skiing that had so absorbed him at first ("After five days it palls"). One afternoon, the twenty-first of December, after taking their last run, he put his arm around her shoulder and said, "Let's go. We've done it here."

"Why?" she asked, her eyes turning to his. "We've only arrived— our skiing has just warmed up." Still, he tried to convince her. "The snow isn't good enough," he said, as they continued to walk through the town. "Look at the ice we hit today. The rocks. We'll go to Venice. You'd like that, wouldn't you? And then someplace else for skiing. Austria. Cortina." She tried to be responsive to his wanderlust, but her reaction was merely halfhearted as he spoke of other places.

They walked slowly back to the Palace, her eyes lingering on the shops and streets she knew she would leave tomorrow. All through the air was the scent of pine, mingled with the whiff of sweets from a *pâtisserie*.

They packed that night, after a last dinner in the hotel's enormous dining room—chandeliers, gilt chairs, and hearty soups.

The next morning, in a small red car he had rented, they left for Venice.

The drive to Venice was cold and foggy, the ice-slicked roads treacherous. Few cars could be seen on the autoroute from Switzerland through the San Bernard pass. When they stopped at a roadside restaurant for lunch, the place was empty, a diminutive Christmas tree on the bar beside an array of forlorn cheeses and a small jukebox. They ate quickly and then continued on to Milan, and to Verona, the fog thickening, and darkening, and enshrouding even the most familiar sights in a concealing mist. The lights pierced the road ahead. Alexander sat at the wheel, his eyes fixed ahead, saying nothing, Allegra mute.

At last, the signs for Mestre appeared, and then the first glimpse of the long bridge, with its steel cables and gaudy signs for Campari, that would take them to the Piazzale Roma.

They left the car in a subterranean parking lot. Inside, it was so cold that Allegra's hands felt frostbitten; she kept rubbing them together. A surly porter, a cigarette dangling from his mouth, took their bags. Alexander, fastening his coat more tightly around his neck, called a taxi. At last—slowly in the darkness—the boat arrived, its lights reflecting in the water.

Such a villagelike quiet had come over Venice! For a moment, Allegra hardly recognized the city. The ghostly back canals; the facades of palazzi that seemed to have wrested themselves from dreams. The whooshing of the water; the occasional startling cry or raucous laugh that one heard echoing from an alley or curtained bar.

It was past ten o'clock when they arrived at the Gritti Palace Hotel. Inside, the *faux marbre* and burnished mirrors were intensified by the light and the quiet. The concierge, with his best professional smile, handed them the key to their room—a vast place with baroque furniture, a bed encased in golden yellow silk, and a long sofa with scroll-shaped arms and deep-green fringed pillows.

Not much later, they walked to Harry's Bar for dinner, her head tilted against his shoulder, her hand in his pocket.

Venice had never seemed so silent. All the eastern sounds, the clipped gaits, the lapping of the gondoliers' oars—all had been muffled to a quiet almost funereal in its intensity. No café tables stood on the Piazza San Marco; no songs serenaded tourists. Life in the Venice she knew seemed to have been suspended. Inside Harry's Bar, there was little of the usual high season boisterousness. The rhythm had subsided to a slower pace, and the waiters were unusually solicitous.

When Alexander asked for a table upstairs, the headwaiter responded with a courteous smile, and led them to the second-floor dining room, which was nearly empty. A white-haired man with a professorial air looked up as they entered, nodding politely, then turning to his wife, who murmured something in a Boston accent.

Alexander ordered champagne and immediately began to peruse the menu, as did Allegra, for they were hungry from the long drive through the mountains. In a moment, the champagne was brought and opened with a flourish; and then, turning to Allegra as the foam settled in the glasses, Alexander asked her to marry him.

She was so startled that she could not speak; she could only murmur, and smile, and look from his searching dark eyes and pressing hands to the curved, filled glass.

"Well?" he said, the anticipation in his voice edged with disappointment, for she had not responded immediately and delightedly, as she sensed he had expected. Her eyes still looked more startled than ecstatic.

"I . . ." And here, even surprising herself, she hesitated. "Alex, I'm so happy, I really am, but I've got to think. Let me think, until tomorrow, or the next day." She was so afraid she had hurt him, and yet it was the only answer she could give.

"This is not quite what I expected," he said with a wry look, as he took up the menu again.

"Neither did I," she said, smiling, and taking his other hand in hers.

He looked at her again with a calm, knowing expression; and then, in a shy, almost boyish voice she had seldom heard him use before, said, "Please, Allegra, you know I've never done this before."

She looked away, ashamed she had not said yes immediately.

The meal was completed in a strange silence, each of them speaking without really being aware of what the other had said. There was no other mention of marriage. Instead, they spoke of Venice—its history, art, and architecture. What they should plan to see the next day, where they should walk.

He asked her why the city had been built on stiltlike structures, what had been the reason for such a venture. She had known the explanation once, but could not remember now. She thought, aloud, of different possibilities, none of which were right. He knew it, and looked at her askance.

"I just can't remember," she finally said, her face flushing. "I'll have to look it up." She felt oddly intimidated not to know—she, who had studied Venetian history! "That kills you," he said, cutting his veal. "Intellectually, I mean." She bit her lip.

By the dinner's end, she had hardly touched her food, merely watching and smoking as he made his way through several courses and leisurely finished his dessert.

At last, sipping his espresso, Alexander took a small box wrapped in silver paper from his pocket. Inside, lying on red velvet, was a gold chain with an amulet—a small coral heart, crisscrossed with twisted ropes of gold and pavé diamonds. He could already tell from her eyes that she loved it; murmuring her thanks, Allegra kept turning it one way, and then another, as she clutched it in her hand. Kissing him, she asked him to fasten the chain around her neck, shivering for a moment, as he did, for the charm was cold.

It was utterly silent at the Gritti when they returned at midnight. All one could hear was the lapping of the water, and the distant strains of music from a phonograph.

They made love, their bodies coming together, their mouths churning with kisses; and afterward, she fell into a dream-filled sleep. She dreamt of boats and the sea; of being with Alexander in a placid channel, and then waking to find herself in a tempestuous ocean, waves leaping up and spilling into the rocking boat. Before dawn, she lay awake, her eyes fixed to the ornate ceiling, as she reached for Alexander's arms. He held her closely, telling her to return to sleep. But despite the warmth of his mouth and the strength of his arms around her, she could not. When he awoke later, he found her standing by the window, her robe tied carelessly at her waist. She came back to bed, where again he held her.

Beyond the window, she had seen Venice in all its gray, damp, winter aspect: the water deprived of blue; the facades of the palazzi obscured by mist, their reflections tumbling into the water, their doorways stamped with faded escutcheons of extinct owners. All the shimmer, color, and gold-glinted *bizarreries* of the heady summer city now turned grave and shabby, like a provincial museum closed for alterations.

Later that day, Allegra telephoned her great-aunt, Giovanna Contarin, but was told that the Contessa was in Rome, and would return at the end of January. She put down the telephone, disappointed and vaguely depressed—what a comfort it would have been to have seen her and asked her advice! She thought of her great-aunt's elegant figure, her intelligent eyes and wisdom, and her letters, stamped with her crest, crossing the Atlantic with their well-turned sentences and sage thoughts.

That afternoon, Alegra walked with Alexander to the church which her great-aunt Giovanna Contarin had helped restore, thinking that within it she might find an answer, that she might know whether to marry him. The trees before it were bare now, the surrounding alleys quiet; the immense black-green door was shut. Allegra stood before it trying to see if it would open. Surely, there must be some mistake, she kept thinking, as she continued to call out, and knock—but no, it was locked.

Puzzled and saddened not to have entered the familiar place—and for Alexander to have seen it—she made her way back with him to the Piazza San Marco, and then to Florian's for lunch.

The next afternoon, while Alexander remained at the hotel to make telephone calls, Allegra decided to take a walk.

She went first through the Accademia, her shoes echoing through the halls as she gazed at Venetian Madonnas, with arched brows and waxen festoons of fruit; and then past velvet-dark portraits of merchants, popes, doges.

At last she came to her favorite painting—*La Tempestà*, by Giorgione. She stood before it a long time, staring at its strange sky severed by the white coil of light, and at the surprised, pleading face of the woman—half-clothed, unsuspecting . . . "Of what?" Allegra suddenly wondered, as she looked closely at the figure, and then at the distant Arcadian landscape with its broken columns and frail bridge, encased in a dewy silence. From there she went to the other rooms, but once more, and then again, she returned to the Giorgione, gazing at its cool, unsettling atmosphere of blue and green, of storm and calm.

It was only two o'clock, but it had grown cold, the sky gray and melancholy. Outside the entrance of the Accademia, the newspaper kiosk was being closed up by an old woman in a tattered coat. Allegra stopped, her eyes passing over the magazines. From there, she walked slowly across the bridge, gazing at the water, and then making her way to the Campo Santo Stefano—no cafés there, now—and through the mazelike streets that led to the Piazza San Marco.

And as she walked, she wondered whether Alexander truly loved her, and whether she should marry him, and whether he was the man she thought she saw. She was not sure; nor was it clear to her whether the turbulence of the past year was simply aggravated by her own craving for love and affection, and whether what she imagined should be was overly colored by her notions of romance.

She herself knew—not always consciously, but still she knew—that much of her life, expectations, and longings had been shaped by art, books, and her own imaginings. Suddenly she thought of Emily—she had now reached the baroque façade of San Moisè—and wondered how it was that Emily, too, had fed so much on literature, and yet had emerged with a seemingly dispassionate point of view, so very different from her own.

She came to a glass shop and stopped before its window, thinking how strange it was that she was not ecstatic when he had asked her to marry him, and yet that was what she had wanted, after all! But instead, it had settled on her like a coating of fine dust; she felt she had come to the end of a corridor, and once arriving, did not feel joy so much as a searching contemplativeness. Whether she loved him, and whether it was a love of the right sort . . . She thought it was. But still she walked, her steps making hard, cracked noises, like the sound of a blind man's cane striking stone. She came to the long, narrow street at the back of the square, stopping before an antique jewelry shop with a window of dazzling rings and blackamoor brooches.

Through the columns, she could see the Piazza San Marco, like a stage set that had suddenly and inexplicably been abandoned. It had all the untidy desolation of a carnival that had fallen on bad times. For a moment she stood looking at the crazy unity of arches, paint, and gilt mosaics that made up the unlikely cathedral. And from there—still thinking of Alexander, and his proposal, and mingling memories of when she had been sad with him, and when she had been happy—she entered Florian's, sat down, and ordered tea, pulling off her gloves and shaking out her cold hair from her hat.

Opposite, in the crimson and gold room, there was a young man dressed in mauve, who looked like one's vision of a poet. His hair was pale and fine, and his eyes looked pallid with thought. As Allegra's tea was brought, three American hitchhikers entered, and asked for coffee and hot milk. Allegra watched them and, for a moment, was tempted to strike up a conversation. For Venice, in winter, is the smallest of towns, and no one who is there, then, is really a stranger to another.

But instead she said nothing, for at the moment it seemed the greatest luxury to merely wander and think. Her tea having been finished, she paid the bill and left, buttoning her coat as she walked toward the massive doors of the cathedral of San Marco. Inside, there was almost no one. A priest, walking on a distant part of the altar, and a group of pilgrims in black—from the South of Italy, Allegra guessed—making their way to the front. The ancient floors and brooding mosaic faces gave one the comforting feeling that nothing could ever be truly wrong—not here, inside this place, with its smell of incense and its aura of survival. She went to see the ancient relics encased in their rock-crystal boxes, and then the riot of gems studding the Pala d'Oro. Lighting a few candles, she knelt, bending her head in prayer, and still thinking of Alexander. But always, beneath her imaginings that she had a choice was the deeper suspicion that there was none, and that whatever would be was inexorable.

She stood up, watching the pilgrims, their faces ruddy with poverty and faith, as they chanted an Ave Maria. It touched her so, she began to cry.

It had grown colder, damper, and darker by the time she left—still, it was not late. The water looked dim and choppy. By the Grand Canal, the lion of San Marco atop the obelisk and the gold globe of the Dogana, beyond, resembled surreal mementoes of a lost pageant. She looked once more toward Florian's, and saw the young man in mauve exit, his white hands clutching some notebooks.

It occurred to her then—for it was only three-thirty—that she would visit the Doges' Palace. It stood opposite, daunting and inviting.

She entered, moving slowly from the Senate chambers to the reception rooms, and to others which held maps and armors; and then to immense spaces hung with huge, vainglorious paintings. Finally, she came to the cramped rooms of the Bridge of Sighs, the bridge that led to the ancient prisons. Its walls engraved with ragged, anonymous dates and names, its thick windows of a greenish glass which made the air seem verminous. She stood for a moment looking below at the water, and at the sharp, pitching waves that rose from one side of the canal to the other; watching as the froth grew higher, tumbling from pointed white peaks to the sea. Suddenly she thought she saw a pink object tossed up; it looked like a hand! She gasped, as if she had seen someone drowning . . . Again she saw the water, robbed of its summer blue, now glassy and menacing . . . And in that second, myriad thoughts flickered through her mind: the waves that day at Sagaponack; the dream of the cave; Alex, running . . . She kept searching the water, trying to recover sight of what she had thought she had seen. And slowly, what she had thought a hand now revealed itself to be the arm of a doll, which someone had tossed into the water . . . Shuddering, she turned and made her way back room by room, finally descending the vast staircase.

She returned to the Gritti and told him yes.

PART THREE

Part Three

32

Three bronze griffins guarded the lacy, wrought-iron gates that led to the salon of Pierre Montis. Once inside, one's eyes were drawn to a tall rock-crystal clock, each side a Doric column carved in porphyry. Slowly, it ticked; there were no other sounds, nor did anything seem capable of disturbing the room's Delphic quiet.

Within the main reception room, with its vaulted ceiling, all was gray, ivory, and crystal. Glittering sconces scattered their reflections; eighteenth-century landscapes, with hazy bluish colors and gamboling figures, lined the pale *faux marbre* walls. Golden silk curtains—tumbling to the floor beneath two massive windows—permitted light to enter gently.

Even the guard seemed only remotely human, motionless in his gray uniform, and bowing graciously to Allegra as she entered; then leading her, with a courtly step, to the elevator. Each of her steps made a resonant echo on the black and white marble floor, her eyes drawn, as she walked, to the balustrade above, with its railing of black arrows tipped in gold.

For Pierre Montis was no ordinary couturier, and those who frequented his salon did not expect to find, within it, the hurly-burly of a pedestrian shop. Nor were his designs in the least conventional; indeed, they were rarely seen on the street, but were reserved, rather, for state occasions, formal dinners, balls, and, occasionally, weddings.

Allegra had known him for years, for her mother had been a client. Now she had come to see the sketch of the wedding dress she had asked him to prepare. "I was thinking of something very classical," she had said, on the telephone. "Ah yes," said the voice on the other end. "I know your taste. Leave it to me."

She had come on a blustery March afternoon, the wind nearly blowing her through the gates. Now she stood in the tiny elevator, lined in amber silk, which led upstairs to Montis's domain.

When the door opened, she was met by the overwhelming scent of narcissus and then by a woman in black, who greeted her with the kind, efficient manner of a weathered professional. She was clearly from the school of *vendeuses* one sees in Paris—soberly dressed, faultlessly groomed, selflessly resigned to a life of dressing others. She showed Allegra through.

They passed from one wide corridor, lined with Dutch still lifes, to another, with shelf after shelf of dimly lit Roman glass. Pale green, blue, glimmering with the nacreous surfaces of centuries. Allegra continued to walk, smoothing her skirt, her eyes still drawn to the glass shapes.

At last, they came to a set of high double doors with two gold knobs shaped like the heads of panthers. The woman, who was called Mrs. Collins, knocked. A voice told her to enter.

The door clicked open.

The eye of a television camera, fixed atop the ivory molding, scanned the room, moving to a painting of a *fête champêtre*, first, and then to a still life by Fantin-Latour, and then to the windows that overlooked Central Park; and finally to Montis himself—a tiny man with a startlingly large head, who sat behind an immense Louis Seize desk. His eyes were a translucent blue, his hands fine-veined, white, and strangely young-looking. He extended one, as he greeted Allegra.

She shook his hand, thinking of the times she had accompanied her mother here; then she sat down.

"It has been many years," he said.

"Yes, many. The last time I was here with my mother."

"I have missed your mother's visits. So has everyone here; we were all very fond of her."

"Yes," she said, looking down at her lap, and turning her face to the side, nodding slightly. "Who would ever have guessed? We'd only come here a month before. The deep-green dress, do you remember?"

"Yes. I remember it well. She usually wore black and white, but I had tried, that time, to convince her to wear another color. She was so particular about clothes." He paused, his eyes absorbed in recollection. "One day she brought me a copy of a portrait by Veronese. 'This is the color I want,' she told me, pointing to the fabric in it. And it was perfect for her—dark and rich. We brought out a bolt of silk—exactly that color—and she was delighted. It looked so well with her pearls."

"The pearls, of course," said Allegra, remembering the long necklaces, a present from her father. "I can't remember a day when she didn't wear them, even in the summer, when it was very hot. An enormous hat, and the pearls running down her back."

"She was very beautiful, your mother. One would have been tempted to call her ethereal. I got the impression . . ." But here he looked up, not completing his thought. "Those beautiful hands; it is always her hands and her eyes I remember."

There was a moment of silence, then he asked whether she would like a cup of tea. She nodded, and in a second it appeared, white and gold cups stamped with his cipher.

"So you are getting married?" he finally asked.

"Yes," she answered, with a slight breath.

"Would you like to see the sketches?"

She nodded.

He turned his back to her and—with a movement of his wrist—opened the vault behind him. From it, he took a large envelope in marbelized paper, fastened by a ribbon. Three thick sheets of paper were taken from it and placed on the table.

"Here. Come and look. I did three different sketches for you."

The drawings were beautifully detailed and in color. In the center was a design of a slim dress with billowing sleeves and a soft, columnar skirt. Montis had even gone so far as to draw in Allegra's face, and had draped the fabric of the skirt so that it looked windblown.

"So you remembered me well," she said, smiling, and yet puzzled that the likeness should be so accurate, for he had not seen her in years. She looked up, her eyes wide, her hand resting on the table.

"Of course, would you expect it otherwise?" he said, and then, "Which of these pleases you?"

She pointed to the sketch in the center.

"Ah," he said, content. "That is my favorite. Good. It would suit you." He stood back, scrutinizing her tall frame. "Go over there, by the mirrors."

She stood between the set of mirrors at the back of the room, while Montis watched, seeing her profile reflected, and the fine lines of her body, with its unexpectedly full breasts; all the angles repeated in a myriad of variations. "It would be perfect for you," he said again. Nodding, he stepped away and pressed the buzzer on his desk.

Mrs. Collins appeared.

"Bring me this one," he told her, and she went to fetch it.

It was the custom at Montis to prepare muslin versions of the sketches first, to aid the client in selection. These were made with almost the same attention to detail as the final design; it was only the fabric that differed.

Still he watched Allegra. "You have your mother's hands," he said, "and something of her eyes, but your father's height and chin. And something else of his that is hard to describe."

"You have a remarkable eye, as well as a memory," she said, smiling.

"It is not difficult. They were remarkable people."

He turned his back to her suddenly, looked out the window, and then, impatiently, asked where Mrs. Collins had gone. He rang again; the woman finally appeared; and then Allegra was led to a mirrored dressing room that was connected to Montis's office.

In a moment she stood before him, waiting, hesitantly, before his scrutiny.

"The skirt is slightly too full at the hips." Mrs. Collins made a note on a small pad. "The neck must be slightly lower. The waist is perfect. The sleeves are a bit too long, and the wrists need to be tightened. Otherwise it's quite, quite right. And the length, how does it feel? You brought your shoes, didn't you?"

"I didn't, actually," said Allegra. No one had mentioned shoes. "Does it matter that much?"

"Get her the shoes," he ordered, ignoring her question. Mrs. Collins returned with a pair of white silk pumps.

"How do they feel?" he asked.

She looked up, as she wriggled her foot inside the slipper. "They're exactly my size," she said, astonished.

"I thought so."

He had come out from behind the desk—a dignified figure with a fair, wrinkled face, in a dark gray suit. Now he circled Allegra, checking the motion of the skirt as she moved, and the line of the dress through the shoulders, continuing, as he did, to direct Mrs. Collins and her notetaking. A moment came when Allegra thought it would not be possible to dissect the dress any further.

"Enough," he finally said. Allegra, her neck stiff from standing, went to change. Her hair brushed and the shoes returned, she re-entered Montis's office a moment later.

"You are happy?" he asked, his eyes expressionless.

"Yes," she said, not knowing whether he referred to her, or to the dress.

"And the color," he said suddenly. "Which would you like?"

"Why, white," she said, her eyes puzzled.

He gave a small laugh. "But there are infinite shades of white, my dear; the question is *which* white?"

He rang for Mrs. Collins again, and told her to bring a set of swatches in silk mousseline—every shade of white she could find.

They were brought: silks that ranged from the palest ivory to others almost ecru. Allegra looked through them, all the while sensing that Montis knew exactly which she should choose.

"This is the one," he finally said, pointing to a piece. "The color of a baroque pearl, only the tiniest suggestion of pink. Yes, that would be perfect." It was decided.

"And now," he said, "you must let me see your hand." This did not take her by surprise, for it was well known that Montis was an expert palm-reader, that he could tell one's fortune within the lines, hills, and valleys of the hand. She extended hers eagerly—long narrow palms crossed by blue veins.

But it was her new ring which had caught his eye—a pear-shaped diamond mounted on a gold band. "It is the wrong cut for you," he told her, disapprovingly. "It should have been emerald or marquis-shaped."

"Should it have?" she asked, looking hard at her engagement ring. He nodded. "You ought to return it."

"Oh, but I can't!"

"No?" He shrugged. "Well, that is up to you."

"And the rest?" she said, eager to hear his augury.

He kept turning the palm over, and then back again, looking at its network of lines, and the nearly imperceptible blue threads of veins. At last, he looked up, his clear eyes suddenly opaque, enigmatic.

"You must not be frightened," he said in an even voice. "You must remember who you are, and what you represent."

A moment passed.

"Tell me more," she urged him.

He shook his head, his expression impassive.

The clock struck three.

"And the dress?" she asked, her voice almost inaudible.

"It will be ready in several weeks. Mrs. Collins will call you." He looked down at his desk, fingering its only object, a gold paperweight in the form of a falcon.

"I am only sorry that your mother did not live to see you in it," he said, after a moment's pause.

"Who would ever have known?" she said, softly.

"No one. That is the point." He stood up, and took her hands in his. His eyes had reassumed their clear blue. "Mrs. Collins will show you out."

Shaking his hand, she thanked him for his help, reiterating how happy she was with the wedding dress. But then, approaching the door, she suddenly turned around. "And the shoes?" she asked.

"They are yours. They are already wrapped."

"Thank you, that wasn't necessary."

"No, no it wasn't, but there, it is done."

She said good-bye and a moment later, passed through the reception room again, with its motionless guard and three griffins. Outside, the buildings cut into the sky, and the green of Central Park was a distant vision. She buttoned her coat, and began to walk up Fifth Avenue to the rectory of Saint Benedict, where she was to meet Alexander.

Véronique de Séguiers's maid was brushing the crumbs from the dining-room table. The damask cloth was strewn with the remnants of a luncheon for two; a few bites of dessert lay on one plate, and a fork and spoon sat haphazardly on another.

Véronique and Alexander were in the library—he by the window, looking out; she, on the couch, waiting to pour the coffee.

It had not been a pleasant month for Véronique. She had been troubled with searing migraine headaches, first, and then with a stomach virus. For the former she had taken painkillers and daily massages; for the latter, she had consumed vast amounts of Contréxéville mineral water. (It was her belief that this particular water, bottled in France, rid one's body of impurities and kept one thin. This was only one of her many maxims on beauty: another was that caviar, as a source of protein, maintained the hair's radiance; and that buttermilk, when liberally applied to the skin, preserved its whiteness and fineness.) It was only on this day, in fact, that she had begun to feel right, which was fortunate, as it coincided with Alexander's coming to lunch.

She had instructed her maid, Claire, to prepare her outfit in the morning, as was her custom. The purple suit, with its silk blouse, hung in the closet; below it, the high-heeled shoes, plumped with small pink silk cushions. Véronique herself would select the jewelry— the pearl and diamond earrings which Stern had given her, and which flattered her small, full mouth and slanting green eyes. It was nearly one o'clock when she had looked into the mirror to see the complete apparition, thinking to herself, as she did, that the facelift had been a great success, well worth the trouble and expense. It had freshened up her looks, as it were, and only in the inner recesses of her ears— hidden to everyone—could the vestige of the scars be seen.

But at this moment, her facelift forgotten, she turned her attention to Alexander.

"You are sure of this, then, Alex? It's a big step to take. And you—well, you have been *such* a bachelor." She smiled, looked up, and handed him a demitasse cup. "It's simply so difficult to imagine you married."

"Why?" His voice was genuinely questioning, for he himself had grown accustomed to the idea, and it was she who had first suggested it, after all.

"I simply can't imagine you as a husband." She had given a peculiar emphasis to the last word, letting it resonate with a vague distaste. "You're so restless, for one thing, and you don't like to feel constrained. That's so much part of marriage, you know—constraint."

"It's strange to hear that from you," he said. "From what I've observed, you have devoted all of last year to pursuing Ed Stern. And towards what end? Marriage, I assume."

She smiled, clucking her tongue, her voice brimming with a sly, corrective tone. "Ah well, that's another matter. That's mutual convenience, if you will. He has grown tired of his wife; I can be useful to him, and he to me. Both parties perfectly aware of what the other side can contribute. An alliance. You are talking about love; this is not the same." There was a moment's pause, as she bent over to pour herself some coffee. "And you did tell me that you loved her?" She took a sip.

"Yes."

"Of course," she answered, her expression indicating that she did not, in the least, believe it. "As I told you, I think it's a very good move. She completes you—takes the edge off your newness. That's good. The whole thing is divinely clever."

"It isn't meant to be clever."

"It was, when you first met her." He did not respond, which made her say, caustically, "Wasn't it? That's a change for you, Alex. There's always been a *raison d'être* to your affections; at least, that's the way it has seemed." Her voice, which had been bitter, now assumed a more pleasant tone. "But now you talk of love. It's charming, really. I wish you luck, you know that." Her tone did not betray her inner fury: that he should separate himself from her, with his noble motives!

The maid entered, carrying a silver vase with tall coral roses. Véronique glanced at them and then returned to Alexander. "Did I tell

you that David Riffner came to dinner? No?" Riffner was Alexander's
superior at the bank—a venerable member of Atlantic Trust who had
worked for the firm forty years. "Oh, I didn't tell you, then? Yes. I
had him here with Ardeshir last week. He's very intelligent, don't you
think? He's impressed with you—he told me you're one of the best
the bank has. We had a long talk. I told him I knew you very well."

"What did he say, exactly?" Alexander was always eager to know
what others thought of him.

"That you had good instincts—for money, for people. For power.
That he trusted you. That's a compliment, isn't it?" A pause. "He
told me he thought you were very well-rounded. That you seemed to
like to work hard and live well. That you were very ambitious." Her
lips parted as she went to sip the coffee. "He got along splendidly with
Ardeshir. They had met years ago in Zurich, apparently."

"And what did you say about my liking to live well?" Alexander
asked, with a sharp look.

"I can't remember." She glanced up. "I told him about the girl.
About Allegra. That she was rich, so you see . . . He knew her
name, of course. I think he had known her father."

For a long while Alexander said nothing. Then, "I thought Ed
Stern didn't much like your seeing Zahedi."

"That's true," she said, with a nod. "But Ed's in Europe now, and
there's no reason for him to know that Ardeshir was here, is there?"
She picked up her purse and took a compact from it. Dabbing her
nose with a puff, she looked up, rubbing her lips together, to blot the
fresh lipstick. "What about Nazif—when will you take care of him?
The money? He told me you seemed reluctant about it, when he met
with you in Saint Moritz." A second's pause. "That would be very
stupid, Alex. Very. You should be able to get something from Allegra,
now, or after the wedding."

"I haven't decided."

"You know," she said, "I've seen Allegra quite a bit recently. At
Sotheby's. She's helping me with my collection . . ." Their eyes met.
"I think I've impressed her with my dedication, my connoisseurship.
'How do you know so much?' she asked me, last week. 'By studying,'
I told her, 'and by knowing what one wants.'" She bent her head
slightly, so that her smile—which at any other angle would have

appeared dangerous—now merely seemed contemplative, even be-
atific. "One thing you must remember, Alex. She's very charming,
your fiancée, but she's not stupid, remember that. Trusting, perhaps . . . And there's really no need for her to know everything
about your life. It's better to keep a little mystery, don't you think?
Be discreet. Things can get so . . . misconstrued." She sat back
against the pillows, fingering a silk tassel.

"I've got to go," he said, as if he had heard, but not fully acknowl-
edged her words.

"So soon?"

"I've got an appointment at the bank, I'm already late."

She took his arm, leading him to the front hall. Within a few
minutes, Alexander was walking quickly up Park Avenue, on his way
to meet Allegra at the rectory.

Allegra had reached the church before Alexander, and slowly
walked up the steps to the brick rectory, still thinking of the meeting
with Pierre Montis.

Saint Benedict's was a distinguished church. The wind, and the
tempestuous March weather seemed to emphasize everything that was
angular and dark about it: the gaunt steeple, and the front gate, with
its cold, clanking latch. No light filtered through the stained-glass
windows; only the outline of the black lead was visible, so that it
was impossible to imagine the panes ever being luminous.

A moment later, she knocked at the door. Then she knocked again.
At last it was opened by a wizened old woman with straggly white
hair and suspicious eyes. She walked with a limp, and thick stockings
sagged about her ankles; occasionally, muttering, she would adjust
them as sounds escaped from her thin, twisted mouth. Once or twice
she turned to peruse Allegra's face, as she led her through the dark
hallway, past the reception room, to another with haggard, stiff furniture and thick beams. Here the woman told her to wait.

Allegra sat down, adjusting herself on the cushionless chair, and
took a breath. The odor of food, of a recently finished lunch, perme-
ated the air; not a delicious scent, but one which was heavy, and
redolent of inferior ingredients. Suddenly she wondered what priests
here ate, and whether such things mattered to them. She doubted it.

The clock ticked. She glanced at it, and at a crucifix nearby, and then at a lugubrious study of Saint Benedict. How long it had been since she had come to this church! For she almost never attended mass in New York; what she thought of as the real church she associated with Europe. "Here it's so cold, and preoccupied by fear," she had once said. And yet, even so, she could not imagine being married outside the church, for she associated the act with the ceremony and the ritual, with its powerful words.

The room, with its lack of light, suddenly brought back a host of memories of church school, and of Irish nuns with rough, chafed faces and small inquiring eyes. They had often been suspicious of Allegra's first name. ("It sounds Spanish," one had once said.) She had always waited to escape the nuns and their unsympathetic voices; the way they rapped the splintered desks after an incorrect answer, or some wrong response to a question about the catechism. But it was always Saturday afternoons, when she was led to the screen-slit silence of confession, that she dreaded most: that moment of confrontation before the terrifying, implacable screen; and then, afterward, the utter relief of absolution.

It had been a revelation for her to go to Europe and see the church of her mother's background: the jolly paunches of priests who drank wine with lunch, the glorious music, and the ancient churches over-ripe with beauty, history, and art. Life-enhancing, rather than life-fearing, it had seemed.

But Alexander had just arrived; she quickly kissed him, as he sat down with her and waited. She noticed immediately that he seemed edgy and uncomfortable, but she said nothing, knowing that churches made him ill at ease. Once she had asked him why. "I'm a pagan," he had told her. "I've little experience in these things."

A tall, hearty man with a distinguished face, an assured gait, and a crop of white hair entered the room. It was Monsignor Melvaney, whom they were to meet, and who would review their marriage papers. They shook hands, and then were immediately shown into a small room to the side, where there was a desk and several thick, leatherbound volumes.

He asked whether they had brought their birth certificates and baptism documents.

He looked at Allegra's. "Born in France," he said, smiling. It was a practiced smile; even so, she returned it. "Yes," he continued. "I've been to Tours, and Paris, too. How long ago? Ten years." He smiled again, as if recalling some pleasant memory, continuing to pass through the documents methodically. It seemed that everything was in order.

"Your parents?"

"They died when I was seventeen."

He looked at the papers again, and said, his fingers drumming the desk, "Philip Clayton, Philip Clayton—the financier? Forum Industries?"

She nodded.

"I remember reading something about him recently. Something to do with the public library."

"The foundation had given money, yes," she answered.

"Ah yes." He turned to her again, with what seemed to be renewed interest—asking her questions about her childhood, her job at Sotheby's, and where she lived. At last, having finished with her, he turned to Alexander, and quickly perused the documents. There were only two—his birth certificate and his American citizenship papers.

"And your religion?" the Monsignor asked, with another crisp smile.

"I wasn't raised with any," he said. Allegra looked to the side, and then at Alexander, afraid that he might grow testy.

"No religion?" The Monsignor repeated this again, attempting not to sound incredulous.

"No."

"But you do believe?"

"In what?"

"In God?"

He did not answer. The Monsignor cleared his throat.

"And in life in the world to come?"

"I believe in life as I know it."

The Monsignor tapped the table with his gold pen. "And you came to New York when?" he said, looking through the papers.

"When I was twenty-four," said Alexander, impatient.

"And you are a banker?"

"Yes."

"Where, may I ask?"

"Atlantic Trust. The international division."

The Monsignor's voice changed slightly, inflected with a new liveliness. "My nephew works there," he said, going on to mention his department, and various other people whose names Alexander recognized.

"What do you think is going to happen with the market?" asked the priest, leaning forward, and continuing to tap his pen.

Alexander gave his prognosis; the Monsignor listened, asking a few more questions to do with finance. And then he said, "Now, back to our original subject." He went on to say that, while it was not necessary for both of them to be Catholics, it was nevertheless crucial to understand the gravity and splendor of the Holy Sacrament of Matrimony; that one entered it for life; and that the vows would bind them to each other until death. He then offered several pamphlets on the subject, and asked whether they would like to attend a special church workshop series.

Allegra took the pamphlets, not daring to look at Alexander as she did so, for she felt his disdain.

"And the date?"

"May thirtieth," she said.

The Monsignor looked at her, and then at Alexander, saying, "You're a lucky man."

"I know," he replied, taking Allegra's hand.

Then the Monsignor escorted them outside; the old woman with the limp reappeared, and led them through the first door, and then the second.

They had just said good-bye when an old man appeared—a derelict with a thin jacket, raw pink ears, and grizzly cheeks. His thin shoes flapped with holes. He looked cold and hungry, and extended his gnarled hand to the Monsignor.

"Father, can you spare something to eat?"

"Oh, don't mind him," the priest answered, with a whisk of his hand. "He's here every day. Come on," he said, turning to the man, "be off with you."

The man slowly made his way down the steps, pulling his jacket close to him, and went down the street, wavering with each gust of wind.

Allegra could not believe what she had seen, and turned to look at Alexander; his face was triumphant. "So you see what your church is really like," he said, under his breath. The Monsignor, who stood away from them on the steps, merely smiled and waved. "We'll see you then, before the thirtieth."

The wind raced behind them as they walked toward Park Avenue. They came to the corner, where the beggar stood, cold and shaking.

"Alex, please give him something!" cried Allegra, tugging at his jacket.

He pulled some bills from his pocket and gave them to the man, who thanked him profusely. Allegra saw his red ears again, and his tattered shirt; her eyes suddenly filled with tears, and with contempt for the church. Impetuously she opened her handbag and thrust a twenty dollar bill into his hand. "Here," she said. "Go get something to eat."

"God bless you, ma'am," he stuttered. "You're a pretty lady, you are."

He turned and walked in the other direction.

"How terrible to see him turned away like that—how cruel," she said to Alexander.

"And then you ask me why I don't believe." He shook his head, taking her arm in his.

They crossed the street, Allegra occasionally looking behind them to see if the beggar had disappeared.

And then she turned to Alexander and said, "Tell me, how did your lunch with David Riffner go, at the bank?"

33

arch 30.

"Dearest Laura:

"I haven't heard from you in ages, so I wanted to write and tell you that we have set a date—May 30. Will you come? I hope so. I can't wait for you to meet Alexander, and know you will love him, as I do. I've told you about him, of course, but meeting face to face is always so different.

"But now I must ask you this: I'm going to be in Boston in early May, on a rather strange mission. Do you remember that scar from my water-skiing accident? It's begun to bother me so much this past year, and I've decided to have it removed. There's a specialist in Boston who has been recommended to me by a friend here, who's also a surgeon. I've spoken with Doctor Stowers about it, and I've decided to go through with the operation. They're talking about Z-plastys and God knows what, but if I don't think too much about it—well! He tells me it's a relatively simple procedure. I've chosen to have general anesthesia, though, because the thought of people poking about with scalpels and things gives me shivers. I'd rather they knock me out. I've scheduled it for May 1, and thought, if it were possible, that I'd come and stay with you and recuperate that week. (They tell me the anesthesia can make you woozy for a while.) Would that be all right? And would you write me to tell me if it is— or isn't?

"It's fairly quiet here, although several friends have given parties for us, which has been fun. I feel strangely tranquil and expectant, as if I had completed one chapter of my life, and were ready to go on to another—one that is more complete, and, hopefully, very very happy.

"I miss you, and was so proud to hear about your award in London; many thanks for sending on the photographs of your last paintings. Your 'new style,' as you call it, works wonderfully well. I can't wait to see the work in the flesh.

"In your last letter you asked if I'd been painting. Sadly, all last year, very little. I felt too buffeted, and my mind too blurred by other preoccupations, to really want to take refuge in the solitude of the studio. But now, funnily enough, I feel quite different—calmer and full of images I want to explore.

"I miss you, and send my love to you and Jeremy,

Allegra."

"April 6.
"Darling child:
"Of course you must come. If the good doctor who is going to take care of that scar is in Boston, then you must visit here, afterward. Unfortunately, Jeremy and I won't be here, because of the show in London, but the cook will, and a funny old gardener called Cynthia Burgon. She's a spectacle, I promise, but friendly and good-natured, if eccentric. She's rumored to keep a wheelbarrow in her living room, and is descended from an old Boston family, a fact of which she's fiercely proud.

"Will leave the key and they'll be waiting for you. Am longing to see you, and hope it won't be too long before I do; of course we shall see you May 30, at the wedding.

"When you visit, do feel free to use my studio if you like. I'll tidy it up, and you can set up your things and work away to your heart's delight. I should think it would be a good time to explore those images you spoke of; try, and tell me how it goes. Remember what I've told you: it is the daily routine that seems to unlock one's inner barriers, and that helps to achieve the flow. Remember: the same time, in the same shirt, with the same cup of coffee, every morning. I will be thinking of you and hope all goes well.

"Do give my best to your Alexander, and much love to you, my dear friend,

Laura."

34

May came, and with it, Allegra's trip to Boston.

The operation proceeded with the inevitability of a dream; indeed, from the moment the sodium pentothal had been inserted in her vein, she remembered nothing—only to awaken hours later, her mouth dry, her stomach nauseous, the stillness of the hospital room all around her, and a nurse gently holding her wrist, saying, "It's all over, it's all over." There were bandages stretched across her chest and a dull ache throughout her body.

She lay there and thought. It seemed so odd to have awoken, for she had never remembered sleeping; there was a feeling of resurrection about this rest. The sheets felt cool, all the more so because of her hot, dry throat and the awful turbulence in her stomach.

Gradually, though, this gave way to a new sense of relief and freedom—that the scar existed no longer; that beneath the bandages lay fresh unmarked skin; and that what had once haunted her, and driven her obsessively to remove it, had miraculously disappeared. It had not been unchangeable, after all! Nor had its ugliness, for which she had blamed herself, been past repairing. And now—at last—she was free of it!

Her head dropped to the pillow, as she tossed and tossed in a drug-induced sleep. In several days, still walking unsteadily, she left the hospital.

Once at her godmother's, it seemed she had never been at the hospital at all, had never known its sterile green light, or slept in a foreign bed with crisp sheets, which were cold and once inhabited by strangers.

Laura's house, though empty, was still full of her—the sweet grass outside, the trees her husband Jeremy had planted, the needlepoint pillows, the English touches; and the studio, to the side, which Allegra remembered so well as a child. It was surprisingly warm. The trees had blossomed early, the air was fragrant, and the birds sang as one awakened. The lawns stretched beyond, shaded by trees; horses grazed beyond the fences.

"Darling girl," Laura's note had said, "make yourself at home. There's plenty in the kitchen, and anything else you need you must simply ask Joanna to fetch. She's a bit deaf, but very dear and means well. Just rest up, paint, and should you care to meet an eccentric stranger—do say hello to Cynthia, the gardener. With my love, Laura."

She had remembered Laura's words about painting ("The same time each morning, the same cup of coffee, the same shirt") and suddenly, with the scar erased from her body, it seemed that her mind had been set free, and with it, her desire to paint. And now, this lock having turned within her, she moved restlessly about the house, walking outside, and then, approaching the studio, peering within it. It was exactly as she had remembered; only the sofa—sagging with age, like a double chin—had changed. Laura's new works stood inside; they, too, had changed, but only slightly. Their style had matured and grown more complex—finer, more abstract—and yet, within it, one could still see the thread to the earlier self that had expressed itself on canvas.

On the first day, Allegra did not enter the studio. But on the third morning, she awoke very early, for her dreams had become stirred with a vague, restless activity that cried for an outlet elsewhere, as if she now had to free herself from other thoughts that had, during the past year, existed behind a closed gate. Like inmates, limping to their freedom, they seemed to want to struggle from their cell onto canvases that stood, empty and expectant, in Laura's studio.

She opened the door to the studio slowly, almost nervously; then, after closing it, took up a brush. At first, she felt stiff, afraid, and unused to holding it. But after a few hours of groping, and even more intensely by the next day, what had seemed difficult now began to flow in a way over which she had no control. That sense of satisfaction, and the clean feeling of relief and absolution now swept over her. During the days that followed, she hardly knew that she had been painting when, four hours later, Joanna knocked at the door, asking if she would like lunch. She had quite forgotten her hunger—and the fact that Alexander had not called for two days.

Four days after arriving at Laura's, she wandered out to the garden, holding a warm mug of tea as she walked down the flagstone path. Roses, blooming in white, coral, and pink, stood at one end; great soft blossoms on tall prickly stalks that wove through the white lattice of the veranda.

She went to pick one, setting down her mug as she did.

"I'd be careful about that, if I were you," she heard a voice say, in a raspy New England accent.

Allegra turned around, and saw a funny-looking gray-haired woman dressed in lumpish clothes, with several rows of pearls, and an apron whose pockets bulged with scissors, spades, and other gardening utensils.

"Who are *you?*" said the woman, narrowing her eyes.

"I'm Allegra Clayton—Laura's goddaughter. And you?"

"Cynthia Burgon." She extended her hand. "How'd you do? I hope Mrs. Hilliard told you about my work here."

Allegra said that she had, and that she had been hoping to meet her. "But why did you tell me to be careful about picking the roses?"

"Usually, I'm the only one who does it; Mrs. Hilliard's very fussy, you know. Anyway, when they're gone, they're gone, I always say."

"Well, not exactly. They do grow back."

Cynthia's eyes looked scornful. "The others may grow back, but not *those.*"

Allegra smiled. "Well, I don't want to disturb you."

"You're not disturbing me," she said, in her Boston accent. "I've just come to look at that tree." She pointed to one, opposite. "It's a mulberry. Such an awful nuisance. So messy. Always dropping something." Her face wrinkled into an expression of disgust.

Her hands on her hips, she walked over to the tree. Allegra, fascinated, followed.

"Who lived here, before Laura?" she asked, after a moment.

"What do you mean?"

"Well, who owned the house?"

"A family. A little odd, I remember. They had brought over a lot of things from Europe for the garden, rather indiscriminately. A lot of Roman heads kicking around, and I *do* mean kicking around. Then, who knows, they sold the house and just disappeared." She looked over to some vines climbing up the arbor, took the scissors from her pocket, and began to snip away, muttering, "Oh, these do get so *invasive.*"

"How long have you been working here?" Allegra asked, sipping her tea.

"Oh heavens, years and years," she said, continuing to cut. She paused for a moment, shaking out her apron and absentmindedly fingering the two thick watches around her wrist. "It was after Mrs. Hilliard was married, she'd come here with the professor. Years and years ago. The garden was in terrible shape. She knew about growing things—the English do, don't they? And at the beginning we worked together. But that was before she started painting again."

"She had stopped painting?" Allegra looked surprised.

"She wasn't painting when she first moved in. That room"—and here she nodded to the studio—"that had been used for something else. A guest room, ah, I can't remember for the life of me. No, she hadn't been painting at all. I remember it very well, funnily enough; she was always out riding, full of energy! Not pretty, but handsome, I think you'd say. She smoked and smoked. I remember seeing her first, that tall slim figure on the horse, coming up the path, her cheeks all red from riding. She'd jump down, take the horse to the stable, rub it down, and immediately come back with a cup of coffee, asking what was to be done that day. She did everything with me, too—weeding, planting, getting the lawn in shape. It looked a different place by the time the two of us got through with it."

"And when did she start painting again?"

"When did she . . ." Cynthia muttered, starting to snip again. The head of a flower fell on the path. "Well, I'd say it was after the tragedy."

"What tragedy?"

"You didn't know?" She scratched her chin. "No reason that you should, I suppose. Her sister. She had a favorite sister, in England; she came here, once, and I met her. Pretty. Prettier than Mrs. Hilliard, though you mustn't tell her I said so! Not long afterwards she was killed in a plane crash. She was young, too. Only thirty or so."

"How awful."

"Yes, a pity, wasn't it? Mrs. Hilliard was undone—I never saw her like that, before!" She gathered the flowers, and then walked to another part of the garden. The late afternoon light had begun to dim, and there was a hazy coolness perfumed with the scent of flowers, damp grass, and trees.

"But her painting?" Allegra asked again.

"Oh yes, her painting—my, you don't forget, do you? That's what they call persistence, deary. It was after that. She suddenly didn't come and help so much with the garden, and I noticed one day that nearly everything had been moved out of that room. She'd brought in the pictures and the brushes. The paints. Then she started her routine—every morning, as she does now." She looked at the two watches she wore. Allegra noticed that one said five-thirty, the other four-thirty. "I'm tired," said Cynthia, matter-of-factly. "So it must be five-thirty." She tucked a pair of scissors into the pocket of her apron, and fidgeted with her pearls.

"I'll be off," she said. "Just be careful with the roses."

"One more thing," said Allegra, calling to her. "Is it really true you keep a wheelbarrow in your living room?"

"How did you know that?" She nodded, and then, in a low voice, said, "The worst thing is what happens when one stores fertilizer. The smell is very *noticeable*." She walked away, not glancing back once, and disappeared down the road.

The following day, Allegra painted and painted, with such speed and concentration that she thought she would exhaust the ideas and appetite to express them. But that did not happen; it merely seemed to uncover more that needed an outlet. She sketched, as well—flowers in the garden, and even one funny portrait of Cynthia, who was pleased to pose for her.

It was the first time in a great while that she had not thought obsessively about Alexander. This puzzled her. It even puzzled her that she was not troubled that he had hardly called, or that when she had tried to reach him, he was either in a meeting, or out of the office. It did not set her mind and her heart spinning as it might once have done; whatever was occurring between herself and the canvases seemed to have soothed it.

Six days after the operation, the stitches were removed, and by the seventh, she saw the fresh, scarless skin that lay beneath the bandages. It filled her with hope, and wonder, just as the painting did: there was a sense of the newly made self, and of the possibilities of life, and the sudden realization that what had seemed ugly and irreparable had been vanquished.

Alexander was to come and take her home the following weekend. She was suddenly mad with excitement to see him; for the freedom she felt, and the sense of wholeness and delight from painting, not only surged within her, but surged within her toward him, as if she wanted to impart, through caresses and love-making, the flow of what she felt inside her.

She took a long walk on the afternoon he was to arrive, for she was skittish with anticipation—glancing at her watch, and barely able to conceal her delight and the fact (and this, with pleasure, she kept reminding herself) that the scar no longer existed!

When, at six o'clock, the car approached the driveway, she ran to it, and then, into his arms, with a delighted, all-embracing kiss.

He held her hard around her waist, kissing her hungrily. "Are you all right?" he kept murmuring. She noticed immediately that he looked tired; there were circles under his eyes, and he looked ill-shaven.

He seemed preoccupied and yet concerned about her, asking about the operation and looking to see the handiwork of the surgeon. She led him to the studio to see her fresh paintings. Casting his eyes about, he murmured that they were good, then kissed her forehead and asked if he could have a drink.

That evening she sat at dinner alone, and waited as he received several telephone calls. An hour later, when he appeared, he found her quiet, and the dinner cold.

He hardly let her sleep that night. "Come here, don't leave me," he kept saying, holding her tightly and caressing her. His kisses deep and needy, his hands pressing again and again over her flesh.

When she awoke in the morning, she went to the window and saw him in the garden, his hand grazing a rose as he walked up a path.

They took long walks along the country roads, Alexander with his arm around her, unusually contemplative. During one such moment he turned to her, saying that he needed some help.

"Tell me, what is it?" she said, her eyes on his face, thinking that this must be the reason for his strange mood.

"I need to ask you for some money," he said, grasping her shoulder and lightly kissing her hair. "To invest in an oil-drilling venture that's come up." He went on to say that Edward Stern had brought him the project, which involved drilling in Louisiana, and that a group of other businessmen—here, he gave some names—were investing in it, as well. "It's a sure thing," he said. "If Stern hadn't brought it to me, I wouldn't be as set on it, but you know how much money he has made, and he's never yet steered me wrong in this sort of thing. Otherwise you know I'd never ask you."

"How much do you need?" she asked, stopping to pick a flower along the path.

"One hundred thousand."

She looked up, trying not to show her astonishment. It was more money than she had imagined—much more. For a moment she said nothing. Then, squeezing his hand, "I'll have to check. I'll have to see."

"When can you do it?" he said, his voice more urgent. "Soon, I hope—otherwise I'll lose my chance."

She told him she would talk to Morgan Guaranty the following week, and would see if it were possible to arrange. He kissed her, holding her at the waist as he thanked her, his eyes scanning her brow, cheeks, and mouth. For a moment she averted her eyes from his—puzzled, even faintly depressed by what he had just asked her.

"I remember when I first saw you," he said, pulling her closer. "How pure you looked. How different, in the midst of all of that."

"When did you know I was yours?" she asked, stroking his cheek.

"From the first moment I saw you."

She smiled. "You didn't seem to act as if you did. You invited me to dinner, but then it was weeks before I heard from you again."

"That was part of the strategy."

"What strategy?" Her eyes searched his.

"To win you, my angel."

"And you applied strategy to it?"

"Of course. How else do you get anything you really want?" He smiled at her. "You've been spoiled, you know. I don't think you've really been used to fighting for things."

He kissed her again, and took her in his arms.

And so the weekend continued—his caresses, and the occasional hurt that crept into the previous week's tranquillity.

She painted only a little after his arrival. It seemed suddenly much more difficult, as if she had to crack through the ice again. But she realized that once she was able to, she would emerge feeling more serene, stronger.

They left the following Monday. It was on the airplane from Boston to New York, when he suddenly mentioned that he would like to have her sign some papers. She asked, "Which papers?," surprised. "Nothing very important," he said, barely glancing up from the *Wall Street Journal*. "I'll explain it later."

35

The walls of the reception room of Gilbert, McCardell, and Berger were slashed with paintings of the Ellsworth Kelly school: great blanks of pure white, incised with blue, orange, and green. Thick-leaved rhododendron plants sat in heavy containers in each corner; brass letters, mounted on the glass door, announced the name of the law firm.

Two steps from the main door sat a gray-haired receptionist with thick black eyebrows. She wore a pantsuit and sat in a glassed-in cubicle. When Allegra entered, she had just spilled a cup of coffee; now she hopped up and down, muttering to herself, as the hot liquid spread across the Formica desk top. "Oh well," she said, with a smile to Allegra. And then, "Can I help you, miss?"

"I'm looking for Mr. Rodman," Allegra said, stepping up to the glass. "He should be here, with Mr. Para. Alexander Para."

"Oh yes, they told me about you. You're Miss Clay—"

"Clayton. Allegra Clayton."

"Oh yes, that's it. They said they'd been expecting you. Well, take a seat and I'll tell them you're here."

Allegra went into the waiting room and made her way to the

couch, a strict piece of furniture with slick pads unholstered in royal blue. Suddenly she felt the white, and the brilliant colors pressing all around her; it seemed there was no relief from them, or from the sun, which streamed through enormous skyscraper windows.

Men—lawyers, presumably—scurried past, all of them preoccupied-looking, some without jackets. "The bar association must be at fault," said one to another, glancing at Allegra as they made their way from the reception area, with its spotlit ceiling, to a long corridor on the other end.

Allegra, who wore a blue and white flower-patterned dress, leafed through a magazine.

At last, the woman told her that Mr. Rodman was ready, and that she should come this way, please.

The door to his office was ajar; a blond woman, his secretary, met them. "This way," she said, motioning to Allegra, who followed.

Alexander stood up, kissing her quickly, and then drew up a chair for her.

Henry Rodman was introduced. Allegra instinctively did not like him. He smiled a bit too much, she thought, and there was something repulsive in the way his paunch, encased in a pale blue shirt, tumbled over the waist of his pants. He had unruly black hair and small eyes with dark circles. He turned to Allegra.

"Has Alex told you why we've asked you to come?" he asked.

"Yes," she answered. "He's mentioned the papers he'd like me to sign." But here, her hands clutched together; she turned to Alexander, who sat beside her. "But would you explain it again, Alex? I'm not sure I really understand all of this."

He began to speak, but Rodman cut in, smiling, and tilting his chair back. "Let me do it," he said, with a nod to Alexander, then looking at Allegra, "Just so there are no misunderstandings. It's for your protection, you see. A kind of safety valve for the future. Not only is Alex renouncing any interest in any of your assets, and your inheritance, but he's going a bit further. He's placing all of his assets in your name; in fact, he's also turning over to you a deed to the house in Sagaponack, and all the effects of the apartment in New York. We'll arrange for the transfer of all that, to your name." He paused. "Alex just wants to make sure—should anything happen to him, or whatever, God forbid—that you receive the full benefits of everything he's worked for. So it's simple, really."

"Don't you think, Alex," she said, turning to him again, "that I should really discuss this with my lawyer? It all seems so rushed."

But again, Rodman answered, "Your lawyer? You can, of course, but as this is your future husband, I'd think you'd trust him."

"I do, of course," she said, for he had made her feel embarrassed, and worse, suspicious. "Well, I suppose, if it's so simple . . . I guess we can go ahead. What do you think, Alex?"

"It's up to you," he answered. "This is for you, after all—for your benefit. If it makes you feel better to have your own lawyer, fine."

"No, no that's all right. Just as long as I can read it through, and you tell me what it entails."

"Good," said Rodman, immediately. "Let's get the papers." He pressed a buzzer. "Harriet, get me the Para documents, would you?"

They spoke a bit about their upcoming wedding, and then, during a moment's silence, Allegra glanced around the office. There were beige books with red labels—"Motions to dismiss or stay"—and a group of family photographs on the table behind his desk.

The secretary entered with the papers.

"Here," said Rodman, passing them over. "Now, let's go through this with you, point by point."

They came upon a sentence which had a minor mistake; she noticed it. "Does this have to be retyped?" asked Alexander, impatiently. "Oh no, that's all right," replied Rodman, looking at him, and then at Allegra. "Just initial it here."

They came to the end.

"Well?" asked Rodman. "Straightforward enough?"

She nodded. "I think so. Alex?"

He smiled. "Yes, fine."

Rodman passed her the pen, pointing to the place where the signatures were required. "Here," he said, pointing to it, "along that line."

She wrote her name, swiftly, in her strong distinctive style. Alexander then added his.

"Great," Rodman said, with a wide smile that seemed incongruous beneath his small dark eyes. "And when's the lucky day?"

"May thirtieth," Alexander said.

"That's a coincidence," he replied. "That was the date of my own wedding—the first, I mean." He chuckled.

Alexander stood up. "We should go."

"Call me if I can do anything else," said Rodman.

"I will."

"Mr. Rodman," Allegra said suddenly, as she stood up. "May I have a copy of these papers, please—to take with me?"

He smiled. "Oh, of course; we'll send them on to you."

He walked them to the door, but before they exited, he turned to Allegra and said, "One thing, Miss Clayton. It would be better for everyone if we kept this between us. These are private things, you know, and I'm sure Alex would agree that it's not something we ought to discuss with friends, guardians, whatever. It might be awkward— for Alex, that is."

She looked at him, sensing behind the gentle phrasing of his words a certain force and harshness. "I had no intention of mentioning this to anyone," she said, her voice cool. "I'm aware that it's private."

"Good. I thought so. Just so you understand, that's all."

They shook hands. She felt Rodman's warm palm, and pulled away. Winking at Alexander, he said, "She's as pretty as you said."

He watched them walk down the long corridor.

It had grown unnaturally hot and sultry when they came out to the street—a humid city heat that left clothes and skin damp and sticky.

Alexander hailed a taxi. She stepped in front of him, thinking she had spotted one. "What are you doing?" he asked, sharply. "That just confuses them."

At last, a taxi pulled up; he closed the door briskly. "Where shall I let you off?" he asked, taking her hand. She gave an address. And then, after a moment, "Are you OK?" he asked, stroking her cheek.

She nodded, quiet now, in the face of his moodiness, and still thinking of the meeting with Henry Rodman. There were moments, such as now, when she felt uneasy about Alexander, almost frightened of him; when his dark moods would come and it seemed she suddenly did not know him. Yet invariably, the next instant, he would kiss her, or joke with her, and like transient clouds the fears would be banished to another part of her mind. A surge of affection would sweep through her, and she would reach out to touch him, or caress him. Still, even when the doubts reappeared, there seemed no turning back. The wedding arrangements had been made. The dress from Pierre Montis was ready.

She felt the sticky seat beneath her, and turned to say something to him, but he was looking the other way, out the window to the traffic. She mentioned the wedding, and how curious it was that they had not yet received a response from Michel Théron, for it was already May twenty-fourth.

"He's not coming," Alexander told her.

"Your best friend? Why not?"

"His mother has been ill. I just received a telegram from him this morning."

They arrived at Allegra's destination. "Don't wait for me tonight," he said, kissing her. "I've got a late meeting."

"OK," she answered, still puzzled by his tenseness. He shut the taxi door; then, slowly, she walked up the street.

36

The wedding day came, an afternoon of sulky skies, with the threat of thunder, and a moody sun that kept darting between the clouds, only to reappear later, as the smiling bride and groom left the church.

Emily had been invited, for Allegra had insisted that she come, despite Alexander's wishes. That evening, an uncharacteristically terse entry appeared in Emily's journal:

"May 30. Went to wedding of Allegra Clayton, now Allegra Para. Ceremony moving, even to me. Alex, too, seemed affected. Found that heartening. Met Giovanna Contarin, Allegra's great-aunt: tiny, warm, exceedingly elegant. Memorable fin-de-siècle face. It was touching to see her and Allegra together—great bond, obviously. Lunch at the Fitzpatricks'. Delicious, very refined as Maggie would say. Harry trying hard not to look disconsolate. Drank too much champagne, head now spinning. Left at three, as did bride and groom, on their way to Greece. Alex's toast strangely short. Found him tense, bridegroom nerves, no doubt. They left to our shouts and congratulations.

"I gave Allegra a book—*The Greek Islands: An Odyssey*—to take with her. She asked me to inscribe it. I did: 'To Allegra—this odyssey, in the hope that it prepares you for the other.'"

37

He had said very little to her during the first hours of the flight to Athens, hardly turning his eyes from a magazine, and asking her once or twice whether she needed anything.

The stewardess brought them drinks; they flipped down the trays as she arrived with her wine, his bourbon. He took a sip, then absentmindedly watched as the ice moved back and forth within the glass. For a moment, his eyes went opaque with concentration. He turned to look at her, as if to say something; searched her face; and then, turning away, sipped his drink.

"Alex," she said, touching his hand. "What's the matter? Something *is* the matter, I can tell."

He turned to look at her again, and then, in a puzzled emotionless voice said, "Your forehead—it isn't symmetrical." His voice had been full of some uncanny sense of discovery and disappointment, as if he were not speaking of her face at all, but of something more momentous. Some dreadful flaw he had seen.

"Alex, what do you mean?" She looked bewildered, as if she had not believed what she had heard. "What a strange thing to say."

"Forget it," he said, returning to the magazine. "You've no sense of humor."

"It wasn't meant to be funny. You were serious. You seemed so astonished. I've never seen that look before . . ."

The stewardess approached them, a basket of rolls in one hand. "A roll, sir?"

He took one and split it apart. Allegra, still disconcerted, opened the book which Emily had given her, gazing, for a moment, at its inscription. She tried to read, but all her thoughts fled from her, her eyes turning repeatedly to Alexander—seeing how nervously he drank, and how he kept looking out the window.

"Would you like me to read to you about Crete?" she asked, touching his hand again.

"Not now," he said.

She read a few paragraphs, but still could not concentrate. At last she took a sleeping pill from her purse, and, in a moment, turned her head to the side.

When she awoke, they were in Athens. The bright white sun beat through the windows of the jet as the plane rushed to the end of the runway. She stretched, her eyes opening slowly. Suddenly she was so excited to think she was in Greece! Leaning over, she kissed Alexander, who still gazed out the window. He looked pale.

"You had a good sleep," he said affectionately, smiling.

"Yes." She rubbed her eyes. "And you—did you sleep at all?"

"I read and thought—mostly thought."

"And plotted," she added, with a mischievous glance.

He smiled. "I never plot."

She laughed and said, "You don't think so? What do you call it, then?"

"Deep thinking," he said, jokingly. "Profound."

"I never doubted it!"

"You shouldn't. I was thinking about you, and how to make you happy."

"Were you?"

"Yes."

"Were you really?"

He answered her with a kiss.

It was chaotic inside the dingy blue airport—porters scrambling for customers, conveyer belts broken down; an imbroglio.

Suddenly Alexander turned to her and said, in a casual voice, "Michel should be here. He was going to come and meet us." His eyes scanned the crowds.

"Michel? Here?"

"We'll spend the night, have dinner together . . . You don't mind, do you? The boat trip is his present—did I tell you that?"

"No," she said slowly. "You didn't."

Alexander nodded. "Yes. Remember to thank him, will you?"

But Michel had already appeared and stood, waving from the room past customs. He looked as elegant as ever, a blue ascot around his neck.

"Michel!" she said, greeting him. "What a surprise!" He kissed her; she asked about his mother. "She is much better," he said. "Much."

And then, taking Allegra's small bag, he said, "Alex didn't tell you that I would be here?" The two men exchanged looks. "That was very inconsiderate." He looked at Alexander. "Everything is arranged."

"What about customs?"

"I've already taken care of that."

At the Hotel Victoria, doormen in trim gold-buttoned uniforms stood at the entrance, seemingly oblivious to the heat. Inside, the lobby was cool and hushed—thick red carpets, formal furniture, and immense chandeliers. Michel, who had already inquired about the rooms, stood with Alexander showing the passports and registering their names. The next moment they were led upstairs to an endless corridor; and through one hallway twisting into another; and then, to a tall door with the number of their suite.

Allegra kept looking about. She had not liked the serpentine corridors, or the tall doors fitted with high, unreachable windows, but the room itself had a cool, dignified anonymity.

The porter brought up their bags. Michel left. Alexander stood at the window, his arms around her waist, as she looked out at the green and umbrellas of Constitution Square.

"We should take a nap," she said.

"Are you still tired?"

She was not, actually; it was simply that she suddenly longed to be in bed with him. They had just been married, and she was his wife! She wondered how he could not be thinking the same thoughts, and kissed his neck and mouth.

"Come," she said, pulling his arm.

But he looked at his watch. "I've got to meet Michel. I've got some things to discuss with him."

"What things?"

"Business. A deal we're putting together."

"On our honeymoon?" And then, after a pause, "That isn't very romantic."

"Romantic?" he repeated, his voice incredulous. "The romance is over." His voice seemed cold; his hands had dropped from hers. She turned her back to him, and then looked up, out the window, seeing nothing, only hearing the drum roll of those words, "The romance is over." Tears had sprung to her eyes, her stomach and her heart felt strangled; she wondered why he had not held her, or kissed her!

"I'll be back in an hour," he said. "Then we'll do some sightseeing— some of your museums. Michel knows all those places."

The door closed, and she was left in the room, with its afternoon shadows and thick white pillows—cool and now creaseless—which had doubtless comforted the heads of so many strangers.

Shadows began to fill the room; hour after hour passed without Alexander. She waited, looking at her watch, too agitated to sleep, lying on the bed in the white silk robe she had bought for her honeymoon, her head tossing, her fingers lighting cigarettes, only to stub them out a moment later. Again and again she stood by the window, looking out . . .

It occurred to her that she could go out; that she need not wait for him; but he had said he would come, and so she would remain there, listening for his footsteps.

Four o'clock.

Five o'clock.

At last, at six, there was a noise at the door: Alexander, his face drawn, but his voice jovial as he swept her into his arms, with apologies, warm kisses, and promises that this would never happen again.

He told her that they would go to a restaurant by the sea for dinner, and that she should hurry and dress.

It was past midnight by the time they left the restaurant. The waiters stood by impatiently, and looked relieved when Michel made a motion for the check. He swiftly took it from Alexander's hand when it arrived; the next instant the waiter came for the small tray with the money.

The road to Athens was deserted now, the orange and red lights of Piraeus at once gaudy and ethereal. As they approached the city, the Acropolis sailed through the darkness like an ancient, proud ship: desolate, empty, making everything below seem to cower before it, the moonlit caryatids of the Erechtheum like suspended phantoms.

When they came to their room, the sheets had been turned down, and the pillows stood cool and expectant.

She went to the window and looked out again at the square, thinking of the afternoon and dinner. Michel had been nonchalant, as always, urging wine on everyone. He had told her about the boat—the *Persephone,* it was called—and about Istanbul, where they would meet his friend Nazif Keskin, whom Allegra only vaguely remembered meeting at the Iranian embassy, in Washington.

Now she heard Alexander calling to her. "Come here," he said, in a voice gone gentle. "Come here, I miss you."

She turned to see his face, its planes softened by the light. Still he beckoned, taking her in his arms. "Let's forget the last day," he told her, holding her chin so that her eyes met his. "Please," he said, "I need you. My wife." And then, "Now, more than ever."

"Do you?" Her voice was bruised, still remembering how curt he had been.

"Yes."

"How can you? You are so obsessed by your work. Your business deals."

"Yes, I am obsessed . . ."

"By your work."

"By you!"

Her smile was rueful. "I'd like to think that, and maybe I once did, but now I . . ."

He put his fingers to her mouth. "You're wrong. Nothing is so important that I would ever risk losing you."

"If you lose me, it won't be for that . . ."

"For what, then?"

She turned her head away and said nothing, feeling suddenly as if she had trespassed, as if she had just stepped on a crack. It terrified her.

"Come," she said, and took his hand, as they went to bed.

He watched her undressing, as if to etch each movement in his mind. The dress, slipped off (hand wriggling, above); the small snap of her bracelets from her wrist; and the touch of her skin as she crept into bed, next to him. He drew her closer, inhaling the scent from the crevices of her body, and feeling the lines of her neck, and then the softness and roundness of her breasts, as she nestled closer.

The light was still on. He could see the veins across her chest, and the small protruding bone of her wrist. He drew her closer still—for he was restless and could not sleep—and now he began to kiss her, with slow, skin-grazing touches. Never had he been so gentle, it seemed; her body felt stung with sensation, as he moved slowly above her with a feline grace, kissing her breasts and then pressing himself against her, so that she could feel his erection and her nipples, pressing—almost against her will—against his chest.

Afterward they lay together. She had taken a cigarette; he brushed the damp strands of hair from her forehead.

"That was what you needed, wasn't it?" he asked, after a moment.

"I need your love."

"You needed my cock," he said, with a slight smile.

She kissed his chest. "I needed that, too, but not as much as the other."

He kissed her mouth, which was still swollen, almost bruised from the love-making.

Then he sat up, his strong naked body leaning over to the table, as he reached for a bottle. She heard the fizzing sound of a sleeping pill being dropped into a glass of water.

In a moment, his arm gripped around her, he fell to sleep. She lay awake, remembering his caresses and then his words, "You needed my cock," as if—in saying that—he had dismissed what she had really longed for.

Suddenly, almost shivering, she remembered Emily's book, and its strange inscription, "This odyssey, in the hope that it prepares you for the other."

It was hours before Allegra was able to sleep.

38

The ropes lay coiled like snakes on the decks; they were her first sight at the port of Piraeus. The acrid sun beat down on the boats, the water stilled to an eery calm.

Allegra sat in a taxi, shielding her eyes from the sun, feeling all that she had tried not to see about Alexander creeping into a part of her mind she wanted to seal shut. She thought of their wedding. "For richer, for poorer . . ." Those words, like slow drumbeats down stone passageways. And then she thought of Emily, suddenly, and of her warnings; the small smile set in the pale face, and the knowing eyes. "But I *do* know him," she had said. The inscription that followed her, like the dreams, "This odyssey, in the hope that it prepares you for the other."

She had awakened that morning expecting to find his arms around her. But again, he had left. She had had her breakfast alone. Glances at the telephone, waiting for it to ring. But it had not. And when he had returned, he seemed quite different from the man she had fallen to sleep with—his eyes hooded, and his mouth, with its surreptitious curve.

Afterward, they had gone to the Acropolis: a proud giant, pinned to the earth, only to be ravished by hungry crowds lusting for beauty and history; within its museum, heads carved with careful smiles, and lost glimpses of graceful stone ladies. And now to Piraeus, where they would board the *Persephone*.

It was a hot day, the sun so white and high that the black lines of the boats seemed blacker, at once more spindly and more threatening—the angular rhythm of the lines, the masts and ropes jagged and confused. Now she sat alone, waiting for him, feeling the hot torn seat beneath her, and looking to see if he had found the boat. She was sweating, and took a handkerchief to mop her forehead, shielding her eyes from the brightness. Then she stepped out of the car to see where he had gone.

Slowly he came into view; slowly; step by step; she, watching him as if she had never seen him before. A stranger, who was her husband.

His white shirt seemed to accentuate his skin and his dark hair, his mouth set in a determined expression. "Everything is ready," he said, in a strong voice. "Come. Tell him to get the bags out."

She motioned to the taxi driver, who unlatched the trunk which he had fastened with a rope. But one bag, in particular, was difficult and kept opening, and reopening. Something was wrong with its latch. Alexander grew impatient. "Look," he said, wresting it from her. "Must we travel like this—like peasants!" He took hold of it, slamming it shut in such a way that it broke. She stood and watched, her eyes still strained and dry from the heat. Still, he kept grasping the latch, trying to snap it shut, but nothing worked. "Please, Alex, stop it," she finally cried. "Leave it alone. We'll fix it later."

People passing glanced in their direction—nudging each other, as they watched the young couple bickering. He took her arm and led her to the *Persephone*.

A tall, sturdy fellow with a mustache and an air of capability walked toward them: the captain. And then the steward: small, with oily skin and hands nervously clutched together. They seemed friendly enough. Alexander assumed another smile and pointed at the bags.

The name *Persephone*, in spare script, came into view.

It was—as Michel said—a splendid boat. Long, lean with high

gleaming motors and elegant lines. The decks were of warm wood that had been waxed so that the grain was almost invisible. Below, there were two bedrooms—one in deep green, and another in ivory and blue, with the remnant of a head of Aphrodite in a niche.

The motors began to purr, and then to rumble; soon Piraeus, with its vessels and cafés, would recede from view. Fumes curled in the air; the water below rustled. Allegra suddenly felt nauseous, as if the air were strangling the life from her, and went up unsteadily, to the deck. Alexander stood there, his arms fastened on the railing, looking out to the sea, as they set off. The breeze became stronger. He took her hand and drew her near. "Who is *this?*" he said, jesting.

The steward came to offer them a drink. Alexander nodded and asked for whiskey, Allegra for water.

She looked out to the sea, thinking of the December afternoon when she had gazed below the Bridge of Sighs, when she had decided to marry him.

He kissed her slowly, almost absentmindedly, holding her hand, and apologizing for the way he had snapped at her about the baggage. She murmured something in response, excusing him. She had forgotten it already, she said. He drew her closer and said, after a pause, "Sometimes I wonder if I haven't been selfish to marry you."

"Why?" She felt her heart tighten.

He shrugged. "Because you would make anyone a wonderful wife, and I—I am not sure of myself as a husband."

"Do you love me?"

"You know I do."

"Then why do you say those things, if you love me!"

He put his hand to her mouth and said, "No more talk." And then, his eyes turning toward the sea, "Come. Look."

Piraeus was no more. In a few hours, they would arrive at Delos, the birthplace of Apollo.

With infinite slowness, Delos came into sight—low, dry hills with windswept thirsty grass; a lone palm tree where legend had it the god was born. This, the last anchorage place between Europe and Asia; the center of the Cyclades; the ancient island of worship, lustration, plague, and ravishment. The water was blue, ludicrously blue, and the hills, though not high, were daunting by dint of their desolation. There was a smell of abandonment about the island, and about its white, marble-reflecting light, as ancient as the trees, with their long, reptilian trunks.

The sea frothed in small white pointed waves and the wind, blowing about Allegra's neck and face, momentarily erased the bitter heat of the afternoon. She thought of the last time she had been here, with a friend, and of standing before the mosaic of Dionysos riding the panther, and how she had wished then that she had come with a lover, or a husband.

At lunch, on the boat, Alexander had been playful, pulling her over to him, stroking her. But now his eyes had assumed that awful distance; there seemed no way of approaching him. The smallest things seemed capable of igniting his anger—an anger often directed toward her. She had grown quiet in anticipation of it, and inside, increasingly resentful toward him.

The pitching boat arrived at the dock about the same time as another larger boat, teeming with sun-burnt English tourists. Soon Allegra and Alexander were walking up hot, dry paths bristling with parched grass, littered with pieces of marble and glittering bits of mosaics. She felt his warm lips on hers, as he kissed her.

Guides approached them, including one Allegra thought looked familiar. She remembered his brilliant blue eyes, with their kouros-like stare; he wore a tight T-shirt and had an almost absurdly precise way of speaking English, emitting the words like machine-gun pellets. "Alex," she said, "let's ask him to give us the tour. I've had him before, and he's good."

They walked toward him, settled on a price, and began to move toward the ruins of markets, agoras, and Graeco-Roman houses.

They came to the house of Apollo, with its broken columns and the mosaic of Dionysos that Allegra remembered. In his measured voice, the guide explained the history of the house, and then of the panther motif which was, he said, most likely Oriental in origin. Looking at it, she thought of Pierre Montis and the panthers of his great doors; and then, of his augury.

She realized suddenly that Alexander had left, had wandered to the opposite part of the atrium. The guide, glancing at her, said nothing, merely continuing to talk. At last, having finished, he turned to her. "You were here before, I remember."

"Do you?"

"Yes. You were with the English group, no?"

"Your memory is very good."

"It is not so difficult. This is your husband?" He nodded in Alexander's direction.

"Yes," she said.

"I am boring him, then."

"No you're not. Not at all."

"No?" He cast a skeptical glance in Alexander's direction. "Where would you like to go next?"

"That is up to you," she said. He smiled impassively.

She began to walk toward Alexander. "The guide is waiting," she said, touching his arm.

"I'm aware of that." There was a touch of annoyance in his voice. "Don't you want to see more of the island?"

"Of course." He looked at her closely. "Your face is getting red."

"Is it?" She put on her hat.

For a moment they stood looking at the island around them. The isolated trees rustled, the sea lapped in white and blue, beyond; the stone sparkled; Allegra, her hair blowing and her hat, trying to escape.

"There are no sounds," she said, almost wistfully. "It reminds me of Cap du Loup."

"Cap du Loup?" He gave her a long, acknowledging look. "How long ago was that?"

"Almost a year. No, a bit longer, I'd say." (Images of Cap du Loup came to her mind: its blue-green trees, its silence-racked air, its desolation.) "What a strange place. I can't imagine how you would have heard about it."

He looked at her, astonished. "How do you think? I'd been there before, several times."

"What do you mean?" she asked, her fingers pressed to her temple. "You told me it was your first visit."

"Did I?" He smiled, a curt smile that showed his even teeth. "Well, it wasn't. I'd been there before with Michel, he'd told me about it."

"Michel?"

"Yes. I told you that. Or perhaps I didn't. It hardly matters." A pause. "It isn't important," he said again.

She said nothing, her eyes gazing at the water rippling toward the shore in incandescent blue waves.

He took her hand. "Come, let's finish up here."

The wind whipped their faces and everything around them, for they had arrived at the phalanx of stone lions: lean Mycenaean figures carved in stone, slim-haunched from the wind, and brindled by the sun of centuries.

The guide, droning on in English, told of their history and how one had been taken by the Venetians as loot, and how it now stood before their arsenal.

"Don't you remember seeing it, Alex?" she asked. No, he said, he did not. "Would you take my picture?" she then asked him.

She went to stand by one of the lions, her sandaled foot poised on the stone pedestal, as she smiled. "Stand up straight," he told her. She did. The guide watched.

The camera clicked; another tourist came, stood in the same spot, and had his picture snapped. Allegra began to walk around the lion statues, observing them from all angles, and wondering how they would appear at dusk, and then at the deepest, darkest part of night.

The guide approached. "You would like to buy some postcards, now?" he asked.

The postcard shop, where drinks were also sold, was not far from the lions. Thick bottles of sodas and juices stood on the bar; flies buzzed, and postcards stuck to the oilcloth-covered tables as one wrote.

Allegra tried to write some cards as Alexander searched for a telephone. "Dear Maggie," she began, but the pen stopped midsentence, the words tangling in her mind before she could get them on the vacant surface of the paper, the bright images on one side at variance with the disrupted scrawls on the other. Maybe Emily's will be easier, she thought. And so she began another, but it, too, stayed silent. She ripped them up.

Alexander, finishing a beer, told her it was time to leave. Nodding, and glancing once more at the palm tree, she followed.

The next hour, they set sail for Mykonos.

Nights followed at sea. Indigo skies pierced by blankets of stars; little else; no sounds except that of the water, and breezes that blew about one's neck and shoulders.

Each day, another island: Santorini, with its narrow cliff-walk and seemingly endless stone steps, worn by pilgrims. Mount Athos—dark, devoid of women, its priests hidden from view, and its winding roads like the insides of a convoluted shell. And then Samothrace, one morning; the wind lashing the boat, preventing them from disembarking, so that the island's temple, and its marble penetralia remained hidden.

Every night, the sound of the sleeping tablets hissing into water.

It seemed a century had passed by the time they arrived at Istanbul.

39

Nazif Keskin glanced at his watch. He was a plump man, with prematurely gray hair, thick black glasses, and a vulpine smile. Ah, it was much later than he thought: perhaps he should not have indulged in this walk? But it was a radiant, tempting day in Istanbul, with a refreshing salty breeze that seemed to carry the city's slanted sounds. Peddlers hawking their wares; the droning of automobiles; the distant honking of ships.

He had told his driver, Mehmet, to meet him at his office, to which he was now walking; they would go from there to the quai, where they would meet Alexander and his bride. What was the girl's name? Ah, he could not remember.

Alexander's bride. The very words made Nazif smile—a smile edged with sarcasm—for he himself had never married, having remained, instead, a connoisseur of women. It amused him now—as he made his way down the teeming boulevard—to remember Alexander's own cynical words on that institution. They had been having dinner that December, almost two years ago. Where was it? Ah, in Paris, at that Italian restaurant near the Rond Point—yes, the cannelloni had been delicious, if a trifle too *al dente,* and the blonde—yes, he remembered her well. They had been joking about marriage. It had been an amusing lunch with Michel, and the three of them had drunk to their freedom.

He adjusted his tie. It was of thick silk in navy with white dots. He had bought it at Lanvin, on the Faubourg Saint-Honoré. Such things were important to Nazif. Indeed, the tie suited him, and his look of fastidiousness.

He continued thinking. The girl—well, at least Alex had made a reasonable choice. They looked handsome together, and she was rich. That was good, for he knew his friend—like Nazif himself—had always had expensive tastes. Even at Oxford, according to Michel. Wasn't that why he had entered into this bargain with Michel and himself, after all? "Alex will be helpful to you," Véronique had assured them. She had proved right.

Nazif suddenly wondered whether Alexander would bring the next payment. They had been slow in coming, recently. Too slow. That had not been the case at the beginning; not at all. He recalled the day he had first discussed the money with Alexander: "For the excavations," Nazif had said. He wondered even now whether Alexander had really believed him. Well, it had not entirely been a lie, after all—most of the money *had* gone to the digs. But the rest . . . It was important to live well, was it not? He thought of his boat, and his art collection, his mouth forming a satisfied smile.

Still, he continued thinking of the bride, and of the time he had met her in Washington. The girl's family name was good, that was also important. Nazif was conscious of lineage, for his own family was neither distinguished nor rich. Yes, Alexander had been prudent, as always. And the girl was attractive. A bit too tall for his taste, but then she had beautiful breasts, and she was bright. Perhaps a bit too bright? But then Alexander had always liked intelligent women ("For the challenge," he had once said)—almost as much as he liked risks. When Nazif had first met her, he had found her charming. And indeed, not long afterward—meeting secretly with Alexander in St. Moritz—he had said, with a slow chuckle over a glass of whiskey, "This one will get you, my friend."

So he had been right. There was some justice in that. *Enfin.* He sighed, wiping the perspiration from his forehead with a white handkerchief.

Everything will work itself out, Michel had told him. And so, indeed, everything had: the digging at Aphrodisias, the superb apartment overlooking the Bosphorus, the money to indulge his taste for travel and rare wines.

Another chuckle to himself and a glance, again, at his watch, and then at his gleaming black shoes. Little things satisfied him so.

He quickened his pace; spotted Mehmet by the limousine; and then glanced across to the sea, where enormous vessels lumbered into the port. Holding the red leather strap, he told Mehmet to get on with it, and to go directly to the quai.

Twenty minutes later, after a drive through the raucous streets of the city—the skies undulating with minarets and echoing with eastern sounds, the air choked with exhaust—he arrived and saw, within minutes, the lines of the *Persephone*.

He thought the girl—for he could still not remember her name—looked rather pale, although he was too gallant to say so. "My beauty," he said, kissing her hand, as he noted, appreciatively, its delicacy. "It has been such a long time. And now you are married!" And then, to Alexander, "My friend, how good to see you." They embraced. As they did, it occurred to Nazif that Alexander, too, looked rather drawn; perhaps it was because of those distant rumblings, in New York? How unlikely that Alex should worry. But then, that Anglo-Saxon atmosphere would be enough to unnerve anyone.

They got into the car, Allegra having given her bag to the driver. "So . . ." said Nazif, in an exuberant voice, "here you have Istanbul!" He leaned across to Allegra, resting his hand on her knee. "This is your first visit?"

She nodded, still unsure, as she had been from the first, whether she liked Nazif.

"Ah, then we will have to give you the grand tour. Right, Alex?"

He glanced at Alexander, who answered, "After we talk—yes." It annoyed him that Nazif seemed to be in such a jubilant mood. "We have things to discuss, Nazif . . ."

"As you wish, but . . ." He made a casual motion with his hands. "We can leave Allegra with the driver, if you like." His tone, which had been sharp, now softened. He kissed Allegra, caressing her knee, and said, "And then the rest of the day we will be free."

Nazif leaned back, his small eyes squinting. "Of course, you are my guests. Anything."

Around them spun the city—a glorious, yet tumbledown sight which thrilled Allegra, who had never traveled this far east. She leaned her head out of the car window to catch some air. Ramshackle wooden buildings, and the twisting tops of mosques could be seen from a distance. Gradually the sea, and the vast opening to the city, became as distant as the landscape of a medieval tapestry, all interwoven with blues, and greens, and turrets. The air was sultry, and honeyed with an Oriental thickness. She kept wiping her brow, and adjusting her skirt on the hot leather seat.

At last they arrived at Nazif's building—an unprepossessing place with one massive door. They entered.

Michel had mentioned the apartment; even so, she was quite unprepared for its lavishness and grave perfectionistic style, its marbled order and pervasive intellectual aestheticism. It occurred to Allegra that Nazif must be very rich, for the rooms were remarkably luxurious. In the anteroom stood a terra-cotta sphinx, a marble sphere, and a fragment of a classical frieze he had found at Ephesus. Throughout were ancient heads, mounted torsos, and the coolness of ivory, bronze, and stone.

"How beautiful," she said, going to the balcony, and then to the terrace, which was massed with climbing vines and plants. Beyond stretched the Bosphorus.

"I am so happy you like my home," Nazif said, following her, and pointing out the sights. A butler in a wine-colored jacket appeared. "My dear, what would you like?" Nazif asked.

"Something light. I'm very thirsty," she said, and then, "Alex, a drink?"

"A whiskey," he said, sitting down.

Nazif murmured to the butler in Turkish, and then, gathering Allegra and Alexander to him, and casting his eyes about, said, "Glorious, isn't it?," for the city lay beneath them, extended like a bronzed map of color and architecture.

"Come, let me give you a tour," Nazif said, taking Allegra's arm, and leading her to another room. It was lined with Roman sculpture,

Attic vases, and a porphyry head of a Medusa, the surfaces of the walls treated to look like ancient stucco. In each corner, poised as if to take step, stood archaic Greek torsos. Above a fragment of a sarcophagus hung an eighteenth-century painting of Mount Vesuvius.

The butler arrived with the drinks, placing them on the vast center table, which was stacked with art books and volumes of *Antiquity* magazine. The three sat down. Allegra and Alexander talking about their voyage, Nazif about the current excavations at Aphrodisias. "Ah, such a terrible accident last week," he said, with a clucking of his tongue. "Ten men killed, such a pity." In fact, he had been annoyed that the disaster had interrupted his weekend at the Princes Islands, and had only taken a desultory interest as he walked through the rubble, his German shepherd, Orpheus, tugging on his leash.

"You would like to see some photographs of the excavations?" said Nazif to Allegra. She nodded. He went to his desk and took a leather-bound volume, opening it page by page. Allegra kept murmuring, her eyes wide, for the photographs were extraordinary: the stone head of a priest, wearing a diadem; a small statue in translucent marble of the sun god, Helios; the vigorous form of a young Greek athlete. Finally, they came to the last picture, one of the goddess of love herself, Aphrodite, her face masked. At least it seemed so, for a veil of sheer cloth had been draped over the marble, partly hiding her eyes.

"Aphrodite," said Nazif, looking at Allegra. "Venus to you, I suppose."

"Or Aphrodite," she replied, "in any language. How old is this one?"

"From the second century, we think. Yes, it's quite certain. But you see here"—he pointed to the cheek—"how the impurities have penetrated the stone. The cloth, you see, is treated with chemicals to help draw them out. It will take some time, but gradually, they will be removed." He looked at Alexander, saying, "Such a lucky man you are, to have such a lovely wife."

"She is, isn't she?" Alexander said, with an acknowledging smile, as he looked at her proudly, although it was still awkward for him to be married among his bachelor friends.

"You are still painting?" asked Nazif pleasantly, for he remembered hearing that Allegra did something of that sort.

"I am, but I haven't done much for a while. Some things in the spring that I liked, though."

"But you must continue!"

"She'll get back to it," added Alexander. "After the trip—won't you, love?"

She began to answer, but was interrupted by Alexander, asking Nazif about a mutual friend, an Argentinian whom Allegra did not know.

"Oh yes, he's been married a long time now," said Nazif, taking a handful of slivered almonds from a silver bowl. "To Fiona, the Venezuelan girl, do you remember?" Alexander nodded. "He adores her, gives her anything, but can't bear to spend time with her. He has a mistress and stays with *her,* and then visits the wife and children."

Alexander smiled. Allegra, noticing his expression, lit a cigarette.

"And the mistress—is she Argentinian as well?" Alexander asked.

"No, French. Or is it Italian? I can't remember," replied Nazif, taking another handful of almonds. "At any rate, he has had a child with her."

"Really?"

"And the wife knows about it," said Nazif, matter-of-factly.

"That must be very painful for her," she said.

"Painful?" There was an amused smile on Nazif's plump face. "We're not talking about painful or not painful. We're talking about reality." Still smiling, he stood up and asked, "Shall I show you to your room"—a glance at Alexander—"or should I say the honeymoon suite?"

He led her through to a bedroom in the back, with a huge canopy bed carved of wood so dark that it seemed to imbue everything around it with a nocturnal glow. The pillows looked as if no human hand had ever touched them, as if they were carved of marble. There was a huge bathroom fitted with floor-to-ceiling mirrors and impressive, old-fashioned fixtures.

Allegra went inside to wash her hands, and looked into the mirror. The face she saw startled her. Her cheeks were drawn, and the pill-induced rest had given her circles under her eyes which smoking had only exacerbated. How ugly I am, she thought to herself. How pale and old.

She finished washing her hands, and sponged off her face, patting it dry with a thick linen towel emblazoned with a swirling red "K."

Voices came from another room; low murmurs; concerned talking. She could barely hear them. With one last glance at the bedroom, she began to walk toward the library.

She walked softly and reached the foyer. They had stopped speaking for an instant and sat face to face in the library, before the head of the Medusa. Suddenly she heard Alexander say, "The worst that can happen . . ." but he did not finish the thought, leaving Nazif to gaze at him, intently and silently. "And Michel?" Nazif finally asked, leaning forward.

"He is like my brother," Alexander answered. "It is the other . . ." But again he did not finish, and the two men sat, stilled by a dense, ambiguous silence. Then Alexander took an envelope from his pocket and handed it to Nazif, "Here. As I promised. It is as much money as I could get hold of at present." Their eyes so revealing, and yet so opaque, that Allegra turned away, suddenly overcome by fear and dread; she felt nauseous.

They had not seen her. She walked back, her hand on the wall of the corridor, then slowly into the bedroom, where she lay on the vast bed, with its overhanging canopy. A revelation, like a deathly chill, seized her. What have I done? she kept thinking. Why did I ever marry him?

Moments later, they came to get her.

She went alone to see the sights of Istanbul, led by Mehmet, the driver, and for a while, the city's ancient beauty took her mind from Alexander. She entered each mosque as if to find within its walls the mystery of a puzzle, the panacea to the pain.

She averted her eyes from couples who walked hand in hand, and from laughing families taking photographs. Peddlers and canny postcard sellers pursued her, seeing in this young woman alone with a chauffeur an opportunity for moneymaking. Young boys hawking souvenirs followed her and called in English. She bought some postcards, a tasseled slipper, and other things she did not really want.

From place to place she went, like a sleepwalker. First, to the Hagia Sophia, with its bulblike ceiling, vaulted and starry, its paths worn by the hordes of centuries, its pressing sense of journeys. And then to the Blue Mosque, which she entered as one might a sparkling blue wave or magical cavern, the sun streaming through gently, and the feel of silky carpets beneath her feet. And finally to Topkapi, with its flowering trees, its lemon-scented air, and its kiosk shining in mother-of-pearl, ivory, and purple. But now the colors swam before her; all she could think of was the penthouse overlooking the Bosphorus, and of her husband, sitting with a man she did not know, speaking of things which lay like labyrinths beneath their looks.

There was a restaurant at Topkapi where tourists and Turks ate spicy rice dishes along terraces. Allegra was shown to a table, while Mehmet stood awkwardly to the side. Motioning, Allegra told him to come and join her. He looked surprised, even embarrassed by the invitation, but she smiled again, urging him, and he came. They ordered lunch and some cold beer, and ate in silence. People around them laughed and joked; several stared; they ate quickly and left.

It was silent in the apartment when she returned. She stood by the balcony and looked out, seeing how the city, newly quiet, had surrendered its morning noises and frenzy to the approach of evening. Suddenly she felt someone behind her: Nazif. "Did you have a good tour? I hope so. Mehmet took you to the Blue Mosque as well? Good. It is my favorite." He explained its history, and its distinguishing features, and then beckoned her to sit down. "How unlucky that we weren't able to join you, but lunch was all right, was it? In the past, the food has not been bad. *Ce n'est pas Lasserre*, alas . . ." This, with a slow chuckle. He glanced at his watch. "Alex is on the telephone, I believe."

They continued to speak until, after a moment, she excused herself and went to the bedroom.

The sheets on the vast bed had already been turned down. In another part of the apartment, one could hear water running, and the padded steps of the butler. Outside, beyond the terrace, Istanbul had assumed its nocturnal aspect: the darkening, gleaming blue lights across the Golden Horn and the horizon, the minarets lit by a full moon.

Allegra sat before the dressing table as she slowly took off her bracelets, one by one. They made a clicking noise as they fell to the tabletop; she stared at them, her eyes faraway.

The door opened. It was Alexander, looking pale, distraught, his shirt open and rumpled. "Alex . . ." she began to say.

"Come here," he said, taking her shoulders and sitting her down. His grip was painful. "Sit down. I've got to talk with you."

"What is it?" Her throat was dry, terrified.

"It has nothing to do with you," he kept repeating. For a moment, she thought he was incoherent. "Nothing, nothing to do with you; all of it to do with me, and with another part of my life. Before I met you."

"Alex, please tell me, just tell me now! What is it?"

"It has to do with Michel, as well. And Nazif."

"Tell me—what?"

He did not answer. She went to reach for her purse to find a cigarette, and began to light it, her fingers shaking.

"You know I can't stand that," he said, ripping it from her mouth, and flinging the cigarette to the floor.

"Alex, just tell me whatever it is," she pleaded, frightened by his frenzied eyes and motions.

He slumped opposite her, on the bed, his head in his hands. A moment passed. Quite suddenly he sat up, taking both her hands and looking into her eyes, and began to tell the story.

40

His eyes were red and bloodshot, and he stroked the hair by his temple ceaselessly. She went to him, kneeling before him, kissing his knees—all the time frightened, half wanting to flee.

"It began six years ago," he said, looking at her directly now, his face disfigured by anxiety. Then he became calm, his thoughts moving more fluently. "I hadn't known Michel well my first years at Oxford. He was at Balliol—more a friend of Jean Dubois's than mine."

"Jean Dubois?" Allegra asked, for the name seemed only vaguely familiar.

"Véronique's stepson. He had come over once or twice for drinks, that was all. I had hardly ever seen Michel when I went to London, and perhaps only once or twice, when I'd gone to Paris. It wasn't until I came to New York, and went to Véronique's for dinner one night, that I really came in contact with him again.

"I remember it very well." He smiled distantly. "She had a small dinner, mostly people I knew, but I do recall entering the room and seeing Michel there, talking privately with her. I had no idea why he was in New York, and thought little of it. We talked during dinner. He knew I was at Atlantic Trust, and I told him the sort of work I was doing. He also seemed to know that I'd been handed the

Théron account, which was administered by the foundation of Michel's uncle, Lucien. He had made a fortune—a huge fortune—in the thirties, in coal and steel. I had heard Jean speak of him at great length—Michel, only once. He was a legend. Brilliant, self-made, from a small town in the provinces. Rocamadour, I think it was called.

"Lucien had set up the foundation in Monaco, for tax purposes. All that was well known. The money had been relegated to charities, universities, and a great deal of it to art, particularly to archaeology, which was Lucien's passion.

"I hadn't really understood Michel's connection to his uncle; I knew only that they had not been close. Lucien had lived on the Avenue Foch, Michel's family on the Left Bank. They might have lived in different cities; they hardly ever saw one another. Lucien had an enormous apartment, and a famous art collection. You must know some of his paintings?" She nodded, as Alexander continued, "They're in the Jeu de Paume, I'd seen them.

"I had told Véronique about some of my work on the Théron account; as it turned out, she had known the old man. It was she who told me that there had been a rift between Michel's father, Henri, and Lucien. Henri had not been nearly as driven or brilliant as the brother; he did well, but not as well as he would have liked. Michel's mother admired Lucien intensely. Henri knew it, and at one point discovered she was having an affair with him. When Henri found out, he went to Lucien's home and had it out with him. At the end, he took a knife from his pocket and slashed several of his brother's paintings—a Gauguin, a Picasso—Lucien was unable to restrain him, he was like a madman. They never saw each other again. Soon afterwards, Michel's father had a nervous breakdown. All of this was a huge scandal.

"I learned that Michel was only ten when this happened. I knew, too, that almost none of the money had passed on to Michel, when Lucien died ten years ago. His cousin, Philippe, and another uncle, Marc, had received part of it. The rest—about two thirds of the fortune—was put into the foundation. Michel's father had, in effect, been cut out of the will. Lucien had died childless."

Allegra, listening, thought of Michel's home on the Rue de Varenne, and of its quiet lugubrious rooms. Still she watched Alexander.

"Lucien's passion was art, as I told you. Art, and archaeology. He had begun to collect late in his life, but when he did, it was with a fanaticism that was legendary. He would phone curators in the middle of the night, Véronique told me. It was an obsession, she said. She had gotten to know the old man very well, you see." He smiled—a knowing, distasteful smile. "Lucien was fascinated by Heinrich Schliemann, the man who discovered Troy. Like him, he learned Greek, went to Turkey, and then to Pompeii and Herculaneum, as well. He donated enormous amounts of money to the excavations at Herculaneum. Much of what people know of it today is due to him.

"In the last years of his life, his interests had moved from Italy to Greece, and then to Turkey. He had given money to the digs at Ephesus and then—his last project—to Aphrodisias. He had met Nazif by that time—Nazif, who was almost as fanatical as he. Nazif had already won a reputation as a brilliant archaeologist, and had worked in Greece, as well as the British Museum. He got on well with Lucien, so well, in fact, that Lucien made him one of the trustees of the foundation. Not long afterwards, Nazif also succeeded in persuading Lucien to establish an account, which he would manage, in Switzerland—an account set aside for current excavations.

"Nazif had known Michel from London and Paris—they hadn't been close then. It was only after Lucien's death that they became great friends." A pause. "Michel respects Nazif, and somewhat fears him, strangely enough, and yet uses him. I'd sensed this, before, once when we had dinner together in London."

He wiped his brow. "I told you that it was six years ago that I first saw Michel again. The next day he called, and we had lunch. We talked about New York, and what was going on at Atlantic Trust. he himself was not working much. Managing his family's finances, he told me. I had sensed his rancor a long time ago when it came to the subject of Lucien—not only because of the money, for God knows Michel loves money, but from the shame that was connected with him, and with his mother. He will never forget it—the scandal, his father, the slashed paintings.

"He knew that I had been handling the account administered by the Théron Foundation. Various types of investments, most of them to end up as donations, funds for charities . . .

"At the end of the lunch, he told me that he had come to know Nazif quite well, and liked him. More than that, trusted him. 'That is not an easy thing for me to admit of any friend of my uncle,' I remember him saying. He made it a point to praise Nazif. Michel left for Paris several days later.

"The next week I heard from Michel again. He said he had spoken to Nazif and that he, Nazif, had mentioned that money was needed to complete one of the main projects at Aphrodisias, and that it was needed quickly. Then Michel asked me a favor—a favor in exchange for something he had once done for me . . ."

"What was that?" Allegra asked.

There was a pause before he replied, "It was at Oxford, my last year. I had some debts to pay—gambling debts, most of them from London. He lent me some money to pay them." She averted her eyes from his face, thinking of the night at the Casino, in Deauville, and how strange, how foreign his eyes had seemed . . . Then she heard his voice again. "Michel asked me whether I could transfer funds from the Théron account to the Swiss account managed by Nazif. For the Aphrodisias project, he said. It wasn't a lot—a quarter of a million dollars. That was small, when you considered the Théron Foundation—hundreds of millions of dollars.

"I hesitated, of course . . . I told Michel that I would like to help, but that I couldn't make such a transfer without proper authorization, it would be illegal. He didn't press me, but I could feel a sarcasm in his voice. Then I called Nazif. But after listening to me, he only reiterated the request, and said again that the money was needed immediately. Not only for the excavations, but for certain bribes necessary to complete the project. Baksheesh, so to speak. If the money wasn't received soon, the work would be delayed, perhaps for several years. I asked about the resolution from the other trustees, and he assured me that he would get them to agree in the near future. 'Don't be so Anglo-Saxon, my friend,' he told me, 'or you'll never get anywhere.' He hinted that he would make it worthwhile, that I would be taken care of. He then said he had spoken about me to Sharif Saud, a friend of his who had made a huge fortune in the arms trade.

He would recommend me as financial adviser to Saud's family, he told me. I said all right, I would do it, and authorized the transfer to his account." He lowered his voice.

"A few weeks later, I learned that a deposit of fifty thousand dollars had been made to my account in Switzerland. I couldn't understand it. It was an account that I had opened a few years before, almost as a joke. Véronique was the only one who knew about it. I had told her once that I considered a Swiss bank account to be the real sign of success. We had laughed about it. Soon afterwards, I opened it. She was the only person I had told.

"I began to suspect that the gift, so to speak, might have been from Michel and Nazif. I called Michel and asked him. 'A token of our appreciation,' was all he said. And then . . ."

"And you kept the money?" she asked, her eyes searching his.

"Yes." His voice was low, choked; not proud, not self-excusing, but quiet and realistic. "My father was dying. I had no one to turn to, and all his medical expenses to pay. My parents had no money. I took it." His head had gone deep into his hands, he was weeping.

"Please, Alex," she said, kissing his head. "Please."

But he continued, looking up, his face still red, gleaming with tears. "Six months later, I got another call from Michel, asking for another transfer. He was different this time. Cool. 'Look,' he said. 'Just tell me what percentage you want.' I told him I'd call back. The next day I did, and told him."

"What did you say?" she asked, suddenly thinking of Bermuda, and his long disappearances; the calls in Sardinia; his eyes, strangely excited, when he had told her of the risk he had taken in returning clandestinely to Argentina.

He did not answer.

"It went on for about two years; after that, I was better off, and my father—well, I had done what I could for him. I began to be uneasy. The accounts are audited very closely, and without the signature of the president—or a resolution from the trustees—it would have been nearly impossible to make the transfers . . ."

"Nazif had not gotten the trustees to agree, then?" she asked, all the while fearing the answer.

"No." Alexander's smile was ironic. "But I had gotten to know the president of the foundation—an old man who had been a confidant of Lucien—and, fortunately for me, an Oxonian. He trusted me, and let me do almost whatever I liked. There were never any questions. I was able to get his signature the second time, and then the next. It continued very smoothly"—here, a cynical smile. "Nazif got his payments, Michel his cut, and I . . . You must despise me, don't you?" He looked at her directly.

She took a deep breath, not daring to look at him too closely. "And when did all of this stop?"

"My cuts, or the transfers?"

"Both."

"I told Michel at the end of the third year that I wanted no more direct part of it, that it was becoming too dangerous. That surprised him. But I was in too deep. They could have blackmailed me if I had refused to continue the transfers."

"And what about Véronique?"

"What do you mean?"

"Did she know all about this—all the details?"

He hesitated. "Nearly all the details. I wouldn't trust her. And you see, Michel, Nazif, and I had been careful not to be seen too much together. Not to be associated." She looked down at the floor, suddenly remembering that lunch in the country, with Michel. "He doesn't like crowded New York restaurants," Alexander had said. And then it occurred to her: Michel was Mr. Sidney! She turned and asked Alexander if this were true.

"His code name," he said.

She heard the clock tick—a sound which had once been inaudible, but which now seemed deafening. There was a knock at the door; the butler, with a carafe of water. Alexander told him to leave.

"And the papers you had me sign?" she asked, taking his arm tightly, "Why?"

"I wanted it to seem as if I owned as little as possible. I was afraid." His hands swept over his head again; looking up, his eyes met hers. She said nothing, only thinking that the reason for the papers seemed desperate, almost demented. That he had betrayed the bank, that he had lied to her over and over again.

"And the money you asked me for?" Her eyes did not move from his face. "The money, Alex. Why the money?"

It was a moment before he answered. "To pay off Nazif," he said. "He had pressured me to make another transfer, and threatened to expose me when I told him I would not. I needed your help. I needed to placate him. You have never known what it is . . ." His voice drifted off. She kept thinking of Nazif, and suddenly recalled her first impression of his apartment, how its luxury and richness had surprised her. Now she understood.

The confusion and rage which had burned within her now slowly turned to weariness.

"Why has this come up now?" she finally asked, her voice exhausted.

"They were checking some of the transactions, a routine check. They saw some discrepancies. The president, the old man, had been replaced by someone else. I suppose that has to do with it." He paused. "They called me in just before I left."

"What do you mean?"

"David Riffner."

"What did he say?"

"That some irregularities had been discovered. He asked a few questions about the account. Nothing probing. He trusts me."

She said nothing, only slightly turning her head.

"They called me again, from New York, this evening," he said. "I've told Michel. I told him what has happened."

Thoughts ticked through her mind like the sound of the clock. Michel's absence from the wedding, the rushed trip to Bermuda. The telephone calls at Saint Moritz, the coins in his pocket when he went running. The white-outs in the date book . . .

"And now, what happens?" she asked.

"I don't know. I have to call the office tomorrow and speak with Riffner again."

"Who else knows about this?"

"You. Michel. Nazif. My lawyer."

"And no one else?"

"I am ruined, ruined," he kept saying. "Had I known then what I know now!" He gazed at her, a pitiful gaze that cut through her heart. "But you have no idea what it is to see your father dying, and not to be able to do anything. My mother, sacrificing everything . . ."

"Why did you never tell me about this, Alex? The phone calls, the time in Paris with Michel . . ."

"You would have left me."

She looked away, not able to bear to look at him. Her husband, Alexander, the man she had married!

"It has nothing to do with you, or with my love for you," he repeated, moving to her, and holding her head against him. "It was another time of my life, before I met you. One day you will understand." And then, again, "And I was so afraid of losing you." She felt his grip tighten. "Please," he said in a hoarse whisper, "don't leave me now. I need you."

There was silence—a silence broken by the ticking of the clock, a slow monotonous sound that seemed peculiarly relentless against the vortex of her feelings. Anger, that he had used and deceived her. Despair and compassion for him and what had led him to it. Even thrill that, at last, he really needed her. That he loved her. That it had not been her, or their marriage, but this that had caused the unhappiness of the last weeks.

"I need you," he said again, still holding her close. "Understand, Allegra!"

"You know I will try," she said, almost unable to speak.

"I know that." He kissed her feverishly. "Are you my love?"

She nodded, tears running down her cheeks.

41

They set sail for Ephesus the following afternoon—Alexander tense, Allegra quiet, Nazif fingering his gold watch as he stood on the quai, Mehmet solemnly behind him.

She was relieved to see Istanbul recede from view, as if, in departing, she were also escaping the troubles that the city, like a Pandora's box, seemed to have unloosed. His anguish. Her growing fear of him, her deepening distrust. The more she thought about the past, the more lies she discovered.

When at last they arrived at Ephesus, they walked without speaking through the ancient, hot-stoned city of marketplaces, brothels, and theaters. He was silent; she knew he saw nothing. Occasionally he would kiss her, or try to show some interest in the sights, but most often he was brusque, rebuffing her questions or comments. He looked constantly at his watch, waiting to reach a telephone.

So it was in Rhodes. Long walks up bougainvillea-trailed walls; a trip to a beach where they lay silently among rows of parched Scandinavians. And then to lunch, where again she waited and waited, only to find him, later, in a telephone booth at the post office, crescents of sweat under his arms as he spoke with his lawyer.

In bed, however, he remained gentle, as if the sexual domain were quite separate from what occurred elsewhere. There at least, she could still find the thread to the man she had originally fallen in love with. During the day, it had become increasingly difficult to recover it.

He had become nervous and paranoid, begging for her understanding and affection, yet often sarcastic and hostile, if she asked questions. One night on the boat, he demanded her diary of the trip, saying that he must destroy anything that indicated where he had been, or with whom they had met. She refused to give it to him, slamming the bedroom door, and weeping from exhaustion.

"If you won't support me in this all the way," he threatened, his voice low, his eyes enraged, "I'll divorce you!" She looked up in disbelief, hardly recognizing the face that had uttered those words (its dangerous eyes, and the curve of its mouth exacerbated by anger), and then fell to the bed, her head tossing, unable to fully comprehend the nightmare her life had become.

The following day she went to find the diary, for it had become something of a companion, filled with her notes and sketches. But it was nowhere to be found. She tore through the shelves, the closets, and searched beneath the bed. It was gone. He had thrown it into the sea.

They arrived at Heraklion, on Crete, one morning and drove to the Palace of Knossos, where cicadas hummed in deafening roars, as one searched for coolness within the bright walls of the Minoan ruin.

As she walked through the labyrinth of rooms, it seemed the palace only vaguely resembled what she had remembered. The colors had never seemed so garish; the ochers, the bright yellows, the vociferous reds. The shadows, slanting across the rooms, the sharp sounds of tourists' voices echoing from the walls.

Alone now, she came to the room with ancient frescoes of glancing-eyed, wasp-waisted Cretan women, their hair plaited in serpentine styles. The "Parisiennes," they were called. She suddenly thought of Véronique, and of the last time she had seen her. Her expression oddly knowing, triumphant. Véronique! It was she who had brought Alexander to this, and she who had ruined him. Allegra was certain. And yet he trusts her, she kept thinking.

How easy it would be, she now thought, to lose him here! She would go deeper, to the lower level, and there, within the maze of chambers, he would never find her. But everywhere she went it seemed that she knew from where she had come; and every time she thought she had truly lost him, she would emerge quite close to the place where he stood.

They drove across the Cretan countryside to the small port town of Kilatos. Farmers edged primitive wagons along the roads in the scorching sun; all the plants looked parched.

The Hotel Ariadne, at Kilatos, was separated from the town, and buried among trees. There was a main reception building, as well as a cluster of bungalows dotted along the sea. It was quiet when they arrived. The dining room was closed, for it was after lunch. Beyond, near the rocks, people sunbathed and swam.

They were shown to their bungalow; Alexander immediately did not like it. "I was told that it would be right on the water," he said, in an angry voice, to the maid. The porter, who held their bags, smiled meekly and shuffled off. With a glance at Allegra, Alexander turned and went to the concierge, hammering the desk with his fist, and demanding a better room. In a moment, he was handed another key.

At last, settled, she began to unpack, pushing loose strands of hair from her face as she did so.

"You don't like me to do those things, do you?" he said, turning to her, and watching.

"No. I don't like to hear you threatening people like that. I don't. The room wasn't so bad."

"But you like this one better."

"It's a better room, yes," she admitted quietly.

"It's just that you don't like what it entailed to get it, do you?"

"It wasn't worth it to me, no. It wasn't a happy way to start." She went on folding her clothes, putting them in drawers, afraid really to look at him.

"You don't know what's worth it, and what isn't. You don't know what the real world is like—you've never had to know!" His voice was bitter, even gloating. "You're so spoiled!"

She turned to him, watching how he leaned against the doorway; how he stood, staring, his eyes full of rancor. Unable to contain her fury any longer, she ran outside, down the hot stone steps, and then, to the water. He followed.

"I hate you, Alex!" she cried, turning around to him, and slapping him across the face. "I hate you!" He stood motionless, silent, his face still smarting, his arms gripped around her. "Leave me alone!" she cried, wrenching herself free. "Just leave me!" She felt around her neck for the amulet that had been her engagement present. "And this . . ." she said, ripping it from her, "I don't want it anymore, either!" She threw it out to the sea, and watched for a moment as the coral heart descended, curling down into the depths.

It was only after moments had passed that she realized what she had done. She stood, stunned, realizing that it was gone forever. Not knowing whether she had loved it, or whether she had wanted to rid herself of it; the two had seemed one and the same! She folded into a small, knotted heap on the ground and wept. She felt his hand on her neck, his lips on her cheek. "Please stop, my love, please stop," he murmured. "Allegra, I'm sorry. Please."

The beach was beautiful near the Hotel Ariadne, and seldom crowded with too many people. The view from the rocks was chiseled and picturesque: the white of the bungalows, a small barren island in the sea, beyond.

At first he left her alone most mornings, and then, increasingly, in the afternoons as well. She would wander and swim, or try to force herself to paint. The bag with her paints had remained closed until now, the brushes fallen into desuetude. One day, hesitantly, she opened it.

It was curious, after a few attempts, how the painting began to anesthetize the hurt. How it became easier, even pleasurable, to run to it. The flow of concentration would set in, and gradually, she would find it easier to locate the pocket of her mind which would be almost unassailably peaceful—a part of herself which Alexander could not reach, and which fed, paradoxically, on the anxiety that churned in the other.

The long days of Crete. His telephone conversations. (To Michel, once: "You don't think Nazif will talk, do you? How much do you really trust him?") The day when he bribed the concierge to destroy the records of his telephone calls. The other times when he would look relieved, even victorious, if all went well—his delight that no one might ever suspect what he had done.

Toward her, his mood swung—alternately loving and resentful, most vengeful when he was most anxious and threatened.

She had grown to fear the mornings most—the mornings which would come, and which she would confront, in Crete. And with them, on each day's awakening, the thought that haunted her: "I wish I had never married."

Each morning she would lie in bed, covered with the twisted sheets, her eyes fixed on the white ceiling.

Seven o'clock in the morning. Maids sweeping the tiled lobby; the concierge staring into the mirror as he fixed his tie.

In Allegra's room, bright light made its way through the slits of the shutters; all around her, the clicking sounds of insects. The cicadas, and the green snakes that slithered across the paths. She would glance, then, at the other bed: it lay empty, disheveled, no remembrance of the man who had slept there (Or had he? she would think). She would look at the ceiling (hot shadows, deepening, cutting into the white plaster) and then, again, at the other bed, its sheets tossed like disrupted waves. Where had he gone? she would ask herself, then thinking, To the post office, most likely. She would turn over on her side, thinking of other mornings, with their caresses, and of the warm mouth that had so often awakened her.

She lay still, perspiring, her hand by her forehead; the sheets, her nightgown, hot and moist, unbearable suddenly. Her hand, searching for the cool part of the pillow.

The sun. The silence. The deep white walls. She thought of the room, how empty it was, and how quiet; and suddenly of vacant-eyed blue figures out of Munch and Hopper.

Down the road from the Hotel Ariadne, in the port, the cafés were slowly opening up—dim doors that yawned to life with color and scent. Umbrellas twirling into bright colors; the smell of coffee. The first hint of the bleached white light which would take over the day. The sea blue, and calm; a lone swimmer in the distance, a few boats, nothing more. An occasional listless wave.

She lay on the bed and put her hand to her face; her body felt still and heavy, her throat parched. The sheets too comforting to abandon—to get up, to face the day, to face him. Even the shadows seemed disheveled, warped and crossed against the ceiling. Suddenly she ripped the covers from her, took the telephone, and ordered breakfast. For she had come to eat almost nothing during the day, and now she was ravenous.

Why are they taking so long? she thought, as she waited. Still, no footsteps. Nothing but the salamanders scurrying. Breakfast had not yet come: that eagerly anticipated tray of honey, milk, and toast—the comforting food of childhood.

That it's come to this, she suddenly thought—her honeymoon, a cortege of famished mornings.

She turned to look at his bed and remembered the times when she had desired him—how distant they seemed now! Still, she had not grown accustomed to the fear, and the indifference, and the way she inwardly recoiled when he touched her. There were moments—mostly at night, after some wine—when she could almost lull herself into wanting him. Not out of real desire, but out of reassurance, as if the mere wanting would obliterate the rest. Love-making had turned into an act she hardly recognized—the grim thrill of sex, as tantalizing as a sword-box.

Had her memory not been so keen, these silent alone awakenings might not have tortured her so much. But it was always the vivid recollections of other times—when he had been tender and loving— that pursued and confused her, and made the loss more aching. "Come here," he would say (she smiled, now, thinking of it), enfolding her in his arms. "I need to protect you." A brusqueness, a serviceability had entered into it now: he would take her and leave her, wordlessly. The quiet terrified her.

The room seemed ominously still and empty. She moved her hand across the pillow, and then to her forehead, to wipe away the beads of perspiration. Her mind was hazy, her eyes thick and heavy, her lashes wet with tears. She looked exhausted, yet she had slept.

And then, once more, she thought of other times, and of sex, and whether it was not this terrible need, in the first place, that had brought her to this. To marrying him. A failure after two weeks!

"The romance is over," he had told her. And with it, too, she now thought, all those other moments; images that moved like slow figures across a hillside—deep embraces and kisses at unexpected instants, or others throughout the hazy-motioned night. Now he had assumed a bitter smile she did not like. The desultory kisses on the airplane to Athens; the way he had left her alone in Istanbul, in Rhodes, and now, in Crete.

How stupid I was, she suddenly thought. The telephone calls. Mr. Sidney. Why didn't I suspect?

There was a knock at the door. The young man, with her breakfast. He wore a white jacket and had a youthful stance, his eyes clear and bright. He was good-looking; she had noticed that the first morning.

"*Efkaristò*," she said, knotting the robe at her waist, and pushing some strands of hair from her face.

He looked at her curiously, saying nothing, but his eyes conveyed the strangeness of the scene: this slender young woman, alone in a silent white room. She felt his eyes, as if they were accusing her—of being alone, a bride alone on her honeymoon. (No doubt they would be snickering about that, in the kitchen. Room X. Strange goings-on; this they would be saying, in Greek.)

He put down the tray. As he did, she wondered, watching him, whether he had a lover. And then she thought, what sort of woman seduces waiters, gondoliers, taxi drivers? In books, in films, not in real life, surely?

She was happy to hear the door shut, as if it shut her off from herself. Glad that he had left her here, alone, with the tea and toast, and the honey which supposedly came from Mount Hymettus (although now she did not believe it, she did not believe anything). Quickly spreading the napkin on her lap, she began to eat swiftly, the crumbs falling to the side. She licked some jam from the knife, then sliced open an orange, gripping it with her teeth until the acid juices flowed down her throat.

From the terrace outside, she could already feel the heat of the sun. She brushed a strand of hair from her face, and then a tear, and then another; brushing them back, again and again, softly, then angrily, sipping the tea until the tears ran into the cup.

She had come to want to die.

More than once at the Hotel Ariadne, she had wandered into the bathroom, clutching the bottles of sleeping pills, aspirins; labels marked with skull and crossbones, and warnings about overdoses. They would come in the morning, and occasionally at dusk, these terrible thoughts; and he would find her here, before the bathroom cabinet, her thin face reflected in the mirror, shaking the vials and gazing at them, like a young madwoman. Seeing him, she would hurriedly shove them back inside. Until now.

Not back yet, she thought. He must be telephoning, still.

She put on the same clothes she had worn the day before, and headed to the beach.

It was the sea that saved her—the icy, opalescent womb into which she plunged, compulsively. She dove in, greedily feeling the water around her and smoothing back her hair, as the cold throbbed around her throat; then emerging to feel her hands, and then her feet, on the hot stones of the path that circled the sea. She clutched the basket with her sketchpads and paints; they had become her companions now, and seldom left her side . . . So vacant were the mornings here, so still, that one seemed to hear the sun beating on the white cottages, and the paths. The other guests, still closeted in their rooms, had not yet appeared.

No one ever asked her who she was, or why her husband was never with her.

By now the early morning coolness had ended, and the sun beat on her skin. She walked to the edge of the water and dove in again, the cold bringing her to life, her arms moving against the current, her hair streaming in one piece. He can't reach me here, she kept thinking—still wishing, even so, that he would want to try. She plunged deeper, deeper into the sea, the colors here more intense and sapphirelike. Holding her breath, she glanced through the water, with its prismatic life: the shadows of a school of fish, and beyond, the outlines of a labyrinth of coral, its lacy phantasmagoric shapes spotlit by the sun . . . She edged closer to it, fascinated by its beauty, all the while knowing that it could cut her . . . In a moment, kicking her feet, she would be sucked to the surface, emerging with a brisk movement and then up again, propelling herself to the top, so that the rays of sun hit her back and her arms, windmilling through the water.

Yet she could not stop thinking of the day before, when he had taken her in a small boat to the island beyond. She had grown frightened. I know too much, it had suddenly occurred to her; all it would take would be one push. He could say it was an accident.

She began to swim faster, her arms pulling her through the water—faster, more furiously.

Her skin glistening, she dried herself and gathered her things.

She set up a canvas with a sketch she had begun the day before, and then, with a flick of her hand, began to paint, almost forgetful of him, at that moment, and of his new smile . . . The touch of a sky; the foamy top of a wave. The sea before her was calm, and yet, in her painting, it was disturbed and ominous—choppy waves where they were tranquil, the water a sinister green rather than its clear, light-shot aquamarine.

Almost every afternoon, she would lunch alone. There was a small restaurant nearby that was attached to the hotel. Everything about it was a clear and constant white: the walls, the jackets of the waiters, the tablecloths, and the sun streaming through the windows. A table in one corner would invariably be reserved for a family who would usually appear about the same time as Allegra. She thought they were Swedish. The woman—the mother, the wife—was very handsome; tendrils of blond hair, bleached by the sun, blew around her face. There was nothing in the least equivocal about her happiness. Her husband; her home, surely. Her children, who chirped in their foreign tongue like beautiful little birds. One day they were showing photographs of themselves on holiday, as Allegra arrived. Laughing and talking, they looked at her and, at one moment, raised a glass of wine. She was seized by an aching sadness, and then by jealousy, and then by anger, but most of all by a cutting sense of failure and shame. "He humiliates you in public," Harry had told her. But she had not wanted to listen.

To be alone had seemed too terrifying, until she had confronted this.

She wished the afternoon would pass; that was all she had come to expect from it. The sea, crowded with people; the occasional whiff of tanning oil; the colors of bright umbrellas that tinted the smooth backs of the toffee-skinned women. Beyond, by the harbor, the water churned with children and rafts.

She returned to the room to find it chaste, silent, and empty. On a table, the skin of an orange, now devastated and juiceless. The beds smooth, uncreased, it seemed, of their troubled nights. Fresh flowers in a vase; a maid-created anonymity with everything in order.

There was still no sign of him.

A guidebook to Crete lay on the table. It had a bright blue cover with huge yellow letters, and a photograph of a "Parisienne." Again she thought of Véronique—how could Allegra not have suspected? Véronique who knew of the account in Switzerland, Véronique who knew David Riffner and had him come to dinner; Véronique, inscribing the catalog in her worldly hand.

She went outside and walked up the paths, drifting into the lobby, with its high ceiling, its fan, and its rows of magazines in languages she did not understand. The concierge would assume his unctuous pose and officious smile.

Seven o'clock in the evening. A moon, clear and white, incised in the sky. She began to get dressed—dressed in the bright, hopeful clothes she had chosen for the honeymoon.

The telephone rang. Allegra picked it up, thinking that it might be Alexander. Instead, a ragged click. The clock struck eight.

Old fears, new fears, began to batter her one by one. The fear about having lost what she loved . . . She went to the terrace, and then to the bed, taking a flower from the vase and tearing the petals apart, bit by bit, as she thought: What is this aloneness that men don't seem to fear, or even understand; or if they do, it's not so harrowing to them. Not to men.

She decided to try and call the Fitzpatricks, picking up the telephone and asking the operator to reach the number.

"Allegra!" A strong voice, calling her from the door. She jumped; it was Alexander. He stood at the doorway, his tone harsh, accusatory, his eyes mocking and dark.

"There you are, daydreaming again," he said, walking into the room.

"Where were you?"

For a moment he did not answer. "In town," he finally said. "So you're checking up on me, now? That was supposed to come later, not after two weeks."

"I've been alone all day."

"So have I."

The telephone rang. She answered it. "Your New York number has come through," the operator said. For a moment Allegra listened to the ringing, but then—seeing Alexander's eyes—hung up.

"It's time to go to dinner," he said. "Are you ready?"

"Yes."

He looked at her appraisingly. "I don't like that dress."

She made no move to change it, merely watching as he went into the bathroom, where he stood by the sink, washing and washing his hands. She saw them twisting with foam—the hands that she had originally disliked.

Again the telephone rang. She moved to answer it, but he reached it first. His voice was subdued now, his answers curt. She dared not ask who it was.

Moments passed. Fixing his tie, he stood before her with an absent gaze.

"Alex," she said, gently taking his arm, "come, let's go and have a drink."

He looked at her sarcastically. "A drink? Why? You don't drink."

She turned away, her eyes filled with tears, and then sank to the bed, her head buried in her hands.

He took them, kissed them, brushing his lips against her cheek as he said, "My wife, my beautiful wife . . ."

And so, with those words, he would win her; for they would kindle a relief, and a hope, within her. That perhaps he still loved her, that he had never meant to hurt her; and that he had never lied to her.

Her hand was in his when they went to dinner.

One night, when the moon had lent their room an eery light, Allegra stood by the door in a thin nightgown, her back turned to him, a few strands of hair blowing. The sky was particularly beautiful that night, the moon chalk-white.

She thought he had gone to sleep, but then she felt his hand, and then his breath, and at last his mouth, soft but insistent now, as he kissed her neck, her cheeks, her breasts—sucking her nipples from the silk of the nightgown. Why this now, so suddenly, she wondered, for in lovemaking, too, she had grown suspicious. Closing her eyes, she wondered whether it was wrong to give in to the mindless pleasure; if it were all right to let desire run its course apart from the rest, from what she feared was so.

Still he held her from the back, stroking her between her thighs, and then, bending over again, so that his mouth enclosed the roundness of her breasts, and then her nipples, tensed now, deeper in color.

The smooth bed waited for them, as if it knew—as she did—what the gruffness in his voice had meant. His eyes were already filled with all the elsewhereness of sex.

He held her tightly, whispering to her and asking—and yet, no question, this—whether she was ready for him.

She was silent—repelled by his voice, his gestures, his hands. Suddenly she felt each part of her locking itself against him, room by abandoned room. Even now, as he touched her, she held her breath, for she did not want to lose herself in him, or ache for him to touch her, or feel her senses choke with desire and pleasure. I wonder if he knows, she thought; he must. But he continued to kiss her harder on the mouth, almost biting her; and then on the neck; but still she felt nothing. No moisture between her legs; no warmth at the thighs; no sweet aching chills as he kissed and kissed her . . . She stood before him out of habit, but her mind and body were sealed against him, against the hurt, against the suspicions of those weeks, with their silent walks and dinners, their lonely still afternoons.

He had begun to suspect it. "Allegra," he kept murmuring, "my wife, my lovely wife . . ." She turned from him as she felt his tongue, probing and licking her ear, her neck.

He pulled the nightgown up to her waist—she, desperate, not knowing what to do, looking at the ceiling . . .

His hands clutched her waist, as she fought them off. But still, he grabbed her, stroking her more furiously, then parting her thighs and touching her. "You're still dry," he said threateningly, as if she had disobeyed him. He began to stroke her more furiously. "Take this off," he told her. "Go over there and spread your legs for me."

She shook her head. "No," she said, backing away. "Not now. Not now, Alex." The moon had thrown maze-patterns of light against the walls; she thought of Knossos.

Suddenly his arm tightened around her; his eyes had grown fierce. "Get on the bed," he commanded her again. "Now."

"Not tonight!" she cried.

"That's not up to you," he said, throwing her down, so that her head grazed the table; she could feel herself bleeding. "Please, Alex, no!" she cried again, her voice desperate.

He pulled her up from the floor, and as he did the flower vase fell to the ground and shattered; now the broken bits lay by her feet. He began to drag her to the bed. She felt the glass cutting into her foot, and screamed, but he clapped her mouth shut, so that no sounds could escape.

He flung her on the bed; blood stained the pillow slip; she was crying. "Please, Alex, stop it . . ." Her face, turning away from his kisses and his wine-stenched breath. "You must always want me, be ready for me," he told her, close to her ear. "Not just at the beginning. Always."

Proud, commanding, he knelt before her on the bed, forcing her to look at him. She turned away, but he pulled her toward him again, with his hand. Never had he seemed so hard, immense, gorged with lust. He pulled her mouth to his penis and had her take him, thrusting himself down her throat; she felt she was choking, choking, that everything was spinning darkness, no light, no escape.

The shadows had darkened from black to purple.

He pushed her down, holding her shoulders so that they faced one another. Her terror, his distended face. Now she turned her mouth away, for his lips, too, seemed foreign and unfamiliar. They disgusted her. He began to cut her mouth with kisses; she went chilly with pain, praying that he would stop. But he continued to press her with kisses that were not kisses, but transmuted into other gestures—vengeful, wound-resembling.

"Are you ready for me?" he asked, holding down her hands.

She started to scream, but again he clapped her mouth shut.

"Do you want me?" he said again.

Her eyes gave him no response. She tried to wrest herself away, but he pushed her onto the bed, forcing himself into her, pulling her pelvis against him to take her more closely. She felt the searing pain of the dryness, and cried for him to stop, but he kept moving more furiously, more insistently, until she felt nothing, only exhaustion and silence.

He flung her to the side, until he had turned her over, her stomach on the bed, grasping her buttocks to him. He stroked her between the thighs; she felt her face, chafed by the sheets, and the tears being rubbed dry, and the stopped screams within her. Still he stroked her hard, as if to flay her, again and again between the thighs.

He turned her around again—her head tilting back listlessly—and told her to suck him. "Take it," he said, but she only kept shaking her head, and spat it out. Now she was no match for his strength, or his fury. He began to kiss her hard, wanting to excite her, but only making her bleed. He touched her again and again, his hands gripping her shoulders as he moved into her, filling and thrusting into her as he watched her deadened face, its closed eyes with their tight fringe of wet lashes, her bruised neck and bleeding mouth.

Suddenly she heard the door close; her hand moved across the bloodstained sheets.

Then, across her mind's eye, stalked a procession of emptiness. A black velvet curtain slowly grazing a stage. No light. Nothing. As if she had entered the cave's darkest part.

42

It was late—nearly midnight—when Emily began to write. She had been standing by the window looking into the garden, out at the sky; and then, contemplatively, she took up her pen.

"July 30.

"I have just seen Allegra Clayton—yes, no longer Allegra Para! I hardly recognized her when we met at the Chinese restaurant (the little sordid one, around the corner). How she has changed! It is in her eyes that I noticed it most, for she has grown older so suddenly; it took my breath away, when I first saw her ravaged face. She had rung me up yesterday and asked if I would have dinner. Of course I said yes.

"When I think of seeing her for the first time! That face, with its odd beauty, and her almost girlish ways. There is hardly a trace of that left (except for the hair, which is beginning to grow long again). In a way it saddens me, all these changes, for she has grown very very thin, and her arms look so frail. 'The Fitzpatricks tell me I've got to eat,' she said, picking at her dinner. She has been staying with them since she left Alex.

"Of course I knew what had happened; everyone does, or *thinks* he does. And then one hears whisperings about it in the most unlikely places. At Bookends, the other day; and once, at Millefleur, when I stopped to inquire about Allegra from Maggie. Two matrons came in and started to gossip about it. I began to say something to them, but Maggie—with an uncharacteristically fierce look—gripped my arm and said, 'No. *Please.*' Of course, everyone now delights in saying how suspicious they were of Alex in the first place. In fact, this was not so. He was invited everywhere, and much-praised.

"A strange end for him, who was held up as such a bright, promising man. It seems they returned from Greece and he was suspended immediately from his job at Atlantic Trust. He submitted his resignation shortly thereafter; apparently he has returned to South America. He is ruined here, that's certain, but no doubt he will turn up again.

"As I said, we met at the restaurant. I was very glad to see Allegra. 'Maggie and Charles have been good to me,' she said, sitting on one of those ghastly red vinyl chairs. 'I'm so sorry,' I said, somewhat duplicitously. For I'm not really at all, and she knows it. It would never have worked; Alex was terrible for her; and I'm sure it was only in the end, when he had destroyed everything he loved most, that he realized what he had done. I told her that. 'He had a genius for destroying your confidence,' I said. 'You seldom read, or painted, or laughed.' I could see her flinch when I described him in those terms— in a peculiar way, she does not like to hear anyone speak ill of him.

"She smoked a great deal during dinner, and drank only a bit of her wine. I, on the other hand, was famished, and polished off everything.

"She asked about my book. I said that it was starting to go better— which is true—and that I had a new idea which seemed to be turning it around. 'That's wonderful,' she said, with that look of hers. 'I can't wait to read it.' And then, leaning forward, 'You must continue, Emily. I have such a feeling about it!' That touched me, although it gave me a twinge of guilt, as well.

"Still skirting the issue of the abortive marriage, I asked about Sotheby's, for she returned there after her leave of absence. 'Oh, thank God for my job!' she said. 'It has helped so much. I've been working like mad, and feel like a sinner who's come back penitent, and willing to do anything to be absolved. They've given me lots and lots to do—cataloging, appraisals, anything. And Harry, too—what a friend!' A slight pause. 'I happened to be having lunch at a funny little French restaurant last week, and I saw a painting on the wall. I thought, that's a Gérome! I asked the owner about it. He told me he'd bought it in Paris, at the flea market. I told him we should take it to Sotheby's . . . It *is* a Gérome, quite a good one. Harry was appalled, though he was proud that I spotted it.' She smiled. 'Harry happens to loathe Gérome and thought this one—a portrait of an Arab horseman—was especially cloying. He told me it was better off in a second-class bistro!'

"The food came. Her eyes drifted into a long, absent gaze, and then she finally said, 'You know, Emily, perhaps I knew—at least subconsciously—all about Alex, without his ever telling me a thing. Maybe I simply didn't want to recognize it.' I said nothing. 'I think *you* knew about him,' she said, 'from the beginning. You never liked him, but believe me, there were parts to Alex that I . . . You see, I had loved him!' But here she stopped, as if a thought had just occurred to her. Her voice lowered. 'Emily, did you ever have an affair with Alex?' No, I quickly replied (unlike her, I'm an able liar). I asked what had prompted the question. 'Things you had said about him, and that he had said about you, that's all. Just a vague feeling I've had.' Mercifully, she let the subject drop.

" 'What really happened?' I asked then, as if there were actually an answer to that question. She told me about the trip, and the first night in Athens, and his strange behavior; and each stop, in the Aegean Islands, with his growing more feverish, more fearful, and more brutal. 'I learned about it bit by bit,' she said. 'At first, I simply couldn't understand. I thought it was because he was trying to escape from me, and that he hated being married, and having a wife. I had no idea it was guilt, or rather, I should say, fear. I don't think he ever really felt guilty. And in the end, when I realized that, I knew I would have to leave him.'

"She leaned back in the chair, tilting her head to the side. 'I began to realize, in Crete, that it was hopeless. There was one night, when the moon was full and bright; I'd hurt my foot . . .' Here, she stopped and then said quickly, as if something were too painful to relate, 'I'd stepped on some coral and cut my foot, when I was swimming . . . I knew that night it was the end, as if my body were telling me what my mind wanted to deny.

" 'Several days later, we flew to Athens. We'd left the boat and took a plane from Heraklion. When we got our suitcases back, mine was splashed with cheap wine. A bottle of retsina must have spilled on it somewhere. My dresses inside were all stained. They stank, and I said something about it. Alex yelled at me, and said all I cared about were such things—my dresses, my wedding. I wept. We returned to the Hotel Victoria, and again he met with Michel.

" 'All during that time I tried to keep sketching and painting; somehow, I found that it helped—just as you had said! And it was that, together with the fact that my scar had been removed—that it had not been irreparable—that helped me get through. Gave me courage, somehow, a certain freedom. Still, there were moments when I was so frightened of him, afraid he might hurt me.' Her face had gone white, her hands against her cheeks. 'The next day, in Athens, he took me to Demeter, a jewelry shop on University Street.' I said I knew their things—great barbaric pieces, copied from ancient Greek designs. 'I couldn't understand it,' she continued, 'since all during the trip he had been castigating me about money. And here, suddenly, he wanted to buy me a present. "The wedding present I never gave you," he said. We went to the shop, and he asked me what I liked. I saw a pair of earrings carved like ancient shells in rock crystal, edged in gold. "No," he said, "I want you to get something *all* gold." Then it dawned on me—it wasn't a present he wanted to buy me, but something he could buy with his European money, and sell off later! He had an account in Switzerland, you see . . .

" 'All those things started to occur to me: the way he always paid cash, the way he spent money so freely in Europe . . .

" 'He was suspended immediately, when we returned. I have never seen anyone so distraught, and yet in such a silent way. It would have been better had he wept. But he did not. I felt for him, even though, by that time, I neither trusted him, nor loved him anymore. All I could think of was that he had cheated the bank, he had lied again and again to me. Still, when he would ask, "You're not going to leave me now, when I need you, are you?" I felt as if a knife had gone through my heart.

" 'I still didn't know what to do. I kept thinking that this was not really happening, and that, if it was, it was not happening to *me*.

" 'That was a Thursday,' she said slowly, looking at me with those blue eyes. 'The next day, we went to Sagaponack. Silently, in the car, I told him what I thought about Véronique. That she had set him up in this and ruined him. She had asked David Riffner questions, she had made him suspicious, I was sure. Alex wouldn't listen, though. We arrived at the house. There were some old phone messages on a table. I picked them up. Mr. Sidney, they said—Michel's code name. And then—then I realized that this had continued all through the time we were engaged, and married! He had told me that all of this had been in his past. But it was greed that had gotten him into this, not his parents! I thought of the phone calls, and the expensive clothes, and the trips, and the Jaguar, and I knew that here, too, he had lied!

" 'I confronted him with it. "I never told you otherwise," he said, his voice as cool as crystal. "I never misled you," he told me. He had no conscience!

" 'I went into the bedroom, weeping. As much as I distrusted him, and knew there was no chance for this to ever be, I still could not really face it, and kept hoping, in an absurd way, that he would come and kiss me, and comfort me. But this time he did not. An hour or so later, I went into the living room. He lay on the couch, with a blanket pulled over him, trying to sleep. I asked if he was coming to bed. "No," he said. "If I'm going to be alone, I might as well get used to it . . ." ' Her voice had gone quite low, almost choked.

" 'The next day, things got worse. I came back to the house and found a note he had left me. I stood there, shaking, just at the sight of his handwriting! And then I made my decision: that I would never, ever live in such fear again, and that I would end this.

" 'We returned to the city. That night, I came home and found another note, saying that he had an appointment with his lawyer. That he would be back later. I felt desperate—desperate, and still haunted by Véronique, and wanting to know what she had done.

" 'It was seven o'clock by then. I took a cab to Véronique's apartment. Her doorman knew me, and let me up without announcing me first. When the elevator opened, the door to her apartment was just ajar. I thought that was strange. I went in, anyway, and then down the hall to her bedroom'—here, her voice faltered—'inside, I could hear her and Alex talking, could see them reflected in the mirrored screen that stood in front of the bedroom door. Véronique sat on the edge of the bed, swinging her foot, Alex pacing up and down. She looked very pale without her makeup, almost sickly. He was questioning her—asking about David Riffner, what she had told him, when she had him come to dinner, what questions he had asked. Once or twice he stopped, taking her shoulders very tightly, shaking her. She denied everything. "I never lied to you," she said. "Never. You know that." Still, he kept questioning her. Finally he sat down. I could see he was exhausted.

" 'Then Véronique asked him about me—the girl, she said, Allegra. "She's going to leave me," he said. I heard his voice crack. Véronique's expression became strange, eery. "You don't need her anymore," she told him. "You got the money, the cover. You got what you wanted out of it, as you said you would, from the beginning." ' Allegra looked up, straight into my eyes, with a pitiful expression. 'Oh Emily, if you *knew* what I felt when I heard that! I wanted to die, I wanted to kill myself! . . . But still I stood there, frozen, outside the door, watching Alex's face and hers!

" 'Then very quietly Alex said, "I never wanted it to happen this way. I loved Allegra." Véronique smiled in that awful way of hers. "You're lying, Alex, you know that. And you know I know that." He saw her face, and her terrible eyes, and suddenly he said, "What's the matter, Véronique—didn't Michel give you a large enough cut?" The next second she had sprung to her feet, grabbing a letter opener on the table, and went for his eyes. But he caught her hand, and threw her down, screaming, on the bed. "You had it out with Riffner, didn't you?" he cried, while her nails cut into his face. "You betrayed me, you whore!" I fled down the corridor and went downstairs, where I called Maggie from the nearest phone booth. She came immediately and helped me get some of my things from Alex's apartment, both of us terrified that he might come and find us there! But luckily we escaped in time. She took me home with her.

" 'He guessed where I was, though, and the next evening he came to see me, at the Fitzpatricks'. Charles came to tell me. "Your husband is here," he said. My husband! I never had a husband! They showed him up.

" 'I was shocked when I saw him. He'd been weeping, and his

clothes were all rumpled, his eyes red. He was so nervous, too! I had never seen Alex nervous—brushing his face with his hands, crying, asking me not to leave him.' She stopped for a moment. 'Oh Emily— he *repelled* me! I felt my heart cleft in two, the pain was so great; I wanted to comfort him, I felt for him, and yet I knew I no longer loved him. I just pitied him. "Don't you still love me?" he asked, his eyes like a child's. I felt my throat stop, and all I could do was shake my head and whisper, "No." She had started to weep, burying her head in her hands, and I didn't know what to do. I gave her a napkin to stop up her tears. In a curious way, I felt both for him, and for her.

"But she continued compulsively, talking through her tears. 'And then, before he left, he turned to me and said, "This is an Allegra I don't know." And I said, "There are many Allegras you don't know." '

"I poured her some more wine, trying to comfort her, for she was still crying. 'Alex called Harry that same night,' I told her. 'Harry never liked Alex, but he couldn't bear to tell you. Harry only saw him because he sounded desperate, almost suicidal.' I said that when they had met, Alex had told him, 'Don't worry, I won't kill myself. It's not my style.'

"She said nothing for a moment, as if she were reenacting the scene in her mind. I asked her to continue. 'The next day,' she said, 'after a sleepless night, I walked to work. Alex was waiting for me on the corner of Madison Avenue and Seventy-sixth Street. He looked so pathetic! "I'm not asking you to return," he said, "just come and have a cup of coffee with me." I began to cry and said, no, no I couldn't.

" 'At work, all I could think of was his face, and his voice. I needed to speak with someone. I called the Monsignor who had married us, and said I needed to talk with him, and could he see me for a moment. I explained why. No, he said, he couldn't. It would be a waste of my time and yours, he told me. Then he hung up.' Her voice had taken on a bitterness I had never heard before.

" 'The papers have been drawn up,' she told me. 'Divorce doesn't take much time, you know.' I asked on what grounds it was being granted. 'Mental cruelty,' she said.

"She was still terribly shaken up, as I was, too. She reached for a cup of tea, spilling it over her skirt and leaping up, so that she wouldn't be burnt by the scalding stuff. A fitting conclusion!

"I asked what had happened to Alex since. 'I don't know where he's gone,' she said. 'He's left for Europe, they say. I hear there was a woman who came to stay with him awhile, and helped him to pack up. I don't know. There's so much I don't think I will ever know.'

"She lowered her voice, and looked at me directly. 'Sometimes I wonder whether he didn't marry me just because he thought I knew too much. What do you think, Emily? Do you think he ever really loved me, or do you think he only meant to use me?' No, I said, it wasn't for that, but then how could I ever tell her otherwise? It would be too cruel.

"She paid the bill, which was kind, for she knows I never have any money. We began to walk home and arrived not long afterward at my building. The half-moon lit up her face, and I saw her eyes, the pale skin, and the wide, trembling mouth. And suddenly I wished everything one would want for her—a husband, a child, fulfillment in her painting.

"We said good-night; I told her to go and get some rest."

PART FOUR

PART FOUR

43

"What about this one?" Maggie asked, gazing at a brooding Manet portrait of a gypsy. "Don't you think it's marvelous?" It was late September; the three women were looking at paintings in a gallery at the Metropolitan Museum.

Emily and Allegra came up beside her to look at the gypsy's mesmerizing face. "Well, you know what they say about gypsies," Emily said, with a sly look.

"What?" asked Maggie.

Emily whispered in her ear; Maggie went red, her eyes wide. "Emily," said Allegra, shaking her head, "what are you telling her?"

"The gospel truth," she replied, with an impish smile.

Allegra raised her eyebrow. "Don't believe a word of it, Maggie," she said, moving to the next picture. "It's all invention."

They came to the Twachtman painting of the reeds, one of Allegra's favorites. "It reminds me of your country house," she said to Maggie, looking at its gentle colors, and the wistful motion of the tall grass.

They continued to move from one painting to another, Allegra telling the history of one, or an anecdote about its provenance. Finally they came to the wing with Renaissance paintings, which was empty. The guard stood against one pillar, looking decidedly uncomfortable.

Suddenly Allegra said—as if addressing both friends, and yet as if she were thinking aloud, for the events of that summer were never far from her mind—"You know, it's so strange. I've been married and divorced—all in one summer—and yet all these men I used to know are calling me now. For dates." She wrinkled her nose, as if she had uttered a distasteful word. "You'd think they'd be frightened. Instead, it seems almost a plus. Why, do you think?"

"It's because you're so pretty," said Maggie, who had been looking at a Madonna by Crivelli. "Besides, everyone knows what happened."

Emily shot a glance in her direction. "Don't be ridiculous. Allegra, don't you see? Now at least they know you can screw—before, who could have been sure? For all they knew, you were just some overachieving virgin, marching around trying to figure out who painted which ear in that Botticelli." She nodded to one opposite. Allegra was laughing. "Emily! You've always got an explanation for everything."

The guard, looking in their direction, asked them to quiet down. Maggie, in the meantime, had wandered to a triptych by Fra Angelico.

"Emily," Allegra asked, in a whisper, "do you think it's really possible to know someone else? I mean to *really* know, what they are, and what they're really thinking, and to be so close that—"

"I doubt it," said Emily, interrupting her. "And if you did, you probably would never fall in love with him. It's the distance and sense of risk that creates the electricity—not one self that falls in love, but one of several, don't you see? Besides, you always love what you cannot quite have, or aren't totally sure of knowing. Don't you think that was true of Alex?"

"I don't know," Allegra answered. And then, as an afterthought, "So that you can never *quite* merge!" She paused. "Sex is such a deception . . . Of course, who knows, if you're really lucky . . ." But her thoughts dwindled off, as they tended to, these days, and her brow furrowed. "Where's Maggie?" she asked suddenly.

"Over there," Emily said, pointing to Maggie, who stood before a Bronzino portrait of a young nobleman.

"Come," Allegra said, moving toward her.

"It was impossible to ever really know Alex," said Emily, her footsteps echoing. "Do you think anyone ever did? You, or Véronique, or Michel, or any of you? I doubt it."

"Sometimes I thought Michel did, but who knows? Alex was brought up to survive, and he grew up in a place where, in order to survive, you had to lie and scheme. Or do you think that's just excusing him?"

"Could you ever forgive him?" Emily asked.

"No. And yet I don't hate him." She looked down at the ground, and then up at the painting before her—a huge, beribboned sky by Tiepolo. She thought of Venice, and of the moment when she had looked below the Bridge of Sighs. "If I had known then," she said to herself. And then, to Emily, "Come on, let's go."

Maggie left them at the corner of Park Avenue, hugging Emily to say good-bye, for Emily was to leave in a few days for Paris, where she had decided to live and finish her book.

"What about your job?" Allegra asked, crossing the street.

"I've left it. Or at least I've taken a leave of absence."

They spoke about Emily's book. It remained a mystery still, for she would not disclose its new plot. "I'm superstitious," Emily would say. "You'll read it when you read it." She mentioned Paris, and where she would live, and when—if ever—she would return. "I've no idea," said Emily. "I don't think about it much."

Emily's apartment was more helter-skelter than usual. Heaps of clothing lay on the bed; worn suitcases, plastered with the stamps of foreign countries, stood gaping open and ready to be filled. Emily took Allegra's jacket and put it on a chair; the cat scampered to it. "Go away, Simon!" she said.

"I thought her name was Damedith," said Allegra, looking at the cat.

"Well, it was," Emily said, with a shrug of her shoulder. "But I got rather bored with it, so I changed it to Simon. Easier on the tongue. She *looks* more like a Simon, wouldn't you say?"

Allegra looked hard at the cat, who was moving toward the cluttered desk. "You don't think this might give him, her a complex?" She sat down, an amused expression on her face. "Female, then male . . ."

Emily cut in, her voice edged with disbelief. "You don't really imagine that animals have any sexual identity, do you? Of course they *fuck*, but I don't think they actually think about it."

"You don't give animals much credit, do you?" said Allegra, drawing up her feet on the sofa.

"No." Emily watched the cat lope into the bedroom. "No, I don't. In fact, I'm not even sure I like animals, which is probably my most atypically English characteristic." She stopped for a moment, lighting a cigarette, her ringed hands in the air. "But then Anglo-Saxons are such maniacs about animals. When I lived in London, there was a family next door with a dog and a little child, a girl. Every so often the dog would take a terrible bite out of the child's face, and off the parents would trot with the kid, to the local doctor, to be stitched up. Well, I happened to meet the doctor once, and I said to him, 'Why the hell don't they get rid of the dog?' He just shrugged. 'They won't,' he said."

"That would never happen in Italy," Allegra said. "They'd *shoot* the dog first."

"True. I've never thought of Wops as being very dog-conscious. Anyway, if Simon didn't have such an exemplary personality, and hadn't been through so much with me—well, I just might give him away." She stopped, and then said slowly, "No, I don't think I would."

Emily went to pick up some letters which lay on the doorstep, flipping through them and at one point saying in a low, delighted voice to herself, "Oh, that's marvelous. Here's one from John."

"John?" It was a name Allegra had never heard her mention before.

"John Durham. My new friend—didn't I tell you about him? No? Well, he's become a great chum, and he's encouraged me with my book. He's an architect, a very good one." She went into the kitchen and put on the tea water. "Tea? Or a drink? I'd better have a drink, or I'll never have the courage to face this. God, how I hate to pack!"

"Tell me more about him," Allegra said, sensing there was a story behind it.

Emily paused, one hand on her hip, another brandishing a cigarette. "You've met him, actually, although I daresay you probably don't remember. At Véronique's dinner party, that December—it must be two years ago now." She smiled to herself, her eyes following a trail of smoke in the air. Then, looking intently at Allegra, "You were so dazzled by Alex that you hardly paid any attention to John."

"I vaguely remember . . . What does he look like?"

"Medium height. Intelligent eyes. Marvelous hair."

"Dark? Light?"

"Neither. Somewhere in between." Emily sat down, and then—almost impatiently, as if she were eager to recount the story—said, "I saw him again in June, not long after your wedding, at a dinner party. Not the most scintillating one I'd ever been to. In fact, I wound up getting sloshed. Really drunk. I don't think you've ever seen me *really* drunk, have you?" She gave Allegra a keen, self-amused glance. "It's not a pretty sight, so I'm told. Anyway, I'd seen John at this party, and we'd spoken quite a bit, and finally left together. I was really soused, and can't even remember—or don't want to—what I said. We got to my door, and I hung on him, and asked him to come in. For a drink. 'No thanks,' he said. 'I think you need some aspirin and some sleep.' I told him, no, that what I needed was a good fuck." She assumed that curved, angelic smile and lit another cigarette.

"You didn't!" said Allegra, shocked, delighted.

"Why not? I've never been one to subscribe to the noli me tangere approach."

"What happened then?"

"He led me inside, took off my shoes, and got me to bed. In truth, I can hardly remember what happened then. In the morning, when I awoke, it all seemed like a haze—this attractive man, rather serious, at my door. Taking off my shoes! Anyway, I staggered from bed to the kitchen, where, on the counter, I found a note. Here it is, I've saved it."

She rifled through a mass of papers and finally succeeded in unearthing it. It was written in a strong regular hand. "Call me if you need more help. You probably will. John Durham."

"And you called him?"

"Yes. Actually, I called him just to say thanks, and he invited me to dinner."

"And you slept with him?"

"Of course."

"That night?"

"Was it?" She knitted her brow. "Memory fails."

"And how was it?"

"Wonderful. He did not discard me at the end, the true sign . . ." She stopped, thinking to herself, strangely quiet. "And yet in some respects the encounter had all the tragicomic aspects of a failed cake. There was not something exclusively sexual about it, which is strange, because he is the most manly of men. No sense of groping toward the other. No, it was sensual, and yet I felt as if I were sleeping with an older, treasured brother. Perhaps it is because he is so protective. I don't know. But in fact, by morning, although neither of us said so, we realized that we were better off, and in a way closer—that is the paradox—as friends." Looking out the window, and holding her cigarette midair, she said, "I suspect I'm too much of a gypsy for him."

"And so, now you have a platonic relationship?" Allegra's voice was teasing. "The sun will be setting in the east next."

"Well, why not? I've never tried it." There was a pause. "He likes artists, writers, and he likes what I write. In another century, he would have made the perfect patron."

"And you've continued to spend time with him?"

Emily nodded. "He invited me to his country house, a farm in Connecticut. Heaven! He took me there for the weekend, several times, and in a curious way, he gave me courage, even when I was quite dispirited and might very well have gone on being a damn fashion editor. He lent me money, that was the first thing, and that in itself so relieved the anguish and terror of those bills that I was much better able to write, simply because I loathed myself less."

She turned to Allegra, her train of thought suddenly interrupted, a trace of bitterness in her voice. "You don't know what it's like to have to ask for money, do you? You've no idea how humiliating it is."

"I can imagine," Allegra answered quietly, in the next moment adding, "But Emily, you could have asked me. I could have lent you money, I would have been glad to help you."

Emily looked down, touched, unable to respond. For a long while she said nothing. "I should have asked, I suppose, but . . ." She shrugged her shoulders, then continued in a determinedly brisk voice, "Anyway, there were still moments when I felt blue—depressed and tired, and fed up with my job. I said I wasn't getting enough done, and that what I had written wasn't good enough. 'Well then, do it again until it is,' he told me. I said it was a question of time—there wasn't enough time during the week! 'You should be working weekends, then,' he said. I was furious. 'The weekends!' I said. 'I get up every morning at five, gulp down the coffee, try to write, am at the goddamn typewriter for hours, and then I go to the office, and you tell me I should be working every weekend, too!' I was furious; my nerves were just shot, you see.

"I remember sitting there, looking at him, in such a rage that I can't even begin to describe it. In a moment he said quietly, 'In your profession, there's no such thing as weekends.'

" 'That's right—me and the whores, same schedule,' I told him. At that, he burst out laughing, and told me to keep eating, because he knew it was probably my one good meal of the day. Anyway," she said, smiling to herself, "I could never be angry at John for too long. He's hard on me, but unfortunately he's almost always right."

She looked at Allegra, and then settled back on the sofa, turning her feet this way and that, and watching their pointed toes now propped against the faded pillows. "I'd grown very snappish and irritable by early summer. I was tired of my job, and the book itself seemed nothing but a hopeless labyrinth. John had invited me to the country several times, but one morning—Sunday, because the *Times* was spread about—remains quite vivid in my mind. I daresay I hadn't been the most amusing guest. He had picked me up late one Friday afternoon. It was sweltering, and I was in one of my most peevish moods. He has a sports car, and I remember that his shirt was open and his eyes scrutinizing as he looked at me. 'You're looking a bit pale,' he said, perusing my face. I blew up. 'You'd be pale, too,' I said resentfully, 'if you'd been bent over the damn typewriter all day, churning out copy for fashion victims.' Anyway, I was in this explosive state all that evening, and by Sunday, I wasn't much better. We'd been talking over the newspapers, and somehow we got on to discussing one of my heroes, whom John quickly described as a 'shrewd, repressed WASP.' 'Well,' I snapped back, 'it takes one to know one.' I instantly regretted my spiteful words; it was only one of the many times when my tongue has gotten the better of me. 'Oh, I'm sorry,' I finally said. 'It's just that I'm not very happy.' I was swinging in a hammock and he was sitting on a chair opposite. He looked up, and then said in his deep voice, 'Well, of course you're not happy, you little fool! You're not writing.' He immediately got up, and took me by the shoulders so tightly that it hurt. 'Emily,' he said, 'there's one thing that you'd better do and you'd better do it fast.' 'What's that?' I asked meekly. 'Get going on your goddamn book.' 'I have,' said I. 'It's just that it's not good enough.' 'Do it over until it is, then. You can write here, or anywhere you want—but *do* it!'

"He went back to the newspapers, and I lay there, stunned, at once happy and aghast. This was what I had wanted to hear, wasn't it? And yet I felt as if someone had led me to the edge of a cliff and said. *'Jump!'*

"The odd thing was that I did begin to really write the next day—clearly, swiftly, as if a wrapping had been lifted from my subconscious. Some dense fog that had been obscuring my creative powers. He helped me enormously, you see. I owe him a great debt that has nothing to do with money."

Her face had become so reflective that Allegra hardly recognized her normally mischievous self. Slowly Emily stood up and went to her desk, where she took up a blue leather box. "John gave me a present to take to Paris, for good luck," she said. "Here. Look." The box was lined in silk and within it was an exquisite pen, worked in red enamel. "Isn't it heavenly?" Emily said, beaming, as she turned it over in her hand. "He told me it once belonged to an English writer who lived in France."

"Which one?" said Allegra, examining the pen.

"He wouldn't say. He said it might influence me."

"When do you leave?" asked Allegra, after a moment.

"Day after next."

"As soon as that?"

Emily nodded. "Will you write me? I expect I'll be at a little hotel somewhere, and God, it would be marvelous to get some letters."

"Of course, just send me the address." Allegra put her hand on Emily's shoulder. "Good luck with your book; if you can do it anywhere, it should be in Paris." She had taken off the gold bracelet around her wrist; it was Victorian, with a granulated design in the Etruscan style. Emily had often admired it. "Here," Allegra said, "a present. Think of me when you wear it."

The two women embraced, Emily murmuring her thanks.

Allegra was just leaving when she suddenly stopped, looking around the dusty, book-piled room, as if to fix the image in her mind. One last glance at the bulletin board, with its snips of papers and old postcards. And then, at a strange word printed in great block letters on a long sheet of paper. "What does that mean?" asked Allegra, pointing to it.

"It's got three completely different meanings, depending on the context—can you imagine? I can't remember where on earth I came across it."

"Are you sure you didn't just make it up?"

"On my honor," Emily said, with mock solemnity.

Smiling, and trying to conquer her sadness, Allegra waved, and left.

Emily stood by the window, watching her walk toward Park Avenue; and then, with brisk, determined movements, began to pack.

44

Emily's first letter arrived several weeks later. It was written on tissue-thin white paper with "Hôtel de la Fontaine," in burgundy script at the top. There were strange spots on each side which Allegra noticed as the paper unfolded.

"October 17.
"Dear Allegra—

"*Me voilà*. I've found myself a little room at the Hôtel de la Fontaine—a suitably scruffy and questionable establishment not far from the Rue Jacob. There's no telephone here, except for one in the lobby, a dismal little affair with cut-velvet curtains and the smell of something that approximates boeuf bourguignon in the air. It's really straight out of Jean Rhys, which I'm sure you will appreciate.

"Do excuse the spots of coffee on the paper. I'm sitting at the Deux Magots, sipping a café crème, and making my way through a baguette. It's eleven o'clock in the morning, and the march of the more fashionable Parisians has yet to begin. Lord, they are vain, but very very chic. I loathe that word, but can't find another that *gets* them as well.

"You will wonder what my room is like. It's covered in toile—demented shepherdesses being chased by wild-eyed cupids—and is fitted with an immense, creaking armoire, an astonishingly virginal bed, a good worktable, and a small sink with mushrooms sprouting up between the baseboards, across the mildewed walls. Naturally, all my book-writing paraphernalia has invaded the place—notes, books, papers, pens; it's a bit of a mess now. But then it isn't always possible to live as exquisitely as one would like, while you're writing.

"There are curtains at the window, and when I look out, I can see the goings-on around me, and the squabblings of the Spanish couple on the top floor.

"The whole atmosphere is marvelous for my writing. I work early morning, as I always do, and then stop about eleven for more coffee, and something in the stomach. In the afternoon, I sometimes walk across to the Luxembourg Gardens, or occasionally take the metro to the Parc Monceau, and watch the nannies and kindly grandparents shepherding spoiled and invariably well-dressed children. I don't much like children, particularly French ones, so there's a touch of masochism to these visits.

"You will ask about my book, too, in your persistent way. It's going well; I've turned the plot around, and have basically scrapped everything I originally began with. I have a feeling you will empathize with the new incarnation.

"Do write. And have you heard from John? I did ring him up, as I said I would, and he promised that he would try and reach you.

"As ever,

Emily."

"October 30.

"Dear Emily,

"Your letters make me laugh so—I treasure them, and love hearing your vision of Paris. I practically felt I *knew* your room.

"You don't seem to be lonely there. Is it the beauty of the city that cancels it out for you? I remember being so lonely there at times, even though I loved Paris. But those little round tables at the cafés! I always felt they were meant for two, and that to be alone at one seemed pitiful.

"You asked for news. The first is that I've found an apartment. It's lovely—in a small building off Madison, on Sixty-sixth Street. I've a fireplace, and lovely high ceilings, and wonderful quiet. I've just finished moving in—how strange it seems to be totally alone! I still haven't gotten used to it yet, and wake up much too early each morning. It has been a warm fall, and only now is there a touch of chill in the air.

"Miscellany: The Fitzpatricks have found a house in Water Mill. It's slowly being finished, and should be ready about Thanksgiving time. Harry, Maggie, and I go around to shops looking for the right things. 'Is it really *me?*' she keeps saying, when we point out a table, or chair. We've all been trying to come up with a name for the place—I've suggested La Contenta (thinking of its opposite, in the Veneto), partly because the house is so peaceful.

"I've only painted a little, but what I have done, I've liked.

"I suppose I think a great deal about this summer, and Alex, and the strange past few years. There are moments when I think I see him; this fills me with dread, I catch my breath, I can't move, as if my head were suddenly severed from my body. It happened once when I was walking to lunch with Harry, and he thought I'd seen a ghost. Well, you see, I *had*—if only in my mind. But isn't that enough?

"So I am obsessed with that awful time, this summer—the death-in-life of a disastrous marriage. I still haven't figured it all out. Certainly there were signs, and then I was unhappy so much. How is it that you don't *know* if you're unhappy? I think I even knew it wasn't right, and yet I went through with it, as if I had no choice. As if it were ineluctable. It was simply that I was so eager to get on with my life! And what I had been leading before, alone, never seemed complete, or real.

"I've thought of seeing a psychiatrist—Charles has recommended someone, in fact. Perhaps that would help unravel it all . . .

"But the last news: John Durham did call me, and invited me to lunch last Sunday. I met him at Chez Madeleine; he was seated in a booth, surrounded by lots of newspapers. I recognized him immediately, without having to ask the waiter to direct me, which was strange, because I'd never met him before. I felt at once as if I'd known him forever. How peculiar, because in Alex's case it was the opposite—the more intimate we became, the less we really knew one another. Sex masked it, for a while, and so did my terrible fear of losing him, but the fact remained that we were really strangers. I felt too much his prisoner all the time; and it was only after I was married, weirdly enough, that I realized that I myself held the key to the bolted door.

"But I'm rambling. Back to John. We talked so much about you; it was relaxed, and so easy that it must have been around four o'clock when we left. He walked me home, and said we must have lunch again. I found it hard to say good-bye to him, so I asked whether he wouldn't like some tea, and to see some of my paintings, since you'd mentioned them to him. He came upstairs—I've a large room which I use just for my painting—and my things were all around. Harry has gotten me interested in botanical drawings, and has been teaching me all about Redouté; some of my new work has been inspired by that. The others I've been doing are immense, floor-to-ceiling studies of the coral labyrinths I saw in Crete. Almost every day during my 'odyssey,' as you call it, I would swim to them—fascinated and yet fearful. How beautiful they were, and how dangerous! Their shapes pursue me still, even as I try to transform them in my paintings.

"John kept walking around them and finally said, 'They're good. They're very good.' You can imagine how pleased I was to hear him say that! He said they were almost 'humanoid,' and that there was something 'animalistic' about them.

"Thank you for having him call me. He is a gift. It is rare to find that combination of vigor and intellect.

"Love—

Allegra."

"November 13.
"Dear Allegra—
"Many thanks for the last letter. I didn't expect such an epistle, but Lord, I welcomed it.

"It has become cold and rainy here. Went to the bird market near Nôtre Dame last weekend, and even that was pretty dismal. All those soggy little things, flapping away. I came back and promptly ordered a whiskey grog at the Magots.

"Book's going well, am quite pleased. If only Madame Chamouse (the owner of the hotel) would get off my back about the typewriter noise, everything would be perfect. My God, but she's dreadful.

"I see very few people, and I walk a great deal, pressing my nose against all the shop windows, dreaming of the day when I can afford some beautiful clothes. Yesterday, I went to Christian Dior—pretended I was a rich Arab lady on a shopping spree. Wore a suit, high heels, swarthy makeup, and a choking scent. They were getting out everything for me—shoes, evening dresses, perfume. Raising my eyebrows, and dismissing it all, I said I would have to think about it, as my husband, the sheik, had seven wives and was rather particular about clothes. Didn't like too much repetition, etc. Oh, you should have seen their eyes! I marched out and walked down the Avenue Montaigne, collapsing in giggles, and then went to the Bar du Théâtre, where I ordered a steak-frites and watched the cadaverous models from Dior (a scene out of *Cabaret*) pick on their yogurts and crudités.

"I hardly have a friend here, but the bookshops are good, so it doesn't matter much. Anyway, with good books, you hardly need people; books don't bore you as human beings tend to, or betray, or disappoint. Funnily enough, as much as I love to observe, I don't really like the human beast that much, save for a few close friends. The rest hardly seem worth bothering about.

"Do you think it's true, as Nabokov said, that you really only need to know six books, but very very well? I tend to think he's right.

"With my best—

                                                                        Emily."

The next letter which Emily received was written in a vigorous hand on thick white paper, with deep blue initials, J.L.D.

"December 11.
"Dear Emily,

"I've been thinking of you, but have been traveling a lot, and have only been in New York intermittently. This is the first quiet time I've found to write.

"It has been a peaceful, but busy winter. I've spent most weekends at the farm. The house has had leaks, and the horses have needed more care this year. You'll be glad to know that Sykes, the caretaker, has decided to stay on. I remember how he used to make you laugh.

"The projects I'm working on have gone very well, particularly the one near London. It seems I will, most likely, be going to Europe next spring, if not earlier—hopefully I will pass through Paris and see you.

"I did call Allegra Clayton, by the way. The more I get to know her, the more my original impression has been confirmed: she's an interesting and lovely young woman who seems to have mastered her shyness. Clearly she is still preoccupied with her marriage, and its events. I could tell this from her eyes, although she hardly ever discusses it. She always refers to Alexander Para as 'the man I married,' never as her husband. At one point, turning to me, she said, 'The man I married had no earthly idea who I was; none at all; and yet it was not entirely his fault. I was too afraid to let him know, fearing, I suppose, that it would drive him away. The more deeply I became involved with him—certainly this was true by the time of our marriage—the more I felt annihilated. I kept having nightmares about my mother's death, the avalanche, that feeling of being engulfed. Oh well, it's over now.'

"Of course it really isn't. Her face shows it, although she looks less drawn than when we first had lunch. Thank God, though, she has stopped smoking and has slowly recovered her laugh. The last time we met, there were even a few signs of what I imagine to be her former playfulness. She has been working hard—that's her refuge, obviously. Hopefully, she won't give up the painting, for she's gifted. I sense it completes an essential part of her.

"I look forward to hearing from you. Write me if you need anything.

"Best—

John."

"March 4.
"Dear Emily,

"I'm so excited! I'm to have a small show of my work at the Beresford Gallery, and have been working night and day to get the things done. Your advice has been wonderful. As you said, I've gotten used to that early morning gulp of getting down to work: the breaking through the barrier of vanity and fear that seems to prevent one from self-expression.

"John has become a great friend, although I've hardly seen him much recently, as he's been traveling. I didn't know he came from such a large family—two sisters, and three brothers. The father died when they were quite young, and he's the eldest. I sense that he takes care of them all. When he's in town, he occasionally calls to invite me to lunch. I've come to consider that the true sign of caring in a man, rather than mere lust (although there's nothing wrong with lust!). With dinner, a man can always hope for more; that is seldom the point of a lunch.

"I love to listen to John talk, particularly about Greece and its architecture. He knows so much about it, and can really bring a place to life—about the Greeks and their temples, and the influence of the landscape; or how, in Italy, the Medicis *thrust* their palazzi on the squares. Strangely enough, when he speaks about Greece, I feel I see it more clearly than I did when I was actually there, last summer. Then it seemed so convoluted, even shabby. The Greece I had remembered—the Greece of the crystalline sea, and the moving sculpture—all this, John has brought back to me.

"He is, of course, intensely analytical, and yet I sense that he feels deeply. Through upbringing, through responsibility, he has been taught that it is better not to show emotion, and to rein in what may surge below the surface.

"You asked whether there was any news of Alex. None. Although Harry told me that he thought he saw him one day, here. Who knows? I was called recently by the people at Atlantic Trust. They asked me some questions—that was very hard.

"As for Véronique: she seems to have succeeded. They say Stern is divorcing his wife, and the two are to be married. There is even talk of his being named to an ambassadorial post, to some South American country. Can you imagine? Véronique, an ambassador's wife? There's a perverse triumph in that.

"Write me soon—

Allegra."

"April 1.
"Dear Emily,
". . . As for Allegra, she seems happier and stronger, though I'm sure it will take a bit longer to forget last year. She spends a great deal of time, on the weekends, with Maggie and Charles Fitzpatrick. They're fine people—I like him, particularly. Apparently they've recently bought a house on Long Island, in Water Mill—La Contenta, they've called it—and Allegra often stays with them there.

"She makes me laugh when she talks about Long Island; she can barely disguise her rebelliousness toward the place. And yet she loves the Fitzpatricks' house! I asked her to explain that—after all, it's in the midst of all that. 'They have their own universe there, their own paradise,' she said, her eyes going deep with that funny gravity of hers (and making me understand, at that moment, how Alexander would have fallen in love with her). 'They rarely go out and they are the least demanding hosts. You are always free to read and wander, and the food of course is wonderful—always exactly what you'd love to eat, and yet always something unexpected. Domestic perfection! The only givens are that lunch is at one-thirty and dinner is at eight-thirty. The last time I was there, I'd had all my wisdom teeth out, and was wandering around like a ghost, in a catatonic state, due to the pain-killers, my mouth, roaring with aches. They're awfully good to me . . .'

"You should know that she then added thoughtfully, 'I feel I've learned so much from Maggie, just as I have, in another way, from Emily. One is so gentle and the other almost ruthless, and yet they have both affected me deeply. How can that be?'"

The letter continued for several paragraphs; and then, at the bottom of the page, was signed, John.

"May 18.
"Dear Emily,
"My show was a success. I sold quite a few things, including one of my favorites to John. He insisted on buying it, although I had wanted to give it to him, as a gift. But he refused.

"John mentioned that he'd told you that I'd been spending time at the Fitzpatricks', on Long Island. At first I dreaded going, for my last memory of that place is awful. But at the Fitzpatricks' house, I've managed to lull myself into thinking that it isn't really *there*. The gates close; the fence is high; and the trees shade the house. And then you are left with the quiet, and the lovely lawns, and the rocking of the little boat by the dock.

"Maggie has been taking me to her exercise class, by the way, and I've grown addicted to it. You come out, at the end, all stretched, and perspiring, and happy—the muscles quite sore. But then I am still Catholic enough to equate effectiveness with pain.

"The house in Water Mill is completely finished, although Maggie is still unsure whether it is really 'her.' But then she never will be sure, and I know it will go through endless changes as she searches. Seeing in every stick of furniture, in every scrap of chintz and linen, something of her own psyche being added or subtracted. Funny, isn't it? And yet, isn't that what I do with each of my brushstrokes, and you with your sentences? Constantly rearranging the self; remaking it. For me, with another painting, for you with a book, for Maggie with a room. Only at the end of creating does it really seem irrevocable, and yet, even then there is always another style to try, or a new technique. It's all the same.

"I suppose the only difference, really, is that a room doesn't help you *see* more clearly; it doesn't mature your vision, or give you insight. It may be memorable, and pleasurable, but it doesn't imperceptibly alter the mind's eye. That you must leave to the other things.

"You asked about the next series of landscapes I'm working on. I know what I want to do—it's all within my head—and now it's just a question of succumbing to it. You see, I still don't completely trust that part of me that creates.

"Harry asked me a question the other day: what did I most want in life? 'A happy marriage,' I said, without a second's pause. 'And to paint.' He asked me whether I thought the two were mutually exclusive. 'Of course not,' I said. 'Except that you must be a whole self in order to do both.' Do you think I gave the right answer? It's what sprang to mind.

"I've been thinking of returning to Venice at the end of the summer, perhaps sometime in September. It would mean so much to see Giovanna, and to see Venice, once more, but in another light. The last time I was there, with Alex, was in winter; the door to the church Giovanna helped restore was locked, and the city itself was so frigid and sinister, almost unrecognizable from the Venice of my childhood summers. If I do decide to come, I'll try to stop in Paris, first, to see you.

"John has been encouraging me to go; the best trips are always quests, he said. Isn't that wonderful—and true?

"Your letters have been lagging—a good sign, though, I suppose, which means your book is coming along. Is it?

"With love—   Allegra."

45

"ay 30.

"Dear Allegra—

"I am sitting at a small café near the Place des Vosges—oh, but it's heaven to be in Paris, in the spring. I feel quite dazed by it. The French are as arrogant and crotchety as always, and yet, dear souls, I do love them. The weather is perfect—blue skies—and all the cafés are suddenly sprouting on the sidewalks.

"I'm still a bit sleepy-eyed from it all, but mostly from the event about which all of Paris has been talking—La Fête Violette, held last night at Maxim's. Everyone was asked to wear a mask. The beau monde did not disappoint, let me tell you. It was really the sort of spectacle one might see once, perhaps twice, in a lifetime. I can't deny the Parisians their elegance—truly it is a delight to see them all done up. Jewels of every hue glittering, one more gorgeous than the other. A fleet of peacocks descended from heaven, strutting about in silks and taffetas, could not have been more splendid. The general ambience of lengthy *soins* and the mingling of costly perfumes and matched parures. Even the child violinists (twenty of them, roaming as they serenaded) were a sight to behold, decked in lavender Mozartian garb. But of course the French take this very very seriously, this aptitude for costumes. Part of the national collective unconscious, I should think. For it is work, after all, to transform oneself with makeup, jewels, and the appropriate Yves Saint Laurent—such clothes! My mouth can't help but water, just to think of them.

"You will ask about my own dress. I found it last Sunday at the Marché Biron, at the flea market, in a small stall that sells antique clothes. It is Belle Époque, I think, and I feel indebted to the poor dead creature for whom it was made, for it is exactly my size. She must have been tall, a rather freakish Victorian, no doubt.

"But back to the fête itself: lots of gossip and the most heady wines. The food, too, was deliriously good. Swans spun out of sugar on cakes, a procession of pâtés . . . There was a group of musicians—Russian, I think—who played wonderfully well, and I danced a great deal. By early morning, I was quite breathless from the music and the sights and the chatter.

"I danced several times with a tall man who had graying hair and an elusive manner. Charming, I thought. I had other partners, too, but this one . . . Perhaps it was his style of dancing which suited me. Firm grip on the waist; a way of going with the beat, even at its most capricious.

"At last, very hot and out of breath, we sat down. I sipped a cognac and, as we took off our masks, I saw Alexander! I must have gone dead pale, and of course he noticed. I felt as if I were sitting with a bloody resurrection! I told him I'd heard from you. I'm sure he thought I seemed half-witted, stammering as I did. He asked news of you. I told him that you were well, and that you were painting.

"I must tell you that I studied him very very closely, as one always does the *inamorato*—past or present—of a friend (protectiveness tinged with the curiosity of a postmortem? What did she see in him, etc?). Well, in his case, I must tell you, there *is* something. Hard to put the finger on, but it's there; perhaps I noticed it more, thrown into relief by this foreign setting. He's both charming and dangerous—a seductive combination. Here, my writerly instincts fail me. I can only say that I can see why you were attracted to him, for you are, indeed, his opposite in every way.

"I expect he is even more appealing now than when you knew him.

He has obviously suffered; men, I think, grow more attractive after their mettle has been tested. (This is true of women, too, but the sobering physical evidence—lines, thinness, etc.—is simply more desirable in the male of the species.) I must tell you that he did not seem like someone defeated. Perhaps you will feel something of disappointment at this news? If I were you, I should like to sense that he has really been through the mill (but then, I'm less generous). Instead, he seems to have survived quite nicely, thank you very much. In fact, everyone seemed to know him. And when the time came to leave, it was a splendid, if vacuous redhead who came to fetch him. She did not open her mouth once and had something of a model's professional elegance.

"But now the plot thickens. I may be wrong of course, but here: clearly he is still in love with you. It's not my instincts which tell me this—he told me so in what is commonly known as plain English. 'I'm still in love with her,' he said. Why? You will ask, if you are human and have brains, which of course you do. Because he will never have you again! What could be more tantalizing than a half-grasped love affair, lodged in the mind like a stunted seed? Familiarity, they say, breeds contempt; so, in love, does too complete a realization. That's the bitter truth, but you, who love impressionism, should understand it.

"Anyway, he left with her. I watched them wend their way through the crowd and, for a split second, I thought—for she, too, was tall and slender.

"But now, news of myself. First, the physical symptoms: high blood pressure, quickened pulse, skipping heartbeat. That could only mean one of two things—either I'm writing well, or I'm in love. *Both* are true! I knew it would happen here, in Paris. Today, alone—two entire chapters! Perhaps it's being in France that prompts this image, but I feel like a pastry chef, squeezing it all magically on the face of a cake. But that's only part of it.

"At the same party where I met your ex, I met another man, who was not masked. He is French, but educated in England—a writer, too! Medium height, fair, with a wonderful mouth and a gallant, weathered look. Rough-hewn features. I spent most of the evening with him, madly chattering, and then suddenly quite withdrawn, almost morose (with me, the inevitable signs of infatuation). He, too, reads Rilke and loves Oxford. Excuse him, then, for being a Frenchman!

"We spent last night together; I hardly slept, yet the hours disappeared so quickly. Today I look exhausted, but feel ecstatic. I will see him tomorrow at a bistro near the Musée Marmottan. I feel like some besotted character wandering around the Forest of Arden, tacking the trees with lunatic verses!

"Other signs: I am sure to be wearing too much perfume, and my eyes are drawn to such *common* items in shop windows. Today, for instance, in an arcade, a pink crepe de Chine slip, embroidered with hearts and edged in black lace, pinned up in the window, as the French do it, with the delicacy of a scientific specimen.

"I can see you laughing and shaking your head with amazement. I suppose all of this must sound like the sex-starved hallucinations of a bluestocking.

"Well, as I've said before, you have curious ideas of what it means to be an intellectual, not to mention an artist. As if creative women had to be soul mates of Savonarola! That's American nonsense, so shake yourself out of it. Think of Edith Wharton and Mary Cassatt— your very own countrywomen.

"I loved your sketches and am so glad to hear that you have come to trust your own obsessions.

"As for Alex: don't you think you should, in a way, thank him for that bittersweet creative hurt? It has made you what you are.

"Emily.

"P.S. *Do* return to Venice this September, as you mentioned you might. It is to you, I think, what Paris is to me. As ever, E."

46

The peaches were unusually ripe and sweet that summer, the weather gentle, and the short rains frequent, so that the grass, trees, and flowers were even more generous, fragrant, and glistening. At the Fitzpatricks' house, there was the scent of roses, and the soft purply-blues of hydrangeas. The quiet of early September approached, with its vestige of summer sun, its breezes and formidable pastel sea.

Allegra had spent many weekends with her friends at La Contenta: lazy afternoons, punctuated by long walks, reading, delicious meals, and painting. The house had assumed its own way of being, and its own rhythm of domestic life. The table set for lunch under the trees, and dinners on the long veranda, looking out to the glimmering pond. In the distance, the rumbling of the ocean.

For Allegra, the events of the previous summer and those people she had known with Alexander, had slowly begun to resemble players in some vivid, but waning play; the faded figures of a fresco.

She had hardly seen John Durham since April, for he had been in Europe most of the summer. Toward him, she felt an enormous debt and warmth, a closeness. She longed to see him, not out of a fervid, aching desire, but out of deep affection.

Now she sat on the steps of the veranda, the morning of the first Saturday in September, when Maggie—looking delighted—came quickly down the porch and said that John had called, and that she had invited him for lunch.

"He's coming, then?" said Allegra, looking up, as she finished her breakfast, one hand holding a piece of jam-brushed toast. She took a sip of tea, and then put down the cup. "When will he be here?" she said, her voice excited. "It's been how long? Three months, I think. At least."

Gathering her skirt, Maggie sat down beside her; the two women looked out past the *allée* of trees to the water, where a flock of monarch butterflies darted among the reeds. "It's already warm, and it's only nine," said Maggie, leaning back and fanning herself. "What do you think we should have for lunch?"

"Salads, don't you think?" Allegra said, sipping her tea. "The one the other day with tomatoes and basil was delicious." She looked at Maggie as the latter devoted her attention to the menu. It always amused Allegra to see her concentrating on it so, for it seemed no sooner was one meal finished than Maggie was thinking of the next.

"Yes, some salads, some ratatouille," Maggie said at last, thoughtfully. "And maybe some mussels . . ." She swatted a bug that flew past.

Allegra nodded. "I'll help. I'll bake the bread I made last week."

"He should be here about one," Maggie said, her eyes scanning the garden. Then, standing up, she said suddenly, "How could I forget. John said he's brought you Emily's book! The manuscript."

When Allegra saw John at the other end of the lawn, it seemed he had not changed at all. The same stance, the open shirt, the wise candid glance. He walked briskly and carried a thick brown package.

She ran to him; they embraced, standing together for a moment, happy to see one another.

"Your hair—it's grown so long!" he said.

"Too long, do you think?"

"No, it suits you—keep it that way."

She asked about his work, and his traveling; and he about Sotheby's, and her painting. For a while, they sat on the lawn talking, John mentioning that he had been in London and before that in Paris, where he had seen Emily.

"Her manuscript," he said, gesturing toward the package which now lay on the grass. "Emily asked me to bring it to you, and said that you were to read it first. And her letter, as well. She was very adamant about it." He chuckled, almost to himself. "She was finishing her second *mille-feuille* at the time. I remember her looking up, very seriously, licking the whipped cream from her mouth. So here it is." He glanced at the package.

Allegra picked it up. "It's grown! And it's heavy. I remember when it weighed only a few ounces." And then, propping her head on the grass, "How *is* Emily?"

"Very well. I was amazed, she looked so French! Her dress, the way she fixed her hair." He smiled to himself. "She looked pale, too, and rather undernourished, so I took her to lunch."

"Where did you go?"

"I told her to pick any place she'd like. Without a moment's pause she said Taillevent. She told me you'd once told her about it."

"Taillevent," repeated Allegra, remembering a dinner there with Michel and Alexander.

"Yes," he said. "I asked why she was so fixed on it—she said she needed it for her book." He laughed. "That's Emily for you."

He stood up, his hands in his pockets, gazing at the tranquil settings, and then at Allegra. "You're not smoking anymore."

"I've given it up."

"Good. You look so much more relaxed and well than you did last fall."

"I feel very well," she said emphatically, standing up.

"How's the water? We should go for a swim before lunch."

"It's great, but a little cold."

"You're scared," he said, smiling.

"No—well, maybe a little."

He took her hand. "Come with me."

The beach was clustered with people when they arrived, the water rhythmic and glassy. He beckoned to her, but she hesitated, still remembering that other afternoon in September, with Alexander. "Another time," she said. "Now I'll just watch." For a moment he insisted, but seeing her reluctance, went ahead alone.

She watched as he swam through the waves, waiting, then diving through them; and then swimming again, his head bobbing in the water. After a few minutes, she felt very hot suddenly, and wished she had gone in with him, for the water looked cool and refreshing. "Perhaps he'll come back and pull me in," she thought; for part of her had wanted that he insist, just as another part had wanted to make its own decision.

In a moment he emerged—invigorated, content.

"Next time?" he said, blotting his face with the towel she had given him.

"Next time," she said.

They read the *New York Times* after lunch, the papers spread across the grass.

Allegra, who was reading the Book Review section, suddenly stopped and asked, "What do you think about this? It's for Emily and Charles—both!" Smoking his pipe, Charles listened as she bent her head and read, " 'With a novelist, like a surgeon, you have to get the feeling that you've fallen into good hands—someone from whom you can accept the anesthetic with confidence.' " She looked up. "Don't you think Emily would like that? I should send it to her." She began to tear out the page.

"How *is* Emily?" asked Maggie. And then, recalling Emily's rhapsodic letter about the evening at Maxim's, Allegra said, "One of her last letters was amazing, written in a completely new style, almost surrealistic." She paused, thinking of the part about Alexander; it had saddened her. "She described a party she had been to, and then went on to tell me about her new lover. French, went to Oxford, reads Rilke. Did you meet him?"

John looked puzzled. "New lover? No. She seemed very much alone. Didn't mention anyone. Strange."

"Strange," echoed Allegra, who lay on the grass, looking at the blue sky, with its puffy clouds. It occurred to her then that the Frenchman was, most likely, an invention, and that the mere precision of the description, and its realism, probably meant that he never existed at all.

"Well," said Allegra, amused, "you never know with Emily whether she's telling the truth. Anyway, her version of the truth is always strangely tinted. I used to wonder if there really *was* a book, or whether it wasn't another of her inventions!"

"No doubt it is that," John said, with a wry smile.

"More coffee?" asked Maggie, who was already beginning to think of dinner, and exactly why that shade of chintz looked so wrong in the green bedroom.

More coffee was served, and their talk, like a piece of driftwood, moved from one subject to another.

Allegra did not dare to open Emily's package until the late evening. She was filled with all the dread and complicity one feels before confronting the work of a friend. "Will I like it?" she kept thinking, as she stared out the window, her eyes drawn to the manuscript which lay on a bamboo chair. "And if I don't like it, should I lie? But if I lie, she'll know. I can't lie to Emily."

At last, she picked up the package, untied the ribbon, and took a letter from it, addressed to Allegra Clayton.

"August 20.
"Dear Allegra—

"This is not the same story I first told you I would write—it is a different book altogether: what I have written here you will know very well. I told you I could only write about what I know; and, you see, I feel in a peculiar way which even I find hard to articulate, that I *do* know you, and what you have experienced and felt, although we are so much the opposite of one another. Try to understand that I haven't used you in the way Alex did; but you know, when it comes to material gathering, that it is hard for me to exercise restraint. I can't refrain from using a good story; it's in my nature to want to transform everything. But if my writing exorcises that experience of yours, and illuminates what was painful and bewildering, am I not, then, forgiven? I never meant to hurt you by it.

"So now you will probably understand why I had to go to Paris. The distance, you see.

"You will ask what I think about the book, and what I felt when I came to the end of it. The day I finished it was almost like any other; I capped my pen, looked out the window . . . I felt not so much relieved, as bereft and stunned, as if I had come to the end of an exceptionally clear dream. And then, of course a book—like anything else—never quite matches the fantasy. I say 'matches'; mark that I did not say 'surpasses' or 'equals.'

"I still haven't decided whether novel-writing is extraordinarily generous, or egocentric in the extreme.

"Do be careful with the manuscript. I shall have to send it on, fairly soon, to my publisher. It's to be translated into the American, they tell me.

"What an awful snob she is, I can hear you saying. I won't disagree.

"Write to me soon.

Emily."

Allegra read through the night, turning the pages one by one, and seeing in them herself, and Alexander, and all the aspects of their love affair; not mirrored, but hazily reflected in a magic, undulating glass of whose transformations and inventions only she and Emily knew the extent. She read and read, and as she read, she often wept, for there were moments that Emily had made so clear, and so vivid, and there were other moments when she felt nothing but rage: against Alexander, against herself, and then against Emily, for having *used* it all.

It was dawn by the time she finished. She set the manuscript down, on the bed table—her head leaden with the confusion that comes with not sleeping. And yet she felt strangely exhilarated and excited, as if now, it were truly over. And this excitement came upon her as a sudden, immense energy: she did not want to sleep, she did not even want to rest.

She would go to the beach, and watch the ocean, and perhaps she would paint. The cleansing freedom of understanding had come over her, and with it, a sweet peace and inner sense of order; like tea leaves in a cup, swirling to some divination.

All around her, the house was still asleep, its bedcovers settled in a deep, late summer quiet.

Downstairs, the windows were latched; she opened them one by one, and looked across the veranda, and then to the lawns and sky.

There were great swooping-winged birds in the sky, and in the distance, a fleet of swans sailing across the pond's surface. The grass was still moist, the air with a heady scent; the reddish-gray reeds whispering and swaying. The trees fluttered and the sea, beyond, was nothing but a distant roar.

Suddenly she thought of lunch the day before, and the wine that had spilled on her dress, and how Maggie had taken a cloth and rubbed it out. And then she thought of Venice, and of returning there later in September.

She dressed quickly, gathering her paints, brushes, and a fresh canvas. Then she walked downstairs to the kitchen. Everything was in clean, sparkling order—the kitchen expectant of the invasion of scents and sounds that would eventually become lunch, and then dinner. She waited by the large black stove, with its paunchy front, rubbing her hands as the water boiled. Then she poured the tea into a thermos and looked for some bread and jam. In a moment, she had packed it all into a basket.

It was not a long walk to the beach—the trees made a light arbor, and the grass felt cool under her feet. Within her was a sense of joy, as if everything had suddenly become quite, quite clear. Sparkling, translucent.

She climbed past the dunes to the beach, which was deserted. Gulls cried. No one was out; no sounds of people; and the water dense and choppy, the waves breaking in tiers. The early morning sun hitting the peaks of water. A few bright pink-gray cracks of light creeping through the still dim sky.

She looked down the road at the small maritime museum, with its blue shingles, and, above its door, an inscription from the Bible: "All the rivers run into the sea, and yet the sea is not full."

She had come to love the sea in September. There was an infinitely more grave and natural quality about it, as if, at last, it had taken rightful possession of the sand and dunes. That it, too, was at peace.

Carefully, she set up the easel, and arranged her paint boxes. It was cool and windy; she blew on her hands and pulled the hood of her sweater closer, looking around. Suddenly she felt very hungry; she took a slice of bread, covered it with jam, and sipped the hot tea. Each taste was so vivid, as if she had never eaten before.

She sat and watched the water awhile, thinking, and waiting for the colors and lines to assume a shape within her mind. At last, sensing it was the moment to begin, she took the brush and dipped it into the pigment. One stroke, and then another. It seemed she had never painted so quickly, so effortlessly.

Suddenly she heard a dog barking and turned around: it was a small dog followed by an old man with a black mustache she thought she had seen before. He was jaunty and eccentric-looking, as if he had come from Deauville, or the steps of Montmartre. He wore a striped shirt and carried a cane.

Smiling to her, he tipped his hat and said good morning. The dog ran from him to her, and back again, as she continued to paint, glancing at the canvas, and then at the ocean.

The old man approached and, asking her permission, glanced over her shoulder, a look of surprise on his face. What she had painted only vaguely resembled the sea before them. For her sea was clear and luminous, with no hint of turbulence . . . He looked at her again, wondering if he were seeing the same sea.

"You are a painter, then?" he finally asked, with a kindly smile.

She turned to him and said softly, "I paint."

"Then you are a painter."

"Do you think so?" she asked, her eyes at once confirming and questioning.

He nodded, yes.

She continued to paint, but more slowly now, for tears had come to her eyes. A turn of her wrist; a color, daubed and streaked across the empty side. For a moment she paused, lightly resting her hand on the canvas, and then, turning to the stranger at her side, said, "I wonder if . . ."

But he had left.

Still looking at his footsteps, her eyes serene, she took up the brush.